To *Love*
Again

To Love Again

a sequel to *Return to Love*

Anita Stansfield

Covenant Communications, Inc.

Covenant

Other books and books on tape by Anita Stansfield:

First Love and Forever
First Love, Second Chances
Now and Forever
By Love and Grace
A Promise of Forever
Return to Love
Home for Christmas

Published by Covenant Communications, Inc.
American Fork, Utah

Printed in the United States of America
First Printing: January 1998

04 03 02 01 00 99 98 97   10 9 8 7 6 5 4 3 2 1

ISBN 1-57734-260-7

Library of Congress Cataloging-in-Publication Data

Stansfield, Anita, 1961-
    To love again : a sequel to Return to love / Anita Stansfield.
        p.   cm.
    ISBN 1-57734-260-7
    I. Title
    PS3569.T33354T6 1998
    813'.54--DC21   97-43392
                                             CIP

ACKNOWLEDGMENTS

Through the course of writing Janna and Colin's story, there were many people who gave their time and experience for the sake of making this project happen. To maintain your anonymity, I would simply like to express heartfelt gratitude to each of you who have shared your experiences with me, and also for reading the manuscripts. *You know who you are.* I couldn't have done it without you.

Also, a special thank-you to Dr. James MacArthur, for having so much in common with Sean, and for his time and know-how. And to Linda and Carol at *The Turning Point*, for allowing me to pass their expertise along to my readers. And, of course, to my family and friends, who continue to give unending support; especially to Vince, for being my hero. And last, but certainly not least, to my Father in Heaven, for once again sending me the miracles I needed.

CHAPTER ONE
Provo, Utah

*V*alentine's Day. *How appropriate, Colin thought as he held Janna close to him, attempting to comprehend how far they'd come. Sleep eluded him as his mind wandered through the memories. It had been nearly five years since he'd married her—though it hadn't been long since he'd believed they would never make it to their fifth anniversary together. In truth, their third anniversary had been anything but happy; and their fourth had come while they were separated and living in different house-holds. But the nightmare was finally over. And the gratitude he felt to have his family back together was beyond any earthly description. A particular scripture kept coming to mind, when Alma had told his son Helaman that "my soul was filled with joy as exceeding as was my pain."*

To this day, it was difficult for Colin to believe that he had fallen into such a volatile trap. It was incredible that someone with his upbringing and beliefs could make such a big mistake. But that was all in the past now. Janna had come back to him, in spite of how deeply he had hurt her. And everything was perfect; even more perfect than the day they had been married. . . .

Janna laughed as Colin lifted her into his arms, and the multi-layered skirt of her wedding gown rustled against him.

"This is the third threshold you've carried me over today, Colin."

He walked into the hotel room and kicked the door closed. "It's our wedding day," he said as if she didn't know. As her feet touched the floor, he pressed his lips over hers. "And you just can't have too much good luck."

Janna's eyes lit up with her smile, warming Colin through. He'd never believed that he could be so happy. After years of waiting and wondering, he had finally taken JannaLyn Hayne to the temple, to be married to her forever.

Later that night, as she lay sleeping in his arms, Colin's mind reviewed all that had led them to this day. They had jokingly called it a shotgun wedding. And in a way, it was. Though they were both easily temple worthy, they shared a common son. Matthew had been born more than seven years earlier. In fact, Colin hadn't even known of Matthew's existence for many years.

Colin and Janna had been high-school sweethearts, until her mother's death in the spring of her senior year. Colin was attending BYU at the time, and his life got a little off track. Then the trauma of Diane Hayne's death had sent them into each other's arms, a little too late at night, a little too long. They'd gone straight to the bishop, and worked hard together to repent and put the episode behind them. But at the time, Colin had no idea Janna was pregnant. She left Utah after her graduation to live with her aunt in Arizona. She broke all contact with Colin, and it was only a series of miracles that brought them back together years later.

The miracles, as it turned out, were edged with sharp reality; it took several months and some hard knocks before they were finally able to put their relationship back together. But Colin had every confidence they could work through their struggles together, even though the majority of Janna's baggage had nothing to do with him.

Baggage. That was the term their counselor, Sean O'Hara, used to sum up Janna's abuse that had never been faced. Sean believed her baggage had started piling up when she first realized her father had abandoned her and her mother when she was a baby. Janna's mother was a good woman who raised her well. They were active in the Church and strong in the gospel. But Diane Hayne had been hurt deeply, and there were things she never talked about. She simply had resigned herself to never marry again, as if any man in the world would only hurt her.

Janna's father came back once, when Janna was thirteen—an impressionable age, Sean had said. Janna had told Colin that her father had been obnoxious and overbearing. She hadn't told Colin until many years later that he'd sexually abused her, using threats and manipulation to keep her quiet. Diane soon sent him packing, and with some help from Sean, Janna seemed to deal well with it.

The JannaLyn that Colin fell in love with was a shy but dignified, beautiful young woman. She had radiated a love for the gospel and a lack of the self-importance and worldliness that most of the girls her age were caught up in. They dated for two and a half years, and everything was fine—until the night Diane died and left Janna alone in the world.

Sean had explained to Colin that all of this had led up to her decision to leave him instead of coming forward with the fact that she was going to have his baby. Janna had truly believed that Colin would be better off without her; she hadn't wanted to hold him back. But it was tough for Colin to swallow the realization that he'd gone on a mission and gotten a law degree with no idea that he was a father. And in the meantime, Janna had married charming, despicable Russell Clark—a temple-recommend-carrying elders quorum counselor who regularly knocked his wife around and inflicted at least two miscarriages upon her with his abuse. If the hypocrisy wasn't bad enough, it couldn't help but affect the way Janna felt about herself.

With some divine intervention, Colin had been able to help her get away from her abusive husband. But Russell had escaped the criminal charges, and eventually he'd found Janna again. The results sent her to intensive care, where her spirit as well as her body faced another long recovery. Nothing short of a miracle finally gave her the will to live and the strength to do it.

News had come just today—during their wedding reception, in fact—that Russell was behind bars, serving the maximum sentence allowable by law. And with Janna and Matthew now sealed to him, Colin had every hope that the future would be as bright as the past had been clouded with heartache.

Colin finally drifted to sleep. He woke to find Janna looking into his eyes, toying idly with his hair. "Good morning, my husband," she said with a little giggle, pressing a kiss to his nose.

"Good morning, Mrs. Trevor," he replied and eased her completely into his arms. "This is heaven, isn't it?" he whispered close to her ear.

Janna made a noise of agreement, then she giggled again.

"What's funny?" he asked.

"I was just wondering if Matthew misses us."

Colin laughed. "I'm certain he's having a marvelous time. Grandma had a whole list of things planned to keep him busy." Colin kissed Janna again. "We'll buy him a T-shirt."

Later that morning, Janna got behind the wheel of Colin's convertible and lifted her face skyward as the top opened up. She laughed as Colin got into the passenger seat and fastened his seat belt.

"Where to?" she asked, putting the car in gear.

"South," he answered with a little laugh.

"Where are we going?" she pressed when they were on the freeway.

"On a honeymoon," he said.

Janna scowled lightly. "Yes, but . . . where?"

"South."

"Colin!" She laughed again.

With dramatic humor, Colin declared, "The castles of Europe, the pyramids of Egypt, the splendor of New York City."

Janna looked skeptical, but he just laughed again. "Oh," he added, "and I thought we'd go to the beach, too."

"California?" She beamed like a child.

Colin touched her face, absorbing the reality of her happiness. After all they'd been through, her genuine smile meant more to him than words could describe.

"Eventually," he said, and motioned toward the road. "Just keep driving, Mrs. Trevor."

Colin leaned back and watched Janna, her hair blowing in the wind, her eyes shining with happiness. He silently thanked God for the evidence of miracles in his life, and pressed her hand to his lips.

They stopped for a meal and gas in St. George, then Janna slept while Colin drove. Her next awareness was Colin nudging her awake.

"Perk up, beautiful," he said. "This is where we're staying tonight."

Janna looked up and forced her eyes to focus. Then she felt them widen. "What is *that?*" The question erupted on a breath of laughter as she sat up straight and took in her surroundings.

"It's a hotel," Colin answered coolly.

"It's a . . . *castle*."

"Sort of," he said, then he laughed.

Janna looked around as Colin pulled into the huge parking lot. "Are we in . . ."

"Las Vegas? Yes, we are. You just walk right past the casinos, and you can find all kinds of good stuff. I came here a couple of years ago with my parents. We had a great time."

Janna knew she had the dumbfounded expression of a tourist as Colin led her through the maze of the Excalibur Hotel. Everything was decorated in a medieval theme, with more glamour and splendor than she had ever imagined. The elevator that carried them up to their room in one of the towers was almost eerily quiet in contrast to the bustling casinos on the main floor.

Janna laughed aloud as they entered their room. It, too, was decorated as if it were truly part of a castle. On one wall was a painting of a knight jousting on a white stallion. While Janna was absorbing it, Colin put his arms around her from behind, hugging her tightly.

"My knight in shining armor," she said, turning to hug him back.

Colin looked into her eyes and caressed her wind-tangled hair. "I love you, Janna," he murmured and kissed her.

For a long moment, nothing existed beyond the two of them. Colin finally broke the spell by motioning toward the window. "Did you catch the view?" he asked.

Janna laughed again as she practically pressed her face to the glass. They could see little beyond the huge towers of the hotel, perfect replicas of castle turrets.

After resting and getting settled in, they went to the basement of the hotel, where they had dinner at a buffet restaurant. Janna had never seen so much food in her life. It was as delicious as it was beautiful. After dinner they stopped to watch a magic show, then they wandered through the arcade and gift shops. Colin won a stuffed animal for Matthew, then they bought him a plastic sword and Viking helmet. Colin also picked out a tiny, glittery sand castle and bought it as a memoir.

After returning their purchases to their room, they walked together over the drawbridge to a point where they could see the surrounding hotels. Janna caught her breath as Colin pointed out a pyramid-shaped hotel, with the replica of a huge sphinx in front of it. He then pointed in the other direction, where a large replica of the Statue of Liberty stood in front of a miniature New York City.

"It's incredible," she said breathily.

"The castles of Europe, the pyramids of Egypt, and the splendor of New York City," he said with the same drama he'd used earlier in the day. He smirked and added, "All in one block."

Janna laughed and dragged Colin toward the pyramid first. Taking in the sights, it was easy for her to ignore the casinos and the occasional evidence of undesirable things that she knew existed in the city. She stood in the lobby of the *Luxor* for nearly half an hour, just gazing at the Egyptian statues and artwork. She thought of the Bible stories that related to these things—Joseph, who was sold into Egypt and eventually became very powerful, and Moses, who was raised by the daughter of Pharaoh.

Janna knew it was late, but she didn't feel the least bit tired as they continued to explore the incredible architecture and sights of the city that never sleeps. She had never considered, before now, the reality that she had lived a very sheltered life. Her mother had been content to stay at home, and Russell had preferred to keep her confined and controlled. Never before had she experienced the exhilaration of seeing new sights and hearing new sounds. With her hand in Colin's, she felt as if she was somehow in the center of a fairy tale. Looking into his eyes, she knew that being anywhere with him—and being his wife—was almost too good to be true. She'd never been so happy in her life, and she told him so as they traversed a walkway over the busy street to *New York, New York*.

As they stood on the street corner, gazing up at the incredible replica of the Statue of Liberty, Janna couldn't hold back a surge of tears. A thousand thoughts seemed to fill her mind all at once.

"What's wrong?" Colin asked, wiping at her damp cheeks.

Janna laughed softly. "It's just so beautiful. I mean . . . I don't know that I'll ever see the real thing, but . . ." She motioned toward it. "I mean . . . to think of what it symbolizes. It's really so . . . beautiful."

Colin put his arm around her shoulders and hugged her against him as she continued to study the statue. Everything else blurred around her. She was only aware of herself, Colin, and Liberty. She thought of the freedom she'd gained; of how far she'd come since she'd first made the decision to flee from Russell's abuse. A subtle nagging in the back of her head reminded her that there were many layers of healing left to be faced before she could be completely free. But with Colin at her side, she believed she could face anything.

After staying out half the night, Colin and Janna slept half the next day. They ate again at the buffet, did some more exploring, then they headed out of Las Vegas toward southern California. Janna was fascinated by the way the scenery gradually changed as they went further south and toward the coast. It was evening before they arrived in Carlsbad, a quaint seaside town near San Diego.

Colin had made reservations at a motel near the ocean, and it didn't take them long to get settled. With a compact kitchen and front room, it was more like a small apartment than a motel room, overlooking a grassy courtyard with palm trees, a pool, a jacuzzi, barbecue grills, and picnic tables. Colin took Janna out for a nice dinner, then they went to bed early, too exhausted from the long drive to do any more sightseeing.

Janna woke up in the middle of the night and realized she could hear the ocean outside the open window. Impulsively she nudged Colin awake, insisting that they go see it.

"Right now?" He chuckled through a yawn as she changed into a long, filmy skirt and top.

"Yes." She laughed and dragged him out of bed. "It's the least crowded time of day."

Colin kept yawning and laughing intermittently as he put on a pair of jeans and a T-shirt. Guided by a high moon, they walked hand in hand across the street and down a long, narrow stairway. Janna actually felt jittery inside as they approached the beach at the bottom of the stairs. She laughed aloud for no apparent reason and Colin stopped her, looking into her eyes, silently questioning her happiness.

"I've never seen the ocean before," she admitted. "It's so . . . incredible."

"Yeah, it is," he murmured, and led her further down the beach. He kicked off his canvas shoes and stepped into the waves, laughing as the cool water rushed over the bottoms of his jeans. Janna took off her sandals and lifted her skirt high, stepping gingerly over the wet sand to stand by Colin as the wave receded. She held her breath as it approached again, then giggled as the rushing water engulfed her ankles. Colin laughed with her, pulling her into his arms. Janna lost track of the time as Colin held her and kissed her, while the ocean waves teased over and over at their feet.

They sat on the beach and talked until the sun came up, then they walked back to their room and slept half the day. After a quick trip to the grocery store, they were equipped to stay close to the motel for the next few days. They barbecued in the courtyard, swam in the pool, and spent endless hours on the beach. Occasionally Colin even painted her toenails, a ritual he'd begun in their youth. It was one of many things he did that made her feel loved and adored. And Janna knew that life could be no better than this. She had no reason not to believe that their future would be filled with happiness as perfect as her endless love for Colin.

The only grim moment came one evening as they sat together in the jacuzzi. As a small group of other motel occupants came to enjoy the nearby pool, Janna had a moment of panic.

Colin was quick to notice her distress. "What is it?" he asked. She seemed to hold her breath as she watched these people closely, then she turned and squeezed her eyes shut.

"What?" Colin insisted, pulling her close to him. She clutched his shoulders and her breathing became sharp.

"Janna!" Colin drew back and looked into her eyes. "Did something scare you? What?"

She nodded and took a deep breath. "I'm sorry." She laughed in an attempt to keep from crying. "It's so silly. I just . . ."

"It's not silly if it scared you. What? Tell me."

"I just thought . . . I saw Russell. That's all. I know that's absurd. I know he's in prison, but . . ."

Colin made a sound of compassion and held her close to him. "It's okay, Janna. It'll take time."

It took her several minutes to calm down. And while she was grateful for Colin's unconditional love and understanding, she hated feeling as if her fears were continuing to haunt their relationship. Forcing unpleasant thoughts away, she relished Colin's closeness and their surroundings, wanting her whole life to be this way.

While it was difficult to leave their honeymoon haven, Janna looked forward to settling into their new life together. It was good to see Matthew again, and to see him doing so well in his grandparents' care.

Janna found it easier each day to put the past behind her. She enjoyed keeping their little apartment clean and orderly, and cooking meals without the pressure of perfection that Russell had inflicted upon her.

Soon after the honeymoon, Colin had a job offer from a law firm in Salt Lake. They prayed about it and decided that relocating was the right thing to do. By the time school started, they were settled into a new home on the edge of the Salt Lake valley. Matthew quickly made friends in their new neighborhood, and seemed to be thriving.

Every once in a while, Janna would recall that Russell still existed, and that eventually he would get out of prison. But she would force thoughts of him away, only wanting her life to go on this way forever. Even so, there were moments when his abuse haunted her. One afternoon on her way to the grocery store, she stopped to put some gas in the car. Her mind began to wander as she pumped the gas, then she glanced at the pump and panicked. Her heart raced, her hands began to sweat, and her stomach tightened into a knot. It took her a full minute to remember that her husband would not be angry because she'd put more than five dollars' worth of gas in the car. And he would not demand to know where every single penny she spent had gone. Janna paid for the gas, then sat in the car for several minutes, willing herself to calm down. She closed her eyes and absorbed the reality that she was Colin Trevor's wife now. He loved her and she loved him. And she knew he would never hurt her the way Russell had.

Janna bought the groceries and returned home to cook dinner. But her thoughts hovered with Russell. Even in prison, he haunted her. She could almost hear him taunting her, telling her that she was not worthy of any man's love. And there were moments when she pondered what an incredible man Colin was, and wondered why he had ever chosen her.

When Colin came home, she managed a smile and forced any disturbing thoughts out of her head. He asked her more than once if something was bothering her. A part of her wanted to talk to him about it, but not wanting anything negative to mar their life together, she just smiled and insisted that everything was perfect.

By the next day, Janna felt better. The hourly evidence that her life was different now helped her get beyond thinking about the past.

Four months after the wedding, Janna called Colin at work just a short while before he was supposed to leave.

"Hello, Mr. Trevor," she said. "This is Mrs. Trevor."

"Yes, I know." He laughed. "What are you up to?"

"I was looking for a talented, handsome young attorney who might take me out to dinner tonight. It's Friday, you know."

"It's either me or no one," he insisted, then laughed again.

"That's what I had in mind. Your dad just came and got Matthew. He'll be spending the night with them."

"How convenient." Colin's voice turned subtly husky, and Janna felt a quiver run down her back. *She loved him so much.*

"So, how about it?" she asked.

"I'll be home in twenty minutes."

By the time Colin came through the door, Janna was wearing her prettiest dress, with her hair in a French twist.

"Wow," Colin said as his eyes absorbed her. "Is this a special occasion?"

"Yes."

"What's the occasion?"

Janna just laughed and changed the subject. "You know that place where they play really classy music, and you can get up and dance if you want?"

"Yes," he drawled.

"Let's go there. I'm in the mood to dance."

Colin only grinned before he left the room to hurry and freshen up. All through dinner, they watched each other through the candlelight, as if they were newly in love. While waiting for dessert, Colin took Janna's hand and they stood up to dance. He held her close and looked into her eyes as they moved easily together in time to the music. She smiled almost mischievously, and he repeated his question of earlier. "What's the occasion?"

"Well," she said as they continued to dance, "several years ago I made a really stupid mistake. There was something I should have told you, but I didn't. I took the cowardly way out and left instead. Of course, you knew all that, but . . . well, what I wanted to tell you then . . . *should* have told you then . . . is . . . well, it's what I need to tell you now."

Colin chuckled. "I'm afraid you've lost me."

Janna's eyes turned serious, filling with mist as she spoke in a trembling voice. "Colin, I'm going to have your baby."

Colin stopped dancing. He swallowed carefully, absorbing the evidence in her expression that she was serious. All the irony of the past and the joy of the present surged through him, and a rumble of emotion erupted from his mouth as he held her as tight as humanly possible.

"I love you, Janna," he murmured close to her ear. "I love you more than life."

Through the next several weeks, as Janna struggled with nausea and fatigue, Colin became obsessed with the baby. It was doubly exciting for him after not being there through her pregnancy with Matthew. He came home nearly every day with something new for the baby, and he worked on Saturdays to transform the spare bedroom into a nursery. Janna was concerned about being able to carry the baby full term after having several miscarriages while she was married to Russell. But Colin kept reminding her to be positive, and he did everything he could to help her so that she wouldn't get too tired or stressed.

As time passed and the child inside her thrived, Janna began to relax and look forward to its birth. A day never passed when she didn't get down on her knees and thank God for giving her such a good life. It was almost too good to be true.

Colin found another great healing moment in his opportunity to baptize Matthew just after his eighth birthday. That, along with everything else, made him wonder how he had ever survived without Janna and Matthew in his life. And now they were expecting another baby.

In the spring, Colin decided that having a second vehicle would be a good idea so that Janna wouldn't have to take him to work every time she needed to run errands. Work was going well and their budget could handle it easily enough, so they went together and picked out a Suburban. Janna insisted they buy the navy blue one, since it was near the color of Colin's eyes.

"I don't care what color it is," he protested lightly. "I just want one that runs."

For some reason, having a Suburban in the garage was just one more thing that made Colin feel like they were a real family—and he loved it!

Being married to JannaLyn was proving to be everything Colin had hoped for. Occasionally he saw signs of her lack of self-worth and her hesitance to believe that he truly loved her in spite of all they'd been through. But as they approached their first anniversary, their life together was good, and he couldn't complain. He had every reason to believe that the little things that didn't feel right would disappear with time. In spite of all the warnings he'd been given prior to their marriage about Janna's *baggage*, there was only one thing that Colin really feared facing. And it came much sooner than either of them had expected.

* * * * *

"You're joking, right?" Janna said, pressing both hands protectively over her well-rounded belly. The baby was due in less than a month.

"No," Colin said, wishing he was, "Russell is up for parole. The parole officer said he would call and—"

"But it's only been a year, Colin." She moved unsteadily to one of the kitchen chairs and gripped the table's edge. The fear making her heart pound was all too familiar.

"I know," he said, sitting across from her.

"One year?" she gasped and shook her head. She couldn't believe it. "It was attempted murder, Colin. He nearly *killed* me! The judge told me he gave him the maximum. How can—"

"It *was* the maximum, Janna. He got one to five. Apparently he's been minding his manners, and he's—"

"Oh, help," she murmured and pressed her head into her hands. "I can just imagine how he'd mind his manners. He'd do everything right—to the letter, just so he could get out and find me again, and . . ."

Colin watched Janna press a hand over the side of her face, briefly fingering the scar on her cheekbone—a tangible reminder of Russell's abuse. He could well imagine her memories of the countless times Russell Clark had hit her there. Her fear was understandable, but he had no desire to see their lives catapulted into fresh misery over it.

"Janna," he took her hand across the table, "if he even comes near you or our home, he'll be breaking parole and they'll send him right back to serve the full sentence. All we can do is be careful and put it into the Lord's hands. We just have to have the faith that you'll be kept safe."

Janna nodded, but she didn't feel convinced. Little more was said after that, but it was difficult for Janna not to think about it. If the fear for herself wasn't bad enough, she was about to have a baby. This was her first pregnancy to go full term since Matthew had been born nearly nine years ago. If something happened to this baby, she wondered if she could cope.

The subject came up again when they were informed that Russell was out of prison. The very thought that he was wandering the streets made Janna angry, when she wasn't downright terrified. Colin reminded her that they were not living in the same area, and it wouldn't necessarily be easy to find them. They had an unlisted number. They'd taken precautions.

"But you're an attorney, Colin. Your name is in the phone book, in bold type. *Colin Trevor, Attorney at Law.* He can find your office without even blinking, and—"

"And what? Follow me home from work?"

"Yes!"

"I'll be careful. We'll keep the door locked. We'll—"

"It's not going to stop him, Colin. I swear he'll—"

"Listen to me, Janna." He took both her hands into his. "A long time ago, you were promised in a priesthood blessing that you would be protected as long as you made your choices according to faith, not fear. We prayed about moving here, and we both knew it was right. If you think we should move again—go out of state, change our names, whatever—then let's pray about it. I'll do it if that's what it takes. But I don't believe that's the answer. You've been given a promise, Janna—from God. It's up to you to make it work."

Janna convinced herself to agree, and she sincerely tried to apply faith toward the problem. She prayed hard for protection, and exerted all her mental energy toward that desire. She had to admit that she knew running wasn't the answer; but still, it was difficult not to wonder if Russell might show up out of nowhere and harm her. She knew his mind, and felt certain that he'd spent his time in prison convincing himself that he'd been wronged by his ex-wife. And he would seek his revenge.

CHAPTER TWO

A pleasant distraction came when Colin's younger brother, Cory, called to say he was coming from out of state on business. Colin agreed to pick him up at the airport since his flight would be coming in late, then he would stay with them for part of the week, and then with his parents in Provo.

The morning after Cory arrived, Colin slept late, since he'd taken half the day off. Janna got up to get Matthew off to school, stopping every few minutes to catch her breath. This baby felt as if it was occupying every inch of her breathing space. Right after Matthew walked out the back door to go to school, she went into the kitchen to see Cory standing at the sink. For a moment she was taken aback. From behind, the resemblance to Colin was startling. She was glad she'd not embarrassed herself by assuming that he was her husband.

"How did you sleep?" she asked.

He turned and smiled. "Like a baby. Colin still snoozing?"

"I think he's in the shower. I'll tell him you're up."

Janna enjoyed observing Colin and his brother as they fixed breakfast together, laughing and reminiscing. Then Cory hurried to get cleaned up, since he had a meeting at eleven.

"You're welcome to take my car," Colin said. "I can drive the Suburban into work later. I don't think Janna's going anywhere."

"Not until I go into labor," she insisted lightly. "I can hardly move from one end of the house to the other, let alone *go* anywhere."

Colin chuckled and leaned over the table to kiss her. He couldn't help anticipating the birth of this baby, especially since he'd missed the first one.

Cory left in Colin's car while Janna was clearing the table. Colin took a basket of laundry down the stairs so Janna wouldn't have to lift it. He'd only been out of Janna's sight for a few minutes, but when he came up the stairs, he heard her talking to someone. Not talking, he corrected. *Arguing.* Was she on the phone? It hadn't rung.

Colin's heart began to race an instant before he heard her scream. He bounded into the kitchen just as Russell raised a hand to strike her a second time. Colin blocked the blow with his left arm and hurled his right fist into Russell's jaw. The surprise in Russell's expression was evident as he reeled back against the counter. Before he managed to recover, Colin took hold of his collar and slammed him against the wall.

"You filthy scum," Colin seethed and slammed him again. Then he took hold of Russell's right arm and twisted it up behind his back, pressing his face to the wall. "Don't you *ever* come near my home or my family again; not *ever!*"

Russell groaned as Colin twisted his arm a little tighter. He glanced over at Janna, who was leaning in the corner, her hand pressed to her face, looking scared and stunned.

"Call the police," he said, trying to sound calm.

Janna nodded and hurried to the phone, barely managing to punch out 911 with the way her hands were shaking.

Russell attempted to squirm free, but Colin leaned his entire weight against him, holding him helpless against the wall. He muttered a string of profanities that made Colin's skin crawl.

"Shut up!" Colin hissed. "I feel hard pressed to keep from killing you for what you've done to her. Don't push me."

The police arrived in just a few minutes. While they were putting Russell in handcuffs, he eyed Janna lewdly, saying with a little smirk, "Don't you worry, my love. We *will* meet again."

Janna clung tightly to Colin and watched as Russell was escorted from the house. Once they were alone, she crumbled. Colin urged her to the couch and let her cry without restraint against his shoulder. When she finally quieted down, he asked, "Are you all right, Janna?"

"Yes," she said and the tears threatened again. "That's why I can't stop crying. I . . . I'm all right, Colin. You were here, and. . ." She became too upset to speak. While she couldn't help but be appalled to realize that Russell Clark had just walked through her back door with no warning, she couldn't deny the reality of how blessed she was. It only took a minute to figure out why Russell had believed that Colin had left the house. He'd obviously seen Cory leave in Colin's car. Janna cried harder as the reality deepened. It was not only an answer to prayers. It was a *miracle.*

With Russell tucked safely back in prison, Janna was able to relax and focus on having this baby—if it would only come. Six days beyond the due date, she was still waiting for some evidence of labor. Matthew had gone to stay with Colin's parents for a few days, and Janna was praying that the baby would come before he returned. She missed her son, but getting to the hospital would be much less complicated if Matthew was taken care of.

Unable to bear another lonely day while Colin worked, Janna decided a good long walk might help get the baby moving. But the summer heat only made her swell up, so she drove to a nearby mall and walked slowly through the stores. She'd been at the mall a couple of hours when she had a sudden urge to leave—or maybe it was a prompting. Either way, she headed back to where she'd parked the Suburban, feeling a subtle ache settle into her lower back. She was just putting the key in the door when her water broke. Gripping the door handle, she glanced around, grateful to see no one near enough to figure out what had happened.

Uttering a quick prayer, Janna got in and drove herself to the hospital. Contractions were setting in hard by the time she arrived. Feeling a mixture of fear and excitement, she walked into the hospital, announcing to the woman behind the desk, "I'm having a baby. Could you—"

That was all Janna got out before she found a wheelchair beneath her and all the help she needed. At the first opportunity, she asked a nurse to dial Colin's office.

"Where have you been?" he demanded when he answered.

"I just went to the mall to walk. I was hoping it would get this baby started."

"Well, I was worried."

"I'm sorry, but—"

"Did it work?"

"What?"

"The walk?"

"Yes, actually."

Janna heard a long moment of silence. Then he asked, "What did you say?"

"I think you'd better come to the hospital, Colin. I've got to go now."

Janna was having an I.V. put into her hand when Colin slipped quietly into the room. She couldn't help laughing at his obvious distress. Then he took her hand and pressed a kiss to her brow. When he pulled back to look at her, there were tears in his eyes, and she felt too moved to speak. He really did love her.

As labor progressed, Colin kept asking questions about how this compared to Matthew's birth. When it became evident that this baby was coming much faster than Matthew had, she told Colin they could analyze the differences later.

Colin attempted to will his heart to beat at a normal pace as Janna was prepped for delivery. In a way, he believed that he had loved Janna the moment he'd seen her; or at least he'd felt drawn to her. And it had taken very little effort to fall in love with her. Through the years and the struggles, he'd only learned to love her more. But he had never comprehended how intense love could be until he witnessed firsthand the suffering she went through to bring a child—*his* child—into the world. He couldn't hold back the tears as Janna gave birth to little Caitlin. It was somehow the ultimate healing after not being there when Matthew had been born.

Janna laughed and cried as the wriggling infant was laid in her arms. She'd wanted another baby almost as soon as Matthew had passed his infancy. Now the years of waiting, the heartache and struggles, all paled before this moment. Then she looked into Colin's eyes, and her joy was too full to comprehend.

"I love you, Janna," he murmured, emotion making his voice quiver.

"I love you, too," she replied and held the baby carefully out to him.

Colin quickly wiped his tears before taking the baby. He laughed at the realization of his love for this child. She was so beautiful; *so tiny*. And it wasn't difficult to see a resemblance to Janna.

Early that evening Colin's parents brought Matthew to see the baby, and Colin used up two rolls of film taking pictures. He could tell that Janna was hurting, but there was a serene glow about her that filled him. He'd never been happier.

After Matthew had reluctantly left the hospital with his grandparents, Colin settled into a big, comfortable chair at Janna's bedside and held the baby against his chest. Janna smiled over at him, and his joy deepened.

"Tell me," he spoke in a hushed reverence that matched the mood surrounding them, "about Matthew's birth."

Janna tried to swallow her regrets as she told Colin the details of his son's birth—an event he should have witnessed firsthand. "You know," she said, "there were many times through the pregnancy that I nearly called you, but . . . I kept trying to convince myself that I'd done the right thing. A part of me truly believed that I had, until . . ."

"Until?" he pressed.

"Until I went into labor," she said with distant eyes. "I realized then that I'd been wrong; that I should have stayed with you." Emotion seeped into her voice. "But then . . . it was too late."

"Too late for what?"

"What was I supposed to do? Just call you up and say, 'Oh, by the way, Colin, I lied to you. You have a son'?"

Colin's smile was poignant. "Yeah," he said, "you should have. But what's done is done." He pressed his lips to the baby's tiny forehead. "We're a family now."

In spite of Colin's reassurance, Janna found it difficult to let go of her remorse. "You should have been there, Colin," she cried. "I was such a fool."

Colin wrapped one arm around the baby and reached out with the other to wipe her tears. "Hey," he said gently, "it's in the past, Janna—all in the past."

Janna fought back her emotion and nodded willfully. He touched her chin and she forced a smile, wishing she could believe him. No matter how she tried, a part of her just couldn't stop regretting the choices she'd made that had brought so much heartache into their lives.

Colin's happiness just seemed to increase as they made this little girl a part of their household. The nightly feedings and constant needs of an infant were a stark adjustment, but Caitlin's sweet spirit more than made up for any inconvenience. Colin felt the unity of their family deepening as they all worked together to care for the baby. Janna seemed tired much of the time, but Colin felt certain it would pass. After all, childbirth was no small thing.

Then, barely more than a year after Caitlin's birth, Mallory joined the family. The second pregnancy was unexpected, and Janna had a difficult time. She often seemed unhappy and frustrated, but Colin figured it was understandable. He did his best to be helpful and supportive, and he felt certain that once they got past the worst of it, they'd be grateful to have these girls so close in age.

But while Janna was recovering from childbirth, something went wrong somewhere. Sean had warned him that things could happen to trigger old memories and expose old vulnerability. Colin believed it was a combination of things that made the difficulties suddenly too intense to ignore, but the real problem started with that birth announcement in the newspaper.

"Here it is, Mom," Matthew called, his nine-year-old head buried in the paper.

"What?" she asked groggily from the couch where the baby lay sleeping against her arm. She'd finally gotten her back to sleep somewhere around four in the morning.

"The birth announcement. Wow, there's a lot of them. But it says right here: 'Girl born to Colin Matthew and JannaLyn Hayne Trevor.'"

"I hate it when they do that," Janna said through a yawn.

"Do what?" Colin asked, coming into the room while he straightened his tie.

"They put those wretched birth announcements in the paper. I can just imagine Russell sitting in his cell reading it right now, making plans. It gives me the creeps."

"Hey," Colin sat beside her and took her hand, "remember the faith thing." He combed his fingers through her long brown curls. "The Lord has proven that he'll look out for you. We just have to keep the faith."

Janna managed a smile. "I know. I guess I'm just paranoid."

Colin touched the scar on her cheekbone. "With good cause, I know. But we've got some time. We'll work on it, okay?"

Janna nodded, but she didn't seem convinced. "You'd better go or you'll be late."

"I love you," Colin said and kissed her with a touch of passion.

"I love you, too," she said, but it sounded weary.

"Hey, Matt," Colin said on his way to the door, "you help get your sister some breakfast before school. Your mother's exhausted."

Matthew folded the paper and looked disgusted. "That's all I do is help with my sister." Matthew was the mirror image of Colin's youth, with thick waves in his sandy-blond hair and rich blue eyes. And according to Colin's parents, he was equally headstrong and stubborn.

"Just do it." Colin pointed a finger, then he smiled and winked at his son. "I love you, Matt. Have a good day."

Colin left the house feeling a bit unsettled. He wasn't so much disturbed by what Janna had said as the indication that her fear still existed. He had no idea if Russell Clark was reading the newspaper, but he found out two days later that Miles Hayne had. And apparently he'd gone straight to the phone book to find *Colin Trevor, Attorney at Law.*

"Who?" Colin asked when his assistant stuck her head in the door to announce he had a visitor who said he was determined to wait until Colin would see him.

"Miles Hayne," she repeated in a loud whisper. "He said he's your father-in-law."

"Oh, help," Colin muttered under his breath. Then more loudly, "Tell him I'll see him in about twenty minutes." He needed that long to figure out how to handle this.

Colin leaned back in his chair and pressed both hands into his hair with a firm sigh. He'd never even seen a picture of Janna's father, let alone met him. From the way Diane and Janna had talked about him, he could well imagine the guy being pretty scummy. Could he face the man who had defiled the woman he loved when she was little more than a child? Obviously he had to. The man wasn't leaving until Colin saw him. But for what?

Twenty-three minutes after he'd received the news, Colin finally concluded that he could meet him. But he didn't have to let the man into their lives. He didn't see any reason why Janna would have to see her father at all. He felt sure it would only dredge up things he'd rather not think about.

Taking a deep breath, he pushed the button on the intercom and said, "Okay, Judy, send him in."

Thirty seconds later, the door opened and Colin rose from his chair. He didn't know what he'd expected, but this wasn't it. Miles Hayne looked young and firm for his age, with neatly-styled dark hair, graying at the temples. He was well groomed and dressed nicely. Colin wondered if he'd been anticipating some vagrant derelict. He reminded himself that appearances could be deceiving as the man extended a hand and a warm smile.

"You must be Mr. Trevor, according to the name on the door."

"That's right." Colin shook his hand, trying to imagine the things Janna had told him this man had done to her.

"Miles Hayne," he said and Colin nodded. "According to what I read in the paper, you are the father of my new granddaughter."

Colin folded his arms. "Janna and I have three children. The oldest is nine. Obviously you've missed something." He couldn't help the curt tone.

Miles chuckled nonchalantly. "I really didn't expect to be greeted warmly, Mr. Trevor. But you could at least give me a chance to explain myself."

Through a long moment of silence, Colin observed Miles Hayne more closely, piecing the image before him into the facts. Actually, he fit his character well. He was smooth and suave, like the devil himself. Colin could well imagine him as a young man, deceiving Diane into his bed with promises, marrying her against her better judgment when she got pregnant, then abandoning her to raise his baby alone. He felt a little sick to imagine the man coming back into their lives with promises of restitution and a good life, all the while privately abusing his daughter. And here he stood. Everything inside of Colin felt repulsed and disgusted. His instincts told him to get rid of him now—and fast.

"I don't need an explanation, Mr. Hayne," Colin said, using his courtroom prosecuting manner. "You have no connection to my family that is valid. The two weeks you actually spent in your daughter's life left scars that still haven't healed."

"I'm certain I don't know what you're talking about," Miles said, but there was a brief flicker in his eyes that Colin had learned to recognize. It was that lying-under-oath look, which usually got tripped up sooner or later.

"Well, whether you know what I'm talking about or not, you are not welcome in my office, or my home, or with any member of my family. It's as simple as that, Mr. Hayne. It's not negotiable."

Miles Hayne smirked as if this were all just an amusing misunderstanding. "You *talk* like a lawyer, boy."

If for no other reason, Colin hated him for the way he said that word "boy."

"I must say," Miles went on, "I was surprised to learn that Janna actually snagged a lawyer." He glanced around the office as if he was taking inventory. "And a successful one, at that. I wasn't sure she'd make it with *any* man."

Colin swallowed the urge to just belt him in the jaw, the same way he'd hit Russell Clark when he broke parole. "You may go now, Mr. Hayne."

"Court is dismissed?" he questioned with a little laugh that bristled Colin's nerves. "A man has a right to see his family, Mr. Trevor."

"If you think you've got rights, then get a lawyer and I'll talk to *him* about it. If you so much as breathe in the direction of my family, I'll have you slapped with a court order so fast you won't know what hit you."

"And you're a *feisty* lawyer." He erupted with that intolerable laugh again, and Colin noted a slight physical resemblance to his wife that was disturbing.

"The door is open, Mr. Hayne. Feel free to use it before I lose my temper."

"Are you threatening me?" Miles asked.

"Yes, I am. And if—" Something fell to the pit of Colin's stomach when he realized Janna was standing in that open doorway, her eyes fixed on her father as if she'd turned to stone. She looked positively gorgeous. But why, of all days, did she have to come today and surprise him with lunch out?

"Well, hello, JannaLyn," Miles bellowed with jubilance. She said nothing. He walked toward her and Colin became taut and alert, like a lion ready to pounce.

"How are you, sweetheart?" Miles asked, giving her a quick hug that evoked no response whatsoever from Janna. She didn't even flinch.

Colin told himself to stay calm and not do anything stupid. Miles put his hands on Janna's shoulders and squeezed them, then he stepped back and looked her up and down as if she were something he could buy and hang on his wall.

"You've grown up very beautifully, my dear. It's so good to see you."

Colin saw something finally come to life in Janna's eyes. What was it? Hatred? Fear? Contempt? Whatever it was, it made Colin's heart beat faster as he could almost feel her thoughts racing wildly. He held his breath when it seemed she was trying to say something. Instead, she pressed her lips firmly together and slapped her father hard across the face.

Colin's concern was briefly overshadowed with pride. He knew it took a lot of courage for her to do that, and he felt certain it solidified the point he'd been trying to make before she came in.

"It would seem she echoes my sentiments, Mr. Hayne," Colin said. "If you will excuse us."

Miles looked at his daughter with hard, accusing eyes. "If your mother were alive, I don't think she would turn me away so coldly."

"If Diane were alive," Colin said, "she would spit in your face."

"You're a cocky little thing," Miles snapped toward Colin.

"Whatever it takes," Colin said, motioning elaborately toward the door.

Miles sneered as if to say they had not seen the last of him, then he brushed past Janna and disappeared.

The moment Miles Hayne was out of sight, Janna visibly crumbled. She took hold of the door frame as if it could save her. Colin rushed to pull her into his arms. He eased the door closed, then adjusted his footing to support her.

"Are you all right?" he asked, urging her to a chair.

"I don't know," she murmured. "I'll tell you when my heart starts beating again."

Colin squatted beside her and held her hand, waiting for a reaction. Just when he thought she would start breathing normally and talk to him, she wrapped her arms around her middle and doubled over in apparent pain.

"Janna?" he demanded. "What is it?"

She groaned and shook her head. Colin put his arm around her and eased her head to his shoulder. After a minute, she took hold of him and groaned again. He could feel her trembling.

"Are you okay?" he asked when she finally seemed to calm down.

"I will be . . . I think." She sighed deeply and straightened herself, then pushed some stray curls back off her face. "What was he doing here, anyway?"

Colin hesitated. "He apparently read the birth announcement in the paper. It seems he wanted to meet his grandchildren. I told him to—"

"I heard what you said." She sounded angry.

Colin tried to figure out where she was coming from. When he couldn't, he came right out and asked. "Did I do something wrong, Janna?"

She looked surprised. "No!" She chuckled tensely. "Heavens, no. I mean . . . the last thing I want is to have him hanging around and . . ." She shuddered visibly, then said nothing more.

"What are you doing here, anyway?" he asked.

"Oh," she smiled and seemed to relax, "I just had to get out of that house. Joyce offered to take the babies for a couple of hours. You know what a good neighbor she is. And I thought we could have lunch. I was honestly going to call. I just . . . forgot."

"Well, I'm certainly glad to see you." He kissed her quickly. "But I wish you'd have come ten minutes later."

"What? And come across my father in the parking lot? Heaven forbid."

"Okay, *twenty* minutes later."

Colin watched the way she fidgeted with her purse and the subtle glaze that rose in her eyes. A distinct uneasiness crept up the back of his neck. He'd not seen her look quite that way since he'd married her. It had been well over two years since she'd suffered any depression. But he wondered now, just as Sean had warned him, if her struggles had merely been hidden somewhere all this time.

"Hey, are you sure you're all right?" he asked. She looked like she didn't know what he was talking about.

"Of course," she laughed. "I mean . . . I was a little shaken, I'll admit. It's unbelievable. He's hardly changed at all. He looks just how I remembered him." She shook her head, then smiled. "I'm fine now . . . really."

"You're sure?"

"Yes, yes."

"Well then, let's go to lunch."

Driving to the restaurant, Janna talked about how good it felt to be out of the house. She smiled and added, "I think I forgot how it felt to not be pregnant."

Colin laughed and took her hand. "Well, I know it was tough, but the results are marvelous. I have two of the most beautiful little girls in the world." He pressed her fingers to his lips. "Not unlike their mother."

Janna only turned to look out the window, and that glazed look came back to her eyes.

"Are you certain you're all right?" he asked gently.

"Yes, Colin, I'm fine," she snapped. "Drop it, okay?"

Colin was taken aback by her tone of voice. He couldn't recall her speaking to him like that since they'd been married. While he was tempted to get angry and defensive, he reminded himself that she'd just encountered a nightmare from her past.

"Okay," he drawled, then said nothing more until they had ordered lunch.

"I talked to Robert Taylor this morning," Colin said, attempting to make conversation. As soon as he said it, he wondered if bringing up the lawyer who had handled her divorce was a good idea.

"Oh, how is he?" she asked, apparently unruffled.

"He's doing good. He told me the firm is looking for another good corporate attorney." Colin watched her eyes closely, wishing he could explain the way he'd felt when Robert had mentioned it. It was difficult to put into words, but something inside told him it was the right thing to do. "He said that Charles would take me back in a minute if I wanted to come."

Janna's eyes widened, but not with interest.

"He said Charles is fed up with lawyers working for him who have no values. He wants somebody with integrity." He paused and added carefully, "He wants *me*."

The compliment warmed Colin all over again as he repeated it, but he felt immediately deflated when Janna said, "You can't possibly commute, Colin. You'd be away from home far too much."

"I know, Janna. I don't want to commute. But if we moved back to Provo, we'd be closer to Mom and Dad. And they could be there to help more with the babies. You know how Mom says she misses the kids every time we talk, and—"

"I don't want to move, Colin," she interrupted tersely. "I'm finally making some friends. I like my house. I like it here."

Colin took a deep breath. "I know, Janna," he said gently. "I like the neighborhood, too. But . . . it's this firm I'm with, Janna. I've told you how there are things going on that I'm just not . . . comfortable with. It's nothing serious; it's not outright dishonesty. But I don't want to get caught up in it."

Janna sighed as if she was exasperated with him. "Do you think you're the only man who doesn't enjoy his job, or—"

"I *do* enjoy my job, Janna. But I can do it somewhere else and work with good LDS people who don't use foul language and tell crude jokes; who don't stretch the truth for the sake of a buck."

"I don't want to move, Colin," she said as if he were a child and she was trying to be patient.

"Listen, Janna." He took her hand across the table. "We don't have to make a decision on this in one afternoon. I'm going to fast and pray about it. I know you can't fast, nursing the baby and all, but will you pray about it? And then we can talk?"

Janna hesitated, then nodded. But Colin didn't like the uneasiness he felt. She almost had that *lying-under-oath* look he'd seen in her father earlier.

Colin's uneasiness didn't lessen through the following weeks. While he prayed for an answer concerning this move and change of employment, he also prayed for Janna's heart to be softened. It didn't take long for him to be certain that moving was the right thing to do, but when he approached Janna about it, she became immediately angry.

"Have you prayed about it?" he asked in a soft voice that he hoped would calm her down.

"No," she snapped, "and I'm not going to. I don't *want* to move."

She handed him the baby and left the room abruptly. Colin patted Mallory's little back and tried to convince himself that this was the woman he'd married. He could let her sharp tone slide if he had to. And he could understand that she was having a tough time. But there was one point he couldn't swallow.

He entered the bathroom to find her putting Caitlin into the tub. "Janna," he began, "forgive me for being presumptuous, but I was under the impression that you and I, having been married in the temple and all, were committed to making our decisions by spiritual methods, for the benefit of the family. Am I wrong in this assumption, or—"

"That sounds like something you'd say in a courtroom," she retorted.

"I'm just trying to understand what's going on here, Janna. I feel like I've had an answer to my prayers. I need to know why you're not even willing to ask for one."

"If you were really concerned about what was best for your family, Colin, you wouldn't be wanting to drag me away from my home and my friends."

"I don't recall saying anything to indicate that my reasons were—"

"You didn't have to," she interrupted. "It's like you just don't want me to get too comfortable, or enjoy my life. I'm actually starting to like it here, and you're ready to pull the rug out from under me."

"Janna," he protested, "it's not like that at all, and . . ." He had to stop when the baby began to cry, as if she could sense his tension.

"Now look what you've done," Janna said sharply, taking the baby from him. "Get Caitlin out of the tub while I nurse her."

Colin suppressed his anger in order to enjoy a little time with Caitlin. He said nothing more about the move, praying inside that Janna's heart would be softened, hoping with everything he had that she would get beyond whatever was eating at her.

Two months after Mallory's birth, Colin woke up to realize that there had been no intimacy between him and Janna since long before the baby arrived. In the past, their lovemaking had always seemed to help smooth over the rough edges. He knew it was an important part of a good marriage, and he felt certain it had been far too long. But when he gently approached Janna about it as she crawled into bed that night, she simply told him she wasn't up to it and went to sleep.

Colin brainstormed for a way to approach the problem. He made arrangements for the children to stay with their grandparents and took her out for a nice dinner. But when they came home, she wasn't in the mood. He brought her flowers, but she was too tired. He came home from work and cooked dinner, hoping to show her that he was willing to ease some of her stress. But, again, she just wasn't in the mood.

Colin tried to tell himself that he was not going to get upset over this. He would not be so petty as to think that this tension between them was based on sex; he knew there was a great deal more to it than that. He just had to be patient. He gave her some time. He bought her a new dress—a sleek-looking oriental thing with a mandarin collar that zipped down the back.

"I can't wear *that*," she said, taking it out of the box.

"Why not? It's your size. You could at least try it on."

"What are you trying to do?" she asked, wrinkling her nose as she held it up. "Turn me into some geisha girl who—"

"Oh, for crying out loud. Just because I went on a mission to Japan doesn't mean I'm trying to change you, or—"

"And it's black, Colin. I've never worn black well."

"I always thought you looked good in black. But like I said," he sighed, realizing this was pointless, "I thought you could at least try it on. If you don't like it, fine."

Janna put the dress away. To his knowledge, she never even tried it on. She never said another word about it.

Colin's next tactic was a combination. He came home from work with flowers. Then he cooked supper, fed the kids, bathed Caitlin and put her to bed, put on soft music, lit candles, and helped Janna with the baby. When the babies were asleep and Matthew had gone to his room to do homework before going to bed, Colin urged Janna to dance with him. It felt good just to hold her close, but after a minute she tensed up and tried to pull away from him.

"What's wrong?" he asked, trying not to feel angry.

"I just don't . . . like to dance," she insisted.

"You *used* to like to dance."

"That was a long time ago, Colin."

"Or is it that you don't want to be anywhere near *me*?" he asked.

"Don't be ridiculous," she said as if the very idea was absurd.

"Well, what exactly should I be, Janna?" he demanded. "I have tried everything I can think of to let you know I care, to help ease your stress. But you hardly give me the time of day. Mallory is nearly four months old, Janna. It's been a lot longer than that since you've let me get anywhere near you."

"Is that what all this attention is for?" she asked. "Sex?"

Colin put his hands on his hips and swallowed hard. "It's called lovemaking, JannaLyn, and it's part of a good marriage. You know, that's what we are—married. Though it's difficult to tell these days."

Colin stopped talking before the anger set in. Three days later, Janna told him she was sorry and made it clear that she was willing to make love. Colin's immediate relief was immense. He felt rejuvenated and replenished from her kiss alone, and just holding her close soothed everything else away. But by the time it was finished, he wondered what had gone wrong. She was so cold and withdrawn that he almost wished it hadn't happened at all.

Colin prayed far into the night while Janna slept beside him. When Mallory woke up to be fed, he got up as usual to change her diaper and bring her to Janna. By morning, he felt prompted to take some action. He called his old family doctor in Provo, who was also a family friend, and asked straight out for some advice. Dr. Reynolds told him that the hormones producing milk for a nursing mother often subdued sexual desire. It was nature's way of focusing the mother's attention on the child. He also talked about postpartum blues, he called it, which could be twice as bad with two babies born close together. He advised Colin to be patient and give Janna some time.

Colin felt a little better, but instinctively he knew it was more serious than that. Hormones, blues, and whatever else she might be struggling with were only making a big problem worse. There was something deeper eating at Janna, and he knew it. He hesitated calling Sean O'Hara, even though he knew Sean could help him see the situation more clearly. He didn't know if it was pride or fear that held him back, but he felt hesitant to open up this whole counseling thing again.

Three weeks later, after the tension in his household had steadily worsened, Colin finally broke down and made the call to Dr. O'Hara. Just his luck—the man was vacationing with his family for another week.

Feeling desperate, Colin prayed more fervently and tried to think logically what Sean would tell him. He reminded himself that Janna had been the victim of a good deal of abuse, and it had all been inflicted by the men in her life. It wasn't difficult to see that Janna's attitude was stemming from that abuse. He doubted that she was intending to hurt him; she just didn't know how to handle what was going on inside her.

Recalling that all of this had started with the appearance of Janna's father, Colin felt the urge to hunt the man down and beat the hell out of him. Did Miles Hayne have any comprehension of the pain and suffering that had resulted from one abusive incident fifteen years ago? And then he had to show up and *remind* them of the dreadful thing. Colin had spent years trying to teach Janna that she was a woman of value, a daughter of God, someone worthy of respect and a good life. Then Miles Hayne walked in and crushed it all beneath the heel of his boot in five minutes.

CHAPTER THREE

*J*anna tried to concentrate on the task before her. At this rate, it would take most of the day just to get these dishes washed. She hummed the melody of one of her favorite hymns, attempting to will away the disturbing thoughts that continued to plague her. But no matter how hard she tried to concentrate on something positive, unspeakable images stormed through her mind.

"Please, help me," she prayed aloud, but even that seemed pointless as memories merged with fears in a grip so seemingly powerful that nothing good could penetrate it.

The babies are all right, she thought over and over. The impulse she felt to check on them again was ridiculous, and she knew it. It hadn't been five minutes since she'd peeked into their little beds where they were napping peacefully. The doors and windows were locked. The girls were fine. But her thoughts spiraled into the same old cyclone. She just couldn't rid her mind of the endless possibilities, visions of the heinous things she knew that people in this world were capable of doing to innocent children. People like her own father and her ex-husband. Every day the newspapers were full of stories: rape, abuse, kidnappings. Janna couldn't even pick up the paper anymore without feeling her heart race at the thought of coming upon more evidence of how horrible the world was. She couldn't watch T.V. at all. Even the commercials sent her mind reeling with the horrible possibilities of what could happen to her or the children; things she just couldn't live with.

"Oh, help," Janna muttered and threw the dishrag into the sink. She almost ran down the hall, checking first on Mallory, then on

Caitlin. They were as safe as she'd expected them to be, and she returned to the kitchen telling herself how ridiculous this compulsive fear was. She hated herself for being so out of control, and wondered for the millionth time why she couldn't just enjoy her life and appreciate all that was good in it. She had a beautiful home, healthy children, and a husband who was too good to be true.

But maybe that was part of the problem. Perhaps a part of her knew it *was* too good to be true. To this day, it was difficult for her to believe that someone like Colin Trevor had even taken notice of her at all, let alone committed himself to her for eternity. She had no doubt that eventually he would discover what kind of woman she really was. And when he did, life as she knew it would cease. If Colin had any idea what was going on inside her head, she felt certain he would realize the absurdity of their relationship. Surely he would see what she had seen all along. They simply weren't suited for each other. No man worth having could ever really love a woman with so many problems . . . so much shame in her past.

Again Janna attempted to make some progress with the dishes. But if her mind wasn't consumed with her fear that Colin would realize he'd made a mistake by falling in love with her to begin with, it was obsessed with the fear that something horrible was going to happen. And she just couldn't live with it.

The kitchen still looked awful when Mallory began to cry, but Janna was relieved to be able to hold her baby and know that she was safe and secure. She had barely finished nursing the baby when Caitlin woke up. Janna changed their diapers and sat on the nursery floor to play with her babies. She only wished she could fully enjoy their time together without being plagued by these dreadful thoughts and feelings.

"Please, help me," she prayed aloud. But in her heart she believed that her prayer hadn't risen above the ceiling. She knew from experience that God expected her to do her part to solve the problems in her life. But there was no avenue she could take that didn't terrify her. She'd gone the counseling route before, and at the time she had believed it had helped her immensely. But at the moment, she couldn't see how it had made any difference. If it had, then why would she be struggling so much now? And the prospect of opening it all up again was just too much to bear. So she just had to live with it, hoping deep inside that one day all these wretched fears would just magically go away so that she could be happy.

Noting what a beautiful day it was, Janna longed to take the babies out to play on the lawn, or perhaps even for a walk to the park with the stroller. But she hardly even dared open a window.

When Colin came home, she felt embarrassed by the condition of the house. She tried to get motivated enough to fix some dinner, but before she could talk herself into it, Colin was busy in the kitchen. She knew she ought to apologize for not being more organized and on the ball. But she felt certain it would only remind him of her many inadequacies, further proving to him that she was not worthy of his love.

"Thank you," she managed to say when dinner was over and he was loading dishes into the dishwasher.

"I know the babies wear you out," he said, but she could hear the frustration in his tone.

Janna nearly asked what was bothering him. But she knew it would only open a can of worms that she was trying too hard to keep closed. She knew he wanted her to get out of the house more, to do things with him and the children. But how could she tell him that just walking out the door made her heart quicken with some indescribable fear? She was *always* afraid, but she felt safest at home.

Janna didn't crawl into bed until late, hoping that Colin was already asleep. But as soon as she slipped between the sheets, he moved toward her and put an arm around her. She felt herself go tense as unwanted memories leapt into her mind.

"Hey," he whispered, "is everything all right?"

"Of course," she retorted, wishing it hadn't sounded so defensive. "I'm just tired."

Colin gently rubbed a spot on her lower back where he knew she often ached. She remembered a time when such efforts would have eased her tension. But now his touch only increased the thoughts and feelings she was trying so hard to fight.

Knowing deep inside that her problems had nothing to do with him, she forced herself to relax. She didn't protest when his touch became intimate, but through the course of their lovemaking, her thoughts became more intensely consumed with nightmarish memories of the abuse from her past. She felt guilty, knowing her mind should be with her husband. She felt as if she was somehow betraying him by her wandering thoughts.

"What is it, Janna?" he whispered when it was done and she eased away. When she didn't answer, he added, "There was a time when you wanted to be close to me . . . all the time. But now . . ."

"I'm just tired!" she snapped.

In a calm voice he replied, "Is it necessary for you to get angry with me?"

"I'm sorry," she said, but her tone of voice still betrayed the turmoil going on inside her. She just didn't know how to explain it without threatening what little was left between them.

"I love you, Janna," he said, sounding as if he was about to cry.

Janna squeezed her eyes shut, and silent tears leaked onto her pillow. Why was it so difficult for her to believe him? "I love you, too," she said. She fell asleep praying that he wouldn't touch her anymore. She couldn't handle the turmoil.

Early the next morning, while Janna was nursing the baby, Colin sat beside her on the bed, straightening his tie. "It's Friday," he said. "Why don't we get a sitter and go out this evening?"

Janna's fear of leaving her home and children erupted in frustrated anger. And then, to make it worse, he brought up his desire to move. While she attempted to cover her fears, their argument escalated. A part of her knew she was sounding like an utter fool, and she could understand his frustration. But for the life of her, she didn't know what to do about it.

Through the weekend, Janna found herself avoiding Colin as much as possible, since his presence alone seemed to encourage her guilt and confusion. Deep inside, she truly believed that he couldn't possibly love her as much as he claimed. And the very idea made her unexplainably angry.

For Colin, time passing didn't eliminate the problem, but he found if he handled things carefully, he could all but alleviate the tension. In moments of frustration, he stopped to remind himself of all that Janna had been through. Focusing on empathy and compassion, he resolved to be patient, certain that she would be able to get beyond this eventually.

When Mallory was six months old and he could count on one hand the times that he and Janna had shared any intimacy, Colin reached a new low. It wasn't so much the lack of intimacy itself as what it represented. They shared practically nothing beyond passing the babies back and forth to keep them happy. Janna didn't want to go out, either with him or as a family. She only went to church about half the time, and his offers to make arrangements for them to go to the temple were passed off and ignored.

Evaluating the situation again, Colin realized that this could go on indefinitely if he let it. Again, he seriously considered talking to Sean O'Hara about it. He nearly called him, then he realized that this wasn't *his* problem. He and Janna *both* needed to talk to Sean if this was going to get fixed.

Colin fasted and prayed about approaching Janna with this idea. When he knew it couldn't be put off any longer, he gathered all his fortitude and snuggled up close to her in bed. She tensed up immediately and he said, "It's okay. I just want to talk."

Janna relaxed some, but not completely.

"Janna, honey," he said softly, "you know . . . I'm concerned . . . that things just aren't right between us. I mean . . . nothing's been quite the same since your father came, and—"

She turned to glare at him so quickly it was startling. "Are you trying to say that all of this is *my* fault?"

Colin prayed for guidance. "Janna, I'm saying that *we* might need some help to work this out. I was thinking that maybe we should talk to Sean. It's been a long time, but I know he'd help us. If we could nip this thing in the bud, and—"

"Oh, that's just what we need." She turned her back and fluffed her pillow fiercely. "If we go talk to Sean, he'll have me dredging up all that garbage from the past and analyzing it. I have no desire to talk about it—at all."

"Well, maybe that's what we need, Janna. If he can—"

"Colin, do me a favor. Stop treating me like some kind of psycho, and let me get some sleep."

Again Colin forced back the anger and resolved to be patient. Over the next several weeks, he noticed the house getting progressively less orderly. He certainly didn't mind having his home look lived in, but it eventually got so bad that he had to clean it up himself or go crazy. He started assigning Matthew more chores around the house, much to the boy's dismay. And when Matthew didn't follow through, Colin came up with some consequences that would make him do it or lose privileges. He began to realize that Janna was not disciplining Matthew at all in his absence, and Colin was left to try and keep the boundaries clear in the hours that he was home.

Gradually, a routine developed that kept Colin too busy to be frustrated. He cleaned and did the grocery shopping on Saturdays, not to mention the usual yard work. On weekdays he worked an average of ten hours, then came home to cook dinner, help with homework, bathe the little ones, do a load of laundry, and pick up the house.

On top of that, it seemed that everything he didn't like about the firm he was working with got worse. He couldn't walk down the hall without hearing some foul word or part of a crude joke. He'd expect it from construction workers, perhaps. But these were attorneys, for crying out loud. Then he reminded himself that scruples were not limited to white or blue collars.

Colin was vaguely aware of two rookie lawyers the firm had hired who were studying for the bar and attempting to work themselves into the business. One was a young man named Don Hammond, and the other a woman, Lily Greene. Colin was too busy to do more than exchange greetings in the hall, but he could hardly refuse when Don came to his office and specifically asked for some help. The following day, Don and Lily both came to his office with some questions regarding the bar exam, and the day after that the three of them ended up having lunch at Colin's desk while he drilled them with questions. Colin actually grew to like Don, but he thought Lily was headstrong to the point of being subtly obnoxious. It was as if she was determined to make it as well as, or better than, any man, and she was going to let everyone around her know it. He couldn't deny that she was attractive, although her sleek blonde hair and chiseled features appeared almost doll-like—as if she wasn't quite real. She always wore long jackets and short skirts, a style that was somewhere between masculine and feminine. He thought she would do better to cover several more inches of her legs, especially as skinny and shapeless as they were.

But gradually a sweeter side of Lily emerged, and he couldn't deny that she had more scruples and class than most of the people in the office. He wondered why Don and Lily had attached themselves to him. Was it possible that the other attorneys were too stuffy to be willing to answer some questions and help out a rookie?

Things at work seemed to improve a little by having someone to converse with who wasn't crude and lacking integrity. But the situation at home only seemed to worsen. When Mallory was nine months old, Colin became so frustrated that he feared he couldn't take it anymore. An argument erupted between him and Janna that seemed to have absolutely no bearing on anything, but it reached a point where he actually felt like hitting her. This realization alone was enough to give him a mental slap in the face. He withdrew and left the house before he had a chance to do something he would really regret.

Needing something to release his nervous energy, he crawled beneath his car to change the oil. He'd taken good care of the little teal-blue convertible; he loved it, and right now it was the means to hide from reality. When the job was finished, he put the top down on the car and went for a drive. He wondered what was wrong with him, that he would actually be tempted to hit a woman—and Janna, no less. After the way her first husband had treated her, he could well imagine what such a thing would do to their relationship. The next morning he finally broke down and made an appointment with Sean, during work hours when he could go to Provo without Janna's knowledge.

"It's so good to see you," Sean said, giving him a quick, brotherly embrace. "I hope you're not going to tell me that you're here because you need me."

"I'm afraid that's exactly why I'm here," Colin stated. "Don't take it personally or anything."

"I know how busy life can be," Sean said easily. "But I'm not sure I've seen you since the wedding."

"Probably not."

"You moved to Salt Lake, right?"

Colin nodded, briefly bringing him up to date on the status of his family and job.

"So, what's up?" Sean asked when the small talk had run down.

Colin took a deep breath and just started talking. Sean listened attentively, making an occasional note on a big yellow notepad. When Colin felt he had summarized it fairly well, Sean cleared his throat and said, "Well, Colin, congratulations. You are officially a codependent spouse."

Colin recalled Sean warning him about such a thing, but he couldn't remember enough to understand what he meant. Whatever it was, he didn't like it.

"Janna has made herself an island, Colin, and you have become the sea surrounding her. You buffer her from the world. She doesn't have to go anywhere she doesn't want to go. She doesn't have to do anything she doesn't want to do . . . all because you smooth it over and take care of it. You're patient. You swallow your anger. You justify it all away with the fact that she has reasons for behaving that way. And what are you getting for it?"

"Hell," Colin stated.

"Pretty close," Sean said. "She's punishing you for it. Oh, not consciously, of course. But somewhere inside, Janna is hating you because you allow her to treat you that way."

Colin wiped a hand over his face and tried to absorb this. He couldn't deny the truth in what Sean was saying. And the truth hurt.

"Now," Sean continued, "I know Janna and her circumstances well enough to make a guess at why she's behaving this way, but I can't fix it. At the moment, she's not willing to talk to me or admit she needs help. And your codependency is making you a part of the problem. You're going to have to make some changes in order to make her face up."

"How can *I* fix it?" Colin snarled.

"I didn't say you could fix it, Colin; at least not the core of the problem with Janna. She's the only one who can do that. But you can control how she affects *you*. You can choose how you respond to her behavior. It's tricky, but it's possible. The bottom line is, she won't change if you don't change. And right now, your behavior is allowing her to remain sick."

"So, tell me why she's acting like this," Colin said, wanting to understand this one step at a time.

"I don't have to remind you of Janna's history. My guess is that she has two goals. Again, these are not conscious. If you were to confront her with this straight out, she would likely have no idea what you're talking about. But it seems to me that, first of all, she's trying to convince you that she is not worthy of your love, and going along with that, she's determined to prove it. She is pushing to get you to prove that you love her in spite of *anything* she might say or do, secretly believing that it will prove the opposite, and that she was right all along. She believes she is a woman worthy of nothing good. It's a self-fulfilling prophecy thing. She pushes you away, and then she can say, 'I was right. You didn't really love me after all.'

"The second thing," Sean went on, "is this bubbling hurt inside her that has nowhere to go. And there is likely a lot of fear connected to that hurt. You're the only one in her life who will allow her to vent it—and you just happen to be a man, which puts you in the same category as her father and Russell. So she's punishing you for that hurt, and you're letting her do it." Sean allowed Colin some time to absorb his words, then asked, "Is this helping any?"

"I . . . think so," Colin muttered. "Just . . . answer one more question."

"Okay."

"Tell me why I felt like hitting her. I mean . . . the very idea just repulses me. Do you know how many times I have promised her that I would never hurt her the way Russell did; that no matter how angry I got, I would never get physical with it? So what is it inside of me that actually wanted to just. . . *hit* her?"

"Well, what were you feeling?" Sean asked.

"I was just . . . angry!"

"And beneath the anger?"

"I was . . . frustrated; helpless."

"Well, why does a child hit a sibling or a playmate?" Colin said nothing, and Sean continued. "It's a natural-man thing. We instinctively want to lash out at what's frustrating us. The trick is in learning to put off the natural man and rise above it. I don't think there's anything wrong with you, Colin. In truth, she may subconsciously be trying to provoke you to hit her." Colin looked surprised and he added, "Wouldn't that prove this 'you don't really love me' thing? The fact that you withdrew and got away when the impulse came is some credit to you. The trick is to learn to keep the situation from getting that intense."

Colin listened attentively as Sean gave him some suggestions for communication skills that would help ward off the anger. He wondered why he hadn't seen Sean months ago, though he still went home discouraged and concerned. But at least he understood more about what was going on, and he was determined to follow Sean's advice for taking some steps to get beyond this codependency thing. The part he didn't like was Sean telling him near the end of their session, "It'll get worse before it gets better."

Colin arrived home to find the house in total disarray, and Janna watching a video in her nightgown. While he tried to find a place to start putting things in order, it occurred to him that he was the patriarch of a dysfunctional family. The thought made him a little sick, but he was determined to get beyond it.

For several weeks, Colin attempted to declare his boundaries firmly and with love. He helped Janna with the children and the home, but he didn't cross the line of assuming her responsibilities as a homemaker. He told her that he'd watch the kids so she could go out without them, even encouraged her to get a friend and go to a movie or something, but she never took his offer. When she spoke disrespectfully or with anger, he simply said, "Is it necessary for you to use that tone of voice?"

Janna seemed agitated by the changes in his attitude, and she attempted to argue with him frequently. But after a few tries, the communications skills Sean taught him began to work—to a point. And Colin was learning at what point to just walk out of the house and let it drop.

On a particular morning, Colin was already late for work because he'd had to deal with Matthew's refusal to take a shower before going to school. On his way out the door, Janna asked Colin if he would pick up a gallon of milk before he went into the office.

"I'm already late, honey," he said gently. "I'm sorry, but I just can't."

She started into a tirade about how insensitive he was, telling him he had no idea how difficult it was for her to take both babies to the store.

"Well," he said, "if you planned ahead a little, I would be happy to watch the children in the evenings so you could go and get groceries without them."

At this, she told him he was a male chauvinist who treated her like a child. And she actually swore at him.

"No, Janna," he said, forcing himself to say calm, "I'm treating you like the healthy adult you are, who is capable of keeping her home stocked with groceries. I have to go now, so I can bring home a paycheck."

"Yes, well at least you're good for something around here."

Colin told himself to take hold of the doorknob and walk out, but the words just held him motionless until they erupted. "I cannot believe, after all I have gone through for you, that a paycheck is all I'm worth."

"What do you mean, all you have gone through for *me?*" she retorted.

"I mean, Janna, that if it weren't for me, you would be running scared with an illegitimate child, if not dead."

Colin regretted letting that come out, even before she drew her hand back and slapped him hard. He closed his eyes and took a deep breath as the sting settled into his face. He remembered watching her slap her father in much the same way. Was it as literal as Sean had said? Was she punishing him for what Miles Hayne had done to her? Did it matter *why?*

"You know," he said in a calm voice that he hoped would keep him from hitting her back, "if I did that to you, you would scream spouse abuse, and—"

"If you're not going to help me, then get out of here and go to work before I really lose it."

"Fine," Colin said and slammed the door on his way out.

He forced the episode out of his mind in order to cope through the day, knowing even as he did that he was likely promoting his own denial. But he didn't know what else to do.

Colin was the last one to leave the office, and he made certain the doors were locked behind him. It was raining a little as he walked through the nearly empty parking lot. Then he noticed Lily, with the hood up on her car, staring down at the engine as if she could fix it by osmosis.

"Do you think if you stand there long enough, you're going to figure out what's wrong with it?"

She looked up in surprise as he approached. "And I suppose *you* would know what's wrong with it?"

"Maybe."

"I thought you law-school boys were opposed to getting grease under your fingernails."

"Tell me, Ms. Greene, do you always slap people into categories?"

"Sorry," she smiled slightly. "I'm standing in the rain and my car won't start. I'm not in an especially good mood."

Colin noted her appearance briefly. With her hair wet and most of her makeup washed away, she was almost pretty.

"Okay," he said, "since you apologized, I could maybe take a look at it."

"Are you telling me you *do* know something about cars?"

"I've kept my own cars running for the most part since I was sixteen." Without her permission, he got in the car and turned the key in the ignition, resulting in a grinding noise.

"So what do you think?" she asked when he got out.

"It won't start," he stated. She glared at him in disgust and he laughed. "It could be something in the starter. It could be the flywheel. Whatever it is, you're going to have to have it towed. I don't think it's moving until it's fixed."

"Oh, that's just great," she snarled. "Like I can afford a car repair bill now."

"You know, Lily," Colin observed as he closed the hood, "if it wasn't such a vulgar car, it wouldn't cost so much to keep it going."

"Vulgar?" she repeated as if he were speaking a foreign language.

"Come on," he said as the rain worsened. "Let's go call your husband, or—"

"He's working late," she stated. "He can't be reached."

Colin only hesitated a moment before he offered, "I'll give you a ride home."

"What do you mean, *vulgar?*" she asked as he pulled out onto the highway.

"It's a vulgar car. It's all for show. You could own a nice, brand-new car for a fraction of the cost, and the repairs wouldn't be so expensive."

"And that makes it vulgar?"

"It's a Mercedes, Lily."

"And what about this sassy little convertible?" she retorted. "It's not vulgar?"

Colin chuckled. "I've had this car for years." He lifted one eyebrow. "It's a Ford, Lily."

She shook her head as if she didn't understand him in the slightest. "You keep your Ford. I'll keep my Mercedes. Okay, Trevor?"

"Okay," he said.

She gave him directions to her condo, and he barely stopped long enough for her to get out.

"Thank you," she called. He waved and drove away.

Colin went home to the usual chaos, added upon by the fact that Matthew had been refusing to do his work, and he and Janna had been arguing. As if things weren't bad enough, Colin had to smooth over her lack of discipline with the child and try to convince him that his mother really did love him, even though she'd been screaming at him about his messy bedroom.

Colin continued trying to keep a balance between patience and solving the problems. While he told himself he was almost getting accustomed to being celibate, he tried to avoid the arguments and ignore all that she was unwilling to do in the home. He kept thinking about the things Sean had told him and tried to define his boundaries, but his gentle declarations to his wife always resulted in his being slapped in the face—sometimes literally—with accusations of being too critical.

"You have no idea how difficult my life is," she said after one such attempt to talk to her.

"I would if you'd tell me about it," he answered calmly.

"You don't know how lucky you are, Colin. You work with *real* people, who appreciate what you do."

"If you want to get out more, Janna, it can be arranged." He went on to remind her of his previous offers to take her on a weekly date, to take her to the temple, to watch the children while she went to the mall or a movie with a friend. She argued his every point with things that made absolutely no sense to him, until he regretted having brought it up at all. She finally agreed to go on a date with him, but she backed out when the specified evening came. And three more attempts ended in the same way. When he tried to ask her why she was so unwilling to spend some quality time with him, she told him he was cruel and unfair, and he expected too much of her.

Colin also felt the need to at least attempt to express his feelings about their lack of intimacy. He waited for what he felt was the appropriate moment, then reminded her of the love they shared and of their history together. He took her hand, saying gently, "Janna, honey, I don't want you to get angry. But something's not right. There are things that I always believed were appropriate in a marriage relationship; intimate things. But you seem so uncomfortable with it; in a way, you always have. I believe something's wrong, and I believe it has to do with the abuse."

For a minute, Colin thought she might actually open up and talk to him; but it didn't take long for the same old argument to erupt. Once again, he wished that he had just kept his mouth shut.

Colin talked to Sean on the phone about the problem in general, expressing his intense frustration and helplessness. "I'm not equipped to handle this, Sean."

"Well, she's depressed, and she's in denial. It's not an easy situation." Sean paused and added, "I talked to her on the phone."

"And?" Colin pressed, feeling some hope.

"Well, it's not my common practice with clients, but I called her and invited her to come and talk with me. I reminded her that we had worked on some pretty heavy stuff together in the past, and I'd like to know how she's doing."

"And?" Colin said again, trying not to be impatient.

"She's not interested in talking, Colin. She didn't say much, but I got the impression that she's blaming you for whatever isn't right."

Colin sighed loudly. "So, what do I do?"

"Maybe you should consider a separation," Sean stated.

Colin chuckled. "You're joking, right?"

"Colin, I don't believe Janna wants to be separated from you, but maybe that's what it would take to learn to appreciate you and let her know that you won't allow this to continue. Sometimes it takes something drastic to force the solving of big problems."

"I'm not sure I can do it."

"Well, maybe you won't have to. Maybe just giving her the ultimatum will be enough to light a fire under her to get some help. But you can't bluff, Colin. Think it through carefully. Decide what you can live with; what you're willing to do. Then let her know, and keep your fence-lines clear. That's the only way you're going to keep her problems from hurting you and making a bad situation worse."

"But . . . what if she chooses the separation?"

"What if she does?" Sean asked. "Can you force her to be happy? Can you force her to stay with you? If she's not committed to making your relationship work, Colin, there's nothing anyone can do." He paused and added, "It's only a suggestion, Colin. What you do is up to you."

"I'm not sure I can do it," Colin repeated, feeling something close to despair.

"What do your instincts tell you, Colin?" Sean asked gently.

"We're supposed to be together. She loves me. She's just hurting, and I understand why, but . . ."

"But you can't live like this?" he guessed with accuracy.

"That's right."

"Think about it, Colin. I'm here if you need me."

Colin almost told Sean about the intimacy problem, but he figured the advice he'd already been given applied to that as well. And he simply didn't want to get into it. The very idea of implying that the problem rested on the lack of intimacy in his marriage just seemed so . . . what? Selfish? Chauvinistic? Whatever it was, he didn't want to talk about it.

Colin thought about it until his head hurt. While Sean's theory made some sense, he couldn't comprehend actually separating from Janna—or even proposing it. Was it the memory of living without her all those years that held him back? Was he just plain terrified to be without her? He knew he should pray about it, but it just seemed so wrong that he couldn't bring himself to even ask the Lord.

A few days after his visit with Sean, Janna erupted over some petty thing, and with little thought, Colin blurted out, "If you don't stop treating me like this, you might be on your own, Mrs. Trevor."

"What do you mean by that?" she demanded.

Colin had to think a moment to realize what he'd said. Now that he'd opened the door, he said more softly, "Maybe we should separate for a while, Janna, until we can—"

"What? So I can take care of these children alone *all* the time?"

Colin sighed and stared at the floor as she told him how impatient, intolerant, insensitive, and selfish he was. He nearly told her that they might as well be separated already since they shared nothing, but he bit his tongue. He went to bed that night feeling so discouraged and alone that he just wanted to go to sleep and never wake up. Knowing that was not an option, he prayed for help and guidance. The feeling came strongly that they needed to move to Provo. He believed it would be beneficial to all of them. His parents could help more with the babies, and Matthew would get away from some friends that were not having a good influence on him. And he could get away from the things at the office that made him uncomfortable. But Janna's reaction, when he brought it up, was exactly what he'd expected.

After that day, Colin began going through the motions of his life as if he were somehow watching himself from a distance. He often thought of the scriptural phrase *past feeling*, and believed it described him well. He was depressed, plain and simple. He felt frustrated, helpless, and completely out of control of his life. He worked at the office. He worked at home. He decided that trying not to be codependent was just too painful. So he deemed himself a classic codependent spouse, because he didn't know how to fix it without provoking a war that he simply wasn't prepared to fight.

Colin loved Janna. He always had. Why couldn't she see that? Why couldn't she understand that it was *her* happiness he wanted, as much as his own? He tried to force thoughts of it out of his head and concentrate on his work, but it wasn't easy.

Following a typical phone conversation with his wife concerning everything that was wrong at home, Colin walked across the hall to Lily's office to ask her a simple question. The door was open, but as he entered, he saw immediately that she was crying.

"What do you want?" she snapped, turning her back to him while she wiped at the tears.

"I just want to ask you about the—" Colin stopped abruptly, realizing that she was *really* upset. It was an interesting contrast to see this apparently tough businesswoman crying as if her heart had broken. "Lily, what is it?" he asked gently.

She glared at him a moment, then said, "Shut the door, before the whole place knows I'm crying."

Colin closed the door and leaned against it. "Do you want to talk about it?" he asked.

"There's not much to say, really." She sniffled and blew her nose. "Tyler just called and told me he wants a divorce." She snapped her fingers. "Just like that." She chuckled bitterly. "I didn't even know anything was wrong. Am I that *stupid?*"

Empathy rose sharply into Colin's chest. He knew all too well the heartache of such struggles. He sat on the edge of her desk and listened to her spill all her feelings, offering some words of compassion and encouragement. He found himself repeating advice that Sean had given him at times in the past. Then, without hardly realizing it, he told her what was going on in his own home. He was embarrassed when he started to cry himself, but she handed him a tissue and just held his hand and listened. Before he left her office, Lily rose and hugged him briefly, saying with fresh tears in her eyes, "Thank you, Colin. I think I feel better."

A few days later, Lily's car was in for repairs due to overheating. Colin took her home. The next day her car wasn't ready yet, and he did it again. As soon as she got out of the car, he told himself this was not a good idea. He wasn't attracted to Lily Greene, and the last thing on his mind was any kind of inappropriate involvement. But he knew it wasn't right for him to be having personal conversations with her, and it certainly wasn't good for him to be giving her rides.

A week later, Lily asked if he would take her home. "The car's getting a new fuel pump. By then it should practically be as good as new."

Colin gave her a ride, but he told her as she got out, "Buy a new car, Lily." He couldn't help his terse tone. "Because I'm not taking you home again."

"Is there a problem?" she asked with obvious surprise.

"I'm a married man, Lily. Next time, ask Don; he's single. Or get a cab."

Lily hardly spoke to him the next few days, which made him wonder if his declaration had somehow made her angry. But he quickly put it out of his mind. He simply didn't care what she thought. He had bigger, more important problems in his life. Lily's struggles were none of his business.

The day following Mallory's first birthday, Colin came to work feeling especially glum. A year had passed since her birth, and his relationship with Janna had gone steadily downhill. Then an issue came up at work that reminded him of why he wanted so desperately to move back to his old law firm in Provo. He felt compelled to stick up for his beliefs during an awkward moment, but he ended up feeling like a fool and wondered if he would have been better off being a plumber. He was contemplating a change of career when Lily came into his office without knocking. She wore a white silk blouse that was too thin to be modest.

"Did you need something?" he asked, trying not to look at her.

"I just wanted to tell you that I was proud of you for what you said out there. It took guts."

"Or stupidity," he murmured.

"You're a Mormon, aren't you?"

Colin hesitated, wondering what she was getting at.

"Yes, I'm a Mormon," he said.

"I thought so." While Colin perhaps hoped for a comment about his effort to maintain his integrity, she added, "I thought I heard somewhere that Mormons were a little stuffy about things like . . . well, giving women rides home, for instance."

Colin pressed his lips together and forced an appropriate answer into his mind. "It has nothing to do with religion, Lily. It's just good common sense."

"I suppose," she said with a little smirk. "Personally, I think it's a Mormon thing."

Colin swallowed his anger. "Okay, it's a Mormon thing," he said, relieved when she left his office.

"Get me out of here," he muttered under his breath. He daydreamed about what it might be like to work elsewhere, to live elsewhere, to have a wife who actually shared a *relationship* with him. But the thoughts only discouraged him further, so he forced himself to concentrate on his work and tried not to think about it.

The next day, Lily apologized to him for being obnoxious. He asked how things were going; she told him that Tyler had filed for divorce, just as he'd threatened, with little explanation.

"I'm sorry," Colin said. "That must be rough."

Lily gave him a stilted smile. "I'm sure I'll manage. How about you?"

Colin felt the urge to just pour his heart out to her, and he didn't understand why. "I don't want to get into it, Lily," was all he said.

That evening, he begged Janna to let them move to Provo. But she wouldn't bend; wouldn't even talk to him about it. He wondered if it might make a difference if she knew he'd been struggling with inappropriate thoughts concerning a woman he worked with. But he couldn't bring himself to tell her, knowing it would only provoke an argument. She would end up telling him that it was *his* problem, and he was being cruel and unfair to expect her to move. Colin felt as helpless as if he'd been locked in some ancient torture device. And any moment, the pressure was going to make him scream.

CHAPTER FOUR

*C*olin gradually felt something shift inside of him. *Indifference.* He just didn't care anymore. A part of him knew that he loved Janna; but it was a logical part. In his mind he could tally their history, the love they'd shared, the struggles they'd endured, and the feelings behind all of it. But on an emotional level, he didn't like her. He didn't like living with her, and he simply didn't care. He seriously contemplated a separation, but a part of him just couldn't bring himself to do it. Perhaps it was just too much work. Or perhaps, deep inside, he wanted to believe that eventually Janna would realize how unhappy he was, and she would fix it—for him. But in the meantime, he felt just plain weary.

Colin loved his children and did his best to be a good father. But when it came to Janna, he found that he was actually quite good at tuning her out. She could complain and try to argue with him, and he could spout off emotionless, mechanical responses. When the anger would take hold, he'd just walk out, fearing he'd go over the edge and do something to hurt her if he didn't leave. Plain and simple, he was *past feeling.*

On a cold morning in October, he got out of the shower feeling especially frustrated. Maybe it was the way he'd gone to sleep with echoes of an argument between Janna and Matthew storming through his mind. Maybe it was having to hunt down a semi-clean towel, and finding the shampoo bottle all but empty. Maybe it wasn't having anything in the house that he could eat quickly beyond some sugary kids' cereal. Or maybe he was feeling particularly selfish and belligerent. Whatever it was, Janna's incessant complaining about some inconsequential thing just set him off.

"You know, Mrs. Trevor," he said on his way to the door, "I didn't abuse you when you were thirteen, and I didn't beat your face in every time you messed up, but I'm sure as hell getting punished for it. And I'm just plain fed up!"

Late in the afternoon, Colin became briefly distracted from his work. He stared toward the window while his mind wandered through times when life had seemed worth living. He thought of the way Janna had been the motivation behind nearly everything he'd done since the day he'd met her. Even through his years without her, he'd always had the hope of finding her. He'd always believed they would be together—and happy. But now, for the first time in his life, Colin could almost understand how a person might become suicidal. He had no intention or desire to end his life. In spite of it all, he could see much that was good. He had children to live for, if nothing else. They needed him. But even the gospel seemed so abstract and difficult to grasp when his emotions were so battered.

"Is anybody home?"

Startled from his thoughts, Colin realized that Lily was waving her hand in front of his face.

"Boy," she smiled, "I don't know where you were, but it wasn't in this world."

"Sorry," he said. "Did you need something?"

"Yeah. I know this goes against your Mormon values and all, but I was wondering if I could bother you for a ride home. I'm finally taking your advice. I'm getting a new car, and I can pick it up tomorrow. The other one just died again, and I couldn't take it anymore. I'd ask Don for a ride, but well . . ." she shrugged her shoulders, "he's out today with the flu. And the rest of these people are just pathetically stodgy, you know."

"Yes, I know," he said tonelessly.

"So, I just . . . thought I'd ask. If you can't do it, I'll take a cab, but—"

"I can give you a ride, Lily," he interrupted. "It's not a problem."

Colin became lost in thought again, wondering where that had come from. He looked up a minute later to see Lily watching him, looking concerned. Her presence made him uncomfortable for reasons he didn't want to analyze.

"Are you okay?" she asked.

"I'm fine," he insisted. "I said I'd give you a ride home. There's no reason to make a big deal of it."

"Okay," she drawled, backing toward the door. "I'll just . . . stay out of your way in the meantime."

"Good idea," Colin muttered to himself after she'd left. Then he forced himself to concentrate on his work, not giving Lily or Janna another thought.

On the ride home, Colin turned the stereo up unbearably loud, perhaps hoping to avoid any conversation with Lily, or maybe to muffle his emotions. Either way, it worked until Lily nudged him and shouted, "Hey, could you hit the dome light for a second?"

Colin turned on the light and turned down the music. "What's the problem?"

"I can't find my flashlight," she reported, digging into the huge purse she carried.

"Why do you need a flashlight?"

"Well, the light switch for the living room is broken. I need a flashlight to get to the bedroom where there's a light switch that works."

Colin made no comment and she went on, still digging in her purse. "A neighbor told me he'd fix it, and I bought the stuff a long time ago, but he . . . I got it!" she declared, pulling a ridiculously small flashlight out of her purse.

Colin turned off the dome light. "But he what?"

"Oh, he's a real nice guy, but he's busy; gone a lot. He just hasn't gotten around to it."

Colin pulled the car up in front of Lily's condo and put it into park. The gesture surprised him. In the past, he'd barely put his foot on the brake long enough for her to get out.

"Thanks for the ride, Colin," she said, opening the door. "You're a sweetie."

Colin turned off the ignition as she stepped out.

"What are you doing?" she asked, seeming as surprised as he felt. He didn't want to go home. It was as simple as that. Home was hell. He felt like being needed and appreciated. And if a ride home and a simple repair could do it, fine.

"I thought I'd fix that light switch for you," he said. "Unless you don't want me to, or—"

"Oh, that would be *great,*" she said as if she'd just won a Caribbean cruise.

Colin followed her into the apartment. He heard the door close behind him and stood there in the dark, watching the beam of her flashlight move away. A few seconds later, a shaft of light burst through a doorway, illuminating the room enough to see.

"Excuse the mess," she said, moving a pile of unfolded clothes and stacking some magazines.

"It makes me feel right at home," he said, feeling the scorn bite his tongue.

"I'll just get the stuff and . . ." Her voice faded as she disappeared into what was apparently the kitchen. Colin, still leaning against the front door, noticed the condo had an unusual layout. He reached over and flipped the switch. Sure enough, nothing happened.

"Hey," he called. "Did you try changing the lightbulb?"

Lily stuck her head around the corner and scowled at him. "Very funny. Are you implying I'm a simple-minded female who would struggle with a flashlight for weeks rather than trying the obvious?"

Colin shrugged his shoulders. "Just checking."

She disappeared again, returning a minute later with some tools and a new switch set in its package.

"I already turned off the breaker," she said.

"Very good," he drawled.

"Are all Mormon men so sexist?" she asked while she held the flashlight for him.

"Sexist?" he echoed

"Well, you don't seem to have a problem with my being a lawyer, but my ignorance of cars and electricity has certainly amused you."

"Forgive me," he said, concentrating carefully on his task. "I certainly never intended to offend you."

"You didn't," she said. Then she suddenly seemed to get shorter, which moved the light.

"I can't see it," he said.

"Sorry," she said, adjusting the flashlight. "I couldn't take these shoes another second. It's not fair, you know. You men can wear comfortable shoes with a suit, but we have to wear these heels or look like a frump."

"A frump?"

"Flat shoes and pantyhose just don't cut it, in my opinion."

"Well, in *my* opinion, whoever invented those shoes was sexist."

Lily laughed, a sound that felt achingly unfamiliar to Colin.

"But they got even," he continued, "when they invented the necktie." As if to prove his point, he set the screwdriver down long enough to undo his tie and leave it hanging around his neck.

"Okay," he said, "let's try it."

"Already?" she asked.

"It's just a switch, Lily."

She left with the flashlight to turn the breaker on, and returned to a well-lit living room while Colin put the switch plate back on.

"Wow," she said, "I'd almost forgotten what it looked like in here after dark."

"Okay now, Lily, watch closely." She stepped toward him, and he flipped the switch up and down. "You turn it off. You turn it on." He chuckled at her scowl.

"You're making fun of me," she laughed, slugging him playfully on the shoulder.

"Yes," he admitted, setting the screwdriver on an end table, "but what do you expect from a sexist Mormon?"

She folded her arms and smiled at him. "You're really not that much different from other men, you know."

"Yes, I know." He put his hand on the doorknob to leave. "It's only the people who *don't* know us Mormons who believe we're weird. Well, maybe some of us *are* weird."

She smiled again. "Thank you, Colin. I really appreciate it. One of the hardest things about being alone is feeling so ignorant about fixing stupid things."

"You're doing just fine, Lily. I'm glad I could help."

She glanced down briefly as if she felt emotional, then she looked up with a forced smile. "Maybe if I could learn to take care of my own car and replace light switches, it would be easier in the long run than putting up with all the . . ." She stopped and bit her lip, obviously feeling overwrought.

"Yeah," Colin said cynically, "we men are just a bunch of insensitive jerks."

The alarm in Lily's expression quickly merged into huge tears that welled up in her eyes. Colin felt momentarily helpless. "Hey," he said while she was attempting to gain her composure, "I'm sorry. That had nothing to do with you."

Lily shook her head in apparent frustration and pressed a hand over her eyes.

"Hey, Lily." He put a hand on her shoulder and kept the other on the doorknob. "You're a strong woman. You're going to make it."

She looked up at him with a stilted smile, then wiped at her tears with an embarrassed chuckle. "You're really sweet to me, Colin . . . in spite of it all." She put a hand to his face and kissed his cheek. "Thank you . . . for everything."

Something inside Colin panicked when she put her arms around his shoulders to hug him. He had no reason to believe it wasn't innocent, but the contact felt so good that he impulsively returned her embrace. She drew back a little without moving her arms. Their eyes met, and it felt like they'd both heard a silent fire alarm go off somewhere in the distance. Colin told himself it was absolutely the most stupid thing he'd ever done to be standing here in this situation, feeling the way he felt about his life. But at the same moment his heart began to pound, igniting something in him that he hadn't felt since long before Janna's father had come to visit.

He briefly tried to read Lily's eyes. There was nothing seductive or provocative; nothing to indicate she was tempting him to do something he shouldn't. But it was evident that she really wanted to be with him. That alone was compelling. He couldn't remember the last time his wife had looked at him that way.

Colin heard his thoughts come back to him and cleared his throat tensely, telling himself to let go of her and leave. But he felt as if he'd turned to stone. In the brief moment he'd had his arms around her, he'd somehow lost his ability to make his mind connect to his body and respond.

"I'm sorry, Colin," Lily said, as if to explain her apparent hesitance in letting go of him. "I guess I'd forgotten how good it feels just to be close to someone."

"Yeah, me too," he said. A voice in the back of his head screamed in panic, telling him to let go! Back up! Get out! But something bigger and stronger held him there. Something human and primal; a lonely, frustrated aching that quickly drowned out any voice of logic or virtue. While Colin just stood there looking into her eyes, as if some invisible force wouldn't allow him to let her go, he felt her hands soften against his chest. She looked briefly at her fingers, as if she was surprised by their response. Was she as helpless as he? As lonely? As aching? Her eyes shifted back to his, and the answer was evident. The evidence deepened as her fingers pressed gingerly beneath the straps of his suspenders. Colin squeezed his eyes shut tightly, as if it could make his heart slow down or keep his breathing from sounding so sharp. Or maybe if he didn't look at her she would go away. He felt as if his heart would pound right out of his chest. Equal to this compulsion to just hold another human being and feel needed was a fear beyond description. But the fear itself only seemed to feed his desire to stay.

He felt her fingers sliding between the buttons of his shirt. A thousand protests screamed in his mind, but all that made it through to his lips was a weak, "Lily, no." It was like something out of a movie. How many times had he seen it on T.V.? Two lonely people going to bed together because it was *no big deal*. She pulled off his tie and tossed it.

"Lily, we mustn't," he said, but he didn't mean it.

"I know," she said, pressing her lips to his. A moment ago he'd been as solid and immovable as ice. Now he was kissing her, holding her. He was somebody else; somebody who wanted only one thing at all costs. Something almost fatalistic happened inside him when he pulled her up into his arms and walked toward the bedroom, abandoning everything he'd ever been taught, everything he'd ever believed in, just to have her.

"God forgive me," he muttered as he kicked the door closed. And the rest was like hovering somewhere between a dream and a nightmare. For a few brief moments, it all seemed so perfect, so right. Then he pressed his face into the pillow and groaned as the agony rose up from the pit of his stomach to suffocate him.

"Janna," he murmured, as if he'd just now remembered that she existed. She was everything to him, the center of his life since he was a teenager. She was the mother of his children, the keeper of his heart. And he had just given somebody else what he had once promised God he would give to Janna alone.

Colin rolled onto his back in an effort to ease a sudden constriction in his chest. He attempted to fill his lungs with much-needed air, but they refused to respond. Somewhere on the brim of his coherency he heard Lily saying, "Colin, are you all right? What's wrong?"

He sat up abruptly and gasped for breath. He forced himself to breathe deeply and calm down, then he lowered his head into his hands and groaned again. "Dear God above, what have I done?"

He felt Lily's hand on his face and turned to look at her. "Oh, Lily." He pulled her head to his shoulder and collapsed back onto the bed, holding her desperately close as if it could make the reality go away, or at least keep it at bay—just a little longer.

While questions and emotions tremored through him like a threatening earthquake, Colin found it impossible to make sense of anything beyond a deep, piercing heartache. He couldn't define its source any more than he could hold it back. He felt like a lost, abandoned child as he buried himself in Lily's arms and cried. It started with a little whimper, then it rushed out in torrents on the crest of a long-subdued wave of disillusioned love and broken dreams.

He lost track of the time as his emotions erupted, barely conscious of Lily's soothing voice, encouraging him to let it out. Gradually the emotion was replaced by a mindless shock. He lay staring at the ceiling, afraid to look elsewhere for fear of the evidence assaulting him with reality. As the numbness began to dissipate, he closed his eyes, aching to hold onto it, knowing that in its absence lay nothing short of the jaws of hell, waiting to swallow him.

* * * * *

Long after Colin had left for work, Janna sat on the couch and stared at nothing. It wasn't so much what he'd said, as the way he'd said it. Instinctively she believed that he had reached his limit. A part of her knew she hadn't been fair with him, but how could she possibly put into words the things going on inside of her? There was no avenue of dealing with her feelings that didn't frighten her. But for the first time in months—maybe longer—the fear of losing Colin was more intense than anything else. She didn't know why; she couldn't explain it. But deep inside, she knew that something had to change.

The babies were unusually cooperative as Janna dug in to clean the house. She knew it needed some deep, thorough cleaning and organization, but within a few hours she had it looking relatively decent on the surface. All the while, images of Colin's cold, hard eyes kept storming into her mind. Occasionally she had to stop and try to will the echoes of his declaration out of her thoughts. *I didn't abuse you when you were thirteen, and I didn't beat your face in every time you messed up.* She managed to finally push it away, only to have it replaced with harsh reverberations of *I'm just plain fed up! I'm just plain fed up!*

She nearly called her husband at the office, but she didn't know what to say. What would a simple "I'm sorry" do to fix the problem at this point? The urge to call him was strong, but she talked herself out of it, fearful of how he might react if she admitted there was a problem. Instead, she just kept cleaning, hoping he would come home to notice that she was trying.

When Matthew came home from school, Janna asked if he wanted to go to the grocery store with her. She wondered if she'd been such a horrible mother as he looked at her with complete surprise, then behaved as if they were going to the circus or something. He helped get the little ones in and out of the Suburban and the grocery cart. She let him pick out some snacks, then he helped her fix dinner while they talked about what he'd done at school.

It wasn't until Colin was an hour late that she finally told Matthew they could go ahead and eat. She expected him any minute, but she got the dishes washed and the babies to bed without any sign of him. She called the office but got no answer. She wondered if he'd been in some kind of accident or something. Horrible images flashed through her mind of losing him now—just when she was on the brink of being able to admit that he'd been right. They *did* need some help.

Janna became so worked up with concern that she called the hospitals and the police department, then she scolded herself for being paranoid when it came to nothing. She forced herself to appear unconcerned when Matthew asked where his father was.

"I'm sure something came up," she insisted and sent him to bed. She put off getting ready for bed herself, certain that Colin would come any time. Then she'd heat up his dinner, and they could talk. Exhaustion finally forced her to go to bed without him, but sleep wouldn't come. All things combined, she couldn't get rid of the horrible dread rising inside her. Why hadn't he come home? Why hadn't he called? Was he trying to tell her something? Was this his way of letting her know he'd really meant it? *He was just plain fed up?*

Janna cried into her pillow as she came to her own realization. *She was just plain scared.*

* * * * *

Colin sat up abruptly when the pain began to constrict his chest all over again. Lily sat beside him and touched a hand to his face. With a desperation he didn't understand, he pulled her close and held her for just one more moment. "Forgive me, Lily." He drew back to meet the alarm in her eyes. "I have to go," he said and eased her away from him.

"What?" she questioned. "Where are you going?"

"I have to go home, Lily. I have a wife and three kids who need me."

"*I* need you, Colin."

Colin looked at her briefly, trying to comprehend how this must appear to her. "I'm so sorry, Lily," he said, briefly touching her face. Big tears welled up in her eyes, and he forced himself away.

While Colin was scrambling to gather up his clothes and get dressed, Lily sat on the bed, wrapped in a sheet, crying.

"I should have never come here with you, Lily," he rambled, if only to ease the tension of listening to her cry. "I should never have given you a ride *anywhere*. I should have let you take my car, and I should have walked home in the rain. I should have never talked to you, or laughed with you, or cried with you. I should have never looked at you twice."

"But you did."

"Yes, I did, and there will be hell to pay—for all of us." The thought made him feel a little weak as he sat on the edge of the bed to put on his shoes.

"This is it, then," she said with an edge of scorn. "I'm a one-night stand to you."

Colin stood to look at her as he buttoned his shirt and tucked it in. "I never intended to be a one-night stand to *anybody*. I didn't plan this. It just *happened*, that's all."

"Why are you shouting at me?"

Colin took a deep breath. "I'm sorry. I didn't realize I was." His heart began to pound again as their eyes met. She was so eager to be close to him, so warm, so sweet.

"I have to go home," he insisted.

"Yes," she snarled, "home to a wife who treats you like dirt. What kind of masochist are you?"

"I love her, Lily."

"And me?"

Colin looked at her long and hard. He took hold of her chin and kissed her quickly. "I'm so sorry, Lily," he muttered. Then he left before he had a chance to think too hard about what he was leaving behind.

Colin drove a few blocks and had to pull over. He was gasping so hard he feared he'd hyperventilate. He forced himself to breathe deeply and calm down, then his mind catapulted through the possible repercussions of what he'd just done, and it started all over again. He wrapped his arms around his middle and curled around them, groaning from the literal, physical pain erupting inside him like some kind of volcano from hell.

It took Colin nearly an hour to calm down enough to drive home. Then he sat in the driveway for twenty minutes, gathering the courage to go inside. It was past eleven o'clock. The kids would be in bed. Maybe Janna would be, too, and he wouldn't have to face her tonight. How could he tell her? What would he say?

"Heaven help me," he murmured under his breath and lumbered toward the door, trying to absorb the reality that he had no business expecting heaven to help him now. Like Esau in the Bible, he had sold his birthright for the sake of gratifying his hunger.

The house was dark, and Colin willed his heart to be calm as he walked toward the bedroom. The hall felt a mile long. He groped his way to the bed and sat down to take off his shoes and socks.

"Where have you been?" Janna asked through the darkness.

Colin squeezed his eyes closed. He knew he had to tell her. But the reality was only still sinking in. He just couldn't bring himself to say it out loud—not yet.

"I ran into a problem," he said.

"I thought you might be trying to avoid me." She sounded almost sorry. But if she only knew . . .

"Maybe I was," he said and hurried into the bathroom. He leaned against the door for a minute, then he turned to look in the mirror at a man who had cheated on his wife. *Adulterer!* a voice taunted from the back of his mind; the same voice that had lured him to do it in the first place.

"Oh, dear God, help me," he whispered and leaned his head over the basin as the blood rushed from his head. Looking down at himself, he noticed that his shirt was buttoned wrong. Grateful that Janna hadn't had the chance to notice it, he peeled off his clothes and got into the shower. Feeling suddenly dirty, he scrubbed himself almost raw, wishing it could wash away the reality of what he'd just done.

Janna was apparently asleep when he finally crawled into bed. Normally he would have wanted to kiss her and snuggle with her just a little, in spite of her resistance. But tonight he stayed rigidly on his side of the bed, afraid to make any contact with her at all, as if his sin might contaminate her. He squeezed his eyes shut at the thought, and tears trickled into his hair.

Colin got out of bed early with practically no sleep behind him. He showered again and got ready for work while Janna slept, realizing as he did that the house was significantly cleaner than it had been yesterday morning. He peeked in on the sleeping children and pressed kisses to their foreheads. The sickness smoldering in his stomach deepened when he realized that he had sinned against them, as well. He was on his way to the door when Janna's voice stopped him.

"You're leaving awfully early. Did you get any breakfast?"

"I'm not hungry, thank you," he said, unable to look at her.

"Did you have any dinner last night?"

He wasn't ready to tell her, but he couldn't lie to her. "Actually, no. I don't seem to have much appetite."

"You don't look so good. Are you all right?"

Colin looked at her then. She actually seemed sincere.

"No." He shook his head. "I'm not all right, but I . . . I have to go." He opened the door.

"Don't I get a kiss?" she asked.

Colin turned again. He'd never left the house without kissing her, even if it was to mow the lawn. But he just *couldn't*. Not while another woman's kiss was so fresh on his lips. Though he knew it wasn't completely fair, he said tonelessly, "I was under the impression you didn't need that sort of thing, Mrs. Trevor."

He saw the hurt in her eyes, but it was quickly replaced by a familiar malice that he was sick to death of. Except that now he deserved it, even if she didn't know that yet.

She said nothing more, and he hurried out before he started to hyperventilate again. He got to the office before anyone else, and just sat in his chair, staring out the window at nothing. He wondered what to say to Lily when she arrived. Could he even face her? He couldn't imagine how he must have hurt her. But as horrible as that was, it didn't compare to how he had hurt his family. And above all that, he had offended God. He had broken covenants. He might as well have cut off his right arm. *And for what?*

Colin stewed over what to do, how to handle it. But there was only one possibility. If he lied and attempted to cover it up, it would only deepen the problem and prolong the misery. There was hell to pay, and the sooner he started making payments, the sooner he could be free of the debt—if such a thing were even possible. What if Janna wouldn't forgive him? The thought provoked that tangible pain again. He couldn't even consider the possibility. She had to forgive him. She just *had* to. Of course it would take time. He had to expect that. It would hurt her deeply, and he would face the consequences— whether he was prepared for it or not.

"You're here." Startled, he looked up to see Judy standing in the doorway. "Getting an early start?"

"Uh . . . yes."

"Lily left a message on my machine," she said, setting some papers on his desk. "She's not coming in today; said she's not feeling well."

Colin pushed a hand through his hair, trying to pretend indifference.

"You don't look so good yourself," Judy added. "Are you okay?"

"I don't know." He managed a chuckle as she left the room. "Maybe it's catching."

"Oh," Judy stuck her head back in, "Lily wanted you to give her a call; something about the Sheppard case."

"Okay, thank you," he said, knowing darn well that Lily didn't need *anything* to do with the Sheppard case.

For an hour he dreaded calling her, and accomplished nothing. He finally made up his mind that he had to start facing the consequences. And he'd start with Lily.

"You called?" he said when she answered.

There was a long pause. "Hello, Colin," she said.

"Hello."

Another long pause. "I'm sorry about what happened last night. Like you, I never intended for it to happen."

"Yeah, well . . . I'm sorry, too."

An even longer pause. "You forgot your tie."

Colin said nothing. The memories were nauseating.

"I need to talk to you, Colin."

"There's nothing to talk about. It was a mistake, plain and simple."

"And what if I don't agree?"

"What are you trying to say, Lily?"

"What if it meant something to *me?*"

Colin pressed a hand over his face as if it could make him think clearly. "I'm sorry, Lily," he said again.

"And that's it?"

"That's it. Call me a Mormon sexist fiend. Call me the world's biggest jackass. Throw darts at my picture. Do whatever it takes to get it out of your system, Lily. You have every right in the world to be angry with me, but it doesn't change the fact that last night was nothing but a mistake. I was a desperate man in a desperate situation. And you just happened to get caught in the explosion. I only ask that you—"

"Go to hell," she interrupted and hung up on him.

Colin slammed the phone down and muttered under his breath, "That's a distinct possibility."

Two hours later, Colin realized he wasn't going to accomplish anything in this state of mind. He stopped to buy some lunch, if only to quiet his growling stomach. Then he drove around for twenty minutes, praying aloud for courage and strength, all the while seriously doubting that his prayers would even be heard. He felt a little hope in realizing that the most righteous thing a man in his position could do was confess the truth to his wife and take the first step toward making it right.

Again, he sat in the driveway, feeling as if the powers of darkness would close around him. Knowing he had to get this over with before Matthew got home from school, he forced himself to go inside and face up to it.

He walked in to find the front room clean, and he could smell something baking. He wondered what might have provoked this sudden bout of motivation from a woman who had hardly done anything in months. Then she appeared, looking adorable in a pair of jeans and a sweater.

"Oh, it's you," she smiled. "What brings you home this time of day?"

Colin was tempted to skirt the issue and avoid it, but he reminded himself to be honest. "I . . . uh . . . I need to talk to you." He glanced around. "Are the girls—"

"They're both asleep. It doesn't happen often."

He nodded. Maybe his prayers were being heard after all. At least they could talk without being interrupted.

"Sit down, Janna," he said, and her expression turned severe.

"Is something wrong?" she asked, seeming more like herself than he'd seen in a long while. Was this a reaction to *his* behavior, or merely a coincidence? "Did you lose your job, or—"

"No," he motioned toward the couch, "I didn't lose my job."

Janna sat down. Colin took a deep breath and sat on the coffee table where he could face her. He pushed both hands through his hair, then leaned his forearms on his thighs. His pounding heart made it difficult to hear her when she said, "You're scaring me, Colin."

"Then we're both scared," he said.

"What?" she insisted when he didn't go on.

Colin decided a preamble would be in order. "Janna, I have something to tell you. It's probably the most difficult thing I've ever done in my life. But it has to be done. You are likely to get very angry, and I don't blame you for that. But . . . I'm asking you to hear me out, and remember the history we have together before you go jumping to conclusions. Are you with me?"

"I'm not sure," she said. "Now you're really scaring me." The silence grew torturous. "Colin?" Her voice startled him from his attempt to put the words together in his mind. His heart pounded into his head.

"Uh . . ." he cleared his throat, "I. . . uh . . . last night, I . . . I took Lily home." He looked up to gauge her reaction so far. It was skeptical, but calm.

"Who is Lily?"

"Lily Greene. One of the new lawyers. I told you about her."

"I don't remember," she said, and he wondered how much she heard of *anything* he said much of the time. "Go on," she insisted. "You took Lily home. Is that why you were so late? You were with Lily?"

Colin hesitated. He nodded. Janna leaned back and folded her arms across her chest. "And?" she asked. "I assume there's more by the sweat beading across your face."

Colin wiped his brow and looked at the moisture on his fingers. He pressed his hands together, took a deep breath, and said it. "I went to bed with her, Janna."

Seconds ticked by, and nothing happened. Colin watched her closely. A brief, sardonic chuckle erupted from her lips and she shook her head. She leaned back further into the couch as if to put distance between them. "This is some kind of sick joke, right?" she said with a shaky voice.

Colin shook his head. Janna moaned and looked away abruptly. She closed her eyes tightly and bit her lip. "Let me see if I've got this straight," she said without looking at him. "Are you telling me that you had . . . sexual intercourse . . . with another woman?" She was shaking now, as if she was suddenly freezing.

"That's right," he said, and she moaned again.

"Do you love her?" she asked and bit her lip.

"No!" he insisted. "I hardly . . . know her. I just . . . happened to be with her . . . and I felt so . . . *lonely* . . . and *frustrated*. It just *happened!*"

Janna said nothing more. Colin was contemplating some explanations to help fill in the silence when she erupted off the couch and flew into a rage.

"You know," she shouted, "I was almost beginning to think that maybe you were right; maybe we *did* need some help, and we could work it out. But now . . . now?" He thought she was going to cry, but instead she shouted louder.

Silent tears spilled down Colin's face as she paced back and forth like a caged animal, calling him every derogatory name in the book, and telling him he was the most pathetic excuse for a human being she'd ever met. At first Colin let her rage, knowing her anger was justified. But when she started the same speech over for the third time, he figured she'd said enough. He stood up to face her, saying gently, "Janna, I know this is tough. And I know it will take time." His voice cracked. "But I need . . . to talk to you about it. I need you to work with me. I don't expect it to be easy to forgive me, but—"

"*Forgive* you?" she retorted as if it were the most ridiculous thing she'd ever heard. "I don't think it's in me to forgive you, Colin."

Colin winced as if he'd been struck.

"You have no business asking me to forgive you, Colin Trevor. What you have done is unforgivable, as far as I'm concerned. I'm the mother of your children, for the love of heaven. Do you think you can just . . . Oh," she cried, "I can't believe it. I can't believe you'd do this to me. After all we have been through, you would do this to me?"

"Listen to me, Janna." He stepped toward her, desperation consuming him. If he lost her because of this, he could never live with himself. "You have to give me a chance." He took hold of her shoulders, wanting to shake some sense into her.

"Don't touch me!" She pushed him away and stepped back. "Give you a chance to what? Give me AIDS?"

"Oh, come on, Janna! She's not some prostitute or something. She's just—"

"And how do you know? You just told me you hardly know her. How could you possibly know whether or not she's—"

"Janna," Colin interrupted. He hated to say it, but she had a right to know. "We took precautions."

Her eyes and mouth simultaneously rounded as she squeaked, "Oh?" Colin looked guiltily at the floor. "She just *happened* to have *precautions* available, in case some married man gave her a ride home and—"

"Stop it!" he demanded. "What she did or didn't do is irrelevant. *I* made a mistake. I'm willing to pay for it."

"Oh, and pay you will," she snarled.

"Listen to me, Janna. I'm going straight to the bishop to take care of this. But it will take time. I need you to help me through this, Janna, to—"

"You've got to be kidding, right? Well, let me tell you something. I held your hand the last time you had sex with a woman you weren't married to, but only because it was *me*. Don't think for a minute that I'm going to hold your hand through this. It's all null and void as far as I'm concerned. You've cut your own throat on this one, Colin."

As hard as Colin tried, he couldn't keep the anger from erupting. "Yes, I certainly did that. But *you* cut my throat on the last one, Janna. You ran away and took my son. And I forgave you. Do you think I'm the kind of man who would run out and look for another bed to sleep in just for the sake of doing it—just to hurt you? If I got more than a condescending kiss once in a while, I wouldn't have to look elsewhere."

In one agile movement, Janna reached for the nearest mobile object, which happened to be a porcelain statue of a woman and baby that Colin had given her for Christmas. She drew back and hurled it toward Colin. He ducked, and it shattered against the wall.

Colin looked at her in astonishment, trying to comprehend how unconscious he might be if it had hit him in the head.

"Should we call that attempted murder?" he asked.

Colin knew his statement struck a nerve. How could she not remember the charges that had put her first husband in prison after he'd found her following the divorce?

"Get out of my house!" she growled.

"It's *my* house, too, Janna."

"Not anymore." She hurried past him and down the hall. He followed and found her emptying his drawers into a suitcase.

"You're just going to kick me out in the street?" he asked.

"That's right."

Colin reminded himself that he'd expected her to get angry. And she had a right to be. "Okay. Okay. So, we need a separation. I can live with that. But you still need to give me a chance, Janna."

"Get yourself a lawyer, Colin," she said, pulling his clothes out of the closet and tossing them onto the bed. "Maybe *Lily* would take your case."

"That's not funny."

"It wasn't intended to be."

"I don't want a divorce, Janna. I want to work it out."

"You should have thought of that before you . . ." She stopped and pressed a hand over her eyes. Her chin quivered. "I can't believe it. I just can't believe it."

"Give me a chance, Janna . . . please."

She swallowed her emotion and looked at him with cold eyes. "Either pack your clothes or you might find them on the front lawn."

"Oh, for crying out loud, Janna. We can at least handle this civilly. We can at least take some time and—"

"I don't need time. I need a divorce."

"If you want a divorce, you're going to have to get it." The anger crept in again. "Because I won't do it. And the only way you'll get it is by default, because I'm not signing anything. I love you, Janna. I love our children. And I intend to be with all of you forever—even if I have to go to hell and back to get there."

"You've got a lot of nerve . . . standing there talking about forever, when you've committed the ultimate crime against this family."

Colin crossed the room with fury. She backed away, and he saw fear in her eyes. But he ignored it and grabbed her firmly by the shoulders. "The ultimate crime?" he retorted in a hoarse voice, close to her face. "Perhaps you would prefer that I sexually abuse your children, the way your father abused you. Or maybe it would be better if I beat your face in when I don't like the way you look at me. Or I could always throw you on the floor and kick you in the stomach to kill your unborn babies. Or perhaps I could force you to give what you won't give me freely. I think they call that rape—married or not. What I did was wrong, Janna, and I'm not trying to excuse it. But don't you *dare* try to tell me that it's the ultimate crime. I've walked through hell for you, JannaLyn Trevor, and I got slapped in the face for it. In my opinion, *that's* a crime."

Colin let go of her abruptly and turned to pack his things. She stood silently and watched him fill three pieces of luggage. At first he tried to hold back the emotion, not wanting her to see him cry anymore. But pain overruled his pride, and once the tears began, he crumbled. He sat on the edge of the bed and cried like a baby. He wanted to beg her to let him stay, to talk to him, to give him a chance, but he was crying too hard to speak, and somehow he knew it wouldn't make any difference. He was vaguely aware of her watching him skeptically, as hard as granite. Then she took his suitcases one by one to the front porch. When he'd finally calmed down, he looked up to see her glaring at him.

"You need to go before Matthew gets home."

"I have a right to see my own children, Janna."

"You don't have any rights, in my opinion."

"The courts will say otherwise, and you know it. Surely we can work this out without having to take it that far."

"Don't count on it."

Again the anger came up to briefly numb his anguish. He lifted a finger and said firmly, "Do what you feel you have to, but so help me, if you drag my name through the mud in court, you will regret it. I've been defamed before a judge once for your sake, when Russell slandered me to save his own hide. I'm not going to do it again."

Colin walked past her and into Caitlin's bedroom, where she was still sleeping in spite of all the shouting. He pressed a kiss to her forehead, trying not to break down all over again. He went into the nursery while Janna stood in the hall, looking like some kind of warden. The baby was just waking. Colin picked her up and held her close, wondering when he might get the chance to hold her again. Visitation with children so young could be difficult. He closed his eyes and pressed his lips into Mallory's wispy hair, praying with all his heart and soul that he could find a way to put his family back together. The next thing he knew, Janna was taking the baby out of his arms.

"You need to go," she said.

"I love you, Janna." He tried to touch her face, but she recoiled and moved away.

"Like hell you do," she said, then repeated, "You need to go."

CHAPTER FIVE

*C*olin spent the night in a motel. He prayed more than slept, and cried more than prayed. In the deepest part of the night, he felt as if the darkness would literally swallow him. The pain he experienced was literal, the regret indescribable. He prayed to be released from the agony, at the same time knowing he didn't deserve to be. He had brought this on himself, and no power in heaven or on earth could free him of the consequences.

At seven in the morning, Colin called Sean O'Hara. "I apologize for bothering you so early, and at home."

"I'm up," Sean said. "I wouldn't have given you my home number if I hadn't wanted you to use it."

"I need you, Sean. I'll work around your schedule, but if there's any possible way you can see me today, I've—"

"I'm available, Colin. You sound pretty upset."

"I'm upset, yeah. What time?"

"I'll call you when I get to the office."

"I'm not at home." Colin gave him the number, and Sean called back a few minutes after eight to tell him that his second appointment couldn't make it due to illness. Driving to Sean's office, Colin could almost believe that the other client's illness was an answer to his prayers. He could at least hope that God was hearing him. If he wasn't, there didn't seem to be much point in going on.

"So, what is it?" Sean asked when they were sitting face to face. "You don't look too good."

"So everyone's been telling me."

"Why the motel room, Colin? I take it this has something to do with Janna."

"More to do with me, I think." He pushed his hands almost brutally through his hair.

"I'm listening."

"Well," Colin leaned back and wiped his sweating palms on his pant legs, "I was hoping you could tell me why a man with my upbringing and beliefs would jump off a cliff."

"I assume this *cliff* is a metaphor? I mean, you are still in one piece."

"In a manner of speaking."

"I'm still listening," Sean said when Colin was silent.

Colin wrung his hands together and realized he was shaking. "I slept with another woman, Sean."

If Sean was surprised, he didn't show it. He slowly straightened his back and said, "Whoa. I take it things aren't going well between you and Janna."

"Do you get that impression?" Colin retorted with sarcasm.

"So, how do you feel?"

"Feel?" he squeaked. "I feel . . . *sick*. I get sick to my stomach every time I think about it."

"Why *did* you do it?" Sean asked.

"I . . . I . . . just . . . felt like somebody else. It was a lonely, desperate, frustrated man who took that woman in his arms."

"And why is that?"

Colin started by describing the enormity of his feelings as he'd left home that day, and what had led up to it. He talked about the incident itself, barely managing to hold back the urge to throw up. When he finally ran down, Sean said, "You're obviously very upset. What are you feeling?"

"I'm . . . in shock. I'm *scared*."

"And angry?" Sean guessed.

"Angry at what? At myself?"

"I don't know," Sean said. "That's why I asked. I'm just . . . sensing some anger here."

Colin tried to think it through, but just ended up shaking his head. "I don't know, Sean. I can't even think straight; I can't sort it out."

"How did you feel toward Janna the morning before it happened?"

Colin took a deep breath. "Frustrated . . . hurt . . . helpless . . ."

"Angry?" Sean questioned again.

"Yes, I suppose I was angry. But *you* taught me that anger always has something beneath it."

"That's right. And in this case, it was hurt, frustration, etc., right?"

"Right."

"So, now that this has happened . . . where did the anger go?"

"It's on *me* now," Colin shouted. "I blew it. I did the stupidest thing I could have possibly done under *any* circumstances!"

"So, are you saying you just walked out the front door with your mind made up to sleep with another woman, so you could . . . what? Get even? Hurt her back?"

"No, of course not."

"Then what, Colin?"

"I don't know, Sean, I just . . ."

"What's the truth of it, Colin? Did your feelings toward Janna just magically change because you did something stupid? Don't sit there and try to lie to me—or yourself. You're still hurt. You're still frustrated. And you're still angry—with her, for pushing you over the edge."

Colin's trembling increased as he listened to Sean expressing emotions he hardly dared voice. In a softer tone, Sean leaned toward him and said, "Do you remember when you told me you wanted to hit her? That you were so frustrated and angry, you just had to walk away?" Colin nodded. "You told me in essence that you feared she might push you to a point where you would really hurt her. Well, you didn't hit her, but . . ."

Sean left the sentence unfinished, and Colin slid down further in his chair as it began to make sense.

"Now, what's the truth of it, Colin? You already admitted that you were lonely and desperate, so . . ."

"She pushed me too far. But that doesn't justify it, Sean. It was wrong. No matter how you look at it, it was wrong."

"Yes, it was wrong. And there are consequences to be faced. I'm not by any means telling you that you should blame your choices on Janna, or try to use her as a scapegoat. That will solve nothing. I am telling you that you need to understand *why* you did it. Janna has a lot to do with the trouble in your marriage. Your choice to deal with it this way is yours, but there is meaning in it for both of you. And the shades of gray will never make what you did right."

Colin felt suddenly numb, except for his continued shaking.

"This is going to take some time to jell, Colin," Sean said. "There's one more thing I believe you should be thinking about." Colin nodded, unable to speak, and Sean clarified, "What about Lily?"

"What about her?" he snapped.

"You slept with a woman, Colin. Have you considered the long-range repercussions related to her? Have you considered how this will affect her, and your accountability in that regard?"

The sickness smoldering in Colin's stomach rose dramatically.

"Will you spend the rest of your life hating her, blaming her for this? I'm not by any means suggesting that you set yourself up for any more involvement with her, but you've got to set things straight with her—if only for your own peace of mind. That's my opinion, at least. You can do what you want with my suggestions, Colin. If I'm not making sense, then we can talk through any aspect of this as much as you need to. But what you shared with Lily was—"

"It was sex, Sean," he shouted. "Plain and simple. Nothing more!"

With a hard stare, Sean asked, "Then why did you cry in her arms?"

The question struck so deep that Colin groaned, muttering an agonized, "Oh, heaven help me!"

Sean allowed Colin some time to get his emotions out. Then he spoke gently, "You know, Colin, it's a fact that men who go to prostitutes do as much talking and crying as they do anything else. In my opinion, it's not just sex they're after. It's *intimacy.*" He paused and added, "So let's talk about intimacy, Colin. What's been going on between you and Janna in that respect?"

"Nothing," Colin snarled. "Absolutely nothing."

"On a physical level?"

"On *any* level," Colin retorted. "*You* once told us that intimacy on many levels is vital to a good marriage relationship."

"And that's true."

"Sean," Colin leaned forward, "I can count on my fingers the times Janna and I have made love since the last baby was born."

"And how old is this baby?"

"Fourteen months."

"Whoa," Sean said. "And on the other levels?"

"We don't talk. We don't hold hands. Nothing."

"So you were starving?"

Colin nodded methodically.

"So, tell me, Colin, what if you'd had nothing to eat for about three days, and you were put in the same room with a Thanksgiving feast, and told not to touch it? Would it not take a great deal of strength to resist?"

Colin didn't answer. Sean went on. "When Christ had been fasting and Satan came to him, tempting him to turn the stone to bread, he resisted the temptation. It wasn't that his hunger was wrong. It wasn't that his needs weren't justified. And if he had done it, his Father would have probably understood why. But if he *had* done it, he would have been using his powers at the wrong time, and in the wrong way. And there would have been consequences to suffer."

Sean rested a hand on Colin's shoulder. "It's impossible to justify or excuse what you've done, Colin. But it's important for you to understand the steps that led up to it, in order for you to fully apply the repentance process. Do you hear what I'm saying?"

Colin nodded as a different kind of pain trickled over his face in silent tears. He could never put into words the depth of understanding settling into him. In spite of it all, he believed in his heart that the Savior knew how he felt. And that gave him some hope.

Through the drive back to Salt Lake, Colin tried to make sense of everything Sean had said, but it all muddled up in a knot of confusion. He figured it would take some time to put it all together in his head. In the meantime, he just had to cope. Before returning to the office, he consciously steeled himself to behave as if nothing in the world was wrong.

Colin was glad to avoid Lily as he went to his office and made some phone calls. He talked to his boss, then returned to his office to start packing up his things.

"What on earth are you doing?" Lily demanded when she walked in.

He only glanced at her for a second, but his heart quickened. He directed the adrenalin into packing faster. He had to get out of there!

"I'm putting these books in a box," he said.

"I can see that." She sounded panicked. "But why?"

"I'm leaving. That's why."

"Colin? You can't just . . . *leave.*"

"Yes, I can."

"What about your clients, and—"

"I've worked it out. It's all arranged."

"But . . . where will you go? How can you—"

"The firm I used to work for in Provo gave me an open offer to come back anytime. It's still open, so I'm taking it. I should have taken it a long time ago; then I never would have . . ." He glanced at her again and felt certain she knew what he meant.

"So you're just going to uproot your family and . . . leave . . . because of me."

Colin swallowed hard. "It would seem the family is staying here. *I'm* moving to Provo."

"Colin? You didn't *tell* her?"

He looked at Lily in astonishment. "Of course I told her. She's my wife, for heaven's sake. What do you expect me to do—be a liar and a hypocrite on top of everything else?"

Lily sighed. "Let me guess. She kicked you out."

"Hey, you're good. You should be a lawyer or something."

"You shouldn't have told her . . . at least not yet."

"And live under the same roof with a lie? If I can't live by truth, Lily, I might as well not live. That's why I went into this business, you know."

"Is it over between the two of you, then?"

"No!" he said with determination.

"Be realistic, Colin. She just kicked you out."

Colin sighed. "Lily, this has nothing to do with you. This is between—"

"It certainly does have something to do with me." She crossed the room and he turned, startled. "You slept with me, Colin," she hissed. "Or is that *nothing?*"

Colin reminded himself of what Sean had said about Lily. As much as he hated it, this *did* have something to do with her.

"I'm sorry, Lily," he said. "You're right." He stuffed his hands into his pockets. "It wasn't nothing, but . . . it doesn't change the facts. Like I told you, I never intended for it to happen."

"Neither did I," she retorted. The anger in her voice spurred the same in him.

"Well, you're the one who started undoing buttons first," he snapped. "Don't start taking a man's clothes off, when you have no idea whether or not he loves you, or if he has a life to give you." He saw the hurt in her eyes, but figured it was better that she heard it now. He tried to comprehend what she might be feeling and had to turn his back to her, as if it might keep his head where it belonged.

"I'm sorry, Lily," he added gently. "I wish I could tell you I love you. It might make what I shared with you mean more; I don't know. But I can't lie to you, and I can't lie to myself. I don't know what the future holds; but right now, I have to do everything in my power to put my family back together."

Colin squeezed his eyes shut tightly when he felt Lily's hands on his back. And he wondered briefly what it might be like to have a normal relationship with a woman—a relationship unmarred by dysfunction and abuse. Her touch ignited something in him; something wrong—and he knew it. But how could he deny the need she had filled in him? His emotions were raw. His spirit felt battered. And she actually cared.

"Colin," she said. He could tell she was crying. "Let me be there for you. Just give me a chance."

Colin heard the echoes of himself saying that very thing to Janna just yesterday. And she'd given him nothing but anger in return. That lonely, hurting ache rose up from the very core of him and responded to Lily's gentle touch.

"Lily," he breathed, turning to pull her into his arms. He felt her cling to him desperately, and he knew he was breaking her heart. It was all so *pathetic*.

"Lily," he whispered, "I know I'm not being fair to you. I wish I could go back and change it, for you as well as for me." He buried his lips in her hair and closed his eyes. "But I can't."

Feeling her soften in his arms, a little voice in the back of his head whispered, *You haven't gone to the bishop yet, Colin. What difference will it make if you prolong it a little? The harm's already done.* But, if nothing else, Colin now knew the source of that voice, and he tried to ignore it.

"I know it's hard," he whispered, "but you've got to walk away from me and never look back, Lily. What I did went against everything I've ever believed in. But if I was lonely and desperate then, I'm lonelier now. Don't stick around long enough to make me hurt you twice." She drew back to look at him with tears in her eyes. "Please," he said and touched her face quickly.

Lily nodded and stepped back. "If you ever change your mind," she said somewhere between a laugh and a sob, "you know where to find me."

Colin just forced himself back to his packing.

"Do you have a place to stay?" she asked.

Colin briefly closed his eyes, trying to push away the hidden message. "No, but I'll find something." Colin wondered if he should go stay with his parents until he found an apartment. But he immediately decided against it. His parents had already struggled through so much with him on Janna's behalf. If he had his way, they'd never even know anything was wrong.

Lily didn't say much else, but she insisted on helping him carry his things to the car. The last load was light enough to handle on his own, and she kissed him quickly while his hands were full. He left her standing in his office, crying. Before he left town, he stopped and ordered half a dozen pink roses to be delivered to Lily's apartment. He wrote on the card: *I'll never forget you, Lily. May your future be bright and strong. Forgive me, Colin.* He sealed up the card, imagining the way she would probably hold the flowers and cry. Then he got a dozen red roses to be delivered to Janna. He imagined her throwing them in the trash as he wrote: *I truly love you, JannaLyn. I pray that one day you will forgive me.*

As Colin got into the car, he felt the mask of self-control fall from his face. Like a porcelain replica of his image, struck with a hammer, it crumbled. Now that he was alone, with no valid reason to hold it back, a fresh tide of emotion surged out.

Colin cried through the hour it took to drive to Provo. He got a motel room and settled in, then he called his home. He was relieved when Matthew answered, knowing Janna would have likely hung up on him.

"How are you, buddy?" he asked.

"I'm okay. Where are you? The caller I.D. says 'out of area.'"

"I'm in Provo, Matt. Did Mom say anything about it?"

"No."

Colin sighed. Did she expect their son to not notice? "Where is your mother now?"

"She's in the kitchen. I'm in my room."

"The thing is, Matthew, I'm taking a job in Provo. Your mom and I are having some problems, so I'm going to stay here close to the office for a while. It doesn't have anything to do with you or your sisters. I love you, Matthew, and so does your mother. We just need some time apart. Does that make sense?"

"I guess so," he said after a long pause. "Are you getting a divorce?"

Colin sighed again. "I don't want a divorce, Matt. But your mother is pretty unhappy with me right now. And she has a reason to be. But we'll just have to see what happens. I'll call as often as I can, and I'll try to come and see you soon. I need you to help take care of the little ones, and do what your mother asks. All right?"

Colin heard nothing but a sniffle. Then another. "Matthew, it'll be all right," he said, fighting to keep the mask in place. "No matter what happens, I'm still your father, and I'm always here for you."

"I know," he said.

"I love you, Matthew."

"I love you, too, Dad. Come see us soon, okay?"

"I will," he promised, wondering if Janna would allow such a thing without causing a scene.

Colin wondered if any man on earth had ever cried so much as he hung up the phone and fell apart all over again. When he got control of himself, he called to make an appointment with his bishop the next evening.

The following morning, Colin got settled with the job change; he was grateful for that, at least. If he'd had to keep working in the same building as Lily Greene, the whole thing would be that much harder. He only wished he'd taken this job months ago. But then, if not for Janna's reluctance to move, he would have. The irony was horrible.

Colin fasted in preparation for talking to the bishop. He wondered if he'd ever been so scared in his life. He drove to Salt Lake early and stopped at the house to get some of his things. Caitlin came running the moment he walked through the door, assaulting him with hugs and giggles. He laughed and held her close. Mallory came toddling after her, and he repeated the same greeting. Then he looked up to see Janna, her arms folded, looking as if she might bite him in two.

"I came to get some of my things," he said, "and to see my children."

"You could have called first."

"So you could leave or lock me out?"

"Maybe."

Colin walked down the hall. "I'll hurry. Where's Matthew?"

"He's delivering his papers." Janna watched him as if she feared he might steal something that didn't belong to him. She followed him into the bedroom, where he haphazardly took contents from his drawers and closet. He picked up the quilt folded at the foot of the bed, and she asked, "What are you doing?"

"It's mine, Janna," he said, walking toward the den. "You made it for *me*, remember?"

She seemed upset but said nothing more about it. While he was boxing up some books and papers, she said, "I thought I could gather up some dishes and things we don't use . . . so you'd have something."

He stopped a moment. "Thank you. I appreciate your thoughtfulness, Mrs. Trevor."

A few minutes later she asked, "Are you staying with . . . *her?*"

Colin was briefly stunned. "No, Janna, I am not staying with her. I don't intend to ever see her again."

"How is that possible, when you work with—"

"Not anymore."

"Dad!" Matthew hurried into the room and hugged him tightly. Colin closed his eyes to absorb it, grateful to be saved from any more of Janna's interrogation. Her interest made no sense to him, after the way she'd sent him packing.

Matthew helped him carry his things out to the car, and as any boy his age would, he tried hard to hold back the tears.

Colin arrived at the church building early. He expected to wait, but Bishop Miller was ahead of schedule and called him right in. He didn't feel prepared, and he hardly knew how to approach this. After struggling through some small talk, the bishop asked, "So, what can I do for you?"

Colin took a deep breath. "I'm in trouble, Bishop." He looked at his hands and noted they were shaking.

Colin's confession erupted on a wave of emotion. The bishop listened, saying practically nothing. Then he responded with a lecture that Colin felt certain was supposed to make him feel humble. Humiliated was more accurate. He knew what he'd done was wrong, and he expected to pay the price. He told the bishop that more than once. But he felt like a naughty child, with a parent who refused to listen to any explanation. Sinner or not, he was still an adult. He tried to imagine how Christ himself would handle this if he were sitting in that chair across the desk. And this wasn't it.

Colin recalled that when he and Janna had committed fornication as teenagers, he had come out of that initial appointment with the bishop feeling hopeful and renewed. He had expected the same now. He was well aware of the price of his sin, and the road that had to be traveled to make restitution. But he had expected to feel some evidence of mercy and compassion. Instead, he felt like dirt.

He finally managed to escape the bishop's office, feeling far worse than when he'd come. He drove around aimlessly while tormented thoughts clouded his mind. He thought of the mistakes of his youth and began putting the pieces together. Perhaps what he needed to do was just accept the reality of who and what he was. Maybe it just wasn't in him to be a strong, religious man. He kept hearing the bishop's words storming through his mind; words that put across one blatant message. He felt like dirt.

He recalled his efforts to tell the bishop of the state of his marriage, addressing things that he considered important to the situation. But he had only been accused of attempting to blame his sin on Janna. *Janna.* He groaned aloud just to think of her. Oh, how he ached to just hold her close and know that she loved him in spite of his mistakes!

Colin pulled the car up in front of his home and sat there for several minutes, trying to build up the courage to go in. He prayed that Janna's heart would be softened. He just didn't know how he could ever get beyond this without her. *He loved her so much.*

Matthew answered the door and laughed as they hugged tightly.

"Where are your sisters?" Colin asked quietly.

He realized they weren't alone as Janna snapped, "I was just about to put them to bed."

"Good, then I'll just kiss them good night."

Janna looked at him as if he were leprous or something. She allowed him a moment with each of the girls, but she stood there wearing her warden expression, her arms folded tightly.

"Are you staying, Dad?" Matthew asked.

Colin hesitated, then shook his head slowly. "I wish I could, but . . . I'll see you soon. I promise. I need to talk to your mother alone."

Matthew hugged him again and left the room reluctantly.

"There's nothing to talk about," Janna said the moment they were alone.

"Janna . . . please hear me out." He hated the desperate tone of his voice, and the way his heart was pounding. He quickly repeated the same pleas she'd heard before, knowing in his heart that it would not penetrate her any more now than it had then. "Janna, please," he finished, tears spilling down his face, "just tell me that there's even a grain of hope that we could get beyond this. *Please*. If I don't have you, I'm not sure that life is worth living."

"You should have thought of that before you . . ." She turned away and bit her lip. He knew by her expression that she was struggling to hold her emotion back.

"Talk to me, Janna," he urged.

Janna swallowed the knot in her throat and turned to face him. "Okay," she said, "you want me to talk? Fine, I'll talk." It took little effort to hurl the words at him that had been pounding through her head since he'd spilled his confession in her lap. "You know, Colin, beyond my mother, you are the only person who ever truly loved me. I know I've got some problems, and I know loving me hasn't always been easy. But in spite of everything life has dished out to me," her composure slipped away, "I always believed that . . . that . . . oh, how could you?" she cried. "Don't you understand? You were the only one who . . ." She started crying so hard that she couldn't speak.

Colin took the opportunity to put his arms around her, praying she wouldn't reject his effort to comfort her. "I know I've hurt you,

Janna. Just give me a chance to make it up to you. Please, just—"

Colin's hands against her back startled Janna to reality. She bolted away from him, wondering how he could have the nerve to even touch her after what he'd done.

He wondered where all of her emotion had gone as she glared at him with cold, hard eyes. "Get out of my house," she snapped. "Get out of my life. I have no desire to ever see you again, Colin Trevor."

"You were just telling me that I was the only one who ever—"

"That's all in the past now, Colin. You've made your choice, as far as I'm concerned."

"What do you mean by that?"

"I mean that it's over between us, Colin!" she shouted.

Colin attempted to fully grasp what she was saying. He reminded himself to breathe, then told her the first conscious thought that came to his mind. "If you turn me away like this, Janna, you might as well just put a gun to my head and pull the trigger."

"The way I see it," she said tonelessly, "you already did just that."

Colin turned and left as the hurt suddenly became too intense to handle. He sat in the car for several minutes, trying to come up with any other explanation for what she'd just said. But there was only one possibility. In her opinion, he might as well be dead. The very idea was so difficult to swallow that a pain developed in his chest. When the hurt became too intense to bear, Colin felt it running into anger, where it could hide and smolder.

Again he drove aimlessly, his thoughts swirling. He thought of all the things Janna had said and done to inflict pain on him. He thought of the neglect and abuse that had driven him away, and the encounter he'd just had. Putting it all together, he had to admit to the truth of his feelings. He was *angry*.

While Colin drove, his anger grew. He hated Janna for putting him in this position. He wished that he'd never laid eyes on her. And while his memories reminded him of every hurtful incident in his relationship with Janna, he was surprised to find himself in front of Lily's condo. The light was on. He sat there for several minutes, trying to talk himself out of going to the door. But he couldn't come up with one person on the face of the earth who might show him uncon-ditional love at this moment, under these circumstances—except Lily.

And as he thought of her, the anger and hurt all seemed to momentarily disappear.

Colin knocked at the door and tried to ignore the quickening of his heart. She opened it wearing jeans and a sweater. Her expression of surprise quickly became a grin of delight. *She was happy to see him.*

"Colin! I certainly didn't expect to see you here."

"Yeah, well . . . neither did I." He added as an afterthought, "I came to get my tie."

She looked momentarily disappointed, but motioned him inside and closed the door. He noticed the roses he'd sent sitting on the coffee table just as she said, "Thanks for the flowers. They're beautiful."

Colin made no response.

"Do you want something to drink?" she asked.

"I don't drink," he replied, wondering if he ought to try it. Drinking was a far lesser sin than adultery, but perhaps it could have the same temporary numbing effect.

"How about raspberry lemonade?"

He was surprised. "I love raspberry lemonade."

"I know."

"How do you know?"

"You always drank it during those long lunch study sessions we had with Don."

"Oh, yeah," he said.

Lily went into the kitchen and returned with a tall glass of pink liquid on ice.

"Thank you," he said, taking a long swallow. "Aren't you having any?"

"I hate raspberry lemonade."

"Then why do you have it here?"

"Perhaps I was hoping you'd come by for a drink."

Colin set the glass down on the coffee table, feeling suddenly uneasy. He was trying to talk himself into leaving when she sat close beside him and took his hand.

"So, how are you?"

"I'm awful. How are you?"

"I'm better now," she said, touching his face.

"Maybe I should just get my tie and—"

"Maybe we should talk," she interrupted.

"Okay, talk," he said. He didn't want to leave. Talking was safe. Time flew as he listened to her ramble about her childhood, going to college, her family. And she went on and on about her grandmother, who must have been one of the funniest people who ever lived. Colin gradually relaxed, laughing with her, holding her hand. He'd forgotten how pleasurable good conversation could be with someone who wanted to be with him. He realized then that it wasn't really sex he wanted. He wanted companionship. And acceptance. But then, the emotional intimacy all seemed to mix together somehow with the physical. The thought startled him, and he tried to stand up.

"Oh, don't go," she said, tugging on his arm. He turned to look at her, and wondered how it could possibly hurt to spend the night with her. The damage was done, and he couldn't think of one logical reason to care one way or the other. Janna hated him and had sworn to never forgive him. She'd just told him, in essence, that whether he was dead or alive made no difference to her. He knew she would fight tooth and nail to keep the children away from him. He'd been denounced by his bishop with harsh judgments and no hint that he cared in the slightest about anything except the grievousness of his sins. And here was Lily, wanting only to be with him. He kissed her before he consciously realized that he wanted to. She seemed surprised, but responded quickly. He kissed her again and again. He knew where it would end, but he didn't care. Perhaps tomorrow he would care. But tonight . . .

Colin was just becoming lost in her affection when the phone rang. "Ignore it," he whispered and kissed her again.

"I can't," she grumbled and stood up to answer it. "I'll make it quick."

Colin leaned his head back and closed his eyes, listening to her side of the conversation. "Hello. What? No, I don't. This is not a good time. I'll call you in the morning. No, you can't do that. I said this isn't a good time, Tyler."

She turned her back to Colin and quieted her voice, but he could tell that she was crying now—arguing with her ex-husband in a way that brought memories rushing back. Colin could hear his own torment in her tears. And his thoughts wandered to Janna. Hadn't he told Lily that he had to do everything in his power to put his family back together? Was he turning into a liar as well? Even if he couldn't get Janna back, he had to know that he'd done his best, or he could never live with himself. And on top of that, he knew that what he felt for Lily didn't justify what he'd shared with her. He'd told her he didn't want to hurt her twice. But here he was, ready to do just that. What kind of man had he become?

"What am I doing here?" he muttered and stood abruptly. Lily turned, startled. "I have to go," he said quietly, pointing toward the door.

She shook her head frantically, holding up a finger to indicate that he wait a minute, then she said into the phone, "Stop shouting at me. I don't have to listen to this. You—"

Colin grabbed the phone from her, saying into it, "Are you aware, Mr. Greene, that harassment is against the law?"

"Who is this?" a man's voice snapped through the phone.

"I'm an attorney, and if you have something to say, then you are welcome to do so through legal channels. Otherwise, you could find yourself slapped with a restraining order."

Colin hung up before he could get any response. Lily looked stunned. "Thank you," she said.

"Don't let him treat you like that, Lily. You deserve better." She smiled at him with a silent implication and he added, walking toward the door, "You deserve someone better than me."

"Oh, please don't go. I—"

"Forgive me, Lily." He took her shoulders into his hands. "I should never have come here. I came with hurt and anger, and it's not fair to either of us. I have nothing to give you, Lily. I'm just a confused, lonely man." He pressed his lips quickly over hers and stepped back. "Forgive me," he said again and opened the door.

Lily put her hand over his on the knob and stood to block his way. "Why did you come here, Colin?"

"Because I'm a selfish, wicked man. I'm lonely and confused and desperate, and I have no idea what's right and wrong anymore."

"And I'm here for you," she said, pressing her hand to his cheek and into his hair.

"I have nothing to give you, Lily. My life is so screwed up right now, I don't even know which way is up. You can't expect anything from me except what I've already given you."

She pressed her lips to his. "It's enough, Colin," she whispered and kissed him again.

Colin pushed the door closed and pulled her into his arms. How could he possibly resist? She offered everything he was starving for: acceptance, caring, compassion. And she expected nothing in return.

Colin awoke in the darkness. It took a moment to orient himself, and then he groaned. The confusion and regret pounding in his head were like some kind of emotional hangover. He became aware of Lily sleeping close to him, and his heart ached for her. Couldn't she see what a jerk he was?

Colin stared at the ceiling while the events of the last few days crowded into his mind, and a steady stream of tears flowed into his hair. *He was such a fool.*

Trying to find something good to think about, he imagined taking the path that Lily offered him. He could move in with her, take back his old job, and put aside the religious beliefs that were presently causing him so much anguish. He imagined the two of them doing things together, having fun, laughing and talking. It was a pleasant image, but he knew in his heart that it would only be temporary. Eventually the mask of romance would fall away and the reality of life would come between them. Every minute he spent with Lily was only prolonging reality. And the longer he put off facing it, the more unhappy he would become.

Colin was startled to hear Lily speak when he'd had no indication that she was even awake. "She must have really hurt you."

"How do you figure?" he asked grimly.

"I was married to Tyler for nearly two years, and I never saw him cry as much as you have in the last few days."

Colin turned his back to her, not wanting his emotions exposed, not wanting to talk about it. She moved closer and whispered behind his ear, "It's okay, Colin. Just go ahead and cry."

Colin cried until he slept. He awoke in the predawn light and quietly got dressed. For a moment he watched Lily sleeping, almost wishing that he could feel for her what he felt for Janna. But he just couldn't.

"Forgive me, Lily," he whispered. But she slept on, oblivious to his writing a note for her which he left on the bathroom mirror.

Forgive me for hurting you twice. Take care. Colin. Then he slipped quietly away.

Colin was in the car before it came to him that he'd forgotten to get his tie. Then he realized that he didn't want it. He could never wear it again without remembering something that was better forgotten. He returned to his motel room, praying for strength, begging God to show him some kind of evidence that he had something inside him worth saving.

As he showered and tried to gear himself up enough to put the mask in place and go to work, he felt compelled to call Sean. He couldn't fathom finding the courage to tell *anyone* that he'd fallen again. But at least he felt that Sean would listen without passing judgment. If nothing else, perhaps a psychologist could help him understand why he seemed so bent on self-destruction.

Colin phoned Sean as soon as he got to the office. Sean said to meet him at four. Managing to get through his work, Colin didn't know if he was relieved or terrified to finally be sitting across from Sean. He got right to the point, speaking with a cold edge that was nothing but an attempt to keep from feeling the reality.

"It happened again," he stated.

The disappointment in Sean's eyes was brief but unmistakable. "And why do you suppose it did?" he asked.

"I don't know!" Colin shouted.

"I'm guessing you *do* know. I'm guessing you just don't want to say it."

Colin took a deep breath and pressed his head into his hands. He forced the truth of his feelings into the open while Sean listened and took a few notes. He told Sean about the interview with the bishop and Janna's attitude toward him. He felt angry toward both of them, while at the same time he couldn't help condemning himself, believing that their behavior toward him was justified.

"You know, Colin," Sean said gently, "bishops aren't perfect, and many of them are poorly prepared for facing such situations. Janna is going through her own personal hell. I would suggest that you find something to base your strength on that isn't affected by the attitudes of people. They're only human."

"Like what?" Colin snarled.

Sean didn't seem affected by his sour mood. "In Alma, chapter forty-two, we're told that 'mercy claimeth the penitent.' When a sin is committed, justice must be met, yes. But the Lord is always merciful to those who come to him with a desire to repent. His mercy is unconditional, Colin, even when—or perhaps *especially* when—some people in our lives are not merciful at all."

Colin nodded to indicate he was grasping the point, but he hardly dared speak for fear of having his emotions erupt. Sean leaned his forearms on his thighs and looked directly at Colin. "What you have to face right now is difficult. You're like a man just out of the desert, who finally got a very gratifying drink of water. Now, if you want to put your life back in order, you're going to have to go back into the desert. And being there will likely be even more difficult than it was before. I suggest that you go home and read in John, chapter four. That's where Christ spoke to the woman at the well—a woman who was living in sin, mind you. He said, 'But whosoever drinketh of the water that I shall give him shall never thirst.'"

Sean leaned a little closer. "I know this may be difficult to grasp right now, Colin. But I swear to you if you turn to the Lord in this, he won't let you down. I can't guarantee it will be easy, but it's where the answers are."

When Colin said nothing for several minutes, Sean asked, "So what's on your mind?"

Colin cleared his throat. "I assume you want me to be honest."

"It works better that way."

"I hear what you're saying, Sean, and . . . I understand. At least I think I do. But . . ."

"But?" Sean prodded.

Colin swallowed hard and admitted to the truth, if only to understand it so that he could somehow deal with it. "I just want to go back."

"To Lily?" Sean asked, and Colin nodded.

Unable to hold back his emotion any longer, he sputtered, "How can I possibly. . . feel this way . . . when I know it's so wrong?"

"You know, Colin, when a person commits suicide, it's often because it seems to be the least painful option. In essence, what you've done is like spiritual suicide. I would guess that where you're at now, the choice between right and wrong is overruled by the option that is least painful. The consequences for the sin are painful. The trouble in your marriage is painful. But being with Lily is only a temporary numbing; like a drug, it momentarily eases the discomfort, but in reality it will only prolong the misery. And the longer you put off facing it, the more difficult and painful the road back. Am I making any sense?"

Colin nodded. It made sense. But it hurt like hell. And he truly wondered if he had the strength to see it through.

CHAPTER SIX

*B*efore Colin left Sean's office, Sean made him promise that
he would get an appointment with his stake president as soon as possible.

"You need to see him, anyway," he said. "Perhaps he can put a
different perspective on the things the bishop told you."

Colin agreed to make the appointment, but he didn't know
whether to feel relieved or terrified to find out the stake president
would be available to see him later that evening.

A fresh bout of nerves assaulted him as President Baker
extended a hand and invited him into his office. Their last personal
interview had been when Colin was asked to serve as a counselor in
the elders quorum presidency. The irony was horrible.

"You know why I'm here," Colin said as soon as he found his voice.

"Bishop Miller called me," the president said. Colin hung his
head, fully expecting a lecture, but President Baker added with
compassion, "I can't imagine what you must be going through,
Brother Trevor. Is there anything I can do?"

Colin glanced up, startled. He was certain there had been some
miscommunication somewhere. While he was fumbling for the words
to clarify his reason for being there, the president said, "Perhaps we
should talk."

At first Colin's words came slow and stilted. But as the president
listened with concern and understanding, he was able to spill out the
full truth of what had happened between him and Lily. He finished
with a firm, "I'm scared, President."

"That's understandable, I think. But I want you to know,
Brother Trevor, you're already on the right track . . . just by being

here." President Baker went on with words of encouragement and no sign of judgment. Colin felt nearly in awe of the hope that settled over him as his sin was put on a scale where justice was carefully balanced by mercy.

During a quiet moment, the president said, "You're not saying much. Are you all right?"

"I . . . uh . . . I think I'm still kind of . . . in shock . . . over the whole thing."

"I must say I'm a little surprised myself, Colin. You're a good man, and—"

Colin chuckled without humor. "You don't know me very well."

"I thought I did," President Baker stated.

"Well, let me tell you something about me, President." Colin impulsively pulled his wallet from his back pocket and showed him a tiny copy of his wedding portrait, which included a seven-year-old Matthew. "You see this?" he said. "My son was seven when I married Janna."

The president's eyes widened. "I didn't realize this was a second marriage."

"It wasn't . . . at least not for me." He looked the president in the eye. "Matthew was born *illegitimate*."

"I've interviewed you for church callings and temple recommends, Brother Trevor," the president said in a kind voice. "Obviously this was a long time ago."

"Yes, but . . ." Colin struggled to find the right words to explain what was jelling in his mind. He made a mental note to discuss these new feelings with Sean. "Don't you see? Obviously I'm not such a good man. Obviously I have a problem."

"And it seems just as obvious that you're willing to correct the problem, whatever it may be. I assume that's what you're doing here. It's apparent that you love Janna very much. If she was good enough to take on your son, I'm certain she will—"

"President," Colin interrupted, "Janna is Matthew's mother." As the president's eyes widened further, Colin went on to briefly explain the circumstances of their relationship, leading back to the problem of the moment.

The president listened then asked gently, "So, what do you feel led up to this?"

Colin explained the way things had been at home, doing his best not to sound critical of Janna in spite of his frustrations. The president then asked Colin about his temple attendance and scripture study, and Colin had to admit he couldn't remember the last time he'd done either. He asked about family prayer and home evening, and again, Colin had to admit it wasn't what it should be. The sickness smoldering inside him increased as he began to see a broader perspective. Instead of clinging to the simple, basic things that would keep the Spirit close to him, he'd let them go, rationalizing that he was too busy, too stressed. He also realized that although he hadn't consciously thought about Lily in a sexual way, his thoughts about her had not been appropriate. That, too, had contributed to his downfall. Again, he wondered what was wrong with him. Why couldn't a man who had been raised with the gospel in a loving family stick to what he knew was right and keep himself out of trouble?

"You know, Colin," the president said, "it's not terribly difficult to see what led up to the incident. It seems that Satan knows our weaknesses well, and he plays upon them. Most sins can be traced back to an unfulfilled need. It's the reason kids get caught up in crime and immorality; they feel unloved . . . or unaccepted."

President Baker opened a desk drawer, retrieved a sheet of paper, and read from it. "Ezra Taft Benson once said, 'I recognize that most people fall into sexual sin in a misguided attempt to fulfill basic human needs. We all have a need to feel loved and worthwhile. We all seek to have joy and happiness in our lives. Knowing this, Satan often lures people into immorality by playing on their basic needs. He promises pleasure, happiness, and fulfillment. But this is, of course, a deception.'"

President Baker set the paper aside and added, "The church establishes certain rules to protect people against such things. Unfortunately, many people bend those rules because little things don't seem so serious—like giving a woman a ride, for instance. Obviously we can't have a separate set of rules for people who are emotionally stable and happy, as opposed to those who aren't. I can almost imagine Satan seeing your vulnerability exposed, and placing subtle stumbling blocks into your path, until you were led blindly to the edge of a cliff. The trouble is, no matter what your circumstances may be, the price has to be paid. It's up to you to climb back up the face of that cliff and find your way back to the straight and narrow path."

"I don't know if I can do it."

"You don't have to do it alone, Brother Trevor."

"But . . . I'm not sure it's in me to . . ."

Colin couldn't find the words to explain it, but as the president went on, it seemed he could almost read Colin's thoughts. "I can understand why you would be thinking of yourself as a bad person. But that's exactly what Satan will use to drag you down. I don't see a bad person, Brother Trevor. I see an honorable man with a good heart and a strong spirit, who has made a few mistakes—mistakes that can be corrected and overcome."

Tears trailed silently down Colin's cheeks as the president spoke of the Atonement and how he could apply it in this situation. Colin listened, feeling somehow numb, then he asked, "Can the Atonement bring Janna back to me? Can it make us a family again?"

President Baker was silent a long moment. "We are all free agents, Colin. No one but Janna can determine how this will affect her, or what she will choose to do about it."

Colin hung his head, and fresh tears spilled down his face.

"Unfortunately," the president added, "most divorces are the result of a person's free agency, against the will of their spouse. I can't count the times I've seen a person left holding the ball alone because their spouse suddenly decided they didn't want to try anymore, and there was something better out there. It's a tragic thing. What's important for you, right now, is to personally get your life in order."

Colin nodded. "And exactly what does that entail?"

The president let out a heavy sigh. "I'm certain Bishop Miller informed you that because you are a Melchizedek priesthood holder, the problem has to be taken care of on a stake level. A disciplinary council will be held."

There were a hundred questions Colin wanted to ask, but he couldn't find the voice to even begin. The president ended the interview with some words of hope, telling him that he needed to concentrate on the goal of getting beyond this, rather than focusing on the painful process. He reminded him that repentance and change were what the gospel was all about. He challenged Colin to remember more than anything that he needed faith in Christ to carry him through this.

Colin walked out of the office feeling entirely different than he had the previous evening. He was still scared, but he didn't feel like an outcast without hope. In spite of being keenly aware of the struggles that lay ahead for him, he felt evidence that God did love him in spite of it. During the drive home, Colin felt the hope beginning to dwindle. He began contemplating the time it would take to get beyond this, and just how difficult it would be. If he was excommunicated, it would be a year from his re-baptism until he could return to the temple and use the priesthood. And only time would tell how long it might take to be worthy of re-baptism. Hope came only in the reminders he'd been given of the Atonement and the repentance process—and in knowing that somebody cared.

By the time he arrived at his motel room, the fragile threads of Colin's hope had become difficult to grasp. He felt homeless and helpless. He knelt by the bed to pray, but ended up with his face buried in the bedspread, sobbing without restraint, clutching handfuls of bedding. He didn't crawl into the bed until his knees and back ached, then he curled up in the quilt Janna had made him and cried himself to sleep.

The following morning, Colin forced his mask of normalcy into place and went to work, praying that he could at least hold up there, or he'd really be in trouble. He was arranging some of his books in his new office when a female voice said, "You must be Mr. Trevor."

"Yes," he said. "May I help you?"

"I'm supposed to ask *you* that," she said, setting some papers on his desk then extending her hand. "My name is Lucy. You may call me your secretary, your assistant, your receptionist—whatever. I'm not too concerned about being politically correct. I am here to make your job easier, and I will do anything in my power to do that—within reason. I'll even bring in lunch, as long as it coincides with my own lunch plans."

"Okay," Colin drawled, hating the memories of Lily that bombarded him. "I only have one question. Are you happily married?"

She looked surprised but said, "Yes, of course. I just got married five months ago, in the Provo Temple."

Colin smiled. "Good. Keep it that way."

"I intend to," she said. "Is there anything you need right now?"

"Not that I know of, but thank you."

Sean called in the afternoon to see how he was doing. Colin had little to tell him, but there was some comfort in knowing he had a friend who was mindful of him. After work he called Matthew, then spent Friday evening sitting in a motel room and staring at the wall. He felt disoriented by the empty time and lack of purpose, when he was accustomed to being busy caring for his children in the hours when he wasn't working. *He missed them so much.*

Saturday morning, he went searching for apartments. The only one he found that he considered feasible was not what he considered desirable. The price was right, and the neighborhood wasn't bad, but the apartment needed a lot of work. Still, he took it anyway, knowing it was tough to find a place to live when BYU was in full throttle. And maybe the repairs would give him something to put his extra time and energy into.

Late Saturday afternoon, he stopped by his parents' home, geared up to act as if everything was normal.

"Hello," Nancy Trevor said when he walked into the kitchen and kissed her in greeting. "What are you doing here?"

"I told Dad I'd look at that outlet in the basement he can't get to work."

"Oh, that's nice. You were always so good with electrical things."

An associated memory assaulted him. He turned to look out the window while he steadied his expression.

"How are you, Colin?" his mother asked, looking directly at him.

"I'm okay. How are you?"

She gave him one of those soul-searching gazes she was famous for. He glanced quickly away, fearing she would read his guilt. "Concerned," she said.

"Why is that?"

"Janna called a couple of days ago."

Colin nearly cursed under his breath. He could feel it coming. "And what did Janna have to say?" he asked coolly.

"Why don't you tell me how Janna is?" she retorted.

"Mother, you're not going to trick me into lying."

"Can I trick you into telling me the truth?"

"What? That I can't tell you how Janna is because I haven't talked to her?"

"That's the truth I was looking for. Now, let me ask you again. How are you?"

Colin wondered exactly *what* Janna had told his mother. But he answered honestly. "I've never been worse in my life."

"Never?"

"Never! What did Janna say?"

"She asked if I'd seen you. When I told her I hadn't, she seemed concerned. I confess that I prodded her a little. She told me you left her."

Colin raised an eyebrow. "*Left* her? Is that what she said?"

Nancy nodded.

"Did she say anything else?"

"If you mean did she tell me *why* you left her, no."

"Well, I didn't leave her, Mother. She packed my bags and put them on the porch."

"Do you want to talk about it?" she asked, putting a hand on his arm.

"No, Mother, I don't. I appreciate your concern, and I'm grateful to know you're here for me. But right now, I just need to deal with it myself."

"Okay. Do you need anything?"

Colin shook his head, then he whispered, "A miracle."

"I assume you have a place to stay."

"I got an apartment not far from here. I've moved back to the firm in Provo."

"Oh, I must say that's nice . . . in spite of the other."

"Yes," he snarled, "in spite of the other."

Colin visited with his father while the two of them found the problem and fixed the outlet. Carl Trevor said nothing about the separation beyond a simple, "I sure hope you can work it out."

Colin went to church in his new ward, even though he couldn't move in for a few more days. He tried to make himself obscure, and sat right at the back, hoping to be inconspicuous when he didn't take the sacrament. He went back to his motel room and cried, then he went to have dinner with his parents.

Through the following days, he worked hard and tried with everything he had to not think about his desire to see Lily again. He wanted desperately to see the children, but even talking to Janna at this point was not a possibility. He nearly called several times to ask about seeing the kids, but his instincts told him to hold off and let her cool down a little more . . . if such a thing was possible.

＊ ＊ ＊ ＊ ＊

Nancy answered the phone. It was Janna, and she was extremely upset. "Have you seen Colin?" she questioned.

"Not since Sunday for a while. Is something wrong?"

"I could probably call him at the office, but I didn't want to get into anything while he's at work. Matthew has been absolutely impossible since Colin left. He wants to go live with his father, and quite frankly, I can't handle him on my own."

"Well," Nancy said, "that's between you and Colin. But if I see him, I'll tell him to call you."

"The thing is," Janna went on, "I can't have Matthew stay with his father if he's living with that—" Janna stopped abruptly, and Nancy felt something uneasy prickle the back of her neck.

"I'm not going to pry, Janna, and if there are things I shouldn't know, then I don't want to know. But if you need to talk, or you need some help, I'm not going to beg it out of you."

"I just don't know what to do," Janna cried. "I have no one to turn to, and . . ."

"Janna, you know I'm always here for you. I can't take sides, but I can be a shoulder for you. You should know that. We've been through some tough things together."

"I know," she whimpered. "You're the closest thing I have to a mother . . . or a sister . . . and I can't talk to my friends about this. There's just no one I'm close to."

"Okay," Nancy said, "let's talk about it."

"You're always so sweet."

"So, what's the biggest problem right now—other than being separated? Is it Matthew?"

"I guess it is. Colin sent me some money. I'm managing, I

suppose, but . . . Matthew insists that he wants to live with his father. But Colin hasn't called at all, and if he's staying with her, then how can I possibly tell Matthew that he can live with his father?"

"Staying with who, dear?" Nancy asked, trying to stay calm and not jump to conclusions. While a part of her didn't want to know, and it was really none of her business, if she was going to be able to help Janna—and Colin—she had to know what they were dealing with.

"I believe her name is Lily." Janna's voice turned bitter instantly.

"Lily?" Nancy repeated, trying not to sound shocked.

"The woman Colin slept with."

Nancy sat down unsteadily. "Janna," she said carefully, "are you absolutely certain? Is it possible that you're assuming something, or—"

"He told me to my face, Nancy."

Nancy forced herself to stay unemotional. "Well, then, the two of you have some big things to work out."

"Work out? How do you *work out* something like this?"

"It's been done, Janna."

"Just have Colin call me as soon as you see him."

Janna hung up, but Nancy sat holding the phone long after the call had disconnected. Carl took it from her hand and startled her.

"Who was that?" her husband asked.

"Janna."

"Something wrong?"

"Carl, I think you'd better sit down."

* * * * *

Colin willed himself to stay calm when Lucy's voice on the intercom said, "Your wife is on line three, Mr. Trevor."

"Thank you, I've got it." He took a deep breath and picked up the receiver. "What a pleasant surprise," he said.

"I didn't want to call you at work." Janna's voice was terse and cold. "But you didn't call, and I had to talk to you. Let's keep it brief and not argue."

"All right."

"Matthew wants to stay with you. I don't want him to go, but he's determined and I can't handle him on my own. But I'm not letting him go if you're living with . . . that woman. So—"

"Janna, I am living in my very own apartment, fifty miles from *that woman.* I would be more than happy to have Matthew stay with me. Tell him I'll pick him up tomorrow afternoon sometime. I'll borrow Dad's truck so I can get his bed and stuff."

"Okay, and you can get the rest of your things at the same time. I've boxed it all up. And there are some dishes and towels and stuff you can use."

Colin was caught briefly off guard. He wondered what had spurred this bout of ambition, when she'd done so little for so long. Was his absence so motivating for her?

"Okay," Colin finally said in a dry voice, while everything inside him screamed in agony. After all he and Janna had been through just to be *together,* and now she had boxed up his every possession, implying that he would never be moving back in.

"I'll see you tomorrow," she said, and hung up before he could say anything else.

Colin went to his parents' home Saturday morning to shovel them out of an early snowstorm. He dug right in and finished before he went inside.

"Hello, son," Carl said. "I appreciate your doing that."

"Well, it was bribery," Colin admitted. "I was wondering if I could borrow the truck today. Matthew's coming to stay with me, and I need to go get his things."

"That's no problem," Carl said. "And I still appreciate your help. I must admit I haven't been feeling real good lately."

"What's wrong?" Colin demanded. His father wasn't one to complain about his health—at all.

"He's been having headaches," Nancy said, coming into the room. "We weren't going to say anything, but it's been going on a long time, and it's getting worse."

"What are you saying?" Colin asked, feeling panicked.

"They've eliminated every logical possibility, Colin," Nancy reported. "He's going in next week for an MRI."

Colin tossed his coat and gloves over a chair and sat down. "What do they think it is?" he asked.

"We don't know," Nancy said while Carl looked the other way.

"We just wanted you to be aware of what's happening. We've already called your brothers and sisters."

Colin nodded, wondering what to say. The thought of something serious being wrong with one of his parents seemed more than he could bear on top of everything else. Then he saw a tense glance pass between them before they both looked at him.

"What?" Colin asked, wondering if his guilty conscience was so obvious.

Carl cleared his throat tensely. "We just have to know, son. Is it true?"

He took a deep breath and tried not to sound alarmed. "Is *what* true?" he asked.

"The reason for the separation," Nancy said. "Is it another woman?"

Colin pressed his head into his hands and sighed. "There is no reason on earth why she had to tell you that."

"She has no family beyond us, Colin. Do you expect her to just handle this alone?"

"I would be more than happy to help her handle it, but she kicked me out with no sympathy."

"Is it true, then?" Carl asked.

"And what if it is?" Colin snapped. "Will you tell me to go to hell, too?"

"I told Janna we would not take sides," Nancy said.

"Is it true, Colin?" Carl asked again.

Colin sighed. "I guess that depends on what she told you."

"She said that you slept with another woman."

Colin winced visibly. Just hearing it hurt. He nodded somberly and sighed. "Yes," he croaked, "it's true."

Colin waited for the inevitable outburst. Carl had mellowed through the years, but he was still his father, and he had very strong opinions about his children disappointing him. And of Carl and Nancy's eight children, Colin had caused them the most grief—difficulties often directly related to JannaLyn.

"Well, don't you have anything to say?" he finally erupted when the silence drove him to the edge.

"Actually, no," Nancy said.

"I don't understand," Colin stammered. "Look at . . . at the things I've done in my life . . . that have caused you grief. The trouble . . . the disappointment. And now . . . now I . . . I have just committed the ultimate sin. I've . . . as good as . . . stomped on everything I was ever taught. I've hurt . . . everyone I've . . . ever loved. How can you . . . not have anything to say?"

"Colin, look at me," Nancy said, and he did. "What is this *trouble* and *disappointment*? A delayed mission? An illegitimate son that you loved and took responsibility for as soon as you knew of his existence—a son that you took to the temple to make him and his mother yours forever? Is there some drug abuse or car theft that we're not aware of? Are you a closet alcoholic?"

Colin shook his head. "Of course not, but—"

"Colin," Nancy continued. "We love you. Do you want us to tell you that you should be ashamed of yourself? Do you want us to say that you should have known better; that no matter how bad things were at home, this was not going to help?"

Colin felt his mask crumbling and pressed his hands over his face to hide it. He felt his mother's hand on his arm. "It's evident that you're suffering, Colin. You're a grown man. You don't need us to enforce the consequences. It'll happen all by itself."

What little self-composure Colin had was shattered instantly. He wrapped his arms up over his head and felt the inevitable emotion erupt in painful spurts. He cried harder when he felt his father's arms come around him, guiding him to his shoulder. Nancy took his hand into hers and held it tightly. When the emotion finally settled, he couldn't deny being grateful to have his parents know the truth. Knowing they still loved him in spite of his mistakes already added to his hope. He had to wear that wretched mask of normality nearly everywhere he went. At least he could come here and be himself.

"Colin," his father said gently, leaning toward him, "there's something I need to say. I want you to hear me out."

Colin nodded, fully expecting a lecture of some sort. He was surprised to hear Carl Trevor say, "You told me once that as a youth, you felt like I never quite trusted you to make the right choices. I have to admit that it's troubled me, Colin. I think maybe you were right."

As Carl took a deep breath and seemed to gather his thoughts, Colin wondered if this was being spurred by the possibility of facing a serious medical problem, or because his son had committed a serious sin. Perhaps a little of both.

"I wonder," Carl went on, "as most parents probably do, if there was something in the way I raised my children that might have caused problems for them."

Colin seemed puzzled as he asked, "Do the rest of them have problems? I thought it was just me."

"Personalities can make a difference," Carl said in a voice unusually soft. "I guess I'm trying to say that . . . maybe I've contributed to your struggles. Maybe I was a little overprotective. Maybe I sensed you were more headstrong than the others; more impetuous. But I certainly never intended to make you feel like I couldn't trust you, or didn't believe you could handle the choices in your life."

"Hey, Dad," Colin said, "I'm a free agent. I made my own choices. No parent is perfect, but if this is the only tough thing I had to deal with, I've got nothing to complain about. You've always been there for me; always accepted me, no matter what." Emotion broke his voice again.

"Parenting is a difficult thing," Carl said, "as I'm sure you are learning. It's ironic that we learn how to do it *after* our children are grown. Your mother and I certainly did the best we could with what we knew, and we've raised a good family. We only hope that each generation will improve and correct past mistakes, not the other way around."

Nancy squeezed Carl's hand, and tears brimmed in her eyes. Colin wondered what they hadn't told him about this headache thing. She looked as if she was terrified of losing her husband.

"I just want you to know, Colin, if I did anything as a father that made things tough for you, I'm truly sorry."

Colin wrapped his arms around his father and hugged him tightly. "Don't apologize to me, Dad. There's no reason for it." He realized Carl was crying and held him tighter. "I'm the one who should be apologizing. I know it will take time." Colin's emotion sputtered out again. "But I pray that one day you can forgive me."

"We're here for you, Colin," Nancy said. "As long as you do everything in your power to make it right, we're behind you all the way."

"Oh, thank you, Lord," Colin murmured and hugged his mother as tightly as he had his father. He'd never felt so humbled in his life to realize that he was being looked out for, in spite of his wrongdoings.

Colin was actually relieved when his parents began asking questions about what had led up to the incident with Lily. He was given the opportunity to share the whole picture without trying to blame his actions on Janna. He expressed his love for Janna and the children, with the hope that they could get beyond this and make it right.

While Colin was talking, Carl reached for his scriptures and began casually thumbing through them. At a quiet moment, he handed the book to Colin and pointed to a spot in the twelfth chapter of Alma. "Read verse thirty-four," he said.

Colin read to himself, feeling a different kind of emotion overtake him. *Therefore, whosoever repenteth, and hardeneth not his heart, he shall have claim on mercy through mine Only Begotten Son, unto a remission of his sins; and these shall enter into my rest.*

"There's a difficult road ahead for you, son," Carl said. "But if you remember that," he pointed again to the scripture, "you'll be okay."

Colin nodded and struggled for composure before he said, "There will be a . . . disciplinary council Tuesday evening. I know you can't go in with me, Dad . . . but . . . would you come? Would you wait with me?"

Carl gave him a sad smile. "I wouldn't want to be anywhere else, Colin."

"You can come too, Mom, if—"

Nancy squeezed his hand. "I'd like to be there. But I think I might be more effective taking care of Matthew while you go. I'll be praying for you."

The hope Colin felt from spending the morning with his parents was shattered into fresh reality as he pulled his father's truck into the driveway of his home. Janna was gone with the little ones, and several boxes were left waiting in the garage. Matthew at first seemed glad to see him, but as they loaded the truck, he was obviously quiet and moody.

"Are you sure you want to come with me?" Colin asked. "You don't have to, Matt. You're old enough to decide for yourself. I would love to have you come live with me, but I want you to do what's best for *you.*"

"I *do* want to live with you, Dad," he insisted.

"Then what's bugging you?" Colin asked, but Matthew just shrugged his shoulders.

"Hey," Colin added when they were nearly finished, "you can come visit your mother and sisters any time you want. All you have to do is ask, and I'll drive you up here whenever I possibly can."

"Okay," Matthew said with a stilted smile.

They went into Matthew's room to dismantle his bed, and Colin couldn't help being surprised by how clean the house was. He hadn't seen it like this in months—maybe longer. Again he wondered if his absence was so motivating for Janna. Or was she trying to prove something to him?

On the drive to Provo, Matthew continued to be quiet, almost sulky.

"Hey, buddy," Colin said, "if we're going to be roommates and help each other through this, we've got to talk to each other." He said nothing and Colin pressed, "I know this must be tough for you. It's tough for all of us. But it's not your fault, Matthew. It has nothing to do with you. I'm only sorry that you have to get caught in the middle."

Still nothing. Colin persisted. "Hey, Matt, if you need to understand what's going on, then let's talk about it. You can ask me anything you want."

"Will you answer me honest, Dad?" he asked.

Colin swallowed, knowing there was only one possible response. "Of course I will, Matt."

"Mom said . . ." He hesitated, and Colin held his breath.

"What did Mom say?"

"She said you slept with some babe you worked with."

Colin glanced over at his son and tried to keep his mind on the road. If he had contemplated *this* moment, among many, he never could have gone through with it. What kind of example was he? A role model who cheated on his wife? But he had promised to be honest, and the best he could hope for was that Matthew would see firsthand the anguish caused by sin.

"Yes, Matthew," he croaked, "it's true."

"I thought so," Matthew said and turned to stare out the window.

Colin tried to think of a way to explain himself, but it all sounded so much like excuses and rationalizations. At least he understood the child's solemn mood.

"Do you still want to stay with me?" Colin asked.

"Yes, I just don't want to be around her . . . whoever she is."

"I can assure you that she is nowhere around me . . . at all."

A few minutes later, Matthew turned and said, "Why did you do it, Dad? Is it because of the way Mom treats you?"

Colin wasn't quite sure how to take that. How much did a ten-year-old perceive? At what level did he understand it? "What do you mean by that, Matthew?"

"Well, I mean . . . Mom hasn't been real cool lately. When you got her away from that Russell jerk and married her, she used to laugh and have fun. And I could ask her things and she'd talk to me. After you got married she used to sit on your lap, and you'd make out while we watched movies and you didn't think I was looking. Then she just got all . . . weird. She gets mad over stupid things. And she wouldn't even kiss you without making a big deal out of it."

Colin was grateful that Matthew kept talking, since the knot in his throat was too big to swallow.

"*I* don't want to live with her, Dad. I can't blame *you* for not wanting to live with her."

Colin coughed to avoid crying. "It's not exactly that, Matthew. I mean, yes . . . things have been hard. But I didn't want to leave. She wouldn't let me stay after what I did. And I can't say that I blame her. It was an awful thing I did."

"Are you sorry you did it?" Matthew asked.

Colin forced back the burning in his eyes and kept them riveted to the road. "Yes, Matthew. I've never been so sorry for anything in my life."

"Yeah, well, I bet that babe at the office treated you better than Mom did."

"That doesn't make it right, Matt. There are reasons your mother behaves the way she does; reasons that are difficult to understand. I had no business betraying her like that, no matter how bad things were."

"Yeah, well," Matthew's voice picked up a hard edge, "Mom used to tell me the same thing about Russell." He mimicked his mother rather unkindly. "There are reasons he does what he does; things that are hard to understand." He returned to his normal voice. "That's what she'd say when her face was black and blue and she could hardly stand up, but she'd clean the house and cook anyway or he'd beat her up again. If she knows how it feels to be treated like that, then why did she turn around and treat you bad?"

"I don't know, Matthew. It's a complicated thing. But Sean is trying to help me understand it, and—"

"Well, maybe I should talk to him too, 'cause I think she's got me in this psycho thing."

"What do you mean by that?" Colin asked.

"'Cause I freaked out, just like she does. I told her to go to hell. I told her I didn't blame you for leaving her for somebody else, and . . ." Matthew hesitated, seeming more angry than emotional.

"And?" Colin pressed.

"And I nearly called her some of the things Russell used to call her. The words kept going through my head, and I probably would have said them if she hadn't hit me."

"She *hit* you?"

He nodded. "Real hard. It still hurt the next day. That's when she called Grandma and said she wanted me to live with you. And that was fine with me. Next time, I might say those things."

"What things?" Colin asked, not making the connection until Matthew spouted off a string of R-rated profanity that made Colin wince, not only from the words themselves, but also the reality they represented. This was what Russell had said to Janna often enough that, years later, the child was still plagued by the memory of it.

"I'm really glad you didn't say that to your mother," Colin said. "If you did, *I'd* probably hit you. Maybe you could work on a way to get those words out of your mind and replace them with something better."

"I think I've tried. Maybe what's-his-name could help me with that, too. Didn't I talk to him when I was a kid?" he asked, as if he were now a full-fledged adult.

"Yes, you did, and for a kid who had been around what you'd been around, it was good to have someone like Sean to talk to. He said you handled it all pretty well. He said you're one of those strong spirits with good instincts; that you know what's right and wrong in spite of the struggles from your childhood." Colin got emotional as the memory of Sean's assurance touched him now. "I'll take you to see him next week, if you like."

"Okay," Matthew said. Then he asked questions about where they were going to live. He didn't seem apprehensive about changing schools, especially when he found out he could ride the bus to Grandma's neighborhood and stay with her until Colin got off work. He seemed a little anxious about leaving his friends, but not as much as Colin had expected him to be.

By late Saturday evening, Matthew was moved comfortably into his new bedroom, and Colin had unpacked most of the things Janna had sent. They ordered a pizza and made a list of what they needed to make their new household function.

Sunday morning, they went to church together. Matthew looked up in surprise when Colin refused the sacrament, but he explained why after the meeting.

"Do Grandma and Grandpa know?" Matthew asked when they were driving to their home for Sunday dinner.

"Yes, they know," Colin said. "But nobody else needs to know. I can work it out privately."

Matthew nodded, then Colin asked him how he'd done in his new Primary class. He just said the teacher was *cool,* and left it at that. Matthew called his mother from Grandma's house to tell her they were doing okay, but she refused to talk to Colin.

On Monday, Colin took the morning off to get Matthew settled into his new school, then he worked a few hours and picked him up afterwards. They went shopping and cooked dinner together, and Colin had to admit he was grateful not to be alone. Having someone who needed him every day would make it easier to hang on.

CHAPTER SEVEN

$\mathcal{C}$olin fasted on Tuesday, wondering if he'd ever been so scared in his life as he thought of facing the church disciplinary council. He dropped Matthew off and picked up his father for the drive to Salt Lake City.

"How are you feeling, Dad?" he asked, hoping to divert his attention from the purpose of their drive.

"I assume you want me to be honest." Carl chuckled without humor.

"Have you ever been any other way?"

"Well, your mother tells me I keep too much to myself; I guess that can be a degree of dishonesty. There's nothing like a good struggle to show a man his weaknesses."

Colin didn't like the way that statement hit home for *him*.

"So, how are you feeling?" Colin repeated.

"I blacked out earlier today," he stated.

"What happened?" Colin questioned.

"I just . . . blacked out for a few seconds. That's all."

"Did you call the doctor, or—"

"Your mother did. He says I just need to get that MRI. It's scheduled for Friday. He tells me I shouldn't drive, or do anything that could be dangerous if I blacked out again." He chuckled again, more tensely. "It's a good thing I just retired," he said. "Although I was looking forward to enjoying it a little more than this."

While Colin was trying to think of something to say to let his father know how much he cared, Carl added, "So how are *you?*"

Reality tumbled back down, and he had to admit, "I'm terrified. I don't want to be excommunicated, Dad. But I know it's going to happen."

"It's not always cut and dried, Colin. There are a lot of factors that go into the decision."

It took a moment for Colin to recall that his father had served many years as a stake president, and many more years on the high council. "You've seen this kind of thing before," he stated.

Carl shook his head slowly. "More than you could possibly imagine."

"You mean I'm not the only stupid idiot in the Church?"

"Such things are terribly common," he said. "It's sad to see the traps good people fall into. We live in difficult times." Colin had to admit it was somewhat comforting to hear his father say, "And your attitude already puts you above the average, son. From what I've observed, you already have a broken heart and a contrite spirit. And that's the most important thing."

Colin was grateful for his father's insight as he briefly explained some aspects of the process that his stake president hadn't mentioned.

"You told me it's not cut and dried," Colin said. "What makes the difference?"

"Well, a lot of things are considered. The motive behind it. The circumstances. The effect on others. Your attitude. The specifics of the sin."

Colin's stomach began to smolder on that last one, but he just listened as his father continued.

"They also take into consideration your church calling at the time, and how many people know about it."

"What difference does that make?"

"Well, who knows about it?" Carl asked.

Colin shook his head. "I honestly don't know. I don't know if Janna would tell her friends. You and Mom know. Matthew knows."

"So, you tell me, Colin. Do you want your ten-year-old son to perceive that you can do something like this and *not* be excommunicated?"

Colin didn't answer. But he was getting the point.

"And what about . . . the woman?" Carl asked. "Would she tell others?"

Colin took a deep breath. "Again . . . I don't know. She's not

LDS. I'm ashamed to say I don't know her well enough to know if she'd keep quiet about it or not."

"Well," Carl went on, not seeming upset by the conversation, "the bottom line is that the decision should come from the Lord. These men put together and discuss the information they have available, then they make a decision, which should be unanimously approved by the Spirit. Only the Lord knows what's best for each individual. And sometimes excommunication, as harsh as it seems, allows a cleaner break from the past and an opportunity for a fresher start."

Colin said solemnly, "I can see why excommunication would be the best thing in the long run. And in a way, I think I knew, the minute I realized what I'd done, that it would turn out that way. But I just . . ." He couldn't hold back the emotion. "I'm scared, Dad. I'm just plain scared to be without the privileges and blessings of being a member. How can I cope? How can I make it through this without the help of the Spirit; without—"

"Let me clarify something," Carl interrupted. "There will be a loss of privileges, Colin. And it's going to be tough to make it. But don't think for a minute that God will stop hearing your prayers and doing his best to answer them. And though it will take a lot more work to keep the Spirit close, it is possible. The Holy Ghost manifests himself to many good people in the world who are not baptized members of the Church. It's just that having the *gift* of the Holy Ghost makes it more accessible, and closer. It will be an adjustment, but you're a tough kid, Colin. Whatever happens, you're going to be fine."

"You keep telling me that, Dad," he said, wondering how he would ever make it through this if something were to happen to his father now.

"I only wish . . . that Janna would forgive me . . . eventually. If I thought we could never make it, I'm not sure I could go on."

"One step at a time, son."

Colin nodded, dismayed to realize that they had arrived at the stake center. He'd never felt so alone in his life as the moment he walked into the high council room and had to leave his father behind. His heart beat painfully as he was seated, and his gaze took in the faces of the stake presidency and high council. His bishop was also there. He had worked in church callings with two of these men. The stake executive secretary was one of his neighbors; their families had barbecued together frequently. The humiliation was so intense that he wanted to just sink through the floor and disappear.

Colin tried to contain his emotion as he answered the questions and explained what needed to be said. But the tears wouldn't be held back. If nothing else, he hoped these men would know the regret he felt.

The time dragged while Colin waited in the foyer with his father. He wondered what could possibly take so long. He tried to imagine the conversations going back and forth as half of the council represented him, and the other half took the Church's position. When he was finally called back in, the heart-pounding fear returned. He managed to keep a straight face as he was told with compassion that he was being excommunicated. He felt like a denounced military officer, remaining at attention as his stripes and any indication of rank were publicly torn from his uniform. The mask began to crumble as he was informed of his loss of privileges, and he pressed a trembling hand over his mouth and squeezed his eyes shut while he absorbed it. He was not to pray in any church meeting or make any comment in a class. He could not publicly bear his testimony or serve in any church calling. Not being able to take the sacrament didn't surprise him; not being able to pay tithing did. He was not to wear his temple garments—something that perhaps terrified him most of all.

Colin felt numb as the stake president took a few minutes with him alone afterward. He was kind and compassionate, offering assurances of hope and encouragement. He recommended that Colin go straight to his new bishop to explain the situation and get his help, even before his records were transferred.

"Don't think you can do it alone, Brother Trevor. This is something that calls for the support of those around you. And even though you've moved to a new area, you can always call me if you need someone."

Bishop Miller was waiting when Colin came out of the stake president's office. Colin was apprehensive about talking to him after the way he'd felt in the wake of their last appointment. But Colin felt somewhat renewed as the bishop invited Colin to visit with him for a few minutes. He basically admitted that he wasn't very good at handling such things, and he wished Colin well in putting his life in order. Colin couldn't help being grateful for the opportunity to talk with him, especially when the bishop promised that he would keep close track of Janna and the children, and would do his best to see that their needs were met.

He cried most of the way home, grateful to have his father with him. Carl listened and made it clear that his love was unconditional.

Colin managed to maintain his composure when he picked Matthew up. He thanked his parents with an embrace; then he went home to resign himself to life as an excommunicated Mormon, separated from his wife and babies, wondering if he could ever get past this.

The following days were dark for Colin. He was especially grateful for Matthew's presence in his life. The boy was a continual reminder that there were reasons for holding on. While it was difficult to see that Matthew's needs were met and their little household kept running, Colin wondered if he would be holding it together at all on his own. He often thought of the advice Sean had given him to get a separation from Janna a long time ago. He wondered now if taking that advice would have made it possible to work out their problems without putting this horrible incident into the picture. But he reminded himself there was no point in wishing to change the past, and he kept his concentration on being there for Matthew. They talked about what was happening, and Colin hoped, if nothing else, that Matthew would learn something from the heartache his father was experiencing.

While it was something he dreaded, Colin knew it was important for Janna to know what had happened. It took days to gather the courage to call her. As soon as she said hello, he blurted out, "Now, don't hang up on me. Just let me tell you something, okay?"

"Okay," she said as if she was doing him a huge favor. "I'm listening."

"First of all . . . are you all right? Do you have what you need?"

"As long as you keep sending me money, I'll be fine."

"Okay," he said, trying not to get defensive. "But . . . how are *you,* Janna? Is there anything I can do to—"

"For having to tell me something, you're sure asking a lot of questions."

"I'm still your husband, Janna. I just want to know that your needs are being met."

"They're being met," she said. "Get to the point."

"I just thought you should know . . . well, I was excommunicated, Janna. I just . . . wanted you to know . . . that I'm doing everything I can . . . to make it right."

There was a long pause. "That's between you and the Lord, Colin. Making it right with me isn't going to be so easy."

Easy? He wanted to shout at her. Did she think this was *easy?* He only said, "I'll do whatever I have to do to make it right with you, Janna."

"Don't waste the effort, Colin. I don't think it's possible."

"And that's it?"

"We've had this conversation before, Colin."

"I guess I was . . . hoping you'd changed your mind; that you might give me a chance."

"I'll tell you what, Colin. If a day comes when I can close my eyes without imagining whatever took place between you and . . . *Lily,*" she said the name as if it were a dirty word, "then perhaps I could cope with having a civil conversation. But letting you back into my bed is not an option."

"I love you, Janna," he pleaded tearfully. "At least you could—"

"Don't lie to me, Colin. And don't patronize me. I'd like to see Matthew sometime soon, when it's convenient. Have him call."

Colin stood with the phone hanging limp in his hand long after the call disconnected. He pressed his forehead to the wall, and the tears wouldn't stop. He was surprised to feel the phone being removed from his hand. He watched as Matthew hung it up, then the boy wrapped his arms around Colin and hugged him tight.

"You know, Dad," he said, "she wouldn't be so ticked off if she didn't still love you."

"Who told you that?" he asked, wiping his face with his sleeve.

"Sean did. It makes sense to me."

"Well, she doesn't believe me when I tell her that I love *her.*"

"Maybe she'll get over it."

"Maybe she won't."

"Hey, Dad," Matthew said with surprising maturity, "no matter what happens, I'm still your son."

"Did Sean tell you that, too?"

"No, but he said some things that made me think of it."

Colin managed a smile. At least Matthew seemed to be doing well, even if he had to give most of the credit to Sean.

"You know, Dad, maybe you should go see Sean. It's been a while."

"Yeah," Colin said, "maybe I should."

Spending some time with Sean did help, but he had trouble with the reality that Janna had the right to choose living her life without him. Sean reminded him to be patient and take it one day at a time.

"What if she files for divorce in the meantime?" Colin asked. "I told her I wouldn't sign anything, but eventually she'll get it by default. She's got grounds."

"I guess we'll just have to see, but in my opinion, I don't think she'll do it. I don't think she knows what she wants. She's hurt and she's angry, and she feels helpless. But deep down inside, I don't think she wants the divorce. Just give it some time, Colin. That's all you can do."

Colin had no choice but to accept it—just like he had to accept the other changes in his life that were direct consequences of the sin he'd committed. He continued going to church, feeling somehow like a ghost hovering on the sidelines. Again he was grateful for Matthew, when some Sunday mornings his son was his only motivation for doing the right thing.

Not being able to pay tithing was difficult for Colin. But he felt the first real glimmer of evidence that his prayers were being heard when he took it to the Lord. He laid it all out, voicing his concerns about being able to make ends meet, especially running two households, if he couldn't give that money to the Lord. He expressed through prayer his testimony of tithing, and told the Lord that there just had to be a way that he could continue to live it. The following Sunday, while Colin was helping Matthew fill out his tithing slip for $1.82, the answer came. He talked to the bishop about it in their weekly interview, and he found pleasure in putting ten percent of his income in a savings account, so that he could give it to the Lord when he had the privilege to pay tithing again. His prayer had been answered. It wasn't much, but it helped.

* * * * *

Janna stood near the front room window, watching discreetly through the sheers as Colin dropped Matthew off. He walked around the car to open the trunk so Matthew could take out his things, and Janna hated herself for the way her heart quickened at just the sight of her husband. The blue jeans with a white button-up shirt were typical of Colin. He often came home from work and changed his pants and shoes, but not his shirt. *He was adorable,* and she hated him for it.

Colin hugged Matthew tightly, then he stood with his hands in his back pockets, watching the boy move up the walk. At the same moment Janna felt tears threaten, she saw Colin wipe a hand quickly over his face, as if to dry his cheeks. When Matthew came through the front door to be met by his sisters, Colin got in the car and drove away. Janna was still standing at the window when Matthew approached and hugged her. She held him a moment longer than necessary, thinking how Colin had hugged him so recently. She cursed herself for the thought. All of this would be so much easier if she just didn't care.

Janna felt tense and awkward with Matthew in the house when he hadn't been there for so long. He was cooperative and did what she asked him to do, but he didn't say much. Over the dinner table she asked, "So, how's your father?"

She saw something in his eyes that told her what he was thinking was different from what he said. "He's doing okay."

"Is he seeing . . . that woman?" she asked.

"Give it up, Mom. He's with me all the time when he's not working, and he doesn't even talk to her on the phone. He wants to get back together with you."

Janna sighed. "Well, Matthew, I'm afraid that's not possible."

"Anything's possible. That's what Sean says."

"Have you been talking to Sean?"

"I saw him a couple of times. He's cool. Dad's been talking to him, too." He paused and added, "Maybe you should talk to him, Mom. Maybe—"

"Forget it, Matthew. I have no desire to talk to Sean right now. I'm certain he's thinking that your father's side of the story is all fine and dandy, but—"

"You don't even *know* what Dad's thinking. He cries all the time, you know."

Janna was briefly taken aback, but she covered it quickly. "Well, he *ought* to cry after what he did to me."

"And what about what you did to him?" Matthew retorted.

"Matthew, you have no idea what you're talking about. You're ten years old, so just leave it alone before you get yourself into trouble."

Janna was grateful when he didn't push it. He went to bed saying nothing more to her, and right after breakfast he called his father. Colin arrived in less than an hour, and Matthew ran out to the car, barely saying, "See you, Mom."

Janna sat down and cried, wondering what had gone wrong with her life. The motivation she'd felt initially in Colin's absence had dissipated with time. How could she make sense of this despair that only grew deeper each day, when she couldn't even discern whether she hated Colin or loved him?

* * * * *

"So," Colin said as they got on the freeway and Matthew still hadn't made a sound, "things went well with your mother, I assume."

Matthew turned to glare at him. "Get real, Dad. She hasn't been cool for even a minute since that night you came home late."

Colin pressed a hand over the tightening in his chest. He knew well what night that was. "And how was she . . . *cool* then, Matthew?"

"Oh, I came home from school, and the house was, like . . . clean. And we went to the store together, and bought good stuff, and we laughed, and she talked to me about school and stuff while we were cooking dinner. She made the chicken blue stuff and—"

"Chicken cordon-bleu."

"Yeah, that stuff."

"I love that stuff," Colin said, not liking the picture coming together in his head.

"I know. That's what she said when she was making it. Then she, like, put on this pretty black dress and had her hair fixed cool and stuff."

Colin swallowed hard before he asked, "And that's the night I came home really late?"

"Yeah, an' she was worried about you. She didn't say that, but she was calling the hospitals and the police and stuff."

Colin leaned an elbow on the car door and pressed his hand

over his mouth, trying to keep his concentration on the road. It took every ounce of self-control to keep that mask in place as he tried to imagine where he might be now if he had refused to give Lily a ride, and gone straight home instead. Tears began to leak out as he imagined walking through the door to see evidence that Janna loved him and was making some effort. "Heaven help me," he murmured. While Janna had apparently been reconsidering the state of their marriage, he'd been in bed with another woman. The thought made him sick to his stomach.

"Dad, you're crying again," Matthew said.

Colin forced out a chuckle in an effort to keep from sobbing. "Yes," he managed, "I'm crying again."

When they finally got home, Colin went into his bedroom and closed the door. He turned the stereo by his bed up loud, buried his face in the pillow, and sobbed. *He was such a fool!*

A few days later, Colin talked to Sean about the irony, and cried all over again. Sean offered compassion, but what could he say? And while Colin was gradually beginning to make sense of what was behind all of this, the pain just wasn't going away.

In the meantime, a day never passed when Colin didn't wonder what he would ever do without his parents. If he'd had to pretend that everything was all right, even in front of them, he felt certain he'd go crazy. He and Matthew occasionally had dinner with them. Like so many other times in his life, Colin was grateful for their support in a way that words could not explain. Although a certain tension hovered around them as they waited for the results of the MRI, they kept smiling and making life easier for him and Matthew.

Colin was with his parents when they were shown the results. On some kind of video, they were able to see the evidence for themselves of a tumor growing in Carl Trevor's brain. As his father squeezed his hand tightly, Colin thought of what they'd been through together on *his* behalf not so long ago. How quickly the tables had turned. He wondered if he could bear facing life without his father to lean on.

Surgery was scheduled, but it was impossible to know what to expect. They were told that brain surgery was not nearly as dangerous as it had once been, and they were told many success stories. They were also told that there were possible complications, and unexpected things happened. Not to mention that there was no way of knowing if the tumor was malignant until it had been removed.

Since the situation was not considered an emergency, the decision was made to wait until after Christmas for the surgery. With all of the family notified, they were all going to be together for the holiday for the first time in many years. The irony was horrible for Colin. Everyone would be there except his wife and daughters. Most of his siblings had not even seen the girls.

As Christmas approached, Colin's mother encouraged him to work out something with Janna so that he could see Caitlin and Mallory. He hadn't pushed the issue, not wanting to argue with her or antagonize her. But even Sean agreed that he had a right to see his children.

Colin argued with Janna on the phone for nearly an hour before he convinced her that he had the right to see them—especially for Christmas. He finally had to threaten her with a court order to get her to agree. He wished that she could tolerate him enough for them to all be together, if only for a few hours, but she wouldn't have it. They compromised by agreeing that Colin would get the children on the evening of the twenty-third and keep them for twenty-four hours. Then they would be with their mother for Christmas Day. Colin talked to his parents about it, and they enthusiastically declared they would have the majority of their Christmas celebration a day early. His siblings all agreed, since they would be arriving before then anyway. Colin knew that his mother had informed them all of his separation, but no one knew the reasons, and that was fine with him.

Christmas turned out relatively well, all things considered. When he took the children to be with their mother on the evening of Christmas Eve, Janna refused to see him. But he sent gifts for her from the children, and hoped she would enjoy the holiday. Or maybe he hoped she'd be lonely enough to ask him to reconcile.

Colin hit a new low in the days between Christmas and New Year's Day. This was a time that he usually took off work to be with his children. Janna wouldn't talk to him. Sean had taken his family to Chicago for the holidays to be with his father, and Matthew was with his friends most of the time. Colin's siblings were hanging around his parents' home, and he felt vaguely uncomfortable with them, as if they might figure out how bad his life really was. And to top it all off, he got a call from his old law firm in Salt Lake, asking him to come in and briefly go over something concerning a case he'd been involved with. The very thought of going back there was like throwing alcohol on an open wound. But he prayed for strength, hoping with everything inside him that he could avoid seeing Lily.

Lily. He hadn't dared acknowledge, even to himself, that his thoughts strayed to her far too often. The more time dragged on without Janna in his life, the more he seemed drawn to memories of Lily. He'd stopped himself from calling her a dozen times, wanting to just talk to her. He wondered how she was doing. Better than he was, he hoped. But then, her value system was completely different from his. For her, the whole thing was likely an emotional loss; but did she even comprehend the spiritual loss? He wanted to ask her. He ached to talk to her, and yes, to hold her. In the deepest part of his heart, he knew that it was Janna he truly ached for; but each time she refused to talk to him, she wedged the reality a little deeper. In the end, he had to accept the possibility that he might not have a future with her.

Still, he had brains enough to know that any more involvement with Lily would only set him back. So, he just plain didn't want to see her. In his present state of mind, it was just too risky.

His business in Salt Lake went smoothly, and he was already sighing with relief to be on his way out without so much as a glimpse of Lily Greene. Don stopped him in the hall to ask how he was doing, and they talked for a few minutes. Before he could get away, Lily walked right past, doing a double-take when she saw him.

"Well, hello, Trevor," she said as if nothing but legal talk had ever transpired between them.

"Hello," he said coolly, trying to ignore the quickening of his heart.

"What brings you here?" she asked.

"Business," he stated.

She glanced toward Don and smiled nonchalantly. "Looks like you're shooting the breeze to me."

"Well, that too," Don said.

"Come talk to me before you go," she said lightly and walked away.

"She's a good attorney," Don commented, startling Colin. "Better than me in some ways, I'm ashamed to admit."

Colin forced the conversation back to where it had been before Lily had interrupted, then he moved toward the door as they said good-bye. "Hey, Trevor," Don said, "you'd better go talk to Lily, or she'll probably sue you or something."

"Oh, of course," he said, pretending that he'd forgotten.

Colin took a deep breath and walked into her office, leaving the door open. She smiled when their eyes met. Colin glanced down and stuffed his hands in his pockets.

"So," he said, "Don says you're doing good around here. That doesn't surprise me."

"I had a good mentor," she said. "It's just not the same here without you."

"Yes . . . well . . . life has a way of changing."

"You look good, Colin," she said.

"Do I?" he chuckled.

"Your hair's longer. I like it."

Colin pushed a hand through his hair self-consciously. He closed his eyes, trying to come up with a good line to make his exit. The sound of the door closing startled him. He turned to see Lily leaning against it. The horrible thing was that he wanted more than anything to just hold her in his arms, if only for a moment.

"I've missed you, Colin," she said, sauntering toward him.

"Don't do this to me, Lily," he insisted.

"We're in an office, Colin. What do you think I'm going to do? Seduce you right here and—"

"Don't say it," he interrupted.

Lily took hold of his left hand, fingering his wedding ring. "Still married, I see."

"Amazing, isn't it," he said cynically, unable to keep from watching her eyes.

"But how long has it been since you were kissed?"

Colin pressed his fingers between hers. "Not since the last time you kissed me."

"Yeah, me too," she whispered, lightly brushing the side of her face against his.

"Lily, don't," he said with absolutely no conviction.

"A kiss, Colin," she whispered, pressing her fingers over his lips.

He closed his eyes to indulge in the sensation, just for a moment. "For old times' sake," she added, and he felt her lips replace her fingers against his mouth.

Colin willed himself not to respond, as if he could somehow enjoy the intimacy without actively participating. Sean's Thanksgiving dinner theory popped into his head, and only one thing stood out clearly: *He was hungry.*

Colin had never felt so hypocritical in his life as he muttered a silent prayer for help at the same moment he took Lily in his arms and kissed her long and hard.

"Oh, I've missed you," she murmured, pressing a hand into his hair.

Colin kissed her again, while something in his mind begged and pleaded, *Please God, don't let me fall again. Please!* He felt Lily easing closer, and he began wishing it could go on and on, at the same time knowing it would only catapult him into new depths of misery. He kept his hands pressed firmly to her back, fearing they would wander elsewhere if he didn't.

A quick knock at the door was the only warning before it flew open. Colin and Lily turned simultaneously to see Don standing in the doorway, grinning like the Cheshire cat. "Wow," he said, "I missed *that* class in law school."

Lily turned her back and cursed under her breath. Colin uttered a silent *Thank you, God,* and hurried from the room.

Colin was in the parking lot before he heard Lily call, "Hold on there, Trevor." He turned and she approached quickly. "Am I not even worth a good-bye?"

"I thought that's what it was," he stated. "A kiss for old times' sake."

She folded her arms and scowled at him. "Lighten up, and take me to lunch."

"I can't, Lily."

"Why not? Give me one good reason."

"I could give you several, but you would just argue with me. I just can't. Leave it at that."

She turned her head and closed her eyes. The hurt in her expression was evident. Had he really been so cruel to her? "Hey," Colin touched her chin, "I'm not worth the trouble, Lily. Find somebody who has a whole life and a whole heart to give you." He got in the car and drove away before he had a chance to contemplate kissing her again.

Although Colin figured he'd only slipped a little, and he talked to the bishop about it right away, he still couldn't deny the increased difficulty he felt in his life. His discouragement was more intense, and his ability to feel any evidence of his prayers being heard was almost nonexistent. He recalled his father telling him once that a recovered alcoholic shouldn't be stupid enough to go into a bar for any reason, and a man attracted to a woman he couldn't have shouldn't be stupid enough to be alone with her. He was talking about Janna at the time, since she had not yet been granted her divorce. But he figured the same rule applied here. As he looked back over the struggles of his life in reference to his father's analogy, he realized that in spite of being a basically good person, he had always been prone to bending rules. He'd pressed black and white boundaries into shades of gray during his youth, until he'd fallen into a trap that got Janna pregnant. And he'd bent rules with Lily—simple, seemingly insignificant rules that had left him vulnerable.

Soon after the holidays, Carl went in for surgery. The evening before, Colin went to spend some time with his dad. They talked much the same way they had prior to Colin's excommunication.

While Carl was showing Matthew his fishing things out in the garage, Colin had a few minutes alone with his mother.

"Do you think he's going to make it?" Colin asked.

"I don't know, Colin."

Colin tried to fathom the worst possible scenario, and he impulsively groaned, pushing his hands into his hair.

"What is it, Colin?" Nancy asked. Her husband was going in for brain surgery, and she was concerned about *Colin*.

Colin shook his head, feeling a tangible pain smolder in his chest. "My father could die," he cried, "and I can't even give him a blessing." The tears trickled down his face as he shoved his hands into his back pockets. "I'm the only son he's got within a thousand miles, and I can't do it."

Nancy put her arms around him and hugged him tightly. "It's all right, Colin. The home teachers are coming. And your dad wants you to be here. Your prayers on his behalf are still being heard."

Colin nodded and managed to remain composed when his father and Matthew came back into the house. He exchanged a concerned glance with his mother when they realized that Carl had just given Matthew his favorite fishing pole. Did he fear he wouldn't live to use it again?

In spite of not being able to participate, Colin was comforted to feel evidence of the Spirit close by as his father was given a blessing and promised that he would live beyond the surgery and be able to function and enjoy his family. But how long he would live remained to be seen.

Colin sat with his mother through the long hours of Carl's surgery. Through the days of recovery, he was reminded of the time Janna had spent in intensive care after Russell Clark had nearly killed her. At moments, he missed her so much it hurt. He was surprised when she called late one evening, after he'd returned from the hospital.

"What's wrong?" he asked. "You need more money?"

"That's not funny, Colin."

"No, it's not funny at all that you can't tolerate me for more than that."

"I'm trying to be civil, Colin. Don't blow it."

"I'm sorry," he said gently. "It's been a long day."

"That's why I called . . . I guess. I was just wondering . . . how your father is. Your mother's hard to get hold of. I assume she's at the hospital most of the time."

"Yeah, she is. He's doing pretty well, actually. But it will be a while before we know if the tumor was malignant."

"What if it is?"

"Then we're dealing with cancer. What can I say?"

She was silent for a long moment. "Tell your parents I'm thinking about them."

"I will, thank you."

"And you, Colin . . . in spite of everything, my heart is with you in this."

Colin squeezed his eyes shut in silent gratitude. It wasn't much, but it gave him hope. "Thank you, Janna. That means a lot to me."

She said good-bye and hung up quickly, but Colin felt a little better after that.

Three months after the incident with Lily, Colin was pleased to see that at least his life had settled into a tolerable routine. He was seeing his daughters on alternate weekends, and taking Matthew to be with Janna on the other weekends. Sean had helped Matthew learn to handle his mother without getting upset. Colin worked on fixing up the apartment, and decided that he actually liked it. Matthew's presence helped make it a home. He gradually came to like his ward, and found them supportive without being nosy. He felt good about telling his home teachers why he could not be an active part of the elders quorum. They turned out to be understanding and supportive, and as far as he knew, they'd told no one who didn't need to know. The bishop met with him regularly, giving him hope and encouragement, and his parents were involved in his life as much as possible.

Carl recovered remarkably well from his surgery, and they were all overjoyed to learn that the tumor was not malignant. It would be several months before he could return to normal activity, but there was no reason to think that he would not have many years of quality life ahead of him.

As Colin settled into his work, he found the satisfaction he'd hoped for when he had first considered making the move. The attitude and spirit were immeasurably better than the firm he'd been with; the one where Lily had been in the office across the hall. He felt certain that the environment they'd been working in, where bad language and crude jokes were common, had played a part in their downfall.

One morning in February, Lucy came into his office looking distressed.

"Is something wrong?" he asked.

"Charles is not a happy man," she said.

"Is there anything I can do to help?"

"Not unless you speak Japanese."

Colin lifted an eyebrow. "Well, actually . . . I do." Lucy looked so pleasantly surprised that he laughed. "Well, I mean . . . I did once. It's been a long time, but I think I could likely manage. Why?"

"Well, Charles took on this client, a Mister Ado Kuwata."

Colin tried not to chuckle at her poor pronunciation.

"Mister Kuwata's son speaks English, but he had to leave town for a funeral or something, and Charles needs to get something or another accomplished, but he has no idea how to talk to this guy."

"Well, tell Charles I'd be happy to help."

Lucy narrowed her eyes on him. "Where did you learn Japanese?"

"Japan," he said and chuckled. She looked comically disgusted and he added, "I went there on my mission."

"Oh." Lucy looked so surprised that he wondered what he'd said wrong.

"Is that so amazing?"

"I just . . . didn't think you were a Mormon."

Colin attempted to keep his expression from showing how deep that cut. Had he lost that countenance they often talked about? Was the light of the Spirit so completely absent from his life? The thought troubled him more than he wanted to admit.

Calmly he asked, "What made you think otherwise? I haven't been asking for coffee or anything, have I?"

"I . . . uh . . ." Lucy stammered and looked embarrassed. She finally said, "It's easy to see garment lines under those white shirts you lawyers wear."

Colin said nothing as his thoughts ran deep. "Did I say something wrong?" Lucy asked. "I mean, it's probably not appropriate at all to even bring up something like that. I'm sorry. I talk too much, and—"

"No, it's okay. It's just that . . . well, it's not like it's any great secret. Charles knows. I just didn't realize it was so obvious. Right now, I am an excommunicated Mormon. I did something stupid. I'm working on making it right. We'll leave it at that."

Colin was relieved when Lucy said nothing more about it, and she didn't treat him any differently. He also went out and bought some white undershirts, wondering why he hadn't thought of that to begin with. Matthew went with him and picked out some boxer shorts for his dad in ridiculous prints.

"Now, why would I want to wear something like that?" Colin asked.

"It's underwear. Nobody's gonna see it but me," Matthew smirked, then his expression turned serious. He said nothing more, but Colin suspected his son had motives. Was he trying to say that he should be so embarrassed to wear such ridiculous underwear that it would keep him from doing something he shouldn't? At first the thought bothered him, then he realized that it was actually touching to think of his son looking out for him in his own little way.

The opportunity to work with a Japanese client ended up being another unexpected blessing in Colin's life. He found the opportunity to relearn the language, and he was warmed by memories of his mission. Then he learned that the firm would pay for him to fly to Japan to follow through on some business for Mr. Kuwata.

The day after he was informed of the forthcoming trip, he answered the phone on his way out the door to work.

"Is that you, Colin?" a female voice asked.

"Yes."

"Hi, it's Lily."

Colin hesitated, hating the way his heart began to pound. "Hello, Lily."

"How are you?"

"I'm coping . . . I think. How are you?"

"The same." There was silence. "Has your wife let you come back yet?"

"No."

More silence. "It's just not the same here without you. The rest of these people are so . . . *stodgy.*"

"Law is a stodgy business, Lily."

"I miss you, Colin." The tone in her voice made it clear that she was speaking on a personal level. "I was hoping—"

"Is there a reason you called?"

"I just wanted to see how you're doing."

"Now you know."

"You're not being very gracious."

"I made it clear where I stand."

"You're a stubborn man, Colin. I just can't believe you would wallow over a woman who wants nothing to do with you, and didn't treat you good to begin with."

"Well, Lily, I just can't believe you would wallow over a man who wants nothing to do with you, and didn't treat you good to begin with."

"I am not wallowing over Tyler."

"I'm not talking about Tyler. How did you find me, anyway?"

"You don't have to be a private eye to call directory assistance, Colin. Although I could be a private eye if I had to. Sometimes you have to, to be a good lawyer, you know."

"I've watched Perry Mason, Lily. I'm on my way to work. I have to go."

"So early?"

"I have to get done so I can . . ." He was going to tell her that he needed to be with Matthew, but Nancy was taking him to stay with Janna right after school so that he could go to a friend's birthday party. "Never mind."

"So you can what? What do you have to come home to, Colin?"

"Tonight, nothing. But usually, my son. He's living with me now, but he's going to stay with his mother for the weekend."

"Let's have dinner, Colin."

"I'm a married man, Lily."

"You're a separated man, Colin."

"Still married."

"I just want to talk, okay? I'm having trouble with this. I kept hoping it would go away, but it hasn't." Emotion tainted her voice. "We went to bed together, Colin. Could you have the decency to at least talk to me about it?"

Colin hesitated. "Okay, call me about seven this evening. We'll talk, but it's not going to change anything."

"I'll see you at seven," she said and hung up.

All day, Colin dreaded Lily's call. The problem was that he *wanted* to talk to her. He wanted to have a real conversation with someone who cared and listened. He tried to convince himself that there was no harm in a phone conversation, and maybe it would help *him* deal with what had happened between them. But he purposely waited until after seven to go home, hoping to have missed her call. And if she tried again, he could just not answer the phone.

CHAPTER EIGHT

*T*he minute Colin walked into his apartment, he knew something wasn't right. There was music playing. Had he left the CD on continuous play all day? It was possible. But he knew he hadn't left the lamp on. He took hold of the doorknob to make a fast exit with the intention of calling the police, when Lily Greene came out of the kitchen.

"What on earth are you doing here?" he asked, but she didn't seem affected by his anger.

"I needed to talk to you."

"I told you to *call.*"

"This is better."

"For who?"

"For *me.* Call me selfish if you must, but I needed to see you."

"How did you get in?"

"You left the window open—just a crack."

"Oh, that's just great," he said with sarcasm and turned his back to her while he tried to figure out what to do.

"Colin," she said gently, "I didn't come to seduce you. I just want to talk."

"Well, the last time I came to get my tie. And before that, it was to fix a light switch."

"I still have your tie."

"Throw it away."

"I just want to talk," she said.

"Okay," he turned and pointed at her, "you sit on the couch. I sit on the chair. I'm not going to take you to bed. I'm not going to have a relationship with you. I'm not even going to kiss you."

She smiled and sat on the couch. Colin took a deep breath and sat down.

"Must you look so . . . *stodgy?*"

"I'm a lawyer."

"So am I. Just relax and talk to me."

"You're the one who wants to talk, Lily. I'm listening."

She began by talking about what was going on at the office, both in business and the personal lives of people they both knew. Then she told him what Tyler had been doing to try and provoke her every so often. For the most part she was glad the divorce was final, but she felt disoriented and alone.

When she was apparently finished, she said, "You still look stodgy. Do I make you that nervous?"

"Yes."

"Why?"

"I refuse to get into that. But everything that happens while we're in the same room, I am obligated to tell my bishop next Wednesday."

"Why?"

"Because I need his help to get through this."

"What? The separation?"

Colin leaned his forearms on his thighs and looked at her closely. "Lily, let me explain something to you."

"It would be nice to have you talking for a change."

"When I married Janna, it was forever. There are covenants between us that go far beyond a civil marriage."

"It was one of those temple weddings."

"Yes. And one of those covenants had to do with fidelity. I made a commitment with God that I would never have any intimacy with anyone beyond my wife. I broke that promise. As a result, I have been denied the right to every blessing associated with being a member of my church. I have been excommunicated, Lily. I don't expect you to understand what that means to me, but I am on a very strict probation, and if I do anything to blow it now, I will go back to square one."

Lily shook her head. "Have you ever considered the possibility that being a religious man is what makes this so difficult for you?"

Colin didn't like the implication, but he said nothing.

"If you ask me, you're just bringing a lot of this on yourself. Nobody said you had to go tell your bishop everything, or that God doesn't understand where you're coming from. Isn't it between you and God?"

"Yes," he said, "it is. But there are only certain people on this earth who have the right to officiate on his behalf and help me through this."

"It all just sounds like a lot of technicalities to me," Lily said.

"Okay, let me tell you something that has nothing to do with technicalities. Let me tell you about relationships. I have a relationship with God. I have felt personal evidence in my life, for nearly as long as I can remember, that he hears and answers my prayers, that he understands me and my problems. I could tell you details if you're interested. When I broke my covenants, I offended God. I severed that relationship.

"Now, you tell me something, Lily. Suppose you had one good friend who was always there for you with good advice and a shoulder to cry on. If there was ever any friction between you, it was your doing, because she was always true, and calm, and kind. And let's say that in a foolish moment you did something to betray her. And she had proof positive. What do you suppose it would do to that relationship?"

Lily said nothing, but she seemed interested, so he kept talking. "Well, in a way, God is my best friend. That's the way I see it. I betrayed his trust. I lost my best friend. I have seen evidence that as long as I remain humble and do my best to make an effort each day toward making this right, he is still willing to bless me. But something's missing. Something's not right. And it's going to take time to earn his trust again.

"Now," Colin shifted in his chair, "let me tell you about Janna. I met JannaLyn Hayne when she was fifteen. It didn't take long to fall in love with her. We went together through high school. We dated in groups a lot because we'd been taught to remain chaste outside of marriage. I graduated and started college. In the spring of her senior year, her mother died unexpectedly. Janna's father abandoned her mother and her when she was a baby, and he only came back once when Janna was thirteen, for a couple of weeks. During that time, he sexually abused her; I didn't know about that until years later. But I did know that her mother was the only family she had beyond an aunt who was worse than no relative. The night her mother died, I slept with Janna. We loved each other, and we were under a lot of stress. But we weren't married, and it was wrong. Three months later she went to live with her aunt, and I didn't hear from her for seven years. When I found her again, her husband was beating her up. He caused some miscarriages from his abuse. I also learned at the time that she had a seven-year-old son. *My* son, Lily. She hadn't wanted to hold me back. She wanted me to be a lawyer, to fulfill my dream. So, I was a lawyer. But I was helpless to protect her from her ex-husband when the criminal charges were dropped. Some time later, he found her and put her in intensive care. When she finally got past it, we were married. Whether it was a temple marriage or not, I told her that I would always be there for her, that she could count on me.

"We had two more children together. Do you have any comprehension of what it's like for two people to share the birth of a baby? Our life was good, Lily, until her father showed up and . . . well, our counselor said that just seeing his face triggered the whole thing. All the suppressed pain of abuse just hit her between the eyes. And that's when she started taking it out on me. I'm not the one who abused her, but I'm the one who got her pregnant with an illegitimate child, a situation that pushed her into an abusive marriage. The way she treated me wasn't right, Lily. But my codependent reaction to her problems wasn't, either. Now, try to imagine, for just a minute, the sense of betrayal in that woman's mind. Every man in her life has hurt and betrayed her—including me. I had to look that woman in the eye . . ." Colin made no effort to hold back the emotion. He figured she needed to see it. ". . . And tell her that I gave another woman what I had promised her I would never give anyone else."

Lily said nothing, but he could see the emotion in her eyes.

"Now, there's one more relationship I want to tell you about. My two younger children are too young to understand what's happening. But they're still affected by the absence of their father. Matthew is ten, however. Try to comprehend, Lily, how I felt when he looked at me and asked if I had really slept with some woman I worked with. He was actually pretty understanding. But then, this is the child who was trained to run to his room and hide whenever his mother's first husband started hitting her. He tells me that he used to curl up under the bed and put his hands over his ears so he wouldn't have to hear his mother's screams and the vile things he called her when he hit her. Then he got me as a replacement. And I betrayed his mother."

Colin realized that he was completely relaxed as he leaned forward and continued. "You see, Lily, my religion is not a restriction in my life. It's a guideline for happiness. And I broke the rules. The results are unhappiness for me and for everyone I care about. I have learned that there is no such thing as a private sin. What I have done has affected many lives. My religion gives me the means and the opportunity to go through a process that will make it possible for me to wash away the sin forever. But it takes time. And there's a price to pay."

"Wow," Lily said in a hushed voice. "I don't know what to say."

"Well, maybe that will help you understand where I'm coming from."

"And you really believe you can make it work with Janna—after all you've been through?"

Colin leaned back. "Quite honestly, I don't know. I want it, and I believe in it. And for now, that's all that matters."

Lily said nothing for several minutes, but she seemed deep in thought and Colin let her be. She finally turned to look at him and said quietly, "I owe you an apology."

"For what?"

"The day you were packing in the office, you told me I was the one who started it. And you're right, I did. It was impulsive. I didn't think. I just reacted to the way you made me feel. But somehow I know that you *never* would have started it. And if I had minded my manners, it probably wouldn't have happened. In essence, you told me I had no business starting something like that when I had no idea where your head was, and what was going on in your life. At least that was my interpretation. And you were right about that, too. I feel like I have some responsibility in this, but what can I do to help make it right?"

"You work out your own life, Lily. And let me work out mine."

She laughed tensely. "I must admit, you've left quite an impression on me, Mr. Trevor. In spite of being a little sexist, you treated me like I had some real value. And it was just so nice to talk to someone who cared, and to feel that closeness with another human being."

Colin glanced away and willed his thoughts to stay where they belonged. He was being tested—and he would not fail this time. "Yes, I know," he admitted. "But we could have accomplished the same thing with a dance."

"Dance with me now, Colin," she said.

He looked over at her, trying to discern her motives. But he felt nothing but serenity as he stood and held out his hand toward her. "One dance," he said, "and then you need to go."

She nodded and slipped her hand into his. Colin had been unconscious of the music that had played continually as they'd talked. But now it seemed appropriate. A little sad. A little lonely. Poignant lyrics with not much point to them.

"Now we have to be able to get a Book of Mormon between us," he said as she put a hand to his shoulder.

"What?" she laughed.

"That was the rule at our youth dances when I was growing up." He put his hand at her waist and held her close to his shoulder as he led her into a simple step in the middle of the small front room. "If our chaperones couldn't get a Book of Mormon between us, we were dancing too close."

She smiled, and Colin realized that in a way, this time with her had been healing. His feelings of resentment toward her had faded. "Cheek to cheek, but not chest to chest," he said, and she laughed.

As her laughter faded, Colin became lost in the music. He touched his cheek to her brow and closed his eyes, wishing only for Janna to be in his arms like this right now. The song ended and another began, but Colin kept dancing, allowing his mind to wander to a better time in his life, when Janna had been her real self, well and strong. And she had loved him.

"Oh, Janna," he whispered, not realizing what he'd said until Lily took a step back and startled him to the moment. He didn't know he was crying until she reached up and touched the tears on his face. She kissed his cheek and walked out the door. Colin stood in the middle of the room through another song, feeling very alone. He was grateful that Lily was gone as the darkness suddenly seemed to close in. Then the phone rang and startled him. It was his father.

"Is everything all right, son?" he asked.

Colin felt a little unsettled. "Yes, why?"

"I just had a feeling I should call."

Colin's voice cracked. "Thank you, Dad. You'll never know how much that means to me."

"Maybe not, Colin, but . . . hey, why don't you come and stay here tonight while Matthew's gone, so you don't have to be alone. Your mother made some soup we could heat up. And maybe we could go for a drive or something tomorrow."

Colin tried to compose himself before he answered. "Thanks, Dad. I think I will. I'll be right over."

Colin hung up the phone, turned off the stereo, and threw a change of clothes and toothbrush into a bag. He opened the door and gasped. Lily was about to knock.

"Sorry," she said. "I forgot my purse."

Colin stepped outside and motioned for her to go in. He waited for her to come back, then he locked the door and walked her to her car. He opened the car door for her, and their eyes met. "If it doesn't start, I'm calling a cab," he said.

On the drive to his parents' home, the impact of the evening struck him. In a way, he felt that Lily's visit was a blessing. He'd been able to share his beliefs, and maybe one day up the road, it might make a difference in her life. Either way, he felt that perhaps he'd made restitution with her as far as possible. If her coming had been a test of his strength, then he'd passed. But the more he thought about it, the more he knew in his heart that his father's call was no coincidence. In spite of his weaknesses, God was looking out for him. His prayers were being heard. If his dance with Lily had gotten out of hand, his father's call would have interrupted before it could have gone too far. Then his heart began to pound as he contemplated Lily coming back in to get her purse. What if he'd still been standing there, feeling dark and lonely? "Thank you, Lord," he murmured and hurried home.

While Colin was eating a bowl of homemade soup, Carl sat down across the table and asked, "So what was going on when I called?"

Colin smiled slightly and said, "It was just one of those dark moments that could have gotten a lot darker."

"Well, then, I'm glad I called."

"Me, too, Dad. Me, too."

* * * * *

Colin pulled the car up in front of the house and hurried toward the door. Matthew came out before he got there, and he said, "Wait a minute. I need to talk to your mother."

Matthew stepped back inside and hollered, "Hey, Mom. Come here a minute." Then he went immediately outside, as if he didn't want to stay any longer than was absolutely necessary.

Colin tried not to be shocked by the appearance of the house. He'd not been inside since he'd come to load Matthew's furniture months ago. It had been immaculate at the time, and he had wrongly assumed it had stayed that way.

"What is it?" Janna snapped, emerging from the hall. Then she saw Colin and stopped cold. Her expression of embarrassment quickly turned to scorn as she pushed a self-conscious hand through her matted hair. Colin couldn't remember her looking this bad since she'd left the hospital after nearly dying from Russell's abuse. Her face looked gaunt and thin, her eyes hollow.

"What are you doing here?" she snarled.

Colin handed her an envelope. "Income tax return," he said. "I thought you could probably use it."

"All of it?" she asked skeptically as she took it from him.

"I'm managing."

"Thank you," she said without seeming too bent on kicking him immediately out the door.

"So, how did it go with Matthew?"

Janna folded her arms tightly over her chest and looked at the floor. "Let's just say I'm glad you have him most of the time, so you can deal with his belligerence."

Colin tried to absorb this. "There hasn't been any belligerence, Janna. He's a good kid who needs to know his boundaries. He needs to be threatened once in a while to keep his room clean, but . . ." Colin stopped when he realized she was shaking. "Janna, are you all right?"

"I'm fine," she insisted, turning her back to him. "Thank you for the money, now please—"

"Janna," he said gently, unable to resist putting his hands on her shoulders. She tensed visibly but didn't protest. He closed his eyes, trying to absorb her nearness, as if it alone could heal him. "Please, Janna," he whispered behind her ear. He could hear her breathing turn sharp. "Let me come back, Janna. Let me be there for you, to help—"

"Oh, stop it!" She turned and backed away so quickly it startled him. "It's not bad enough that you cheat on me, then you waltz back in here with a paycheck and expect me to forget that anything ever happened. And on top of that, you've turned my son against me, and—"

"Things were bad between you and Matthew long before I jumped off a cliff, Janna. You can't blame that on me. If you treated him like a human being, instead of—"

"Get out!" she screamed. "I don't ever want to see your face again. Get out!"

Colin hurried outside, hovering between anger and anguish.

"Things went well, I hear," Matthew said with sarcasm as he got in the car.

"Yeah, real good," Colin snapped angrily. But it only took a few minutes for the anguish to take over. In spite of his struggles, Colin could look at his life and see that he was making progress; things were getting better. He had wrongly assumed that Janna was doing the same.

Hoping to glean some information, he asked Matthew, "So, how's your mom?"

"She doesn't say much." Matthew looked out the window.

Colin tried to ignore the increasing uneasiness. Trying to keep the conversation light, he went on, "Well . . . what did you have to eat? Did she fix anything good?"

"We had microwave dinners and stuff; just like old times."

"And how are your sisters?"

"Oh, they're okay."

Matthew couldn't be prodded to say anything more, but Colin called Sean on Monday morning, hoping for some advice.

"Actually," Sean said, "I called her. Maybe I was prompted; I don't know. I told her I was aware of what was going on, and wondered if she needed anything. She pretty much told me to mind my own business."

"In other words?"

"She doesn't want my help, Colin. I can't force her to do something she doesn't want to do."

"I'm worried about her, Sean. What if she gets depressed like she did after Russell tried to kill her? She was practically suicidal. Then what?"

"It's hard to say, Colin."

"My daughters are in her care, Sean."

"You would know more than I do about the legal possibilities, Colin."

He knew what that meant: prove Janna an unfit mother and take the children away. The thought made him sick. He couldn't do it; at least not unless it got really desperate. And to top it all off, he had to leave for Japan. He wished that Caitlin was old enough to use the phone and call her grandmother if she needed something. But that wasn't an option. Colin prayed about it. The answer was slow in coming, but it felt right.

"Hey, Matt," Colin said over the dinner table one evening, "you know I have to go to Japan for a week."

"Yeah, I know."

"And we talked about having you stay with Grandma and Grandpa, but . . . well, I know it's not something you're excited about, but I was wondering if you'd mind missing school a few days to go stay with your mother. I'm worried about her. And I'm worried about your sisters. I'm not sure I can leave the country when I'm still wondering if she's all right. I've talked to a few people who live in her neighborhood, and they've talked to her some, but she won't let anybody help her with anything. She's stopped going to church, and she won't hardly let anybody in the house. I'm afraid she's really depressed, like she was before I married her. What do you think, Matt?"

"What can I do?" he hedged.

"I don't know, Matthew. But you can be there. I just know I've prayed about it, and this is the only thing I can think of to make sure she's all right. Maybe you should pray about it, too. I think you'd be able to get an answer easier than I could."

"I don't want to go, Dad. But I'm worried, too. If you think I should, I will."

"Thank you, Matthew. You're a good kid. I don't know what I'd do without you."

Janna seemed hesitant to take Matthew when Colin called to talk to her about it, but she finally agreed. Colin told her a white lie—that his father was just not feeling good and his mother wasn't up to it. His mother said she'd back him up on it. Nancy was concerned about Janna, too.

Once Colin was in the air on his way to Japan, he forced away thoughts concerning things he couldn't control while he was gone. He kept a prayer in his heart for those he loved, and made up his mind to enjoy this opportunity. Between business meetings, which went well, he was able to go to some of the places he'd worked on his mission. He even looked up some people he'd helped convert. On the flight home, he couldn't deny his gratitude for this opportunity. In spite of the struggles in his life, he felt as if the Lord was blessing him. His bishop had suggested that as long as he remained humble, with a penitent attitude, the Lord would not forsake him. More and more, he believed that was true. He only prayed that things had been all right at home in his absence.

* * * * *

Janna stood discreetly at the window and watched Colin drive away as soon as Matthew emerged through the front door with his suitcase.

"Hi, Mom," he said and hurried down the hall to his room.

Janna followed him. "How are you, sport?" she asked.

"I'm okay. How are you?"

"Okay. So, your dad's going to Japan. He must be pretty excited."

"I guess so. He didn't say much about it, really. I think he's got other things on his mind."

"Like what?" she asked.

"Give it up, Mom. If you want to know what Dad's doing, why don't you ask him yourself?"

Janna tried not to get defensive. She didn't want to start the week with an argument. "I can't. He's on his way to Japan."

"He'll be back in a week." Matthew brushed past her toward the kitchen. She thought he would look for something to eat, but she found him there a while later, washing dishes.

"What are you doing?" she asked.

"What does it look like I'm doing?"

"I didn't know you *did* things like that."

"Me and Dad trade dish nights. He told me I should help you out a little. He said he didn't think you were feeling very good."

Janna thought of a biting retort, but she reminded herself to not afflict Matthew with her anger toward Colin. She looked at her surroundings and told herself she should help Matthew, or start somewhere else and pick things up, even a little. But she just went to the couch and lay down where she could see the girls playing.

Matthew did most of the work of heating frozen dinners and feeding the girls. Then Janna put them to bed and left Matthew watching videos. She went right to bed, but hardly slept at all as the darkness just seemed to close in tighter around her. It felt so familiar. She couldn't remember what it felt like to be without it. But why did it just keep getting worse? Why couldn't she find anything inside of her that was noble and good enough to pull her out of this? Colin seemed to be doing well; her brief glimpses of him showed a man with his usual confidence, as adorable as ever. She told herself there was no need to wonder why he'd turned to another woman. Deep in her heart, she knew the truth of it: she was simply not woman enough to keep a man like that happy. She should have known better than to ever get involved with a man like Colin Trevor to begin with. They may have grown up in the same area, but they were from different sides of the tracks nevertheless.

Janna's mind wandered, as it often did, to Colin's confession of adultery. She still had difficulty comprehending the horror of it. And while a part of her knew she'd been less than fair with him, a much bigger part couldn't comprehend his doing something so low. How could she not wonder about the details? She thought of the intimacy she had shared with Colin, and tried to imagine him doing the same things with somebody else. The thought made her groan as her stomach tightened into painful knots.

"Damn him!" she muttered to the surrounding darkness. And then she cried. She cried until there was nothing more in her. As the emotion settled into an increasingly familiar numbness, she encouraged it to come, wanting only to be free of the pain.

Janna didn't know if she'd slept at all. It didn't feel like she'd lost consciousness, but she was startled when Matthew said, "Mom, are you all right?"

"I'm just . . . not feeling well," she said in a voice that sounded distant and detached. "Would you . . . get the girls something to eat . . . and change their diapers and . . . keep an eye on them?"

Matthew startled her again when he finally said, "Okay."

Knowing he would keep the girls safe and cared for, Janna slipped back into a numb oblivion.

* * * * *

Nancy Trevor answered the phone while she was putting lunch on the table.

"Grandma?" Matthew said, obviously upset.

"What is it, Matthew?" Nancy asked.

"Something's wrong with Mom. I think she's really lost it, Grandma. I'm scared. Mallory's been crying for an hour and I can't get her to stop, and Mom just doesn't move. She won't talk to me or anything."

"What do you mean she won't move?" Nancy tried to sound calm.

"I don't mean she's dead or anything. She just stares at the wall and . . . Grandma, I'm scared. I don't know what to do."

"You did the right thing, honey. I'm getting in the car right now to come up there. It will take me nearly an hour, though. Do you think you'll be all right until then, or do you want me to call someone in your ward to come help you?"

"I'll be all right," he said firmly, "if I know you're coming."

"Now, Matthew, just make certain the diapers are changed and the girls have something to eat. If you've done that and they keep crying, it's okay. Keep an eye on your mother, and if anything gets worse at all, you call 911. All right?"

"Okay, Grandma."

"Is there anything else you want to ask me before I hang up?"

"No, just hurry."

Nancy's prayer to avoid traffic and get there quickly was answered. She found Matthew sitting on the living room floor with some story books, and the little ones asleep at his sides. He looked up with tears in his eyes and said, "I prayed."

Nancy hugged him tightly then whispered, "Where's your mother?"

"In the bedroom."

Nancy walked quietly down the hall and peered in. Janna was lying curled on top of the bedspread, her eyes glazed and hollow. Their occasional blinking was the only sign of life beyond the way she rubbed a hand up and down her arm as if she was freezing. Praying for direction, Nancy approached her tentatively and put a hand to her shoulder.

"JannaLyn?" she said gently. "It's Nancy."

When Nancy couldn't get Janna to say anything at all, she called Sean O'Hara from the kitchen phone. His receptionist said he'd call back as soon as he finished with his current appointment. While Nancy was waiting, she had Matthew help her pack what the girls would need, and they worked on picking up the house a little.

Sean didn't seem surprised over Janna's condition. He told Nancy to call 911 and get her to a hospital, preferably the one in Provo so that he could be close by. Nancy feared Janna's reaction, but she went without argument when Nancy said firmly, "I don't think you're feeling well, my dear. So let's get you to a doctor and find out what's wrong."

With Janna in the care of the paramedics, Nancy took the children to her home and tried to get them settled in. She wondered how long it had been since the girls were bathed as she peeled off their clothes and put them into the tub. But she had to admit feeling greatly relieved to know that Janna was where she could get the help she'd needed for a long time. And all her worrying over the girls was alleviated by having them in her care.

The following day, she and Carl took the children back up to the house, where they cleaned it up more thoroughly, took care of the piles of dirty laundry, and left the house in a state where it could remain empty for the time being.

Nancy talked to Dr. O'Hara on the phone. He told her that Janna had finally emerged from her stupor with a great deal of fear and anger. He was concerned about her, but he felt that under the circumstances, she was where she needed to be. Nancy agreed. She only hoped that Colin would see it the same way.

CHAPTER NINE

Colin got off the plane and went straight to a phone to let Matthew know he'd be picking him up. When no one answered, he tried again, wondering if he'd dialed it wrong. Feeling uneasy, he called his mother. As soon as she answered, he could hear the familiar sounds of his children in the background.

"Mom? Are the kids there?"

"Colin, where are you?"

"I'm at the airport. Are the kids—"

"They're all here, Colin. They're fine."

"What happened?" he demanded as all his earlier concerns came rushing back.

"Janna's in the hospital, honey."

"What's wrong?" His tone clearly expressed his panic.

"We can talk when you get here, Colin."

"Fine, but I need to know what happened."

"She had a breakdown, Colin."

"A *breakdown?*" he echoed.

"We'll talk when you get here. Please be careful."

On the drive home, Colin's mind paraded through the possible scenarios, all of which made him a little sick. He got there just as the little ones were about to go to bed, so he hugged them tightly and tucked them in. While Nancy was busy, Matthew explained what had happened to Janna, then his mother returned to fill in the details. She finished with the assurance, "Colin, she's getting the help she's needed for a long time. Sometimes it takes drastic measures to get things moving."

Colin nodded but said nothing. He spent the night on the family room couch and shared breakfast with his children. He left a message for Sean before he went into the office, and the first thing Lucy said when he arrived was, "A Dr. O'Hara called and asked you to meet him at the hospital at 11:30. Here's the room number." She handed him a paper.

"Thank you."

"Forgive my nosiness, but who's in the hospital?"

"My wife," he said.

"Is it serious?" she asked with concern.

"I don't know. I just got in last night."

He was relieved when she changed the subject. "How was Japan?"

"It was great," he admitted. At least something in his life was great.

Colin hurried to get the mandatory work done and stepped off the hospital elevator at 11:28. He took a deep breath before heading into the psychiatric ward. The tight security only added to his uneasiness.

"How was your trip?" Sean asked.

"It was great. How is Janna?"

Sean ushered him into a small room that reminded him of the rooms at his office where they counseled. They sat down before Sean answered, "Right now, she's not good at all. But that's to be expected. We've taken the first steps to opening up some very old, festering wounds, so we can clean them out once and for all. That's the goal, at least. The results depend a lot on Janna."

"So, what happened? My mother told me a little, but . . ."

"She just . . . shut down, Colin. All her bad behavior toward you was a subconscious effort to cope with pain in the first place. Then she lost you. Then she lost Matthew. I get the impression that most of the people who were close to her at all suggested she get some counseling. But she didn't want to talk to me because it scared her. Your mother was supportive but incapable of fixing anything. She closed herself off from her friends. She had no one, nothing to connect with. So, she just . . . shut down."

"Well," he sighed, "I'm grateful Matthew was there, at least."

"Matthew's being there probably hurried along something that could have been much worse. His being there to see that the children

were safe made her let go of the thread she'd been holding onto of
knowing they needed her. Her sense of commitment to her children
is what kept her hanging on this long."

They talked for a short while longer, while a numb kind of
dread closed in tighter around Colin. He was startled when Sean
asked, "Do you want to see her?"

"Is that a good idea?"

Sean shrugged. "I suspect one of two things could happen.
She'll get angry . . . or she'll be reminded that in spite of everything,
you still care. Most likely a little of both. Either way, I think it will
help spur those feelings along that she's got to face if she's going to get
better. She can't heal what she doesn't feel."

Colin had spent many hours with Janna while she was in intensive care after Russell's attack. He somehow expected it to be the same
this time, but it was not at all the same. He entered quietly with Sean
to find Janna curled up on the bed, wearing her own clothes, staring
at nothing.

"Hello, Janna," Sean said.

Without moving she retorted, "I thought you left. Haven't you
picked my brain enough for one day?"

"Your husband is here," Sean said.

"Well, tell him to go to hell."

"I thought you could tell him yourself," Sean added. Colin
scowled at him.

Janna shot her head up with a scowl that put Colin's to shame.
"What are *you* doing here?" she snarled.

Colin forced his voice to remain calm. "I just . . . came to see
how you're doing."

"Oh, how noble." She sat on the edge of the bed and wrapped
her arms around herself. "Now that you've got me locked up in here,
you can take the house, the kids. I guess everything's just hunky-dory
for you. You've got it all."

"I haven't got what's most important to me, Janna. I haven't
got you."

She called him a hypocrite then, with a word before it that she'd
obviously learned from Russell. Then she told him how it was his
fault she was in this condition, and he was going to have to answer

for it. Colin was grateful when Sean interrupted, saying, "I think you've thrown enough darts at him for one day. I'm certain Colin's looking forward to his next visit."

Sean opened the door. Colin said quickly, "Take care of yourself, Janna." She didn't even look at him.

"I'll be out in a minute," Sean whispered.

Colin had to lean against the wall to gain some equilibrium once he left the room. Sean came out and guided him back to the room where they'd talked.

As soon as they sat down, Colin asked, "Did I put her in here, Sean? Was what I did really *that* hard on her?"

"That's a tough question, Colin. What do you think?"

Colin thought about it for what felt like an eternity. Then he sighed. "I didn't cause the problems. What I did was the last straw."

"I don't think I could have put it better myself. You're doing good, Colin, in my opinion. You really are."

"Really?" he chuckled dubiously. "I feel most of the time like I'm barely functioning."

"Perhaps, but you are functioning, and you understand what's going on. Hang in there. Right now, the most important thing is that you're there for your kids. They need your stability."

Colin nodded.

"Before you go," Sean added, "there's something you need to be thinking about. I know how much you love Janna, and I know the history you have together. But all your faith and hope and prayers will never take away her free agency. All my knowledge and ability will never make her get better if she doesn't want to."

Colin put a hand over his mouth.

"This is one of those things that's difficult for me to explain to someone who doesn't have the gospel, because I don't know how a human being could possibly face such decisions without the help of the Spirit."

"I've been excommunicated, Sean. I'm not entitled to the help of the Spirit."

"Do you believe that in spite of your struggles, God would abandon you to make decisions concerning your family on your own?"

"No," Colin shook his head. In spite of it all, he had to admit that God was helping him through this.

"So, when it comes to Janna, you're going to have to listen to those feelings and instincts. If she's not going to recover, you can't spend the rest of your life raising her children with empty dreams. I admire your commitment to her, and I have every hope that we'll get through this. But you have to face the possibility that you may not have a future with her."

Colin absorbed it. "I'm not sure I *can* accept that."

"If that's what the Spirit tells you to feel, fine. But don't go ignoring it for the sake of being stubborn. The fact is, some people just don't have the strength to pull out of things like this. In my personal opinion, some people just can't see the reality of what abuse has done to them until the veil is lifted and they can see the big picture. Then they'll have their chance to right the wrongs. I believe that Janna has it in her to function in the real world and make a life for herself. But I can't tell you that she's going to want to make it with you. So, leave doors open if you must, but make choices based on your needs and the needs of your children."

Rather than going back to work, Colin drove to the Mt. Timpanogos Temple and sat on a bench on its east side. He was grateful to be there alone as he mourned over the reality of what he'd just been told. He looked up at the high windows and knew that on the other side of the glass was the celestial room. If only he could be there now! If only he could feel the warmth and peace of heaven close to him to get him through this! But he had denied himself that right for the time being, and he had sent Janna over the edge. He prayed fervently for over an hour, then his mind wandered back to the day that he and Janna had been married here. They'd taken pictures in this very spot. He closed his eyes, and the moment felt so real he could almost taste it. How could he let go of something so rare and precious as the love they shared? How could he look back through the good moments of their life and not see Janna's potential? He finally walked back to the car with one thing clearly in his mind. He didn't know what the future would bring, but for now, his faith and prayers would continue toward the life with Janna he'd always dreamed of—the one they'd had a taste of before her father's visit had triggered all this ridiculous baggage.

A silver lining appeared in the clouds as Colin enjoyed getting to know his younger children again on a daily basis, and his parents truly seemed to enjoy helping with them. Through the following days he managed to accomplish his work and pretty much take over the care of the children in the evenings; but he knew he couldn't leave them under his parents' roof indefinitely, and his small apartment just wouldn't accommodate them. He came up with a logical solution, and he talked to his parents about it; but he couldn't do it without Janna's permission. He'd not been back since that first visit, although he'd sent flowers every three or four days, always with the same message: *I love you, Colin.*

He talked to Sean about his plan, and they agreed that it was feasible.

"But even if she tells me it's all right," Colin said, "can't she turn around and sue me for selling the house under these circumstances, claiming that she wasn't of sound mind?"

"She's not crazy, Colin. She's not going in and out of reality or anything. In my opinion, what's best for the children now is more important than the remote possibility of her taking you to court over it later." Sean smiled. "If she does, I can recommend a good lawyer."

The following morning, Sean met Colin at the hospital. "I told her you were coming. I think I'll just wait outside the door for a minute and let you say hello."

"Gee, thanks," Colin said with sarcasm. He took a deep breath and went in. She was sitting in a chair by the window with her feet curled up beneath her, reading a book. Colin stood in front of her until her eyes moved up to meet his. He couldn't believe how just seeing her made his heart pound. How could he ever live without her?

"Hello," he said, wondering if she'd start swearing at him.

"Sean said you needed to talk to me about something."

He nodded, wondering where to begin. "Romance novels?" he asked, taking notice of the book. "I didn't think you were into those things."

"This one's different," she said. "Besides, it's on Sean's required reading list. And he won't declare me sane until I complete his required reading list, among other things. According to him, this is not a romance novel. It's *relationship fiction.*"

Colin smiled. "I'll try to remember that."

She moved her eyes back to the book. "Maybe you should do the required reading list, too."

"Wouldn't hurt."

"So, what do you want, Colin? I've got a busy schedule, as you can see."

Colin sat on the edge of the bed, aware of Sean's coming quietly into the room. "My concern is for the children, Janna. I've talked to Sean about this, and he thinks it's the best thing, but I need to talk to you about it, to know what you think."

She looked alarmed. "You're not having that Lily woman around my kids, are you?"

Colin swallowed his defensiveness. "No, Janna. I can assure you she is having no contact with any of us."

"So, what's your point? Are you going to divorce me?"

"I told you before that if you want a divorce, you're going to have to get it yourself."

"Okay, we're narrowing it down."

"Janna, I'm working here in Provo. And Sean says that when you're ready to leave here, you're going to need time to yourself . . . to adjust. He said it would be good if you had your own place, but it would be better if you were close to him, where he can be there for you. I need a home for the children, Janna—a place where Mom and Dad can help with them, and where I can be close to the office. But I can't do that without selling the house in Salt Lake. I know you loved it there, but I don't know what else to do. I'd like to get you an apartment, Janna, where you have some time to work things out. Then, as soon as you're ready . . ." Colin steeled himself. This was the hard part. "If it's what you want, I'll trade you places, and you can have the house and the physical custody of the children."

"Janna," Sean said when she didn't say anything, "do you understand what Colin's asking you?"

"Of course I understand. I'm not some kind of imbecile."

"Well, then why don't you repeat it back to him, so there's no misunderstanding."

"He wants to sell the house in Salt Lake and buy another one here so the children can have a home. He'll get me an apartment when I get out of here so I can have my space. When I can cope, he'll let me have the house and the kids if I want."

Sean exchanged a quick glance with Colin.

"Janna," Colin went on, "do you have a problem with that, or—"

"It's fine with me," she shrugged. "I don't ever want to go back to the old neighborhood, anyway. Those people just think I'm some kind of psycho now."

"I'm certain they would understand, Janna," Colin said. Janna didn't respond, and he added, "I've already had an offer on the house, and I've found one not far from Mom and Dad's home for about the same price."

"Just take good care of my kids. And keep them away from that tramp."

Colin took a moment to maintain his control. "I'll take good care of the kids," he said.

"Where are they when you're at work?" she asked.

"Right now, they're with Mom and Dad."

"Okay," she said and went back to her book.

"Thank you, Janna. I'll call you."

She said nothing until he was almost out the door. "Hey, Colin." He turned back to see her nose still buried in the book. "Thanks for the flowers."

"It's my pleasure," he said, and left the room with Sean.

He couldn't have expected it to go any better. She didn't argue or make it difficult for him. But he still felt like he'd been hit by a truck. The feeling persisted as he methodically went through the motions of moving his home and family. Having to sort through and box up Janna's things was more difficult than he'd expected. Occasionally he'd come across some keepsake that would make him heartsick. But when he came across the little sand castle they had bought together on their honeymoon, he had to just sit down and cry.

Still, he had to admit he was being blessed when the house sold quickly, and the one he wanted to buy, which was less than a mile from his parents' home, was already sitting empty. A good credit rating and a good realtor got the sale pushed through quickly. He took the papers to Janna to have them signed, with a notary present. She said little, but at least she wasn't antagonistic. With the help of ward members on both ends, the move was made quickly; his parents were great with the transition, spending time with the children during the days at the house and helping to unpack boxes. Colin kept the apartment he already had; Matthew agreed that it would be a good place for Janna when she was released. And they talked about how to make it comfortable for her.

Janna finally reached a point where Sean told Colin to start bringing the children for brief visits. Colin remained in the hall and let Matthew take the girls in. The first time, Mallory screamed and refused to let Janna hold her. But gradually the situation relaxed, and with a little bribery, the girls actually began to enjoy the hospital visits.

When Sean informed Colin that Janna's release was approaching, he put more energy into preparing her apartment. Matthew actually got excited about the project, and together they gathered household items that were familiar to Janna, working to make the apartment a place where she would feel comfortable. A few days before she was expected to come home, Colin walked through the little apartment and tried to imagine her coming here. How he ached to be here with her—anywhere with her! He wanted to hold her and ease the pain for her. But all he could do now was honor her wishes to keep his distance, and pray that she would get past this.

* * * * *

Janna stared out the window of her hospital room, thinking how familiar the view had become. While a part of her felt as if she'd scream if she didn't get out of here, there was something inside that felt just plain scared at the prospect of trying to make it on her own. Sean had said many times that she was ready. He said she'd come a long way, and she knew that was true. But still, the reasons for being here hovered inside her, and she knew there was much healing left to do.

The weeks Janna had spent in the hospital had been like an emotional roller coaster. She couldn't count the hours she'd spent in group sessions, not to mention all the time that Sean O'Hara had spent coaxing her memories and feelings out into the open. At moments she'd hated him, hated what he was forcing her to endure. At others, she wondered how she would ever survive without him; he was her lifeline. She had screamed and raged as she'd spilled things she'd once believed she could never utter aloud. She had cried a seemingly endless stream of tears, suffering through pain so intense and literal that it was difficult to believe it had emotional roots.

Gradually the pain had leveled off, and with Sean's guidance she had learned much about the things that had happened to her and how they had affected her life. She had dealt with many levels of bitterness and hatred toward those who had abused and victimized her. And Sean had helped her sort through that, as well—to a point. She had learned much about the cycles of abuse and dysfunction, and with Sean's guidance she had set goals to get beyond them and overcome them, if only to raise her children to be emotionally healthy people who could stop the cycles.

At this point, Janna knew she had many layers of healing left to face, and much work ahead in becoming the woman she wanted to become. But she felt some hope in the very idea of being out of this wretched place.

At the appointed time, Nancy picked Janna up at the hospital and drove her to her new apartment. They exchanged friendly small talk that was typical of their occasional visits, until Nancy stopped the car and handed her a key.

"There it is. Number three."

"Will you come in with me?" Janna asked.

"I'd love to. I haven't seen it yet myself. But I know that Colin and Matthew have been working hard to get it ready."

Janna felt nervous as they approached the door, then she noticed Colin's convertible parked close by. Pointing to it, she asked, "Is he—"

"Oh," Nancy laughed softly, "no, he just left the car for you, so you'd have a way to get around." Janna nodded and turned the key in the door, wondering why Colin would leave her his precious convertible under the circumstances.

Going inside, she didn't know what she'd expected, but it wasn't the rush of warmth that seized her as she immediately saw her own furniture, her own curtains, her own belongings set out, as if she'd decorated it herself. With Nancy at her side, she walked from room to room. The bathroom was stocked with everything she needed, including towels that were familiar to her—her favorites. The spare bedroom had a little desk and some bookshelves filled with her own things. Her sewing machine and supplies were there, too. In the bedroom she found her clothes in the closets and drawers, her things on the dresser, her favorite comforter on the bed. The kitchen was well-stocked with groceries and equipped with dishes and necessities that were familiar to her.

"Is something wrong, dear?" Nancy asked when tears leaked from Janna's eyes.

Janna shook her head and managed to say, "It just feels like . . . home." She couldn't bring herself to say that she felt the evidence of Colin's love all around her, but an hour after Nancy left, a dozen roses were delivered with the usual message on the card: *I love you, Colin.* Janna held the flowers close and cried, wishing with all her heart that she could believe him. She'd come a long way, and had dealt with many horrible images in her mind that had plagued her for years. But she couldn't force away the images of Colin touching and kissing another woman. Sean had helped her understand what led up to it, and she was trying to make sense of everything he'd said. But it still felt all muddled and confusing, as if she'd put sections of the puzzle together but couldn't get those sections to meet. She just had to keep reminding herself, as Sean often said, that it would take time to heal, and time to understand, and she needed to take it on in layers. For now, that's all she could do.

* * * * *

Once Janna was settled into the apartment, Colin put his full concentration on getting his family into a routine. He found it a difficult adjustment to take over the complete care of his children in addition to his hours at work. Each morning, while Matthew was getting ready for school, Colin had to get the girls up, dressed, and fed. Then he'd drop Matthew off at the bus stop and take the girls to his mother's house before work. In the late afternoon, after picking them up, he had to get them dinner, oversee Matthew's homework if necessary, bathe the girls, and get them to bed. On top of that, he needed to keep the house in order, the laundry done, and deal with every little crisis that came up. He went to parent-teacher conferences, doctor and dentist appointments, and ball games. His parents were wonderful, always going the extra mile in their care of the children while he worked. He told them more than once that they didn't have to be full-time baby-sitters, and that he could make other arrangements. But they insisted that the girls needed to be with family, and he was grateful.

No matter how busy Colin was, Janna hovered in the back of his mind continually. He prayed for her. He ached for her. He continued sending flowers every few days, and occasionally called just to ask how she was doing. At times she sounded indifferent; at others she said horrible things to him, and he'd cry for an hour after she'd hung up on him. He continued to see Sean regularly, for himself as well as to keep posted on Janna's progress. Sean said little about what Janna was doing specifically; he mostly answered with generalities like "she's doing better," or "she's having a tough week."

During this time, Colin began having frequent headaches. At first he blamed it on stress, but when they persisted quite regularly, his mother suggested he see a doctor. Recalling his father's brain tumor, he was downright scared. But it turned out to be nothing more than a vision problem. It took a few days to adjust to wearing glasses, but he was grateful for the disappearance of the headaches.

The evidence of time passing gave him the hope that he could actually get beyond his personal struggles and regain his membership in the Church. But the longer Janna kept her distance from him, the more he began to fear that mending the bridges between them would simply never happen.

* * * * *

Janna felt significantly better as she settled into life on her own. Nancy occasionally brought the girls by to see her for short visits during the days, and Matthew stopped by on his bike once in a while. While she longed to be with her children more, she knew that she needed this time on her own, to sort out her life and become strong enough to be a *good* mother. If she thought too hard about it, she could feel terribly guilty for her neglect of the children, and for all the anger and dysfunction Matthew had witnessed. But Sean had suggested that when she got beyond this, she would be whole and strong and have plenty of time to teach her children who she really was.

While Janna was beginning to feel capable of going to get groceries and keeping things under control without extreme paranoia setting in, she continued to see Sean regularly. She felt progress in their sessions, but there were still things that troubled her—and other things that terrified her.

On a warm spring afternoon, Janna answered the door, taken aback to see a woman who simply looked out of place in this apartment complex of young, conservative families. Her clothes and hairstyle projected opulence, and her self-confident aura intimidated Janna.

"May I help you?" Janna asked in response to this woman's obvious surprise.

"Uh . . . ," she smiled, showing perfect white teeth, "I had a friend who lived here, but he's obviously moved, and . . . I'm sorry to bother you."

Janna felt an uneasiness she couldn't quite pinpoint as she asked, "Who were you looking for?"

"Well, he's obviously not living here now, so I'll just—"

"You're looking for Colin Trevor," Janna guessed with a degree of certainty.

Everything fell neatly into place with a sick thud in the pit of Janna's stomach as this woman replied with bright-eyed surprise, "Actually, yes. Do you know him?"

In the moment that Janna hesitated, she studied this woman in detail, starting at the leather pumps on her feet and moving up over her long, slim legs. She wore a short black skirt, a lavender blouse, and a long tailored jacket. Her blonde hair hung to her shoulders in a sleek, smooth style. While Janna wanted to just slam the door in her face, she felt compelled to talk to this woman. Maybe it was just curiosity. Maybe it was more.

"You must be Lily," Janna said tonelessly, geared up to watch her reaction closely.

She smiled. "Yes, I am." By her expression and tone of voice, Janna felt certain this woman had no idea of who she was. "Do you know where I can find him?" As far as Lily knew, this was likely an acquaintance of Colin's, subletting his apartment, who might know where to forward his mail.

"Possibly." Janna tried to remain vague, perhaps hoping to glean a feel for where things might stand. "Didn't he tell you he was moving?"

"He didn't mention it the last time we talked."

"Is this concerning business?" Janna asked.

"Well, yes and no," Lily answered in a tone of voice that made it easy for Janna to believe the woman was an attorney. "I really need to talk to him. If you could just give me a phone number, or . . ." Lily hesitated, as if she'd finally stopped to question what Janna's connection was. "I'm assuming you know Colin," Lily said as if Janna were on the witness stand.

"Oh, I've known Colin for years," Janna said, managing a smile.

"So, how are things going for him? I mean, with the separation and all, is he—"

"I have no idea how he's doing," Janna interrupted, unable to control the terseness in her voice.

Lily looked a little taken aback by Janna's sudden lack of friendly demeanor. In that lawyer tone, she asked, "Exactly what is your connection to Mr. Trevor?"

Janna lifted her chin and mustered every ounce of dignity she could find. "Beyond three children, very little at the moment."

Lily's brief look of surprise and embarrassment passed quickly. "You must forgive me," she said evenly. "Under the circumstances, you were the last person I expected to be here."

Janna looked at her hard and retorted, "I wish I could say the same."

Janna felt herself being appraised as her identity became evident. She wished she had even a smidgen of makeup on. What was Lily thinking? What had Colin told her? Was she seeing a dysfunctional, abusive wife? A mental patient?

"I never imagined coming face to face with you, Mrs. Trevor," Lily said. "But now that we are, perhaps I owe you an apology."

Janna folded her arms. "And what exactly do you owe me an apology for, Ms. Greene?"

With a steady gaze, Lily said, "Maybe we should talk."

Janna wondered if she was up to this, but she couldn't resist the opportunity. Willfully she stepped back and motioned Lily into the apartment. She looked briefly hesitant, and Janna wondered if the woman feared getting murdered by her lover's psycho wife.

"Have a seat," Janna said, glad the apartment was tidy.

"Thank you." Lily sat on the edge of the couch at one end, and

Janna sat at the other. She glanced around briefly, then set her eyes on Janna.

"You were apologizing," Janna said. Lily was silent and she added, "And I was wondering exactly what you were apologizing for. Was it going to bed with a married man that you're sorry for? Or is it the fact that you're still seeing him? I was hoping perhaps you might be apologizing for the trauma this has caused to my children. Or maybe you regret the way Colin was denounced by the Church and had all rights and privileges taken from him. Or is this a personal apology? Are you regretting the weeks I spent in the hospital, or the fact that I may be denied the right to see my children because of it? Or maybe you're not regretting it at all. Perhaps I'm jumping to conclusions to assume that this apology is anything more than lip service in a tense moment." Janna leaned forward a little. "So, tell me, Ms. Greene. What exactly are you apologizing for?"

With no malice, Lily replied, "The difficulties in your marriage were there long before I came along, Mrs. Trevor. They had nothing to do with me."

Janna was proud of herself for holding a steady expression and an even voice. "There's some truth to that, and I won't deny it. But what happened between you and Colin was like throwing a match into a gasoline spill. Maybe we could have cleaned it up if it hadn't exploded."

"Mrs. Trevor," Lily said, "Colin is a wonderful man. He deserves to be loved and appreciated."

Janna took a deep breath and reminded herself to stay calm. "Yes, he certainly does. But the ring on his finger is a clear indication that you don't have the right to make him feel loved and appreciated."

"Someone had to." There was a trace of venom in Lily's voice, but Janna tried to ignore it and make her point.

"Now, don't get me wrong, Ms. Greene. I am not attempting to put the entire blame for my present situation on your shoulders. I hold some accountability, and I know that. And Colin is certainly a big enough boy to make his own choices. But there's something I want you to think about. Marriage is a sacred institution. You have no comprehension of what two people have struggled through together, and no business trying to intervene. Have you ever stopped to consider the ripples caused by that one rock thrown into the water? Do you know how many lives this has affected? Think about it. And in the future, I would suggest that you find a single man, and leave the married ones to work out their problems with their wives."

Janna expected the woman to get angry or defensive. She couldn't blame her, really. But she simply said, "I'm offering my sincerest apology for the part I played in this situation, Mrs. Trevor. That's all I can say."

Janna nodded slightly, then wondered how to tell this woman that she could leave now. As they briefly sized each other up as *the competition*, Janna tried to comprehend the reality that Colin had shared a bed with Lily Greene. Had he kissed those lips? And touched that silky blonde hair? How had it started? What did he say to her? How had he touched her? The thought began to make Janna feel nauseated.

"So, is it over between the two of you?" Lily asked.

"Not according to Colin," Janna said. "But at this point, it's difficult for me to believe anything he says."

"Is it fair to keep him hanging on like that?" Lily asked.

"Ms. Greene, if my husband wants to pursue a relationship with you, I'm certain he'll let you know. Apparently what transpires between the two of you has nothing to do with me."

"Or maybe it has *everything* to do with you." Lily stood up to leave, much to Janna's relief. "It wasn't my name he said when he—" She stopped abruptly at the same moment Janna's eyes widened. "Never mind," she added tersely and took hold of the doorknob.

"I can't say it was a pleasure," Lily added, "but perhaps necessary."

"Perhaps," Janna said.

Lily turned back with the door open. "I don't suppose you'd tell me where I can find him."

"Since he has custody of my children, I'd prefer that you not see him in their presence." Janna hesitated, reminding herself that Colin had his free agency. "But obviously I have no control over whether or not you respect my wishes." She sighed and added, "His office is in Jamestown Square."

"Thank you," Lily said and closed the door. It wasn't until she was gone that Janna realized Colin had been with this Provo law firm for several months. How could he have any kind of relationship with a woman who didn't even know where he worked, or that he'd moved weeks ago? There was a little comfort in that, she thought. Then she wondered why she cared.

Sean told her the next day that it was probably good for her to have faced Lily, and he was proud of her for the things she'd said to her.

"It took courage," he insisted.

"Then why did I turn to jelly after she walked out the door?"

"It was unsettling, wasn't it?"

"Yes," Janna admitted.

"How did you feel toward her after everything was said and done?"

"I hated her, but at the same time I couldn't bring myself to completely condemn her. Colin's an attractive man; a woman would have to be a fool not to notice. And I can't expect her to live a higher law."

"But you can Colin?"

"Yes." Janna stood up and walked toward the window as they talked. "He should have known better."

"Yes, he likely should have," Sean said. "So, at this point, how are you feeling toward Colin?"

"I hate him, too," she said, knowing from experience that saying anything less than the absolute truth of her feelings would get her nowhere with Sean.

"He hurt you very deeply," Sean stated.

"Yes, he did."

"So, how do you feel about the things Lily said to you?"

"I hated that, too."

"Why?"

Janna rubbed her hands up and down her arms and answered coldly, "Because it was true."

Sean didn't push her on that, for which she was grateful. But she felt certain it would come up again. Instead, he started into a calm tirade about how pathetic Colin's behavior had been. While Janna appreciated the way Sean always validated her feelings, she was a little surprised at his vehemence on her behalf. He rambled on about how insensitive and impatient Colin had been while Janna had struggled to deal with her emotions. He finished with a strong, "You know, eventually a person's true character always comes out. It's amazing that someone with his upbringing could turn out to be such a lying, cheating lowlife with no regard for—"

"Now, wait a minute," she interrupted. "What Colin did was wrong, and it hurt me deeply—as you well know. But that one incident doesn't make him a horrible person. I mean, look at the way he's taken care of the kids. And he's made certain I had what I needed, and he comes from a good family with—" Janna stopped when she caught Sean's subtle smirk. She quickly reviewed the conversation, then snarled, "You did that on purpose."

"Yes, I did," he said proudly. "So, what's the truth of it, Janna? Is Colin a decent person? Or do you hate him?"

Janna felt angry as she admitted, "Both!"

"Do you think it will ever be possible to let go of that one incident and accept him as a decent person?"

"I don't know," she insisted.

"Well, it gives you something to think about. As I see it, even if you don't reconcile your marriage, you still need to come to terms with it and be able to accept him for who and what he is. He will always be the father of your children, and your lives are connected whether you stay married or not. Do you think it's possible to forgive him?"

"At this point, no."

"Yet you told me, not so long ago, that you believed with time you could forgive your father and Russell. Is what Colin did worse than what they did?"

Something painfully uncomfortable erupted inside Janna at the comparison. A memory began to jell in her mind, but it took her a minute to place it.

"What are you thinking?" Sean asked, looking at her intently.

"I'd swear you are the nosiest person on the face of the earth," she snapped.

Sean shrugged his shoulders, apparently unaffected by her criticism. "It's my job," he said. "Do you want to tell me what you're thinking now, or do you want to let it mull around in your head and confuse you and eat at you and then tell me about it next month, or maybe next year? How long do you want to take to get over all of this?"

"Okay, fine," she said. "But give me a minute."

Sean moved his hand in a gesture to indicate she could take her time. She took a deep breath and said, "The day Colin told me what he'd done, I accused him of committing the ultimate crime against his family. He got angry with me. He asked me if I'd prefer that he . . . sexually abuse my children, the way my father had abused me. He asked if . . ." The emotion bubbled out. ". . . if he should beat my face in when he didn't like what I'd done. Or kick me in the stomach to kill my babies. Or . . . rape me, the way Russell had. He said that what he did was wrong, but he said it wasn't the ultimate crime. And . . . I know he was right."

"Yet you don't believe you can forgive him."

Janna hung her head and cried. "Maybe I could forgive him . . . eventually. But I don't know if I could live with him."

"Would you prefer that he spend the rest of his life with somebody else—somebody like Lily?"

The thought made Janna sick. But she said nothing.

"Well," Sean said, "it gives you something to think about. Eventually you'll have to decide which is more difficult—forgiving him enough to share a life with him, or allowing him to live his life with someone else."

Janna was grateful when the session ended. She had far more to think about than she could handle. She drove up the canyon and walked by the river to think, but her thoughts and feelings were still muddled and messed up. It was all so hard.

CHAPTER TEN

 *T*he following day, Janna drove to where Matthew's team was playing a soccer match. She had avoided his games, since he'd told her that Colin was always there. But Matthew had called the night before, saying that his father had to work late and wouldn't be able to go to the game. Janna thought she'd get no better chance to see what her son was doing, and she could avoid Colin at the same time.

Wrapped in a big sweater, she wandered across the field and stood some distance from the other parents, watching her son with pride. At halftime he ran over and hugged her. It was difficult not to notice how grown-up he was looking—and how much he resembled his father. She hated the part of her that still erupted into butterflies at just the thought of Colin Trevor. It wasn't fair. It just wasn't fair.

* * * * *

Colin was relieved to finish his work earlier than he'd expected. He pulled the Suburban up in the parking lot and got out, thinking that it badly needed washing. Janna had insisted that they buy the navy-blue vehicle because it matched his eyes. He hated the way the simplest things evoked memories of her and made him ache to have her back in his life.

He had barely started across the huge lawn surrounding the playing field when he stopped. The pounding of his heart told him that the woman standing alone several yards away was Janna, even before he consciously recognized her. He turned back and scanned the parking lot. Sure enough, the convertible was there, but he'd missed it. Then he turned back to look at Janna. He'd not seen her at all since she'd been released from the hospital. *She was so beautiful.* Watching the wind play havoc with her hair, he ached to just rub it between his fingers, to inhale her fragrance, to absorb her presence.

Knowing that conversation with her would likely turn to confrontation, he held back, just relishing the opportunity to watch her—until he couldn't bear keeping his distance for another moment.

Several minutes into the second half of the game, a voice startled Janna. "So, what's the score, Mrs. Trevor?"

Janna turned to see Colin looking into her eyes through a pair of wire-rimmed glasses.

"What are you doing here?" she snapped, hating her heart for the way it raced just to feel his presence close by. How long had it been since they'd even made eye contact?

"I came to see my son," he stated, not taking his eyes off her. She turned abruptly to watch the game and avoid his gaze. "So, what's the score?"

She looked at him again, as if she feared he intended some double meaning. "With the game, Janna," he clarified.

"I have no idea. Matthew made a goal at the first of the second half. That's all I know."

She wanted to tell him she'd met Lily and watch him squirm. She wanted to ask if *the other woman* had called him at the office. Had he seen her? Kissed her? Touched her? But in truth, she didn't want to know. So she said nothing. She turned again to find him still watching her.

"What?" he asked when she stared at him for a long moment.

"You're wearing glasses," she said, thinking he certainly looked adorable in them.

Colin seemed embarrassed, as if he'd forgotten. "Yes, Mrs. Trevor. It would seem that middle age is catching up with me—or at least with my eyesight."

"Oh, that explains it," she couldn't resist saying as she turned her attention back to the game.

"Explains what?" he asked tersely.

"Why you mistook some other woman for your wife. Obviously you weren't seeing very clearly." She heard him sigh and added, "Or maybe it was dark."

Colin sighed again and looked at the ground. "I guess I deserved that."

"Yes, you certainly did."

He sighed again. "Sean tells me you're doing well."

"He tells me the same thing. Just between you and me, maybe *he's* crazy."

"Because he thinks you're doing well?"

"Exactly."

A few minutes later she said, "I want to see the kids, Colin. I mean . . . Matthew visits, and your mother brings the girls by occasionally, but I . . . I need them."

"I know what you mean."

"I was wondering . . . if every other weekend would be all right with you, like we were doing . . . before."

Colin's heart quickened. "What do you mean?"

"You have custody of the children, Colin. I want to know what my visitation rights are. Can we talk about it, or should I get an attorney?"

"Are you talking about divorce negotiations, Janna?"

"Sean tells me I shouldn't make such decisions until I . . . get past all this. I don't know what I want, Colin. If you decide you don't want to wait around, I guess that's up to you. In the meantime, I want to see my kids. Is every other weekend all right?"

"That's fine," Colin said. "You can see them any time you like."

"We'll try that for now."

"Okay."

"I appreciate your letting me take the convertible," she said.

"You have to get around."

"But it's really a pain getting the baby seats in and out of it."

"I can't afford to buy another car, Janna. Running two households and paying the medical bills has me stretched thin as it is."

"I'm not asking you to buy another car, Colin. I was just wondering if I could use the Suburban when I take the kids. It has the car seats in it. Whoever has the kids gets the bigger vehicle."

Colin took a deep breath and stuffed his hands in his back pockets. He hated this, but he agreed. "Okay. That's fine."

"Good. I'll pick up the kids and the Suburban Friday at six . . . unless you have a problem with that."

Colin wanted to tell her he had a real big problem with that. He wanted to say they should be raising their kids together, and riding in the same car, and living under the same roof. But he knew she would only slap him with that big *adulterers have no business expecting such things* response. And maybe she was right.

"Tell Matthew I had to go," she said.

Colin watched her walk away, then carefully put his mask into place for fear of crumbling then and there. It was only after the children were all in bed and the dishes were washed that he finally crawled into bed and allowed the tears to come. *He was such a fool.*

Colin nearly cursed his opportunity to see Janna when the memory of those few minutes stayed with him for days. *Oh, how he missed her!* The nights became darker, the days lonelier. It had been over six months since he'd lost her, and he felt no closer to getting her back—if such a thing were even possible.

Colin dreaded Friday. He was used to having the children nearly every minute that he wasn't working. How could he bear the silence of an entire weekend without them?

At six o'clock Janna called, and he answered the phone. "I'm on my way over," she said.

"Okay."

"Well, could you have the kids all ready to go so I can hurry?"

"They're ready. Their things are packed."

She was silent for a moment. "What I mean is, could you have them in the Suburban, ready to go?"

"What you're really trying to say is that you don't want to see me—at all."

"That's what I'm trying to say, Colin."

"And why is that?" he asked cynically.

"Being anywhere near you just messes up my head. I'm having enough trouble keeping it straight; I don't need you around to make it worse. I'll be right over."

Matthew helped Colin put the girls in their car seats and load their bags into the back. Colin kissed them good-bye and left Matthew in the Suburban to entertain them. He'd barely walked back in the house when the convertible pulled into the driveway. He watched discreetly from the window as Janna got from one vehicle into the other. She started the engine, backed out, and drove away. It was like some exchange of top-secret documents in a spy movie. And he hated it.

Colin went out to eat alone, then came home and went right to bed. He woke up early Saturday with more nervous energy than he knew what to do with. He worked in the yard until dark, then showered and bought groceries, heated up a frozen dinner, and went to bed. Early Sunday morning, Matthew came to the house to get church clothes for himself and the girls. Colin gathered them up and watched Matthew get into the Suburban from the window. He told himself he should go to church too. But he didn't. Through the day, a nearly tangible darkness seemed to close in around him. Only the children coming through the door turned on the light, and he managed to make it through another week.

The next time Janna took the children, it was raining hard and he couldn't work outside. He tried watching some videos, but they all reminded him of her in one way or another. He tried listening to music, but it was the same thing. He wondered how many songs had been written about love gone bad and being alone. He did go to church on Sunday, but he came home feeling even more depressed. He felt like an outsider—like some fly on the wall who could watch but not participate.

When school let out for summer vacation, Colin had to make some adjustments. Matthew agreed to check in with his mother or grandmother regularly, but Colin was still concerned about him being on his own too much. He quickly realized there was little he could do about it, but he did go to lunch with Matthew once or twice a week, if only to keep their communication open. And the boy seemed to be doing well. If only Colin could feel the same about himself.

Colin quickly got into the habit of not going to church unless he had the children. Fifty-fifty wasn't bad, he told himself. But when Matthew went back to school in the fall, he had to admit that some unsettling things were going on inside his head. He'd not laid eyes on Janna in months, except for an occasional glimpse of her out the window as she exchanged vehicles. He was lonely, and tired, and just plain hated living like this. He could almost literally feel himself spiraling downward. But he did one thing that he'd been too stupid to do the last time: he went straight to see Sean. If nothing else, he could help Colin make sense of his thoughts and hopefully avoid doing something stupid.

"You miss Janna," Sean said with empathy.

"So bad it hurts."

"Is it Janna you miss, or are you just lonely in general?"

"I . . . don't know. I used to know, but . . . well, Janna wants nothing to do with me. She says that being with me messes up her head."

Sean chuckled, and Colin glared at him. "Is it funny?" he asked.

"Well," Sean said, "look at it this way. You're always wondering where her head is. She admitted it to you, but you seemed to have missed the point."

"Apparently I did."

"It can be awfully confusing to hate someone you love, Colin. I think she misses you as much as you miss her. Unfortunately, at this point, the pain inside her far outweighs any loneliness she might feel. Who knows what the future will bring?"

"Which brings us back to where we started," Colin said.

"You're lonely."

"Yes, I'm lonely." Colin talked about what he'd been feeling; about his hesitance to go to church. He rambled on about the doubts and questions churning around in his head.

"I think you'd better clarify that," Sean said at one point, "for yourself as well as for me."

"I don't know if it's true, Sean."

"You're talking about the gospel."

"Yes, I'm talking about the gospel."

"I'd always had the impression that your testimony was pretty firm."

"Well, it seems to be shaken up a little right now."

"It's not so uncommon for someone in a difficult season of life to question their deepest beliefs. I was a convert to the Church, Colin. I didn't join until I had an undeniable witness that it was true. But I know from talking to others that it's not unusual to grow up in the Church and simply never question it. Correct me if I'm wrong, but I get the impression that you always had a testimony. Is it possible that you believed it was true just because it made sense and felt right?"

"That's possible."

"But you've told me of many spiritual experiences; of things in your life where you knew God was there for you, and—"

"Now, don't get me wrong, Sean. I'm not denying that God exists, or that he hasn't been a part of my life. I have no doubt about that. I guess it's . . . the Church in general. I mean . . . the bottom line is that right now, the path is just too hard and rocky. And if that path doesn't lead to the truth, then it's just not worth it."

"So, what do you think you should do?" Sean asked.

"I don't know. What would you do?"

"Test it."

"It's that simple?"

"Simple, yes. Easy, maybe not. My only suggestion is that while you're testing religion, don't go messing with natural laws. Whether the Church is true or not, Colin, the heartache of sin is real."

"You don't have to tell me that. All religious matters aside, my cheating on Janna made me lose her."

"Which makes you lonely," Sean said. "A lonely man questioning his beliefs could lose his respect for natural laws, and that could make him awfully apathetic."

"Maybe that's part of what's troubling me."

"Apathy?"

"Yeah. Sometimes I think that if I can't have Janna back, what's the point? There are my children to consider, but eventually they'll be back in their mother's care most of the time. And what will I have? What is there to lose?"

"I think you're thinking things you don't want to admit to."

"Maybe I am."

"Lily?"

Colin said nothing, hoping the silence would tell Sean he didn't want to say it.

"Okay," Sean said, "I want you to try something. Stand up and move into that chair."

"Oh, not this. I don't have to pretend I'm Janna, do I?"

"No," Sean chuckled, "just sit down." Colin changed chairs and he added, "Now, you are Colin's conscience. You are the little angel who sits on Colin's shoulder and tells him what he *should* be doing. So, tell me about it."

Colin stammered through a list of virtues that was downright overwhelming and depressing. He had to be a good father, patient with Janna, hopeful of their reuniting, faithful that his probation would prove him worthy of re-baptism.

"And what are the consequences of this path?" Sean asked.

Colin talked of eternal promises that seemed too abstract to believe in and too distant to hope for.

"Okay," Sean said, "now move to that chair. Not the one you were in before . . . the other one."

Colin changed chairs again, and Sean explained, "Now you are the devil's advocate. You have permission to be or do anything, with no regard to religion or values. Tell me what you *want*, Colin. Be wicked. Just let those natural-man thoughts flow out."

Colin was surprised at how quickly Sean's permission to feel and think such things kicked in. He talked about his thoughts being consumed with a woman forbidden to him. He speculated on spending his weekends without the children in Lily's company—more specifically, in her bed. He talked about the pathetic hopelessness of pining away for a dysfunctional woman who wanted nothing to do with him, as opposed to the prospect of enjoying himself with a woman who had practically begged him to be a part of her life. He talked about leaving the children in his mother's care until Janna was well enough to take them, and seeing them only when it was convenient. He talked about the money he would have if he divorced Janna and gave her only minimal child support payments.

"And what are the consequences of this path?" Sean asked.

Colin had to admit, "It would be nice for a while, but I know in the long run I would be a miserable man."

"Okay," Sean said, "now move back to your original chair." Colin did so, and Sean continued. "Now, you've listened to your heart, or your spirit, however you want to put it. And you've listened to your head. Put them together, Colin, and decide what you need to do with your life. You can't make long-term decisions on some things right now, because it's out of your hands. But there are some things you can be working on, and there are some things that simply have nothing to do with Janna. So, tell me, Colin, what do you think you should do?"

This assignment wasn't as easy as the other two chairs.

"A suggestion," Sean said. "If it's difficult to define, then break it down into the roles of your life. For instance, you are a man, a father, a husband (sort of), an attorney. You get the idea."

"Well, I have to be a father for my children. Being their father brings that obligation, plain and simple. I love them."

"Okay. That's one aspect of your life."

"And being an attorney is easy. I'm comfortable there. I like my work. It's not a problem."

"That's good."

"As far as being a husband, I guess I have to wait and see what Janna decides."

"Okay, but have you considered the possibility that even *if* Janna comes around and wants to make it work, maybe *your* hurt runs too deep? Is it possible that it could just be too late?"

Colin hated to admit that he didn't have an answer. "Go on," he urged.

"What about the religion thing?"

"I guess I need to test it."

"And I assume you know how to do that."

"Yes, actually, I do," he said, knowing the formulas for receiving such answers very well.

"And what about the role in your life of simply being a man? What does the *man* want? What's feasible with your value system?"

"I don't know."

"So, what do you think you should do?"

Colin was surprised at how quickly the answer came. "Test it."

Sean smiled. "You're getting good at this. So, how would you go about that without compromising your values?"

"I'd have to think about that, but I believe I'm getting the idea. Whatever the future brings, I have to know in my heart that I'm making the right choices for the right reasons."

"Like I said, you're getting good at this."

Colin wasn't so sure, but he did feel like he came away with something he could work on. And that gave him a sense of purpose, not hopelessness. The first thing he did was begin to read the Book of Mormon. He couldn't count the times he'd read it, but he'd not done at all well with his scripture study lately. So he started at the beginning, telling the Lord that he was reading it with the intent of knowing for himself whether or not it was true. He told God straight out that if it wasn't, he intended to make some changes in his life.

Thinking through his loneliness dilemma, Colin decided that the same testing theory applied. He was technically a married man, and he couldn't let go of that without knowing beyond any doubt that he couldn't have—or didn't want—a future with Janna. But perhaps that in itself needed testing. If he was going to pine away for Janna, he had to know it was the best option. And perhaps there were things he could do without breaking the rules that would help him test his ground and know where he stood.

The next time Janna took the children for the weekend, Colin ate an early dinner, then picked up the phone.

"Hi, Lily," he said when she answered.

"Who is this?" she asked in that snappy attorney voice.

"It's Colin," he said, almost hoping she would tell him she'd found someone else and it would take about three minutes to be absolutely certain she was not going to be in his future.

"Hi!" She sounded ridiculously excited. "How are you?"

"I'm . . . struggling. How are you?"

"The same," she admitted.

Pursuing the testing theory, he asked, "How long since you've been kissed?"

"Not since the last time I kissed you," she answered in a dreamy voice that turned his insides to jelly.

"Same here," he said. "But don't go jumping to conclusions. I have no intention of kissing you. I was just wondering how you would feel about a phone date."

"A phone date?"

"It's the only kind I can do legally under the circumstances. But I need some company."

"You're still married, then?"

"Yeah."

"Still separated?"

"Yeah."

"Lonely?"

"Yeah."

"Still holding onto the hope that she'll come around?"

"I guess I am. But it's hard sometimes. I suppose I just need to look at things realistically. I need to test my ground a little."

"So, you're asking me for a phone date," she stated with a little laugh.

"Yes, I am."

"When?"

"Right now, if you're not busy."

"Why would I be busy? It's Friday night. I'm still divorced. And I'd swear there isn't a man in this city worth having. They're either married, or Mormons, or—"

"Both," he interrupted.

"Yes, or they're idiots."

"Some are all three. Like me, for instance."

"You're not an idiot, Colin."

"That's a matter of opinion, I suppose."

"So, where are your children?" she asked. "I understand you have physical custody."

"How did you know that?" he asked.

"It's that private investigator thing."

"They're with my wife for the weekend," he said.

"Then she's doing better, I assume. I understand she was in the hospital for a while."

"How did you know *that?*" he demanded, but she only laughed and changed the subject.

They talked for nearly three hours, and Colin realized how enjoyable adult conversation could be with someone other than his parents or his therapist. Their mutual interest in law was invigorating. They argued about their beliefs on the death penalty and gun control, but she respected his views and didn't make him feel defensive for having them. They avoided talking about anything personal, which was fine with him. He just enjoyed the evening, caring little about the phone bill. He figured it would still be less expensive than taking a woman out for a nice dinner, which was simply against the rules as long as he had that ring on his finger.

Colin slept well that night, and spent the following morning in bed, reading the Book of Mormon. He worked on the house and yard through the afternoon, then called Lily again while he was cooking himself a steak and a baked potato. She talked about her family while he ate, and she asked him to fax her a taste. "I would if I could," he chuckled.

The next morning Colin went to church, then went to his parents' house for dinner. He didn't talk to Lily again until Janna took the children two weeks later.

"It must be Mommy weekend," Lily said when he called.

"It is," he said.

"Well, it's good to hear from you," she said. "But it would be nice if it was a little more often."

"I'm too busy to even think straight . . . except on Mommy weekend."

While Colin was trying to think of some way to open the conversation, she said, "Colin, why don't you get a divorce so we can have a *real* relationship?"

Colin quelled his first defensive reaction, and steered to an opportunity to test his ground. "And what exactly would that relationship entail?"

"Well, we could, like, go out to dinner, or go to a movie. You know, *real* date things. It's a good place to start."

"And then what?" he asked, wishing it hadn't come out sounding so severe.

"I don't know what, Colin." Her voice was equally intense. "I only know that I love you, and I hate the way you keep me hanging on."

Colin was too stunned to respond. He had believed all along that she cared for him, but he'd never dreamed . . . Had he simply assumed that she couldn't possibly have feelings that deep, because he didn't?

"You're awfully quiet, Trevor," she said.

"You can't really mean that, Lily. You know practically nothing about me."

"I know how you make me feel."

Colin sighed and struggled for something to say while battles erupted between his heart and his head.

"You're still not saying much, Colin," she said, sounding irritated.

"I . . . don't know what to say. Surely you can't mean that you—"

"Don't tell me what I feel, Colin. You told me once that you couldn't say you loved me. I don't know if your feelings have changed, but I do know you are one of the most honest, decent men I have ever met. And I know you won't say something to me if you don't mean it. I can't make you love me, Colin, but you can't make me *not* love *you.*"

Colin reminded himself that he had called her; that he was attempting to find out exactly where his heart was and where his future lay. Holding himself to the honesty she had just mentioned, he said, "I . . . don't know how I feel right now, Lily. Things are just . . . messed up. What happened between us has a lot of mixed emotions wrapped up in it. I care for you, Lily. I care about what happens to you. And I want you to be happy. I'm just not so sure that I'm the man who can do it. Right now, I just need a friend. But I have to keep my distance, because . . . well, deep in my heart, I still want to make it work with Janna. Eventually, she'll either take me back, or I'll be able to reach a point where I can let it go. In the meantime, I can't give you, or any other woman, anything beyond this."

"Phone dates," she said, but her tone was light.

"Yeah, phone dates."

"I can live with that . . . for now. I'd like to think there's a future for us, but . . . well, maybe my Mr. Right will come along before Janna decides to dump you, and you might be left out in the cold."

"That's possible," he said.

Through the night, Colin found his thoughts consumed with all the hurt he'd experienced in his life that was connected to his relationship with Janna. He slept little as memories assaulted him, at moments provoking anger, at others, tears.

The following morning, Colin tried to force his negative emotions away, but they refused to relent. He hurried to pick up the house and put in a load of laundry before going on some errands and to the grocery store. He was just about to leave when the doorbell rang. With car keys in hand, he pulled it open and caught his breath.

"Lily," he said, wishing it hadn't sounded so perky. But no matter how hard he tried to feel otherwise, he couldn't deny being glad to see her.

"Hi," she said, seeming almost shy. "You look different. You're wearing glasses."

"Yeah," he said sheepishly.

Lily glanced down, then looked up into his face. "I know this goes against your phone date theory and all . . . but . . . well, I got your address by snooping around the office a little, and I . . . I guess I just wanted to see you."

Colin didn't quite dare admit aloud that he wanted to see her, too. So he just said, "Well, I was just going on some errands."

After an uncomfortable moment of silence, she asked, "Would it be a problem if I came along?" She put a hand over her heart and the other to the square. "I swear it will be pure and platonic." She smiled. "I don't want to give you anything else that you'll have to talk to your bishop about."

Colin closed the door, locking it behind him. "Well, in that case," he said, "it would be nice to have some company."

"Where are we going?" Lily asked as he put down the top on the convertible and started toward town.

Colin handed her his planner. "I have a whole list."

While Colin drove, Lily read his list along with its notations, teasing him and making him laugh. How long had it been since he'd really laughed? Together they went to pick up dry cleaning, get some photocopies, and then to pick up some film that had been developed. Lily looked through the pictures, admiring the children and asking questions as he drove to an auto parts store to get some oil and a filter for the Suburban. He had her divide the pictures into two sets.

"I always get double prints," he said.

"The extra set must be for their mother," she observed.

"That's right," Colin said. The thought struck him deeply, and he unconsciously put a hand to his chest, feeling a little heartache over the reality. A hopeless kind of heartache. Then he glanced at Lily and wondered if he just needed to make up his mind to getting over Janna so he could get on with his life—wherever it might lead him.

"What's next?" he asked after he put the auto supplies in the trunk.

"Matthew's game, it says," Lily reported. Colin must have betrayed his concern when she added, "Maybe it's not a good idea for me to be with you. I won't be offended if—"

"It's okay," Colin said impulsively. "We're only a few blocks away, and I just need to stay a few minutes. You can wait in the car . . . if you don't mind."

"I don't mind," she said. "Will Janna be there?"

"Not likely. She usually just drops him off or sends him with a friend, because the girls are pretty tough to handle at a ball field."

As they pulled into the parking lot, Lily was telling Colin how she had been quite a ball player as a child. He laughed as she told him she was so fast and so skinny that her teammates called her "Zipper."

"I won't be long," he said, putting the car in park. Then he hurried toward the playing field, his eye tuned in to finding Matthew among the mass of boys all wearing identical shirts. He paused at the edge and watched closely once he'd spotted him. During a time-out, he caught Matthew's attention and waved. Then he saw Matthew wave to someone else, and turned to see Janna standing a short distance away. His heart quickened at the sight of her, then it began to pound as he realized that Lily was sitting in the car.

"Oh, help," he muttered under his breath as Janna sauntered toward him. He glanced toward the parking lot, wondering how he had managed to be so distracted that he'd missed seeing the Suburban.

"Where are the girls?" he asked, swallowing hard.

"They're with your mother. I told Matthew I wanted to see an entire game for once."

"That's nice," Colin said, wondering why she had approached him. It wasn't like her.

"Is it okay if I bring them back a couple of hours early tomorrow? I want to go to a fireside."

"Sure," Colin squeaked. "No problem."

He was hoping to get away before Janna noticed that he wasn't alone, but he saw her eye catch something beyond his shoulder—in the direction of where his car was parked. As her cold, accusing eyes shifted to his face, the anger he'd felt earlier encompassed him freshly. He reminded himself that he had a life—and he was tired of groveling and begging and apologizing to this woman who wanted nothing to do with him.

"I can't believe you would bring her here," Janna growled in little more than a whisper.

"Yes, well, I surprise even myself sometimes." He liked the way his words seemed to sum up his entire relationship with Lily.

"Is this what you do with your weekends when you don't have the kids?" she snapped.

"Mrs. Trevor," he said, determined to stay calm, "I have never—ever—attempted to make you believe anything beyond the absolute truth. How you perceive it is up to you. This is the first time I have seen her in *months*, and even if running a few errands with Lily isn't the most appropriate thing for me to be doing, I don't know what difference it makes to you. I was under the distinct impression that you were not concerned with my life one way or another."

"I'm concerned with the way all of this affects my children."

"She has never been anywhere near the children."

Colin watched Janna's gaze move again to the car, where Lily was waiting, apparently oblivious. Her thoughts were so transparent that Colin actually chuckled. "You know, Janna," he said, "one day you're going to have to get off the fence and make up your mind."

"What do you mean by that?"

"I mean that you can't expect me to wait around forever. If you start counting up the years I've spent waiting for you, you'll find that I've already given a lot more than most men would. I don't know how you can stand there with blatant jealousy burning in your eyes and try to convince me that you don't love me anymore."

Janna looked up at him, startled, then she looked away, unnerved at having him read her thoughts. She had to admit, "I never said that I don't love you anymore. If I didn't, it would be easy."

"No," he said, "you've just told me that you hate me; that you never want to see my face again."

She looked angry, but he didn't care.

"Make up your mind, Janna. I'm only human."

Janna watched Colin walk away, hating the dilemma pounding in her head. At the moment, she hated him all the more for being right. She recalled Sean telling her that she was either going to have to forgive Colin or acknowledge his right to spend his life with another woman. But at the moment, one seemed as impossible as the other. She just didn't have the strength to make such a decision—not yet. She figured if he made the choice to divorce her before she came to terms with all of this, she would just have to live with it—if such a thing were even possible.

Colin got in the car and slammed the door.

"Oops," Lily said and he glanced over at her, surprised. She nodded toward the ball field and turned to see a perfect view of where Janna was still standing. "I guess that didn't go so well."

"How do you figure?" he asked angrily, turning the key in the ignition.

"Oh, it was pretty evident that a heated conversation was taking place."

Colin sighed and put the car in reverse. "I'm not sure we know how to have any other kind."

As he drove, Colin was amazed to hear Lily validate the feelings going on inside of him. She finished by saying, "I know how much you love her. I'm not sure any woman could erase the impression she's left on you."

Colin felt certain she was right, but he said nothing as his feelings crept back and forth between hurt and anger. As he pulled the car up in front of the house, he looked over at Lily, wanting with everything he had to just take her in his arms and ease this lonely ache. But he couldn't. He just *couldn't*. He was wondering how to tell her that he couldn't invite her in when she said, "I should go. It was good to see you, but . . ."

Colin nodded, still afraid to speak for fear of erupting.

"Are you okay?" she asked.

Colin shook his head.

"Do you want me to stay?" Lily took his hand and squeezed it.

Colin looked into her eyes, contemplating the choice before him. He hadn't felt any more tempted than this the last time he had taken her into his arms. Truthfully, he admitted, "Yes, Lily, I want you to stay." A serene little smile touched her lips just before he added, "So you'd better go."

Her smiled turned sad, but she nodded in agreement and got out of the car. Before Colin found the motivation to get out himself, she was driving away. The house felt especially empty when he went inside, but he sank to his knees by the bed and immersed himself in tearful prayer. It was the only thing he could do without falling completely to pieces. And he figured one nervous breakdown per family was more than enough. He felt some peace in realizing that he had resisted the temptation; but that seemed little compensation when he felt so lonely and confused.

Colin didn't call Lily again that weekend. And he didn't go to church. He read some in the Book of Mormon, but he found it frustrating and pointless. The next two weeks were difficult. The children seemed crankier than usual, and work became stressful. He didn't dare think about Janna at all, because it would only deepen his discouragement. His only reprieve came with thoughts of Lily. He kept hearing her voice in his memory, telling him that she loved him. And, more and more, memories of their intimacy became a comforting pastime. He asked himself often if he *did* love her. Was it his stubbornness concerning Janna that kept him from admitting it?

An hour after Janna picked up the kids, Colin answered the phone. "It's Mommy weekend," Lily said.

"What do you want?" he asked, albeit lightly.

"Well, since you asked, I want you to get in that sassy little unvulgar convertible of yours, drive up here, walk through my front door, take me in your arms, and—"

"Okay, you can stop now. If you only knew how tempting that was, you wouldn't be saying such things to me."

"And why wouldn't I?"

"I've already hurt you—and myself—twice, Lily. Don't make me hurt you again."

"I wouldn't be hurting if you were with me," she insisted. "I wasn't hurting when we did *errands* together. What harm was there in that?" When he said nothing, she added, "Well, I guess having your wife see us together probably wasn't real good."

Colin had to admit to the thoughts that had been plaguing him. "I don't know. Maybe it was."

"Oh, you mean the classic jealousy tactic. See if the reality of another woman opens her eyes? Is that it?"

"If I admit to that, it makes me sound pretty pathetic. Honestly, Lily, I've never intended to use you or to—"

"Listen, Trevor," she interrupted, *"I'm* the one who came to see *you.* You've never been dishonest with me. I know where your heart is. Don't apologize, okay?"

Colin actually felt touched by her understanding and acceptance. "Okay," he said. "Thank you."

When silence lingered for several moments, Colin tried to think of a way to turn this conversation into something productive. "Okay, Lily. Let's just say, for instance, that I was divorced, and we decided to try it. Where would we start? Move in together for a while to see if it works?"

"Maybe."

"No. That's not the way I work, Lily. We could date—chastely—and decide if we really wanted to get married. And if we got married, then what?"

"Then we're married. It would be great."

"Better than being married to Tyler?"

"No contest."

"Are you sure?" Colin asked. "You don't even know me, Lily. How can you possibly have any idea what being married to me would be like?"

"I know how I feel about you."

"Okay, but how are you going to feel about me when I expect you to go to church with me every Sunday, and support me in doing service work that could take several hours out of my evenings? Could you support me in religious beliefs without being a part of them? Are you willing to participate in daily family prayer and scripture study, and a weekly family meeting? Are you willing to never watch an R-rated movie, or drink any liquor or coffee in my home?

"And how are you going to feel about being a stepmother? The fact is, after my working hours I have children to bathe, feed, and care for. I deal with homework, sibling rivalry, and a lot of dirty laundry. That's reality, Lily. That's real life. You're a career woman, and if I married you, I would respect that. But if you marry a divorced man, you're going to likely marry his children. Eventually Janna may take them full time, but I have to face the possibility that she may not be capable of handling them on her own. That means my second wife would be a mother, and her influence and commitment to my children would be terribly important to me."

Colin took a deep breath. "Now, do you still love me?"

"Yes."

"But could you live with it?"

"I don't know."

"Well, at least you're honest."

"If you give this spiel to every woman in your future, Colin, you'll *never* get married again."

"That would be better than having some woman come into my home to be faced with a disillusionment that will hurt us all."

"But . . . can't love overcome those things, Colin? If two people truly love each other, isn't it possible to deal with the rest?"

"I guess that depends on how committed those two people are." He paused as her question touched something painful, and he had to admit, "I used to believe that true love could overcome any obstacle. I don't know if I believe that anymore."

After thinking about all of that for two weeks, Colin was prepared to call Lily and tell her that there just wasn't a future for them. He appreciated her willingness to fill in his empty hours and be a friend, but he knew he could never be happy with her. He dreaded telling her, but he knew he had to be completely honest with her. It was the only thing that could redeem what he'd done to her life.

Late Friday evening, she called him before he got up the nerve to call her.

"There's something I need to tell you," she said.

"Okay. There's something I need to tell you, too. Ladies first."

"You know, Colin, I've thought a lot about what you said the last time we talked. And maybe actually seeing you with Janna made me think about it a little differently. I don't know. As much as I hate to admit it, you're right. With Tyler, I believed the things that weren't right between us would go away or become easier when we got married. Well, they just got worse. What you and I shared was incredible, Colin. But you're right. It's not enough." She chuckled sadly. "At least not right now. Who knows? Maybe if my feelings haven't changed up the road a little, I might have more courage to take it on. In a way, I believe that because of the way you treat me, and the way I feel about you, I could do anything. But maybe I overestimate myself."

"Lily, I think you could do anything you put your mind to. You just have to decide if it's worth it."

"Well, since you put it that way, I may show up in your life yet." Following a lengthy pause, she said, "So, what did you want to tell *me*? Are you getting a divorce?"

"No . . . not yet, anyway. I just wanted to tell you that I appreciate the lonely hours you've eased for me, and your friendship. But in my heart, I just have to face what I think I've known all along. We shared something. We learned something. But now we have to put it behind us. We're just not right for each other, Lily. It would never work."

He could tell she was crying as she said, "Never say never, Colin."

Lily didn't call on the next Mommy weekend, and he was relieved. He'd tested it, and he knew where it stood. He couldn't determine whether or not he would have a life with Janna, but he knew he could never have one with Lily. Even *if* love could overcome all their differences, he just didn't love her.

CHAPTER ELEVEN

*C*olin nearly panicked when he realized that the days had suddenly become shorter, and fall was easing closer. It had been almost a year since his excommunication. The evidence of time passing discouraged him as he looked at his life and wondered if he'd made any progress at all.

It seemed only yesterday that he had yearned for time to pass and ached to put all of this behind him, but now he felt scared and uncertain. He knew it took much more than time to get his membership in the Church back. He could never be re-baptized while feeling such apathy and lack of conviction. He'd been committing himself to regular study of the Book of Mormon, but he felt as if there was some kind of mist that kept his mind from absorbing what he read. That same clouded feeling was there when he prayed. He just didn't feel connected; it was as simple as that. Of course, he'd been excommunicated. He'd lost the privilege of having the gift of the Holy Ghost, and he knew that. But in the emptiness of his life, it was difficult to even remember what having it felt like. He'd seen some evidence of blessings in his life, but it was all so intangible, so difficult to grasp.

Most of the time, Colin felt too busy to think much about it. But when night fell and the children were asleep, that dark mist seemed to deepen. His loneliness was so intense that he nearly believed at times it might consume him. A part of him kept clinging to the hope that it always gets darkest before the light, and maybe God had a light for him just around the corner. But something in him felt uncertain and cynical. The hurt often clouded the hope, making him believe that another path would be preferable. The road back to the temple just looked too difficult, and if it wasn't the right road, he didn't want to take it. And what point was there in even reaching for that goal if Janna refused to be a part of it?

In spite of the doubts and discouragement, he continued to pray and study, believing that perhaps it was the only thing that could save him. He kept recalling Sean's challenge to test his doubts. He couldn't do that with any conviction if he didn't follow the test through to the end.

It took every ounce of Colin's inner strength to get out of bed and go to church while Janna had the children. It would be one year this week since he'd jumped off that cliff with Lily.

Sitting through his meetings, Colin thought of Janna, wondering if he'd made restitution with her. He'd confessed the sin to her immediately. He'd taken care of her to the best of his ability, in spite of the separation. What else could he do? He'd done everything tangibly possible to right the wrong. The year had been difficult. He'd had his low times. He'd slipped a little a time or two. There was that time he'd kissed Lily, and maybe it hadn't been the most proper thing to have those long phone visits with her. But he'd talked to his bishop about all of it, and time had put it behind him. Or had it?

Colin knew that when the time came to see if he was ready for re-baptism, he would be asked to bear his testimony, and he would be asked if the Lord had forgiven him. How could he respond in this frame of mind? All he felt was a dark cloud hovering around him, holding him back, damning him from any kind of peace at all.

Colin sat down in testimony meeting, but found himself wondering if he should just forego this last meeting and go home. He hated sitting through the sacrament when he couldn't participate. He hated being without his children. He hated this oppression he felt. He wondered if perhaps he was trying too hard to find an answer that he already knew somewhere inside. But where? And what?

Ignoring the meeting completely, Colin leaned his forearms on his thighs and turned his mind to prayer. He begged God to give him some light, to help him get past this brick wall. He prayed that his feeble efforts would be acknowledged; that in spite of his weaknesses, he might be forgiven for what he'd done, and be given a chance to start his life over. He asked for a witness, that he might know beyond any doubt that the gospel was what it seemed to be, reminding the Lord that he had studied the Book of Mormon according to Moroni's challenge.

Colin felt numb as the sacrament song began. When he could think of nothing more to say in his prayer, he tuned his mind to the words of the song, even though he wasn't singing.

I marvel that he would descend from his throne divine
To rescue a soul so rebellious and proud as mine,
That he should extend his great love unto such as I,
Sufficient to own, to redeem, and to justify.

Colin almost felt an emotion somewhere inside—a sensation hovering close to him. He closed his eyes, concentrating, willing it closer, aching to make it tangible. But it was just like everything else in his life, clouded and undefined. His frustration deepened through the sacrament. He felt so cut off. He passed the sacrament trays along, looking at the bread and water as if he'd been in the desert without food or drink.

Through the remainder of the meeting, Colin continued to pray. He concentrated on his private conversation with God, hoping to avoid the testimonies being borne that somehow discouraged him further when he'd been banished from being able to walk up to that podium and bear his own. He nearly laughed inwardly at the thought. And what would he say if he could? Did he even *have* a testimony?

He nearly got up and walked out, and he would have if he'd had the strength to move. *Please help me,* he prayed. *Give me the strength to get through this. I'm afraid if I walk out of this building feeling this way, I'll never have the strength to walk back in.*

Colin stopped praying long before the closing song began. He felt numb; past feeling. Then he thought of Janna, and everything inside of him ached freshly. *He missed her so much.* If he couldn't have her, he had to know that God was hearing his prayers. Without one or the other, he would never make it.

He wasn't going to sing, but the elderly gentleman sitting next to him held the hymn book open for him to share it. He managed to squeak out the first two verses of *How Great Thou Art.* Again he was aware of a sensation that seemed to want to tell him something, but he couldn't quite grasp it. Then something warm began to happen inside him as he sang the third verse. *And when I think that God, his Son not sparing, sent him to die, I scarce can take it in. That on the cross, my burden gladly bearing, He bled and died to take away my sin.*

Colin couldn't sing after that. Hot tears spilled down his face as he closed his eyes and tried to grasp the reality of what had just happened. He expected the feeling to evade him, to go quickly, to leave him wondering if he'd imagined it. But as he attempted to tune his spirit in to the emotional frequency surging through him, it all became too real to deny. The only thing he was aware of outside himself was the completion of that song. As if angels were expressing the feelings of his heart, he heard the phrase resounding through him, *My God, how great thou art!*

Colin could never put the experience to words. He only knew that instantly everything changed. Darkness turned to light. Anguish became joy. Weakness merged into strength. Despair dissipated into hope. There were no words spoken in his head, no vision that came to his mind. But he *knew* beyond any doubt that his prayers had been heard, that the gospel he had been testing was true. He believed that, deep inside, he had known those things all along. But what he hadn't known until now, that couldn't possibly be discredited, was the one simple fact that stood above the rest. He knew he had been forgiven. He couldn't explain how he knew. *He just knew.*

Colin's eyes flew open, startled by the congregation's *amen* following the closing prayer. He frantically wiped at his tears, hoping no one would notice. The gentleman sitting next to him patted him on the shoulder, handed him a tissue, then stood up and moved away.

He hurried out to the car, grateful to avoid any conversation or skeptical glances. During the brief drive home, the emotion struck him all over again. *He couldn't believe it.* In spite of all his weakness, all his doubting and stubbornness, he had been given an incredible, undeniable witness that made all the suffering worth it. Everything was right. Everything looked clear, and fair, and good. And he knew he was going to make it, no matter what the future held.

Colin went straight to his bedroom, grateful for the first time in months to be alone. He fell to his knees by the bed, humbly attempting to express his gratitude, while cleansing tears flowed unrestrained. There was no sense of time passing.

Eventually he crawled onto the bed, where he lay for more than an hour, exhausted and at peace. His stomach began to growl, and he realized he'd eaten nothing since yesterday's lunch. But he felt no desire to get up and fix himself something to eat; he just wanted to stay here and hold onto this feeling forever. He thought of Janna and cried fresh tears, wishing there was some way of telling her that he'd been forgiven. He knew that was impossible; it would only provoke an argument that would defile a sacred experience. But impulsively he picked up the phone to call her anyway, and he was relieved when she answered. Without giving her a chance to say anything, he said simply, "I love you, Janna. I just wanted you to know." He hung up before she could respond, not wanting anything to mar what he was feeling.

As the intensity of the experience began to fade, Colin felt the loneliness creep in. But he found the strength to recognize it and ward it off. He hurried to change his clothes, then he drove to his parents' home. They'd shared his pain; he thought it would be appropriate that they share his joy.

Colin went quietly into the house where his father was snoring on the couch, and his mother was busy in the kitchen, with music playing. He sneaked up behind her and grabbed her, laughing when she screamed.

"Oh, Colin!" she scolded, but he just chuckled. Then she did a double-take and looked deep into his eyes. "You seem awfully happy. Are you—"

"I *am* happy, Mother." He hugged her then lifted her right off the floor, turning around with her and laughing deeply.

"Stop that!" she insisted, sharing his laughter as he set her down but kept her in his embrace.

"What's all the ruckus?" Carl demanded through a yawn.

"Sorry to wake you, Dad," Colin said. "But I've got good news."

"Is Janna—" his mother began, but he interrupted.

"Nothing has changed with Janna." He became briefly lost in the one reality of his life that was difficult. But his present joy outweighed it, and his mood quickly lightened again. "However," he continued, "I have been blessed with the knowledge that . . ." The emotion rushed back, affirming all over again the truth of it.

". . . That my Father in Heaven has forgiven me . . . for what I did."
Something between a sob and laughter erupted from his throat. "I
can't tell you how I know. I just *know.*"

Nancy got tears in her eyes. Carl put an arm around Colin and
hugged him tightly. "You don't have to tell us how you know, Colin.
There's no need."

He had dinner with his parents, grateful beyond expression for
their involvement in his struggles, which gave him the opportunity to
be so open with them now. What would he have done if he'd had to
keep it a secret from them all this time? He couldn't even imagine it.

Colin returned home just a few minutes before Janna brought
the children back. He enjoyed the little bit of time he had with them
before they went to bed, perhaps more than he had in weeks. He felt
alive again. He felt like a man with something to give them beyond
simply caring for their needs.

The following day, Colin went to see Sean about the time he
knew he'd be going to lunch. He waited for only a few minutes before
the receptionist told him he could go back to Sean's office. Sean stood
up when he walked in.

"What's up, Colin?" He did the same double-take his mother
had done the day before, adding firmly, "You look happy."

"It's that obvious, eh?" Colin chuckled. "Well, I just wanted to
stop and tell you something." He slapped him playfully on the
shoulder. "I thought you might like to know that the Church is true."

Sean laughed, giving Colin a firm embrace. "Yeah, I know."

"I know you know," Colin said softly. "But I thought you might
like to know that *I* know."

Sean nodded, briefly seeming too moved to speak. He finally
said, "Come on. I'll buy you lunch and we'll celebrate."

Through the course of the meal, Colin told Sean about his
experience and the hope it gave him. Just as with his parents, it was a
pleasure to share his joy with someone who had shared so much of his
pain and suffering.

Colin actually looked forward to having the disciplinary council
reconvene to determine his worthiness for re-baptism. With sincere
emotion he bore his testimony of the truthfulness of the gospel, and
the power behind all he had learned during the past year. He testified

firmly that he knew the Lord had forgiven him. And he went away with a date scheduled for re-baptism.

Colin felt ecstatic at the reality. He would be a baptized member of the Church again, with rights and privileges, and perhaps most important, with his sins washed clean. His parents took him and the children out to dinner to celebrate when he told them, and later that evening he talked to Matthew about it, sharing his feelings on a level that an eleven-year-old could understand. After Matthew went to bed, Colin phoned his brother in Minnesota.

"Hey, Cameron, I have a big brother favor to ask."

"Okay, what's up?"

"The problem is," Colin said, "I need you to come here, if it's at all possible. I know it's a lot to ask, and if you can't do it, I understand."

"What's going on?" He sounded concerned.

"Well, the thing is, I got myself into trouble."

"Is it money, Colin?"

"No, Cam, it's not money. Just hear me out. Do you remember when I was about five and I took Dad's best fishing pole out of the garage, and I was trying to cast it in the backyard? I made a horrible mess of the fishing line, and when you found me and told me Dad would be furious, I started to cry."

"I remember."

"Well, you helped me untangle it. We put it back. And Dad never knew. You saved me that day. Well, Cameron, I took something I wasn't supposed to, and I made a big mess of it. Dad knows about it this time." He paused to draw courage. "He was with me the night I was excommunicated."

Colin heard nothing but a sharp breath.

"Are you still with me, Cam?"

"I'm here."

"The thing is, I've been praying about this, and I want you to be the one to re-baptize me. We set the date for a week from Saturday, but we can adjust it . . . if it could mean your being here."

Still silence.

"Cameron, I wouldn't blame you if you don't want anything to do with this. I just felt I should ask."

"Why me?" Cameron asked. "You have two other brothers."

"Yes, but . . . you're my *big* brother."

Silence. Then a subtle sniffle. "It would be an honor to rebaptize you, Colin. I'll find a way to be there."

Colin chuckled with relief. "Thank you, Cam. You can't know what this means to me."

"Does this have something to do with the separation, and Janna being in the hospital and all? You don't have to tell me. I was just wondering how things are going between the two of you."

"She's doing good from what I hear, but we're still separated. I still have hope. And yes, it has everything to do with our separation. I *would* like to tell you about it, because I've learned some things that you might find interesting. But I'd like to tell you to your face. When you get here, we'll talk, okay?"

"I'll look forward to it."

Colin laughed out loud when he got off the phone. It just felt so good. Until he thought of Janna. He hurried to dial her number before he lost his courage.

* * * * *

Janna absently answered the phone while she was opening a can of soup.

"Hello, Janna," Colin's voice said gently. Just hearing him speak made something quiver inside her. "How are you?"

Her involuntary reaction put her on the defensive, but she reminded herself to be civil. "I'm okay. How are you?"

"I'm doing good . . . considering," he said.

"You didn't call to tell me I can't take the kids Saturday, did you?"

"No, of course not," he insisted. "I know you have plans for the circus. They're excited." Colin wanted to tell her that he wished he could go with them, but he stuck to his purpose. She hadn't hung up on him, and he didn't want to push his luck. "It's next Saturday I wanted to talk to you about, Janna. I have a big favor to ask you."

Janna's heart quickened. Was he going to ask if he could see her? Did he want to talk? The very idea almost made her tremble. She wasn't ready to discuss her feelings yet. How could she when she hardly understood them? She was both relieved and surprised when he said, "I'm going to be re-baptized, Janna. And I want you to be there."

Janna had to sit down. She didn't know *how* to feel. She hesitated before saying, "I just don't know, Colin. I can't promise."

"Okay," Colin said, feeling his heart break a little more. He felt certain if she could just see the evidence that he was clean again, it would make a difference. "I just thought I'd let you know. It's at the stake center just north of the house, at six in the evening, if you decide to go."

"I'll think about it. Thank you."

Following a lengthy pause, Colin asked, "Is everything all right, Janna? Is there anything you need, anything I can do to—"

"I'm fine, Colin, really. Thank you, anyway."

"Okay. I'm not trying to push or anything. I just . . . want to know that you have what you need, and—"

"You've been good to take care of me, Colin, in spite of everything. And I really do appreciate it, but . . ."

"But?" he pressed, praying he wouldn't regret it.

Janna gathered fortitude and told herself not to get angry. "I'm just having trouble with this, Colin. Maybe it's just me; I don't know. I only know that I can't find anything inside of me that has the strength, or the selflessness, or whatever it might be, to . . . get past this."

Colin didn't have to ask what she meant by *this*. But he did say, "It's been a year, JannaLyn. *A year.* Haven't we lost enough years already?"

"I can't talk about this right now, Colin."

"Okay, when can we talk about it?"

"I'm not sure we're capable of talking at all without just getting angry and—"

"Okay, we'll let Sean mediate," he insisted. "Give me an hour with Sean there to help us. That's all I ask. I have to know where I stand, Janna. I can't go on like this."

"You don't have to wait around for me, Colin. I'm not stopping you from getting on with your life."

Colin wanted to tell her that she *was* his life, but he only repeated his plea. "One hour, Janna. Please."

Janna didn't want to do it, but she couldn't deny that he deserved to know where he stood, even if she wasn't sure she could tell him. "All right. You make an appointment and let me know. I'm flexible. I'll meet you there."

The following Monday morning, Colin arrived at Sean's office. He was so nervous he was practically shaking. Sean came personally out to the waiting room to get him.

"Janna's already here," he said. "She's not very happy about this, but I think it might be good for her."

"And me?" Colin asked skeptically.

"I guess we'll have to see," Sean said gently, ushering him down the hall. Colin's heart pounded into his throat as they entered the room. He felt like a lamb going to the slaughter. Janna was standing at the window, her back to them. She didn't turn as they entered and Sean closed the door.

"Colin, I'd like you to meet Janna," Sean said facetiously. "Janna, this is Colin."

"That's not funny," Janna said and turned around. Colin caught his breath just to see her. He couldn't remember the last time they'd stood face to face. She'd gained weight since her hospital stay, and she looked more like herself. *She looked beautiful.* How he ached to just take her in his arms, if only for a moment!

"Well, it made you say something," Sean responded lightly. He sat down and motioned to the other chairs with his hands. "Have a seat. Just like old times, eh?"

"Not exactly," Colin said as he took a chair, unable to keep his eyes off Janna, while she seemed to want to look anywhere but at him.

"So, where do you want to start?" Sean asked. When nothing happened, he added, "Colin, I believe you instigated this meeting. I assume there's something you had in mind."

"I just need to know where I stand. It's been a year, and I have no idea what's left between us."

"Janna?" Sean encouraged, making it clear he was not going to do the talking. As he had often put it, he was just the referee.

"I'm not sure there's anything left between us," she said. "I don't know if it's my fault, or your fault, or nobody's fault. I only know what I'm feeling."

"What *are* you feeling, Janna?" Colin asked gently. "That's what I want to know."

"I feel . . . confused . . . and *frustrated*. I think . . ." Janna hesitated admitting it, but she'd thought this through, and knew it would be unfair of her to expect him to wait it out. "I think . . . maybe it would be . . . better if you just . . . get on with your life, Colin. I'm not so sure that I was the right woman for you to begin with."

Colin glanced quickly at Sean, hoping for some kind of support. All he got was a penetrating gaze. He thought of a hundred points to illustrate that she was wrong, but he simply said, "I've always believed you were the right woman for me, Janna. But if you don't love me anymore, then—"

"I didn't say that!" she snapped.

Colin's eyes widened. "Then what *are* you saying?"

"I *do* love you, Colin," she insisted, finally turning to look at him. Tears spilled down her face as she said it, but she wiped them away and her eyes turned hard. "But love alone just isn't enough. It's that simple."

"If I love you, and you love me, then—"

"If you love me, then why did you do it?" she shouted. "How can you possibly sit there and tell me that I'm the right woman for you, that you love me, when you went to bed with some blonde woman you didn't even know anything about?"

Colin caught a cautioning glance from Sean that he interpreted as *Don't get defensive. Let her vent the anger.*

"Stupidity," he answered. "I was just plain stupid, Janna. It's as simple as that." Then a thought occurred to him, and he sat up a little straighter. "How did you know she was blonde?" As soon as he said it, he recalled that Janna had seen Lily sitting in the car at the ball field. But Janna's expression made him wonder if there was something he didn't know.

Janna glanced at Sean and he nodded slightly, as if to tell her she needed to be honest. Janna sighed and looked the other way. "She came by the apartment looking for you, not long after I got out of the hospital. We had a little *chat.*"

Colin sank further down in his chair and pressed a hand over his eyes. The very thought of Janna and Lily standing face to face made him a little queasy. He wondered why Lily had never mentioned it in all the hours they'd spent talking on the phone. He was aching to know what they'd said to each other, and at the same time wondered if ignorance was better. It had the feel of a bad scene from a soap opera.

"Tell him the gasoline theory," Sean said with a proud little smile. "It really is a good one."

Janna looked askance at Sean, then at Colin, whose eyes were wide with . . . what? Fear?

"What's the gasoline theory?" Colin asked when Janna said nothing.

Janna cleared her throat tensely. "Lily told me that the problems in our marriage had nothing to do with her." Colin's queasiness increased as he tried to imagine how the conversation must have led up to that point. "I told her she was probably right about that, but . . ."

"But?" Colin pressed.

"I told her that what had happened between the two of you was like throwing a match on a gasoline spill. I told her that maybe we could have cleaned it up . . . if it hadn't exploded."

Colin squeezed his eyes shut, not liking the analogy at all. "Could we have cleaned it up, Janna?" he asked without opening them.

"I don't know."

"And now that it's exploded, and the fire's burned down, now what?"

"I don't know that either, Colin. Which brings us right back to where we started. I can't tell you where to stand, Colin. It's obvious you're getting your life back in order, and what you choose to do with it is up to you. I can't tell you that waiting around for me will be worth it. At this point, I can't make any promises, because I can't even think about you without thinking of *that woman* in your arms. How can I ever trust you again? How can I—"

"Wait a minute," Colin interrupted. "There's a point I'd like to make. I did something wrong. But I didn't sneak around. I wasn't having some secret affair, meeting this woman behind your back. I didn't lie to you, Janna."

"So, are you trying to tell me that it only happened once?"

Colin took a deep breath. "Twice. I went . . . back . . . one time . . . after you kicked me out. It was before the disciplinary council."

"And since then?" Her tone of voice made him feel as if he was on trial all over again.

"I saw her at the office last year during the holidays . . . and . . . we kissed. That's all."

"That's all?" she asked skeptically. "Colin, I saw you with her."

"She was sitting in my car, Janna. And that is the extent of it. Beyond a little drive that afternoon, there has been nothing but conversation, and most of it has been over the phone. I haven't talked to her for weeks. There's no way I can prove any of this, Janna. You're just going to have to believe me. You're going to have to get over it."

"I don't know if I can, Colin. I can't make you any promises. Maybe you should just get the divorce and get it over with."

Colin felt so numb he barely managed to speak. "That's not what I want, Janna. I want us to be a family again. I want—"

"Well, maybe you can't have what you want!" she shouted. Colin winced and turned away. In a softer voice she added to Sean, "I don't think there's anything else to say. Can I go now?"

"Do you have anything else to say?" Sean asked Colin.

Colin thought of a thousand things he wanted to say, but he knew it wouldn't make any difference. He just shook his head, and Janna got up and walked toward the door. As she opened it, he asked, "Will you come to my re-baptism?"

"Don't count on it," she said and slammed the door.

The shock Colin felt was broken only by Sean's declaration of, "I'll be there."

"Thanks," Colin managed, then nothing more was said for several minutes. "What should I do?" he finally asked.

"What do you think you should do?" Sean responded. "We've talked about her free agency. The best thing I can tell you to do, Colin, is to take it to the Lord. He can let you know if it's worth holding on. Logically, it doesn't look very promising. But there's no way of foreseeing the future. I'm starting her into some things that I believe will really make a difference in her life. But again, I can't guarantee how that will affect her feelings toward you."

Colin leaned forward and pressed both hands into his hair, praying inwardly for any grain of hope. He couldn't deny the peace he'd found with the Lord, but the cloud left between him and Janna made him wonder if he could ever find peace with himself.

"Okay, Sean, tell me one thing."

"I'll certainly try."

"What would *you* do?" Colin leaned back and looked him in the eye.

"I can't answer that for you, Colin. I'm just—"

"No, don't tell me that," Colin interrupted. "For just a minute, be my friend, not my counselor, and tell me what *you* would do. I know I have to make my own choices, but I need some grounding here. I don't even know where to start."

Sean sighed and rubbed a hand briefly over his face. "If I were you, and Janna were Tara, I'd hang on for dear life until there was absolutely nothing left to hang onto. If it were me, I don't think I could let go as long as there was even an inkling of hope. I cannot fathom living even a year without Tara, let alone eternity."

Colin filled his lungs with life-giving sustenance. "Thank you, Sean. That's all I needed to hear."

"And as your counselor," he added, "I would say: Be realistic. Listen to the Spirit. That is your key to knowing if there's any hope left."

Colin nodded, resigning himself to more waiting and wondering.

"There's one point I've been thinking about that might be in your favor," Sean said. "Statistically, in adulterous situations, more marriages end because of the dishonesty surrounding the act than the adultery itself. We can only hope that eventually Janna will realize you were never dishonest with her."

Colin nodded and reminded himself not to give up hope. The days leading up to his re-baptism were a roller coaster of emotion. At moments he felt ecstatic—so close to heaven he could almost touch it. At others he ached so much for Janna that the pain was physical. He felt as if his heart might literally break.

Saturday morning, Colin left the children with his mother to pick his brother up at the airport. He and Cameron embraced firmly as soon as he got off the plane.

"Hey," Cameron said when he pulled back, "you're looking good; much better than last Christmas when I saw you."

"Well, that's somewhat comforting," Colin chuckled.

"How's Dad?"

"Oh, he's great. He gets tired faster than he used to, but all in all, you'd never know anything ever happened."

"Well, that's what Mom tells me, but I wanted to be sure she wasn't fibbing."

"Come on," Colin said, "let's get out of here, and we can talk on the way home."

The small talk ran down as Colin eased the Suburban onto the freeway, heading south.

"I really appreciate your coming," Colin said. "It means a lot to me."

"I'm glad I could make it," Cameron answered.

"I'm sure you're wondering what happened. You can't help but be curious."

"Maybe, but it really doesn't matter any more, does it?"

"Well, as of today the sin is technically washed away, but its effect on my life will always be there. It's like a thread in my tapestry now. The trick is to learn from it and move on."

"So, you told me over the phone that you'd learned some things you wanted to tell me about. I'm here."

"Well," Colin took a deep breath, "I'm certain you can guess what happened."

"A woman?" Cameron asked gingerly.

"Yeah," Colin sighed, "it was a woman."

"Well, I didn't think that committing a felony would have provoked a separation."

Colin managed a chuckle. "I guess that depends on what kind of felony it was."

He wondered if Cameron would ask questions about what had happened specifically, but he only said, "So, tell me what you learned."

"Well, I learned that being meek and patient doesn't mean allowing someone you love to push you over the edge. There were problems in my marriage, Cam. I knew there was a lot of unresolved baggage inside of Janna, from the abuse and all, but I never expected it to come between us like that. When it did, I just couldn't handle it. Instead of taking my counselor's advice, I just . . . let the hurt and frustration get to me. I lost touch. And I fell."

"You fell hard, I take it," Cameron said.

"Yeah, I fell hard." He chuckled without humor. "Janna has this gasoline theory. She said that what I did was like throwing a match into a gasoline spill . . . that maybe we could have cleaned it up if it hadn't exploded."

"And how is Janna now?" Cameron asked, breaking an awkward silence.

"It's hard to say. I mean . . . she's come a long way since the breakdown. Sean tells me she's doing relatively well. She's making it on her own. But at this point, she still wants nothing to do with me."

"Is it going to come to divorce, then?"

"Not if I can help it," Colin insisted. "Unfortunately, I'm only one half of the decision. For the moment, I'm just hoping and praying—and holding on."

After another long silence, Cameron said, "So, what else did you learn, little brother?"

Colin felt some peace wash over his discouragement as he said, "I learned that the Atonement is real. I never thought I could say this, but I'm actually glad that I was excommunicated. I needed a clean break; a fresh start. I have a deeper testimony, a stronger love for the gospel, and a much broader perspective on life, and love, and relationships than I ever had before. I learned that bad choices can affect so many lives, cause so much hurt. It took me some time to realize how I'd even hurt the woman I got involved with. If Janna and I had stayed together, I doubt I would have ever talked to her again. But it was difficult to keep from contacting her when things got low. I think a part of her really believed that when I . . . got involved with her, I was ready to leave my wife. It was hard for her to understand why I would be so committed to someone who had made me so unhappy. But how do you explain something like that to a person who has no comprehension of the temple, or of eternity?"

"She's not a member, then."

"No."

"Then I assume you met her through your work."

"She's an attorney. Her office was across the hall from mine at the Salt Lake firm I was with. I'd wanted to leave that firm for months before it happened, but Janna refused to move."

Cameron sighed. "Now, that's an ironic little twist."

"Yeah," Colin said with an edge of cynicism. "The whole thing is pathetically full of irony. I realize now that I should have followed

my feelings and changed jobs in spite of Janna's reluctance. I could
have commuted. Or I could have stayed with Mom and Dad some.
Maybe the distance would have helped us work things out more
productively." Colin shrugged. "But there's no good in speculating
over such things now."

"But hey," Cameron said cheerfully, "today's the beginning of
the rest of your life. You're starting over."

Colin smiled over at his brother. "I'm starting over. I only wish
I could start over with my wife. I wonder how many mistakes I'll have
to make before I learn how to do it right."

"Sounds to me like you've learned quite a bit about doing it right."

"I guess I have."

Colin felt a nervous excitement consuming him as the hour of
his re-baptism approached. But thoughts of Janna hovered in the
back of his mind, making the entire experience bittersweet. Carl
offered a prayer before they left for the church, and in it he prayed
that Janna's heart would be softened. The prayer stuck with Colin as
the meeting commenced. Matthew held his hand while they listened
to the bishop talk a few minutes about the glory of repentance and
forgiveness. Colin wished that Janna could hear this. He glanced
down the row to see his parents each holding one of the girls. His
brother sat at his side, dressed in white, as he was. Sean was there, as
he'd promised. But Janna's absence was starkly evident, and he
couldn't help feeling the heartache.

When he and Cameron stood up to go into the font, Colin
scanned the room. No Janna. Concentrating on the moment, he swallowed his disappointment and stepped into the water, trying to
comprehend what this meant to him. *He'd come so far.* In a way, the
time seemed to have gone quickly, and in the eternal perspective, it
was incredibly brief. Colin reminded himself that this was between
him and his Father in Heaven. As Cameron took hold of his wrist and
raised his arm to the square, Colin closed his eyes and surrendered
himself to the Spirit that surrounded him and filled him to the core.

Colin felt warmth almost literally encompass him as he came up
out of the water. He wiped the water from his eyes and embraced his
brother, then he saw Cameron discreetly motion with his head. Colin
turned to see Janna standing just behind Matthew at the edge of the

font. His joy became full-blown with heart-pounding reality as their eyes met. It was impossible to tell where her thoughts were. *But she had come.* That alone gave him hope.

Colin felt a fresh nervousness as he changed into dry clothes to be confirmed. He combed his wet hair back off his face and returned to where the family was waiting. He was greeted with hugs and handshakes, but Janna was gone. He couldn't deny his disappointment, but he reminded himself that his prayers had been answered. She had seen him come up out of that water, his sins against her washed away.

Colin was confirmed by his father, with Sean, Cameron, and the bishop assisting. He couldn't hold the tears back as he was given back the gift he had lost. Then his father went on with a personal blessing, admonishing him to stay close to the Spirit and stick to the guidelines carefully, as Satan would work especially hard to drag him back down in the coming year as he worked toward returning to the temple. He was blessed with the strength and fortitude he would need to get through the difficult months ahead, and he was told that God was mindful of his struggles, and that his sins were indeed forgiven.

Colin heard his father hesitate. In the moments of silence, he tried to comprehend the joy of being given such promises from his Father in Heaven personally, and at the same time, he wondered what was meant by *the difficult months ahead.* He was almost startled when his father began to speak again, saying in an unsteady voice, "And I promise you that as you remain faithful, you will be blessed with the desire of your heart, to be reunited with your wife, where the two of you will share joy beyond earthly comprehension."

When the blessing was finished, everyone but the little girls had tears in their eyes; even Matthew was crying. Colin just held his son close and tried to comprehend the promise he'd just been given, and what it meant to all of them.

The following day, Cameron went to church with him and the children. Taking the sacrament moved Colin to his usual overflow of tears. He'd never felt so grateful for anything in his life as what the Atonement meant to him in that moment.

As the testimony portion of the meeting commenced, Colin wanted desperately to stand up and publicly express all he was feeling. But he wondered if it was right to be so open about it. Of course, he could bear his testimony without being specific. As his heart began to pound, however, he knew that it was important for him to say the things in his heart. He was just getting up the courage to stand and walk up to the podium when Matthew did just that. Colin did the same, getting a nod from his brother to indicate he'd keep the girls under control.

Colin sat by Matthew in the choir seats while they waited for the woman at the podium to finish. Their eyes met. Matthew squeezed his hand. Colin couldn't believe how much he loved his son. He wondered what he would have done without him through all of this.

Colin listened with growing emotion and humility as Matthew stood up and said that he knew the Church was true because his father had proven that it was. He said that he was proud of his father, and he was grateful for his good example, while Colin became so emotional he wondered how he would ever stand up and be able to speak at all. He was hoping that someone else might come up and go ahead of him. But as Matthew walked past him to go sit with his sisters, Colin realized there was no one else on the stand besides the bishopric. He said a quick prayer, took a deep breath, and moved to the pulpit, taking hold of it firmly on both sides to keep from shaking.

"That was my son," he said with pleasure. "If I had known he was going to say all that stuff to make me cry, I would have made him let me go first."

The audience gave a little chuckle. That was a good sign. He cleared his throat and wondered where to begin. "Bear with me," he said, and took a moment to compose himself. In a clear, steady voice he said, "We've been in this ward for several months, since we bought the house we're living in. And I'm grateful now for the opportunity to stand up here and tell you how thankful I am for the fellowship you have given me, and for the help and support I've received on behalf of my children. This last year has been tough for them, even if the little ones are too young to understand what's been happening. Most of you know that my wife and I are separated. I have been especially grateful for the Primary teachers and scout leaders who have been there to help make up for some of my inadequacies in being both a mother and a father."

Colin felt like he should say something to pave the way for Janna if she were to eventually attend this ward, but he didn't know how to put it. *Help me* he prayed silently, and the words came. "You see, my wife spent some time in the hospital, and for health reasons, I have had the children the majority of the time." *There*, he thought, *that worked*. He'd implied it was a physical illness. "She's doing better now, and we're hoping and praying that we will be able to put our family back together." His composure began to slip, but he swallowed hard and put it back into place.

"I want you to know that I have a deep, firm, testimony of the truthfulness of the gospel. I know that God lives, and that he hears and answers prayers, even when we don't deserve to have them answered."

Again Colin felt his composure slipping, but it wasn't so easy to put into place this time. "I stand before you today to bear witness that the Atonement is real; that repentance is possible because we have a Savior who died for us. I have felt his love. I have felt the evidence of his forgiveness. And I am truly grateful to . . ." Colin squeezed his eyes shut and bit his lip as the emotion became too much to hold back. ". . . to have the privilege and opportunity . . ." He wiped his hand over his face and sniffed. ". . . The opportunity to partake of the sacrament, understanding and appreciating what it means more than ever before in my life."

Colin closed his testimony and returned to his seat, vaguely aware of a number of sniffles in the room. Cameron handed him a couple of tissues out of the diaper bag, then put a firm hand on his shoulder.

Following the meeting, several people shook Colin's hand, telling him they'd appreciated his testimony. A few even hugged him. But the most touching was an elderly woman who looked into his eyes, lifting a trembling hand to his face as she said, "Bless your heart, young man. Your faith has inspired me."

They went to have dinner with Colin's parents, then Colin drove his brother back to the airport. It was difficult to say good-bye, and even more difficult to express his gratitude for having him come for this occasion.

On Monday, Colin took Matthew with him to the bank. "There's something very important I need to do," Colin told his son, "and I want you to be with me." He told Matthew how he had opened a second savings account right after he had been excommunicated, and he had been putting ten percent of all his earnings into that account. With Matthew at his side, he closed the account, getting a cashier's check for the entire amount, including all of the accumulated interest. He hoped that his example would teach his son a lesson that might somehow compensate for the grievous mistakes he had made.

When they got back to the car, Colin showed Matthew the check. The boy's eyes grew wide. "Wow, Dad. This is a lot of money."

"Yes, it is." Colin looked at it a moment himself, briefly contemplating the financial struggles they'd endured through the last year. While he filled out a tithing slip, he explained to Matthew how he'd been supporting two households, paying Janna's medical bills, and dealing with all the little needs of raising children. He told his son how he'd felt it was important to send Janna flowers regularly, since it was difficult to find any other way of reminding her of his love. But each payment to the florist had been stretching his wallet. Looking at the amount that represented ten percent of a year's wages, he considered the family vacation they could take, the luxuries they could buy. But Colin knew in his heart that he'd done the right thing. And even though he had been denied the right to pay tithing for a year, he believed that even the act of setting this money aside had brought blessings into their lives.

Colin explained his feelings to Matthew as they drove to the bishop's house. After they put the little gray envelope into the bishop's hands, Colin took his son home, feeling better about himself as a father—and as a man—than he had in a long time.

In the days following Colin's baptism, he found evidence of what he'd lost by having it with him again. Through the past year he had felt much evidence of God's love for him, and the answer to many prayers. But now that his life was in order, with the gift of the Holy Ghost as his constant companion, it was easy to recognize the difference. If not for Janna's absence, he could say that he'd never been happier.

A week beyond the baptism, however, Colin felt a certain letdown. The children were gone for the weekend, and a familiar loneliness settled around him. He kept himself busy around the house and yard, and even did a little Christmas shopping. But even that was discouraging. Could he face another Christmas without Janna? He'd been told that the months ahead would be difficult. Was this just the beginning? Would it get worse before it got better? Would it *ever* get better?

And if things weren't bad enough, he answered the phone Saturday evening to hear Lily say, "Is it Mommy weekend?"

"Yes, it's Mommy weekend," he said, trying not to express his full dismay at hearing from her. "What's up?"

"I was just . . . wondering how you're doing," she said.

"I'm doing all right. And you?"

"Not bad, I guess . . . all things considered."

"You know, Lily, it's nice to hear from you, but I really shouldn't stay on."

"Why not?"

"It's just . . . not a good idea."

"Are things better with you and Janna?"

Colin winced and forced himself not to snap back. "No," he said straightly, "nothing has changed with me and Janna."

"So, why is it not a good idea?" She sounded angry. "It was apparently a good idea a few months ago."

"Well . . . you see, I've got my membership in the Church back, Lily. I have to be careful." He didn't bother trying to explain to her about how low he'd been a few months ago, and how far he'd come since. "I'm truly sorry that you've been caught up in my emotional challenges. I've always tried to be honest with you, but—"

"But talking to a woman on the phone is a sin?" she asked. "It must be something like giving a woman a ride home."

"It's not a sin, Lily. It's just . . . not a good idea. Phone calls, like rides home, can lead to . . . you know what I mean."

"Yes, I'm afraid I know all too well what you mean."

Colin hated the way disturbingly clear memories surged into his mind. *He was so lonely.* Trying to steer his thoughts elsewhere without sounding too abrupt, he said, "So, how is everything at work? Are you doing okay?"

"Work is good . . . most of the time."

"How many marriage proposals have you had?" he asked, relieved when she laughed.

"None that I know of, unless I missed something. I have been dating some, though."

"That's good," he said eagerly.

"I suppose. If you ask me, it's only convinced me that the really good ones are already snagged."

Colin told himself to get off the phone as quickly and kindly as possible. "Lily, I thought we came to a firm conclusion that we weren't right for each other."

"Well, it's difficult to be too firm on any conclusion when feelings don't go away."

Colin sighed. He really hated this. He could almost imagine Satan whispering promptings into her ear.

"Lily, I need to go. I—"

"Just promise me one thing, Colin."

"What's that?"

"If she ever gets up enough courage to just let you go and get it over with, call me. Give me a chance."

Colin thought it through quickly. "If I get a divorce, Lily, you'll be one of the first to know. I can't promise anything beyond that. In the meantime, keep dating. You'll find someone who isn't a sexist Mormon with three kids."

"But the kids look like you. I've seen pictures."

"Sort of, I guess. My mother thinks they do."

"Well, having kids around who look like you could be interesting."

"You don't think much about what they look like when they're screaming at each other over the breakfast table."

She didn't respond, and he couldn't resist saying, "I understand that you spoke to my wife."

"And where did you hear a vicious rumor like that?"

"From my wife."

"Oh," she chuckled comically, "I must have forgotten to mention it."

"Obviously. I can just imagine what the two of you had to say to each other."

"Well, don't go flattering yourself too much, Colin. It wasn't some cat fight."

"I'm sure it wasn't, but I also realize that it wasn't long after Janna had been in the hospital. I have no idea where her head was."

"She mentioned being in the hospital. She seemed to think that I already knew about it. So I pretended I did. Some kind of breakdown, I assume."

"Something like that."

"Well, if you must know, she was dignified and relatively kind, considering who she was talking to. If I had been in her shoes, I don't know that I would have been that civil. I resent the way she keeps you hanging, Colin, but I have to admit she's not what I expected. She's a beautiful woman with a lot of class."

"Yes," Colin agreed, "she is."

"In spite of that obvious hatred in her eyes for me," she added lightly.

"I know the look well," he admitted.

"Hey, that means we have something in common."

"Not funny, Lily."

She was silent for a moment, then her voice was severe. "I'm having a tough time, Colin."

"I know I'm at least partly to blame for that, but . . . I've done all I can do," Colin replied. "Keeping me in your life is only prolonging your misery. I know more than ever that whether I have Janna or not, I must have a woman who shares my religion."

"Then talk to me about your religion, Colin. Teach me."

"I can't. If you're really interested, I'll arrange for some missionaries to come and talk to you."

"Are they as adorable as you are?"

"They come in all shapes and sizes, but they all have the same answers. I have to go now, Lily."

"I love you, Colin."

"Take care of yourself," he said and hung up. Then he went to his bedroom and prayed. He prayed for Lily to find some peace in her life and get over him so he could stop being plagued by her. He prayed for Janna's heart to be softened. He prayed for hope, and strength, and the courage to just make it through another week.

CHAPTER TWELVE

"So," Sean said to Janna, who was feeling less than enthused to be in his office, "it's been more than a year since the separation. Maybe it's a good time to evaluate where you are and see where you're headed."

"Down," she snarled. "I'm headed down."

"Why?"

"I don't know. I just feel like I'm going nowhere. I really don't like my life, Sean. You tell me I've come a long way, but I don't like myself any more than I ever did. You're the one who's told me that a person who doesn't like herself has nothing to give to anyone else. So where does that leave me?"

"You *have* come a long way, Janna. But right now you are at the crest of a hill, so to speak. If you keep pushing forward, then your healing can be complete and you can put the past away for good. But if you slip back now, much of what you've been through will do little good in the long run. Whatever you do, Janna, don't slip back. In a way, I believe that's what happened before. We did a lot of counseling before you married Colin, and you made a lot of progress. But obviously it wasn't complete." He took her hand and squeezed it firmly. "I'm with you, Janna. Let me help you just a little further, and then you'll have the strength to stand on your own and make some choices about your life."

Janna sighed. "I guess I'll have to take your word for it."

"Okay," he said, "so let's talk about where you've been in the last year."

"To hell and back. Well . . . maybe I'm not back."

"And Colin? Where do you think he's been?"

"The same," she had to admit. "But I think he's already back. He seems to have passed me up . . . once again."

"What do you mean?"

"I don't want to talk about Colin," she said firmly.

"Okay, so let's talk about you."

Janna mechanically recounted the steps she'd been through since her breakdown and the healing she'd experienced. In her mind, she understood the abuse and why it had affected her behavior. But in her heart, she just felt numb and confused and unable to acknowledge that she was a woman of value who deserved to be happy. Sean got her to admit that at least part of her reason for holding back with Colin was her belief that he would be better off without her. And she had to wonder if it was better for the children to be mostly in his care.

"So, now that you've come this far," Sean said, "where do you want to go?"

"I don't know. The future just seems like a black cloud to me, and I'm afraid to step into it."

"Okay, let's look beyond the cloud. What do you see? How would you *like* to see yourself?"

"I don't know. If Colin—"

"No, this doesn't have anything to do with Colin, or your children, or anybody else. This is just you. How do *you* see yourself in the future? What kind of person do you see?"

Janna just shook her head in frustration. Was she so screwed up that she couldn't even define a goal?

"Let's try it this way. What is one of your biggest fears about the future?"

"There are so many, I don't know where to start."

"The biggest."

That was easy. "Facing Russell when he gets out of prison. I know he'll find me. Maybe this time he'll kill me. Maybe that's why all of this just seems like a waste of time."

"How do you see yourself in Russell's presence, Janna?"

As she tried to put words to the image in her mind, enough pain welled up to convince her that she hadn't dealt with all of it yet. Tears accompanied her answer. "I see myself curled up on the floor, my arms over my head, screaming and begging, just praying that he'll stop hurting me."

"In a word?" Sean asked. When she couldn't answer, he provided, "Victim?"

Janna nodded. "That seems to cover it."

"So, how would you *like* to be when you face Russell? If it's inevitable, then what can you do to be prepared for that moment? What kind of woman would frighten *him?*"

Janna chuckled at the absurdity. "He's not afraid of a woman; not any woman. Well, maybe a babe with a black belt in karate or something. But certainly not me."

"Why not you?" Sean asked.

"Oh, come on, Sean. You're a counselor, not a miracle worker."

Sean glanced briefly heavenward, saying lightly, "I have partners in high places." She felt dubious as he leaned forward and added, "Just hear me out. I want you to imagine yourself standing face to face with Russell Clark, your chin high, your shoulders back. There is no fear in your eyes. Your stance is confident and firm. And you tell him to his face that you will not tolerate his abuse—that you will not be a victim anymore, to him or anyone else. Then imagine *him* curled up on the floor, screaming and begging."

"Well, it's a nice thought, Sean, but I might as well imagine myself flying to the moon."

"It's been done," he said.

"Flying to the moon, or—"

"Both." Janna looked at him askance as he went on. "Janna, the minute you walked away from Russell Clark's abuse, you became a survivor. But you were harboring a lot of pain from his abuse, as well as your father's. That pain has made it difficult for you to face your fears and conquer them. And it's caused problems in your relationships. Well, you've come past a lot of the pain. Now it's time to deal with the fears. The death of a fear is terribly exciting, Janna. So I want to issue you a challenge. I want you to get beyond being a survivor. When I think of a plant that's surviving, for example, I imagine it a little shriveled or wilted, with some yellow or brown leaves, although it's showing some hint of green to indicate it's still alive. But take it further, Janna. Imagine that plant with adequate water, and sun, and nutrients. Imagine it being transplanted into a bigger pot to give it the room to grow that it needs. Imagine it *thriving*. That's how I see you, Janna. I see *you* thriving. Can you see it? Can you catch the vision? Do you think it's possible?"

Janna thought about it. "I like the vision, Sean, but I don't know if . . ."

"Right now you don't have to believe in it. You just have to *want* it. I think it's time you took some big steps forward, and I have some suggestions if you're interested. What do you say?"

Janna felt afraid of delving into *anything* new. But Sean had been good to her. He'd never let her down. Hesitantly she agreed, thinking that it certainly couldn't hurt any.

One of the first steps Janna took was to get a job. At first the thought terrified her. She'd *never* had a job. She'd given birth to Matthew soon out of high school, and had married Russell before the need to work had arisen. Colin had taken good care of her since she'd left Russell, and she'd had her divorce settlement from Russell to rely on in between. She had no college education, no skills. She didn't even know where to begin.

Janna knew that Colin would not expect her to work. He was seeing that her needs were met without complaint. But she knew he was being stretched financially, and she felt a desire to help take care of herself. Beyond that, she had to face the reality that one day he might choose to not take care of her any further. If they did get a divorce, she would have to make it on her own. And if he got custody of the children, she certainly wouldn't be getting child support.

Confused and concerned, Janna turned the problem over to the Lord in fervent prayer. If there was anything she had learned through all of this, it was that she couldn't do it without God's help. And whenever she tried, she ended up in a mess. Well, she was trying with everything she had to get out of the complicated mess her life had become. And she felt that getting a job and becoming more independent was a good place to start.

Late one evening, pondering her struggles in general, Janna found it difficult to sleep. She thumbed aimlessly through the scriptures until they fell open to a page in the Bible that was well worn. The scripture, marked in bright pink, stood out blatantly. How could she forget the first time the Lord had led her to this verse? Hebrews, chapter eleven, verse thirty. *By faith, the walls of Jericho fell down.* It had given her the courage and hope she'd needed to get away from Russell's abuse. But as she looked back over the years since, it became clear to her that the invisible walls in her life that had held her back were still standing. Yes, she'd managed to escape the walls of abuse. But their effects still stood around her, invisible barriers to becoming the woman she wanted to become.

With that verse of scripture prominent in her thoughts, Janna turned again to prayer. Looking back over the evidence in her life that, in spite of her struggles, her Father in Heaven did indeed love her, she petitioned his help in breaking down these walls once and for all. And again, she felt like getting a job was a good place to start.

Several days passed with no brilliant ideas. She had looked through the "Help Wanted" section of the newspaper over and over. She had registered with an employment service, but they hadn't sounded very hopeful when she admitted her lack of skills or experience. Way past midnight, Janna wandered through her quiet apartment, wishing she could come up with an answer. Then, when she sat down by her sewing table, it was as if a lightbulb came on inside her head. She *did* have a skill! She could sew just about *anything*. And she was good at it.

The following morning, she made some calls and found a job opening at a fabric store in the mall. She was amazed at how easily she got the job, and at how quickly she felt competent at it. While her work mostly amounted to cutting fabric for customers, she was able to answer questions and give advice that some of the others who worked there were unable to do. The only thing Janna didn't like about her job was the occasional annoying organ music coming from across the mall corridor.

Two weeks into Janna's job, her manager asked if she would be willing to make up some pattern samples to hang in the store. She gladly agreed. The manager was pleased, not only with how quickly she completed the projects, but with the quality of her work. One of the pieces she'd made was a vest with a tapestry front. It got a lot of attention, and after it hung in the store for a week, she had seven requests to do custom sewing at home.

As Janna adjusted to being a working woman, she also became involved in some classes on personal assertiveness and self-development. Gradually she began to see patterns in her struggles and fears, as well as the means to overcome them. She began to understand the phrase *Life happens from me, not to me.* As she mulled the thought over and over in her head, she realized it was the very basis for all she had suffered, and the hope for her future. She had spent most of her life like a cork, bobbing around on an ocean wave, with no control over where she ended up. But now she was beginning to understand that she had the ability within herself to *choose* the course of her life. She could choose her relationships, and she could control how she allowed others to affect her.

Janna also learned that she taught other people how to treat her by what she would allow. She could look back and see that her lack of self-worth had given others the message that she could be mistreated. As she tried to fully absorb the concept, she went back through the major turning points of her life and wondered how different it might have been if she had known all of this years ago. She reminded herself not to have regret, but to look to the future with fresh knowledge and hope.

At the same time, Janna had the opportunity to take some classes in self-defense. She had expected some elaborate training in martial arts, but she was even more impressed as the class commenced with a psychological study of "the victim." She learned that people who attack or abuse are often attracted to people who project a silent message that they will allow themselves to be victimized. She learned to carry herself with confidence and to change her body language. Then she learned some simple moves to stun an attacker enough to get away.

As Janna began to absorb all she was learning, she found herself fantasizing about meeting Russell again, rather than fearing it. Over and over again, she took her mind through the scenario. And it always ended with him on the floor, moaning in agony.

She also attempted to fantasize a happy ending for her and Colin. But at this point, any thoughts of him were tainted with all the hurt between them.

Between her hours at work and at the sewing machine, Janna went to her classes and group therapy, and she also continued to see

Sean. As her new life took shape, she began to see evidence of a self-confident, capable woman emerging. She found the time she spent with the children more enjoyable, and she thoroughly enjoyed telling Colin that he didn't need to give her any more money.

"What do you mean?" he demanded over the phone.

"Well, you're already paying rent on the apartment and taking care of the utilities. There is no need to give me any extra money. I'm sure you can use it."

"Yes, but—"

"I have a job, Colin," she said, and silence followed. She could almost literally feel his surprise coming through the phone line.

"I see," he finally said.

"Is there a problem with that?"

"No," he insisted. "No, not at all. I just . . ."

"Anyway," she went on before he could say something that would make her angry, "I want you to know I really appreciate all you're doing for me. But don't send me any more money. Use it on the kids."

Later, Matthew told Janna that Colin had said he thought it was good for her to be working. He just hoped she wouldn't become too independent.

"I think he wants you to need him," Matthew said.

Janna made no comment. She *did* need Colin. She simply wasn't prepared to admit it. But Sean had once suggested that it might be easier for her to make future choices if she could do so without relying on Colin's financial support. Staying with a man out of fear for survival wasn't acceptable. She knew that well enough.

Janna had been working at the mall nearly a month when she became acquainted with Hilary Smith. Hilary worked down the corridor a short distance in a bookstore where Janna often browsed on her breaks. She was pleasantly surprised the first time Hilary arranged getting a break at the same time and offered to buy her a lemonade. Hilary was so much younger than Janna that she was surprised they could have so much to talk about. She came from a small town about an hour south of Provo, and was attending her freshman year at BYU. Sharing breaks quickly became a habit, and then they began going to movies together. Hilary was waiting for a missionary, and Janna was married to a man she never saw, so they found the arrangement agreeable.

Hilary quit her job at the mall when she was offered a job teaching dance lessons. Janna occasionally met her at the studio, where she enjoyed watching the different classes. She especially liked watching the ballet. When Hilary first suggested that Janna take some lessons, she laughed. But Hilary finally talked Janna into it, and she found it was an enjoyable way to exercise. It also added to the positive changes she was making in her life.

The first Thursday of December, Janna worked vigorously, trying not to think about the upcoming holidays—not to mention Matthew's birthday. The prospect of both made the situation between her and Colin all the more difficult. She was squeezing a bolt of fabric into place when a masculine voice inquired, "Could you direct me to the flannel?"

Janna turned to see a well-dressed man who reminded her somehow of a Viking—blond hair, blue eyes, and something about his looks that spoke of Scandinavian ancestry.

"Uh . . . ," she stammered then turned abruptly, pointing in the appropriate direction, "over there, just past the broadcloth."

"Broadcloth?" he echoed as if he had no idea what she meant.

Janna sighed. Men were generally as lost in a fabric store as women would be looking for hunting and fishing supplies.

"I'll show you," she said, leading the way. Before she could get away, he asked her specific questions about the fabric, telling her that he was picking it up for his grandmother, who was crocheting the edges of flannel baby blankets for her grandchildren.

Janna didn't give the encounter another thought until the following day when he returned, greeting her with a cheerful, "Hi. How are you?"

"I'm fine," she replied. "Did you need something?"

"I was just wondering if I could buy you a muffin or some-thing." He glanced at his watch. "Do you ever take breaks or—"

"Of course I do, but . . ." Janna was taken so off guard she didn't know what to say.

"Well, what do you say?"

"I . . . uh . . . well . . . I don't even know your name."

"Paul," he said. "And you are Janna . . . according to your name tag."

"Well," she glanced away and pretended to be busy, "it's a pleasure to meet you, Paul. But I'm married."

"You're not wearing a ring," he said.

Again Janna was taken off guard. She knew from the things she was learning about assertiveness that it would take little effort to make it clear to him she wasn't interested. But in truth, she was intrigued with Paul. And the thought of some positive male attention was certainly appealing.

"I'm . . . separated," she admitted. "I'm not sure at this point which way it's going to go."

"Oh, I see," he said. "Well, I certainly don't want to put you on the spot. But I would like to buy you a muffin."

Janna consented to take a break with Paul, and learned over hot chocolate and a muffin that he was divorced. He had two children whom he saw regularly.

"And where do you work?" she asked.

"I sell pianos and organs," he stated, "just across the hall from where you work."

"Oh," she laughed softly, "is that you playing that annoying music with—" She stopped when he looked stunned, then he laughed with her.

"Yes," he admitted, "it's me. And yes, it *is* annoying."

Taking breaks with Paul quickly became a habit, which was nice since Hilary had quit working at the mall. She enjoyed his friendship, and found that she really liked him. He was a perfect gentleman, and didn't pry about her situation, for which she was grateful.

A week after she met Paul, Janna left work at the end of her shift, only to find that the convertible wouldn't start. She went back inside to call Nancy, but there was no answer, and she didn't want to call Colin. She was contemplating calling for a cab when Paul appeared.

"I thought you left," he said.

"I did. But my car won't start."

He offered to give her a ride home, and she gladly accepted. He looked at the car before they left and declared that it appeared to be the battery. He called later that evening to tell her that he'd picked up a new battery for her, and he'd be glad to pick her up for work the next morning and put the battery in the car.

Janna had no desire to get involved with another man—especially since she was still married and she knew it wasn't appropriate. Still, she couldn't deny being grateful for Paul's help; it spared her having to call on Colin. And she found Paul's company enjoyable. They began talking on the phone occasionally, which filled some empty hours. His attention couldn't help but make her feel better about herself, when she'd felt so worthless and unattractive for so long. All in all, Janna had to admit that things were looking up. And she was extremely blessed.

* * * * *

Colin felt especially gloomy as he began a session with Sean. The holidays were approaching, and he wasn't certain if he could bear spending them without Janna—again. Sean suggested they concentrate on how far he'd come, rather than on the uncertainty of the future.

"Okay," Sean said, "so go back to, say . . . a month before you got involved with Lily. What would you do differently?"

Colin was surprised at how easily he was able to answer that. "I would follow your advice and get a separation—not because I wanted to be living under a different roof, but because it would have distanced me from the problems and the emotions, and it would have let Janna know I was serious about not putting up with her abuse. And I had tried everything else. I knew in my heart that I was supposed to change jobs and move, but she wouldn't do it. I should have done it anyway. Under the circumstances, I believe it would have been the right thing to do. If I had listened to what the Spirit was telling me, I never would have had any opportunity to get involved with Lily. A separation from Janna would have given me the chance to be in control of my own life in spite of her struggles. I could have put my full effort into solving the problems between us and letting her know I loved her, without this horrible mess making things worse."

"And what if she had chosen divorce, even then?"

"It's like you said, I can't make her choices, but I could not live my life like that. I deserve better."

"You've come a long way, Colin."

"Have I?" He chuckled bitterly and walked to the window, pushing his hands into his pockets. "Then why do I feel so lost and helpless?"

"Helpless, really? Or just lonely?"

"Who knows?"

"And what can you do about that?"

"I guess that's in Janna's hands."

"And what if Janna chooses a life without you?"

Colin turned to face him. "Do you think she will? I mean, seriously, Sean. Where do you think her head is?"

"I honestly don't know, Colin. She's doing beautifully. She's come far. But she's having trouble with this adultery thing. I don't know if she can let it go or not."

Colin sighed and hung his head.

"I have some thoughts about the situation that I'd like to share with you," Sean went on, "even though they go beyond the normal boundaries of being your therapist. Right now, I think the answers you're looking for are more spiritual than psychological."

Colin nodded to indicate he was listening.

"You know, Colin, God knows the outcome. What does the Spirit tell you to do?"

"I keep feeling like I should hang on, but then sometimes I wonder if I'm just being stubborn, or if I'm really capable of feeling anything at all. I wish I could go to the temple, but I can't. It's just so blasted . . . *hard.*"

Sean was quiet for a minute. "Colin, do you remember that blessing you were given when you were confirmed?"

Colin nodded. "I was told there were difficult months ahead. Well, it's been months, and it's still difficult."

"And you were promised that you would have the desire of your heart, to be reunited with your wife."

"In this life?" Colin asked cynically. "And what if her free agency counters the desires of my heart?"

"My opinion? Eventually it would cease to be the desire of your heart. And you would find peace."

Colin sighed. He didn't like the way this was sounding. "How can God possibly know the outcome, Sean, if we have our free agency? I don't understand that."

"Can I give you an analogy?"

"I wish you would," he retorted, wondering how Sean managed to stay calm when Colin was often less than kind in these conversations.

"If I offer my children a choice between spinach and bubble gum, what are they going to choose?"

"It's obvious, of course."

"Okay, but let's fine-tune it a little. Let's say I offer my children a choice between rice and mashed potatoes. What will it be?" He paused. "You don't know, because you don't know my children. But you know *your* children. I have a daughter who would eat mashed potatoes over just about anything. I have a son who hates potatoes of any kind; it's his way of declaring his independence. They are both children of the same parents, raised in the same environment. But I know their differences, and I can predict the outcome of their choices. Our Father in Heaven knows us far more intimately than we know our earthly children. He knows how we will respond to our choices. We have our free agency, but he knows the outcome. It's as simple as that."

Colin had to admit, "That makes sense."

"And does that perhaps make it easier to believe the Spirit can help you prepare for the future?"

Colin nodded. He was thoughtful a minute, then asked, "So, did God know I was going to commit adultery?"

"A series of choices led up to it. Knowing your background, your personality, your struggles, I would guess, in my own inadequacy, that God knew it would happen. But perhaps God also knew that once it happened, you had the strength to make it back and become a stronger, better person than before."

"A stronger, better person . . . without my wife. I know I need to fast and pray about this—to see if I need to keep holding on. But I can't comprehend being without her, Sean. What if she can't get past it and forgive me?"

"So what if she can't, Colin? Then what?"

"I don't know. That's why I asked you!"

"Is there a future with Lily?"

Another bitter laugh erupted. "No, not even close. I considered it; we even talked about it. I just don't love her, and even if I did, I don't think we could make it work. It's difficult for me to imagine being with anyone but Janna."

"You and Lily have come far, too."

"What do you mean by that?" He felt defensive at the suggestion.

"I mean . . . you've made restitution with her, haven't you? There's no bitterness or anger directed toward her. You don't want to live your life with this taboo subject hanging over your head, do you? Every time something comes up to remind you, do you want to feel uneasy? Well, I don't think you will. You've dealt with it . . . for the most part, anyway. It will take time to be complete."

"I suppose."

"So, what did you learn from Lily? Did something good come out of your relationship with her?"

Colin leaned against the window sill and folded his arms. "You're joking, right? We're talking about *adultery*, Sean. We're talking about the most hellish experience of my life."

"Yes, we are. And the more time passes, the more that experience becomes a part of who and what you are. As I've said before, is it possible to pull a thread out of our lives and not have the tapestry become unraveled? Like it or not, Lily Greene has become a thread in your tapestry. Is it possible to separate the sin from the strength you've gained, the humility, the wisdom? I know you've come a long way, and you've learned a lot. But I'm wondering what you learned from Lily. They say that each human encounter leaves an impression; some good, some bad. But even the bad things can teach us something good. Is there anything you learned from Lily?"

As Colin thought about it, he realized there *was* something. And he felt suddenly grateful for the opportunity to admit it aloud in a situation where he wouldn't be judged or condemned. If he was going to be at peace with this, he had to understand it—all of it.

"I assume you learned something," Sean said.

"Yeah, I think I did."

"Something you don't want to talk about?"

"Something that maybe I should be ashamed to admit."

"You're not going to embarrass me, Colin."

"Yeah, well, I might embarrass myself." He cleared his throat and just said it. "You see, Sean, I learned something from my experience with Lily that put other aspects of my life into perspective. I think there was so much guilt associated with it that I couldn't acknowledge it for a long time. But the sin is wiped clean now, and like you've said, I have to understand it."

He was silent for a minute, and Sean said, "That's all true, but you still haven't told me what you learned."

"I realized that intimacy between a man and a woman could be . . . well, let me put it this way. The experience with Lily made me realize that the problems between Janna and me had always been there. It was never quite right. I look back now, and I can see how guarded she always was, how distant—like she didn't really want to be involved, didn't want to be there. Oh, I mean . . . we had our moments. The love was there; I could feel . . . the spiritual unity, the commitment, the rightness of our intimacy because it was within marriage. But it ended there. Emotionally, physically, she just wasn't there."

"And with Lily?" Sean asked.

Colin sighed. "I really hate this."

"Hate what?"

"This comparison thing. How can I possibly compare my marriage to a sinful encounter and not—"

"Why don't you get the comparison over with, and then you can analyze it. And with Lily?" he repeated.

"I really enjoyed it, Sean—at least for the moment." He paused, then added, "I can't believe I just admitted that."

"Admitted what?"

"That I enjoyed committing adultery."

"Did you enjoy the consequences?"

Colin chuckled at the absurdity of the question. There was no need to answer. Sean knew better than anyone the hell of what he'd been through because of his brief moments with Lily. "Enjoyable or not," Colin said, "if I could have foreseen the repercussions, I never could have gone through with it."

"That's just it, Colin. When we sin, we lose control of the outcome."

"Haven't we said this before?" Colin asked, certain they'd shared a similar conversation years ago in discussing his immorality with Janna in his youth. "What will it take to teach me what I need to learn?"

"True repentance is when you face yourself, Colin. I think you've done that. I think you're learning. And that's what we were talking about—what you learned from Lily."

"Well . . . she was *with* me, Sean. I was everything to Lily, if only for an hour. And it made me realize . . ." Emotion rose up to accompany the raw truth into the open. "I realized that I had *never* been everything to Janna."

"Do you know why?" Sean asked with obvious empathy.

"The abuse?"

"Yes, the abuse," Sean said. "But there is far more to it than even *I* had imagined."

Colin turned abruptly to look at him. "What are you saying?"

"Maybe you should sit down," Sean said. "If there's any possibility of your ever having a relationship with Janna again, I think you need to know what she's been dealing with."

Colin moved unsteadily into a chair and told himself not to let his emotions get the better of him.

"There's no reason for you to know the details, Colin. But it's important for you to realize why she couldn't cope or function in a marriage relationship. You see, when she talked to me at the age of fifteen, she told me about her father's abuse, and we talked over the way it affected her. She seemed to thrive on my validation that it wasn't her fault, and that she wasn't dirty or wicked because of it. I assumed it was taken care of for the most part; but I had to admit that when we started counseling together prior to her divorce, I could see signs that it hadn't been dealt with. It has affected her perception and her choices far too much. I don't know if I was just too inexperienced at the time to pick up on the fact that she was only scraping the surface, or if her determination to not go any deeper was just too strong. Whatever it was, she simply didn't face the whole truth of it. The bottom line is that a person can't heal what they haven't felt—and it doesn't get felt while it's buried alive in the soul, festering and becoming toxic."

Sean shifted in his seat, and his expression became even more severe. "Colin, following Janna's breakdown, I was eventually able to get to the heart of it. If not for the breakdown, I'm not sure she would have ever committed to going that deep. But she was forced to get extensive help, and I could work with her more regularly."

"So, what's the truth of it?" Colin asked when Sean hesitated a little too long.

"Janna's abuse was intensely defiling and degrading. She told me things that I had never comprehended, Colin. That's one of the hardest things about my job—being able to cope with the images I have to see in order to help victims heal. And I'm not going to inflict those images on you. Janna has dealt with it now; those old wounds have been opened, cleaned out, and they're healing. But you have to understand what was going on inside of her every time you touched her. She felt, in a way, as if she was betraying you by the thoughts in her head, which only amplified the problem. But all things considered, she is doing remarkably well with it. We've also gone extensively through the abuse added by her first husband."

"Why does it just add on like that? Why would Janna even marry someone like him?"

"Of course, he was suave. But the truth is, people project unspoken messages. Janna's had a "victim" demeanor ever since her father made her a victim. Russell Clark, having an abusive personality, was drawn to her projection."

"So, why was *I* attracted to her?"

"That's for you to decide, but my guess is that you saw something deeper. You saw her potential. It was the *real* Janna you fell in love with, and you had a way of coaxing it out into the open.

"As I was saying," Sean continued, "there are two reasons why you need to know about the extent of the abuse. First of all, you need to understand the reasons behind her struggles with you. And secondly, if you do get back together, you need to understand that in spite of all the healing, it could still affect her perception of an intimate relationship."

When Colin made no response, Sean asked, "What's troubling you?"

"If I had known . . . would it have made a difference?"

"You *did* know, Colin. You knew she'd been abused. You knew there were things going on in her head that had nothing to do with you. The fact is, she was abusing *you*, and whatever she might have suffered does not justify passing it on. She understands that now, and you need to understand it, too. She *hurt* you, Colin. So learn from this; understand it. But don't let it dredge up regret and guilt, and don't try to make it invalidate *your* feelings. Otherwise, you're just encouraging the cycle to continue."

Sean leaned forward and pressed his fingers together. "Abuse is an amazing thing, Colin. Janna's life is a classic example of the horrible things that can result. You take a two-week period in her life, when her father was staying in the home, and then try to comprehend the lives it's affected. Like a pebble thrown into a pond, the abuse and heartache and dysfunction just ripple outward endlessly— until someone puts up a firm bank at the water's edge and forces it to stop. You're that someone, Colin. Even if you and Janna don't make it together, you can still show her through the years that you won't allow the abuse to damn you, or your children, or her. You can press forward with understanding and wisdom, and stop the cycles. Like you, my personal hope is that the two of you can get back together. With what you've both learned, you could accomplish great things. But that remains to be seen."

Following a lengthy silence, Sean said, "So, now that we've talked through some things, where is your head?"

"I have to stick it out. Everything inside of me tells me we're supposed to be together, and I can't give up."

Sean smiled. "My prayers are with you, kid."

The conversation eased into small talk before the session ended. On the way out, Colin said, "You're a genius, Sean. I don't know what I'd ever do without you."

"I'm glad I could help. But hey," he chuckled, "you're paying for my daughter's braces."

Colin laughed. "Glad I could help."

Colin came away feeling significantly closer to healing and understanding. But he still felt down. He realized through the evening that Matthew was in a similar mood. While they were clearing the table together, he attempted to perk him up.

"Your birthday's coming up, Matthew. Have you thought about what you would like to do?"

"Yeah, I've thought about it," he said firmly. "But I don't think it'll go over."

They were interrupted as the girls, fighting over a toy in the front room, both started to cry. Colin hurried to break it up and distract them with something else to play with, then he hunted down Matthew to continue their conversation.

"Why won't it go over?" Colin asked. "Is it expensive?"

"No, it's free."

"Okay," Colin drawled. "What is it?"

Matthew looked up at him, saying cautiously, "I want to have you and Mom together for my birthday party."

Colin took a deep breath and reminded himself to keep his own emotions out of this. "That would be great, Matt, but I don't think she'll go for it. *I* certainly don't have a problem with it, but . . . well, I guess you'll have to talk to your mother."

"If she says it's okay, will you—"

"I'll go along with whatever she says, Matthew." Colin added, more to himself, "It's the story of my life."

Matthew's mood only seemed to worsen through the remainder of the evening. As Colin thought about it, he realized Matthew had seemed despondent since he'd returned the previous evening from a weekend with his mother. When the girls were asleep, Colin went to Matthew's room and sat on the edge of the bed while Matthew was putting away his clean clothes. He came right out and asked, "What's up, buddy? Something's obviously bothering you. Maybe we should talk about it."

Matthew said nothing.

"Did something happen with your mom?"

"No, not really. I mean . . . I think she's doing good. We had fun and everything. She just spent some time Saturday on the phone. And again Sunday morning."

"Was she rude to you, or—"

"No, she just . . ." He stopped and looked at Colin skeptically.

"She just what?" he demanded.

"She was talking to some guy, Dad. Talking and laughing like she hasn't since . . ."

Their eyes met briefly as the realization began to sink in. Then Matthew turned and slammed a drawer closed.

"What guy?" Colin squeaked.

"What are you going to do? Go beat him up or something?"

"Don't be ridiculous," Colin insisted. "What guy?"

"All I know is that his name is Paul. He works at the mall, too. He gave her a ride home when the car wouldn't start, and—"

"What?" Colin nearly shouted as a similar memory slapped him right between the eyes. "I didn't even know anything was wrong with the car."

"It was the battery. I guess Paul fixed it for her."

"What?" Colin bellowed again.

"It won't do any good to get ticked off about it, Dad. You're the one who keeps telling me that she's got to make her own choices."

Colin absorbed his son's words of wisdom and swallowed hard. While he was attempting to come up with an appropriate response, Matthew continued.

"It's just that . . . she's still married to you, right?"

Colin nodded.

"I just don't want her to . . ." Matthew got emotional. ". . . To get a divorce."

Colin hugged his son tightly and murmured, "Neither do I, Matthew. Neither do I."

Matthew pulled back and looked his father in the eye. "I was just hoping if you guys got together for my birthday, then maybe she'd remember . . ."

Colin nodded. "We could hope," was all he said. But he hardly slept that night while thoughts of Janna becoming involved with another man catapulted through his mind. If nothing else, it certainly was a lesson in empathy. He couldn't comprehend how it might feel to imagine her going to bed with another man. He thought of what he'd put her through and cried into his pillow. It seemed he was going to lose her. And he wasn't certain he could accept it.

CHAPTER THIRTEEN

*N*othing more was said about Matthew's birthday until Janna called three days before the date. Colin answered and immediately said, "Matthew's not here. Do you want him to call you or—"

"I need to talk to *you,*" she said tersely.

"Ooh," Colin said dramatically. "What's the occasion?"

"The occasion is our son's birthday. He insists he doesn't want any presents. He just wants to have us together for the party. We argued for over an hour, but he won't bend. So, I guess we're having it here at 6:30. I've picked up that game he wanted, and some clothes. Whatever you want to get him is up to you. I'll call your parents and invite them."

Colin was silent for a long moment. Once he got past the initial shock, he wasn't certain if he was looking forward to this or dreading it. "Okay," he said. "Can I bring anything? I can bring the cake or—"

"I've got all of that covered," she insisted. "I'll see you Thursday." She hung up without a good-bye.

Through the following days, time seemed to drag as Colin was assaulted with butterflies every time he thought of spending Thursday evening at the apartment with Janna and the children. He tried to recall the last time they'd all been in a room together for more than half a minute. He honestly couldn't remember.

When they finally arrived, just a little after six-thirty, Matthew went in without knocking, and the girls scurried after him. Colin stood by the door, aware that Janna was in the kitchen. Crepe paper and balloons were strung from the ceiling, just the way Janna had always done for birthdays. The children were obviously very much at home here, but Colin felt like a stranger. He could hear Janna greeting the kids and talking with them. He became so absorbed in listening to her voice that he was startled when she appeared in the little front room.

"Oh, hi," she said, and for a moment he could almost believe that she was glad to see him. "Uh . . ." She glanced away, appearing as uncomfortable as he felt. "You can put those over there," she said, referring to the gifts he was holding. "Make yourself at home," she added, while something in her body language seemed to add *but not too much.*

"Thank you," he said and set the gifts down.

Colin's parents arrived a minute later, which eased the tension somewhat. They seemed almost as comfortable here as the children. Colin felt like the only outsider. He relaxed a little as the party got underway. It was difficult to keep from watching Janna as Matthew opened his gifts. She looked so beautiful, and her laughter made his heart beat faster. Just being in the same room with her made him ache to hold her.

Colin helped clean up the wrappings when the gifts had been opened, then he lit the candles on the cake. He tried not to think how his life could always be this way if Janna chose to divorce him. They would see each other only on such occasions. He felt certain he couldn't bear it.

When Colin's parents left, the children asked if they had to go now, too. "That's up to your mother," he said, glancing cautiously toward her.

"The kids are having fun," she said without looking at Colin. "Let them play."

She went into the kitchen, and Colin impulsively followed. "Here, let me help you," he said. Without her permission, he started rinsing the residue of cake and ice cream off the children's dishes. He turned on the garbage disposal, well aware of Janna wiping off the counter.

"Ouch!" she cried, then mumbled something under her breath.

Colin flipped off the disposal switch. "What happened?"

"I . . . broke a glass earlier. I thought I had it all cleaned up, but . . . Oh, my." She looked at her finger with concern.

"Let me see that," Colin insisted, taking her hand into his. A large sliver of glass was sticking out of the end of her finger. It wasn't difficult to pull it out, then he tossed it into the garbage. "Ooh, it must have gone deep," he said when blood oozed out of the tiny wound. He grabbed a paper towel and pressed it over her finger. Only then did he stop to realize he was holding Janna's hand. She seemed to realize it in the same moment, as her eyes rose to meet his.

"Thank you," she said.

Colin glanced back down and pulled the towel away, but fresh blood oozed out and he pressed it back over the wound. "A little pressure should stop it," he said, grateful for the excuse to hold her hand a little longer.

He met her eyes again, and his heart quickened further as he caught—however briefly—a glimpse of something he recognized. *She still loved him.* He glanced back at her hand when she looked away uneasily. He then noticed something that stabbed at his heart.

"You're not wearing your rings," he said. Had she been wearing them on their previous encounters through the past year? He honestly hadn't noticed.

Janna cleared her throat and eased her hand away. "I threw them away . . . a long time ago."

Colin shook his head. He couldn't believe it. "You threw them away?" he asked, certain he'd heard her wrong. "Your wedding rings?"

"That's right," she said with indignation. "It seemed appropriate under the circumstances."

"Janna, they were worth at least—"

"I know what they were worth, Colin—monetarily at least. But frankly, they were worth nothing to me." She began vigorously cleaning up the kitchen, as if it might make him go away.

Colin glanced down at the ring on his own finger. He'd not taken it off since the day they'd been married. The thought of Janna being out in the world without her wedding rings bothered him more than he dared admit. But it brought to mind something that bothered him even more.

"Who's Paul?" he asked.

Janna stopped what she was doing and turned to look at him. For a moment, her eyes looked guilty. Then angry.

"What difference does it make to you?" she asked.

"You're my *wife*, Janna. If you're seeing another man, it makes a great deal of difference to me."

"I am not *seeing* anybody," she insisted.

"According to Matthew, you've been—"

"Your son needs to learn to mind his own business," she snapped.

"*Our* son knows that as long as we are married, you shouldn't be—"

"You've got a lot of nerve, Colin Trevor," she growled quietly, obviously hoping to keep the children oblivious to their arguing. "I can't believe that *you* would actually lecture me about spending time with another man."

"At least I was honest about it," he retorted. "I wasn't sneaking around, pretending to be something I wasn't."

"What on earth are you implying?"

"I'm not implying anything. I'm telling you that you are my *wife*. If you can't live with that, then for the love of heaven, get a divorce and get it over with."

"If you want a divorce, Colin, then by all means . . ."

"I *don't* want a divorce, Janna. I want us to be a family again. You're the one who's running around with some other guy, trying to pretend you're not committed elsewhere."

"You have no idea what you're talking about, Colin!"

"Has he kissed you?" Colin demanded.

"So what if he has?" she retorted, taking a step toward him. Looking directly into his eyes, she snarled, "Maybe he *has* kissed me, Colin. Maybe he's even spent the night. Why don't you go home and think about that? Think about it good and hard. And maybe . . . just maybe . . . you'll have an inkling of what you've put me through."

Colin attempted to swallow his emotion. He didn't want to admit that he'd already thought about it—far too much. He couldn't deny the point she'd made. But at the same time, he felt certain she was missing another very important point.

"I'll think about it, Janna. But I want you to think about something, too. If it's vengeance you're after, it's not worth it. Take it from me. *Nothing* is worth breaking those covenants, Janna. *Nothing*."

Colin hurried out of the kitchen and gathered up the children. He thanked Janna for her hospitality, trying to ignore the anger in her eyes. Then he took the children home and put them to bed.

"I guess it didn't turn out so good," Matthew said when Colin sat on the edge of his bed. "I heard you and Mom fighting."

"Well, it was nice for us to be together for your party, Matthew—even if it didn't end so well. But maybe some of the things we said needed to be said. I don't know."

"Are you going to get a divorce?" he asked.

"I don't know, Matthew. I just don't know."

* * * * *

Janna hardly slept at all the night of Matthew's birthday, and she went to work the following day in an especially foul mood.

"Whoa, you don't look so good." Paul's voice startled her from vehemently straightening a table of fabric remnants. "Something wrong?"

"Everything's wrong," she snapped. Then she took a deep breath and forced a smile. "I'm sorry. It has nothing to do with you." She sighed. "Well . . . maybe it does."

"I don't understand," he replied softly.

"Well . . . it's kind of a long story. And I'm not sure you'd want to hear it . . . even if I wanted to talk to you about it."

"Sure I do," he insisted. "How about over lunch?"

Janna's conscience struggled with her battered emotions for just a moment before she smiled. "I'd love to."

Over a burger and fries, Paul opened it back up. "Okay," he said, "so what's eating at you . . . that has something to do with me?"

Janna took a deep breath. "Well, my husband came over last night . . . for our son's birthday."

"And?"

"It seems that Matthew mentioned something to him . . . about you. He wasn't very happy about it."

"You're separated, Janna."

"Yes, but I'm still married. In essence, he told me I needed to make up my mind. Sooner or later, I've either got to reconcile with him . . . or get a divorce."

Janna's heart quickened at the way Paul took her hand and leaned closer to her, asking in a smooth voice, "And what do you want, Janna?"

"I don't know, Paul. That's the problem, I guess."

Beyond that, she refused to talk about it any further. She had a decision to make, but it had nothing to do with Paul. She avoided seeing him after that, insisting that they were getting a little too close for the circumstances. He seemed to respect her boundaries, but a day hardly passed when he didn't pop up in the fabric store to remind her of his interest. As the holidays crept closer, Janna's mind became consumed with a reality she couldn't keep ignoring. She had to get on with her life, one way or another. She wondered every day if she should just file for a divorce and get it over with.

In Janna's frame of mind, she was dismayed to realize that Matthew wanted the same thing for Christmas that he'd wanted for his birthday. "I don't know," she retaliated, "how you could possibly expect your father and me to spend the holiday together, Matthew, when it ended in disaster last time. Is that what you want . . . to have your parents arguing and—"

"I want us to be together for Christmas," Matthew insisted. "That's all."

Janna thought it over and reasoned that even if they were going to divorce, they needed to learn to be on civil terms for the sake of the children. She asked Matthew to invite Colin over for dinner on Christmas Eve, and to tell him he was welcome to come back over in the morning to open gifts with them. When Matthew asked if they could have Christmas at the house instead of the apartment, since it was bigger, Janna insisted that it was either on her territory or not at all. Matthew didn't argue, and she was grateful. She had no desire to explain to him her apprehension about going inside the home where Colin was raising her children the majority of the time. She wasn't certain she could explain it if she had to.

Janna got off work early on the day of Christmas Eve, and became caught up in the spirit of the holiday as she prepared Christmas dinner and cleaned up the apartment. She was surprised to hear the doorbell when the children weren't expected for more than an hour. She opened the door and felt immediately disconcerted.

"Paul," she said, attempting to sound pleased. It wasn't that she didn't enjoy his company. It was just that being with him was inappropriate, and she knew it.

"Hi," he said. "I won't keep you. I just wanted to wish you a merry Christmas." He handed her a beautifully wrapped gift.

"Oh," she stammered, "you shouldn't have . . . really. I mean . . . I have nothing for you. I didn't expect you to . . ."

"Hey," he said, "my intention was not to cause you distress. I'm not expecting anything in return. I just wanted you to know I was thinking about you."

Janna reminded herself to be gracious. "Thank you," she said. "Would you like to come in for a minute?" She clarified the invitation as she closed the door behind him. "My kids and . . . my husband . . . are coming in a while. I don't think it would go over well if you were here."

Paul chuckled. "Probably not." He glanced around. "You have a nice place."

"Thank you," she said, thinking as she glanced around that she owed much of her surroundings to Colin's generosity. At times, she could almost hate him for being so good to her. It made everything so much more confusing.

Janna invited Paul to sit down, and they started talking until she lost track of the time. Then she glanced at the clock and panicked. She could well imagine what a disaster it would be if Colin arrived before Paul left. He picked up on her concern and moved graciously toward the door. But she simply wasn't prepared to have him kiss her. Her pulse quickened and something tingled inside her as their lips made contact, however briefly. It wasn't until he'd gone that she realized he'd awakened something inside her that she'd believed was long dead. Feeling somehow warmed by his affection, she sat down and opened his gift—brass candlesticks with elegant wine-colored tapers.

"Oh, they're beautiful," she said to herself. Then she smiled, wondering if she was finally making some progress toward her future. She didn't know if Paul was the right man for her. But she knew it was time to get on with her life.

* * * * *

Colin was pleased to arrive at Janna's apartment on Christmas Eve and find her in a favorable mood. She didn't seem terribly disconcerted by his presence, and he fought hard to not betray just how much her presence affected him. In reality, he felt as giddy as a teenager at his first dance. His only dismay came when he happened to notice an opened gift stuck between the couch and the end table. While Janna was in the kitchen and the children were occupied, he picked it up. Brass candlesticks and long candles. Then he noticed the tag. *Merry Christmas. With Love, Paul.*

Colin wanted to be angry as he discreetly put the gift back. But in truth, it just plain hurt. He was losing her, and he knew it. Or rather, he'd lost her a long time ago, and it was time he started accepting it.

* * * * *

When Janna finally got the children to sleep and the Christmas offering laid out, she went to her room and crawled into bed, exhausted but not sleepy. Her mind wandered back to Paul's kiss, and the same tingling sensations erupted out of nowhere. Then she reminded herself that she was a married woman with no business having such thoughts.

Struggling with her thoughts was something Janna had worked very hard on. For years her mind had been plagued by memories of abuse, and she had learned to replace those thoughts with positive things. She recalled Sean telling her that it was right and good for her to have intimate thoughts about Colin, and perhaps that was a means to help her replace the negative images. She'd never been able to do it, however, without having her thoughts intruded upon by images of Lily Greene in her husband's arms. So she'd attempted to force *any* thoughts of Colin out of her head. And now? Now, as she lay staring at the ceiling, almost wanting to think of Paul's kiss and relish the memory, all she could think of was Colin. He was her husband, but only in a technical sense. And once again she was faced with the reality that she couldn't keep him hanging on.

Janna finally drifted off to sleep having convinced herself that her thoughts of Colin were only habit. There was simply too much hurt between them to ever repair. But early on Christmas morning, the moment he walked through the door, she felt a rush of butterflies more intense than anything she'd ever experienced. She felt almost angry with him for evoking such feelings when he'd hurt her so badly.

Concentrating on the children, Janna had to admit it was nice to do Christmas this way—for their sake. Matthew's obvious pleasure at having the family together more than compensated for any tension between Colin and Janna. They didn't speak to each other beyond a few necessary exchanges. But they were both able to enjoy the children.

While the kids were playing with their new things, Colin helped Janna prepare breakfast. She didn't say much, but they were in the same room and being civil. The family sat down together to eat, then he offered to help her clean up.

"You really don't have to," she said, finding it increasingly difficult to be in the same room with him—and these feelings. But he insisted, and all she could do was try to work and keep her distance. She could almost feel him wanting to bring up the status of their relationship, and she simply didn't want to get into it. The tension eased somewhat when Colin began telling her about some things the children had been doing recently. She found herself laughing with him, then a tense silence descended and their eyes met.

Colin was trying to decide if the expression in Janna's eyes was an indication that she still loved him, or regret in knowing that they would never be able to share what they once had. Perhaps both. As the silent tension between them grew thick, she turned her back to him abruptly. Seeing her shoulders tremble, he couldn't keep from touching them.

"Janna," he whispered, "what do I have to do to convince you that I love you?"

Janna felt no defensiveness at his question; only a heartache so distinct that she had to put her hand to her chest in an effort to ease the pain.

"I know you love me, Colin. But . . ."

"But?" he pressed when she didn't finish.

While she was searching for the words to explain without provoking an argument, Colin turned her to face him, looking deep into her eyes. "I love you, Janna. Nothing else matters."

Janna held her breath as the intensity in his eyes seemed to hold some kind of power over her. She felt helpless to resist his nearness, in spite of the confusion it spurred in her.

Colin knew that kissing her was risky at best. But his need for her overruled, and he pressed his lips over hers with no thought of what her reaction might be. He heard himself moan as the reality began to sink in. While he nearly expected her to push him away and slap him, he simply wasn't prepared to feel her respond. Instantly, everything changed. They were clinging to each other, consumed with a kiss as passionate as any they'd ever shared. Hope and light filtered into Colin's every nerve. He felt warm tears trickle over his face just as he heard her whimper and realized that she was crying, too.

"Colin, please," she murmured and turned her face, but she didn't attempt to move away. "Please . . . don't do this to me."

"What am I doing, Janna? Tell me. Talk to me," he pleaded.

Janna was tempted to just leave the room and let it drop. But it was becoming increasingly evident that time was running out. She couldn't leave him waiting and wondering any longer. Gathering her courage, she reminded herself of how far she'd come. And Colin had a right to know where her head was. She settled the side of her face against his shoulder, if only to avoid his gaze.

"There were so many times," she began, "when you would hold me . . . and touch me . . . and I couldn't keep myself from thinking about . . . Russell . . . and my father. It was as if the memories of the abuse consumed me. And I felt so powerless."

Janna lifted her head to look at him, and fresh tears rolled down her face. "I've dealt with all of that now, Colin. But . . ."

"What, Janna? Tell me."

"Now . . . now . . ." She pressed a hand to her mouth as the emotion became too intense to handle. She stepped back and shook her head. In response to his obvious frustration, she finally sputtered it out. "Now . . . all I can think of . . . is *her.*"

Colin hung his head, and tears of regret surged out to join the tears of joy he'd shed only moments ago.

"I don't know if I can ever be free of it, Colin," she cried.

Colin took hold of her shoulders. "What do I have to do, Janna, to make restitution for what I've done? What?" he cried. "Tell me what I've overlooked. Tell me . . . anything. I'll do it. By heaven and earth, Janna, I need you in my life." He nearly shook her. "Tell me what to do!"

"There's nothing more you can do!" she insisted on a wave of emotion. "Has it ever occurred to you that the problem is *me*? Did it ever once cross your mind that maybe I just don't have what it takes to deal with something like this?"

"No, Janna." He tightened his hands at her shoulders. "I don't believe it. I love you. Don't you understand?"

"I love you, too!" she shouted. "But . . ."

"What?" he pleaded. "But what, Janna?"

Janna took a deep breath and struggled for a steady voice. She drew back her shoulders and mustered the courage to just say what she knew she had to say. "Maybe . . . there's just too much hurt in our past, Colin. Maybe it's just . . . not fixable."

Colin shook his head. "I don't believe it, Janna. I won't accept it. I won't!"

"Well, you've got to!" she shouted.

Colin felt his heart begin to pound before his brain fully perceived what she was getting to. "What are you saying?" he asked in a husky voice.

"I'm saying that . . . I'm not sure if there's anything left . . . to build on. I'm saying that . . . maybe it's just too late for us."

Colin refused to believe it. "How can you respond that way when I kiss you, then turn around and say there's nothing left to build on?"

Janna took a deep breath and restated her case firmly. "There's too much hurt between us, Colin. Maybe it's just too late."

She turned and left the room. And Colin managed to put that once-familiar mask of normalcy into place for the sake of the children.

When the day was over and they were finally asleep, he sat in the darkened front room of his house and ached to cry. His head pounded with unvented emotion, but it just wouldn't come. He couldn't find the motivation to go upstairs to bed, any more than he could get up and do something productive to ease his restlessness. He finally managed to turn his mind to fervent prayer, knowing it was the only positive thing he could connect with at the moment.

Around two o'clock in the morning, Colin felt an urge to write Janna a letter. He sat at the kitchen table with a notebook and wrote page after page. He poured his heart out to her concerning his feelings when he'd first met her and his intense love for her, right from the beginning. He told her of his regret for the hurt he'd caused in her life because of his weaknesses, and expressed the things about her that made him love her. He ended with a heart-felt plea concerning their future, telling her that he just didn't believe he could accept life without her.

Colin didn't finish the letter until after five a.m. He folded the many pages together and put them into an envelope that he left unsealed, thinking he might want to add to it later. Two days later, he noticed the letter still sitting on his dresser. He picked it up and held it for a moment, then realized he didn't have the heart to give it to her. He felt certain he'd been inspired to write it, but perhaps it was for him, not for her. She was well aware of his feelings, and opening his heart up again just seemed more than he could bear. If she'd made up her mind to divorce him, nothing he could say or do would change it.

The Sunday after Christmas, Matthew was ordained a deacon. It was indescribably painful for Colin to stand back while his father ordained his son, and he was unable to participate because of the choices he'd made that had denied him the right to use the priesthood. He reminded himself that in two years, when Matthew was ordained a teacher, he would be able to do it. But that seemed little consolation at the moment.

It took great effort for Colin to make it through the weeks after Christmas, expecting to be served with divorce papers any day. But he prayed and stayed close to the scriptures, hoping that, if nothing else, he would find peace.

At the end of a particularly low day, Matthew came quietly into Colin's room only a few minutes after he'd gone to bed.

"What is it, son?" Colin asked. "Is something wrong?"

"No, I just . . . wanted to give you something. I've had it for a long time . . . but you should have it."

"What is it?" Colin asked, turning on the lamp on the bedside table.

Matthew placed a small object into his father's hand. It only took a moment to realize what it was.

"Where did you get these?" he insisted, his fingers trembling as he absorbed the feel of Janna's wedding rings.

"I saw Mom throw them away . . . a long time ago. She was real mad that day. When she wasn't looking, I dug them out of the garbage and . . . well, even if you and Mom don't get back together . . . I thought you should have them."

"Thank you, Matthew," Colin said, and the boy hurried away.

Colin held the rings tightly in his fist, not certain why they gave him an abstract kind of comfort. At the moment, it was the best he could hope for.

A few days later, Colin had barely gotten the girls out of the tub when Matthew came running up the stairs to say that someone was here to see him.

"Who is it?" Colin asked.

"I don't know. He asked for my mother. When I said she wasn't here, he said he'd come back, but I told him I'd get my dad. I didn't tell him she doesn't live here."

"That's good, Matt," he said. "You help your sisters dry off, and I'll go see who it is."

Colin thought he'd probably find a salesman waiting on the porch. But everything inside of him reacted when he saw Miles Hayne standing near the door, looking around as if he was taking inventory, just as he'd done in Colin's office. It took only a moment to recall the fact that Janna's seeing her father had catapulted the family into years of misery. And why? Because the man had abused her so thoroughly that she couldn't even cope. A tangible repulsion rose into Colin's throat as he tried to comprehend how sick this man's mind was. He thought of Sean's analogy—that one pebble of abuse thrown into a pond creates seemingly endless ripples in lives and relationships. And this was the animal who had thrown the pebble. The man probably had his own abusive background, but nothing gave him the right to defile a child. Colin could think of no good reason to even attempt a civil tone of voice when he demanded, "What are you doing here?"

Miles Hayne rocked on his heels and said with a lilt of arrogance, "I told you before, young man, I have a right to see my family."

"And I told *you* to get a lawyer."

"I intend to if we can't come to an agreement. I'd like to talk to my daughter about it first."

"Well, she's not here."

"Then I'll come back."

"No," Colin said, "you won't. You will never set foot in my house again. You will never make any contact with my wife or my children. Do you understand what I'm saying, Mr. Hayne?"

The man's eyes moved beyond Colin's shoulder as he said, "There's my little darlings."

Colin turned to see the girls sitting on the bottom stair, wrapped in towels. As Matthew came down the stairs, Colin said, "Matt, take your sisters upstairs, please."

Colin watched Matthew urge them away, then he turned to their visitor as Miles Hayne said, "They're beautiful girls—much like their mother."

It only took a split second for Colin to comprehend the possible undertones of his statement. This man had sexually abused his own daughter in unthinkable ways. The thought of even allowing him in the same room with Caitlin and Mallory sent an electrical current to Colin's every nerve. He drew back a fist and hit Miles Hayne in the jaw before he consciously realized he even wanted to. Before Miles regained his footing, Colin grabbed him by the collar and slammed him against the door. Miles hissed, "You have no right to—"

"You are in *my* home, against *my* will. And that gives me a lot of rights. Why don't you sue me? Why don't you go to the police and do everything in your power to get what you think you deserve? Just give me a chance to get you in the courtroom, you filthy scum, and I *promise* you that you will get *exactly* what you deserve."

"Are you threatening me, boy?"

"You're damn right I am!" He kept hold of Miles' jacket with one hand and opened the door with the other. "Now get out of my house!"

Colin slammed the door and locked it, leaning against it to catch his breath and calm down.

"Who was *that?*" Matthew asked from the stairs. Colin wondered if his son had seen him hit their visitor and throw him out.

Knowing he had to be honest, he said, "That was your grandfather, Matthew." The boy's eyes widened. "He is your mother's father.

He left your grandmother when your mom was just a baby. He didn't come back until she was thirteen, and then he . . . he sexually abused her, Matthew. He's the biggest reason your mother has had such a hard time. And now he wants to be a part of the family, if you can imagine."

"I'm glad you hit him, Dad. You were great!"

"Yeah, well," Colin chuckled, "I don't know if I should have hit him or not, but it sure felt good."

Colin and Matthew agreed that they shouldn't say anything to Janna about her father's visit. Colin only prayed that Miles wouldn't show up again. He wasn't certain that any of them—especially Janna—could handle it.

* * * * *

As Janna lay in the darkness, staring at the ceiling, she suddenly felt more lonely than she had since she'd awakened in the hospital with the realization that she had lost her children because of a nervous breakdown. Of course, she had every hope that with time she would be able to take them on full-time again. But thinking of them now only intensified her loneliness. She wished she could just touch their little heads while they slept and know that they were in her care. Since that was impossible at the moment, she forced her thoughts elsewhere.

For no apparent reason, Janna's mind turned to her mother. It seemed like forever since Diane Hayne had died, yet she still couldn't think about her without aching. She wondered how these difficult years might have been different if she'd had her mother to lean on.

"Oh, Mother," she whispered to the darkness, "if only you were here now. Maybe you could help me understand. You always had a way of seeing the big picture." Silent tears leaked into Janna's hair. "I miss you, Mom."

It seemed that her mother's death from a sudden stroke had been the beginning of a long string of problems. How could she ever forget the way Colin took her home from the hospital that night, holding her while she cried for hours? She'd finally drifted to sleep in his arms. He was there when she woke up in the dark, and the comfort of his kiss quickly became an avenue to hide from the pain of reality. At the time it had all been so incredible, so seemingly perfect.

But from there, everything had gone from bad to worse. A few days after the funeral, they'd gone to the bishop to confess their sin; and three months later Janna had moved to Arizona to live with her aunt, leaving Colin with no idea that she was pregnant. Now her mother had been gone nearly thirteen years, and Janna's life seemed as messed up as it had ever been.

As Janna prayed for guidance and understanding, she found her mind wandering to a fantasy she'd often indulged in through her years without Colin. What if she had chosen to tell him she was pregnant, rather than running from him in fear? As she thought it through carefully, she felt a new layer of understanding settle into her mind. She could almost literally see the long-range consequences of her choice. Of course, they would have had a more difficult beginning. But Janna knew now that her mother, because she worked for a lawyer, had left her financial affairs in good order. When Janna had moved in with her aunt, Phyllis had taken over Diane's assets, and Janna had made no effort to protest. If Janna had married Colin soon after her mother's death, she felt certain that they would have inherited the house free and clear. In spite of starting out with a baby born too soon, she and Colin would have gone to the temple after a year. And rather than having layers of abuse added to her life, Janna would have had Colin's love to nurture her through the healing. She felt stunned as the picture became increasingly clear in her mind. *She'd been such a fool.* The impact on her life of a single choice was amazing.

As sleep continued to elude Janna, other choices in her life came to mind. In her marriage to Colin, she had chosen to resist facing up to the fears inside of her, rather than going to counseling as he had suggested. She had chosen to respond with anger and bitterness, rather than looking at the situation realistically and with humility. And a horrible irony occurred to Janna as she thought back to the morning that Colin had walked out the door, declaring that he was fed up. That was the day Janna had begun to realize she needed to make some changes. She'd almost called him at work to tell him that she was sorry, and to take a step toward making things right. But she had talked herself out of it, afraid of facing it head on. Now she knew that he had taken Lily home that day after work—and the rest was a nightmare. But what might have been different if she *had* called him at work? If he'd had some indication that she actually cared about their marriage, would he have been so drawn to Lily? She seriously doubted it.

Janna turned her face into the pillow and cried as these thoughts tormented her. When she couldn't bear the emotion any longer, she attempted to steer her mind back to the pleasant memories of when her mother had been alive. Concentrating on the images in her mind, Janna felt a definite warmth encircle her. She found some hope in the thought that perhaps her mother was with her, after all. With that in mind, she finally went to sleep, dreaming intermittently of a time when she and Colin had been young and in love, with their whole lives ahead of them. *If only it could be that way again.* But at this point in her life, she simply believed it was too late.

CHAPTER FOURTEEN

*A*fter declaring to Colin that, in essence, there was no future for them, Janna expected to feel better—to experience some kind of relief. Instead, she became consumed by an abstract discouragement. She kept telling herself she should call a lawyer and get the divorce under way, because she felt certain that it was unfair to expect Colin to keep hanging on. But she just couldn't bring herself to do it.

In mid-January, Janna finally broke down and made an appointment with Sean. She'd gradually weaned herself from their counseling sessions and had been managing rather well, for the most part. But as she confronted this final step toward a new future, she had difficulty coming to terms with it.

"So, what's the problem?" Sean asked once she was seated in his office.

"I just need to make a decision, but it's not . . . coming together for me. I can't explain it."

Sean reviewed the decision-making process found in the Doctrine and Covenants. She'd heard it all before. If the decision was right, she would feel peace. If it was wrong, there would be a stupor of thought.

"So, what are you feeling?" Sean asked.

"I feel a stupor of thought no matter *what* path I think of taking. If I leave Colin, it doesn't feel right. If I stay, I'm consumed with all the hurt, and . . ." She couldn't finish.

"Janna, you've come a long way. At this point, I want to emphasize again something that's come up many times through the work we've done together."

"I'm listening," she said a bit tersely.

"Janna, the most important part of any kind of healing comes through the Savior. Perhaps, prior to this point, you weren't ready to fully absorb and understand this. But maybe now it could make a difference." Sean's eyes became intent, and his voice lowered. "Janna, do you really *know* your Savior? Have you personally experienced the unconditional love he has for you?" She said nothing and he added, "I believe you've had a great deal of evidence of his love, but I wonder if you truly understand that he paid the price for your pain, Janna. That's the *only* way you will ever be completely free of what's still holding you back. Am I making any sense?"

"Yes, but . . . how do I do that?"

"Well, it's a personal thing. Of course prayer, study, and fasting are the obvious avenues. Spiritual experiences usually don't just *happen*. As I see it, you have to create an opportunity for them to happen. I believe you'll get out of it what you put into it. Frankly, Janna, I don't think there's any other advice I can give you. You've come through the struggles of your abuse as valiantly as anyone could. Now it's time to find complete peace as you move forward into your future. And no one can do it but you."

Janna couldn't rid her mind of that particular sentence. It hovered with her through the following days as she attempted to make sense of everything Sean had told her. *No one can do it but you.* That was the answer she'd received when she had initially left her abusive marriage to Russell. The Spirit had let her know that, although she was given a great deal of help from those around her, no one could make her choices or find the courage to take those difficult steps except her. And now she was confronted with a new turning point in her life.

Thinking back through her past, Janna wondered why she'd had the courage to leave Colin at the age of seventeen without telling him she was pregnant, yet she couldn't find the courage to go back to him now. The answer came quickly. Leaving him hadn't been an act of bravery. It had been the cowardly way out in the long run, and she'd been paying for it ever since.

Still, the hurt became all muddled up with her thoughts, and she was every bit as confused as she'd ever been. Rather than thinking too much about it, she did as Sean had suggested and concentrated most of her free time on intense study. She read the scriptures fervently, along with many books related to the topics she was struggling with. Sean had given her a reading list when she'd been in the hospital, and she'd learned a great deal from the variety of books he'd suggested. But as she reread some of them now, she felt more prepared to absorb their messages. She felt evidence of God's love in having these materials available to her.

Evidence of another blessing came when she got a call from Karen, an old friend who had helped her during the time she was attempting to get away from Russell. Soon after Janna married Colin, Karen had moved to California to pursue a job opportunity. They hadn't talked for more than two years, and Janna was surprised by the timing of her call. Karen was stunned by the report of all that had happened in Janna's life since they'd last talked. Janna felt the evidence of their friendship as she poured her heart out and received a great deal of compassion.

"So, what now?" Karen asked.

"I don't know. I'm pretty confused at the moment." She went on to explain Colin's apparent frame of mind, and the feelings she was struggling with.

"Now, wait a minute," Karen said. "Are you telling me that he's practically begged you—right from the day this happened—to take him back and to make it right?"

"Well . . . yes."

"And he's been re-baptized?"

"That's right."

"Then, what's the problem?"

Janna attempted to explain the hurt still smoldering inside her. Karen said little, but Janna sensed that she was frustrated. She reminded Janna to follow through on Sean's advice, and before they hung up she finally said, "Janna, you have to make your own choices, but I need to say something. You remember, of course, that my husband left me for another woman."

"I remember."

"Well, I certainly wasn't a perfect wife, and for a long time I wrestled with my feelings over that. I thought that maybe if I had been a better housekeeper, or if I lost some weight, or any number of other things, that maybe I could have kept him. The fact is, Janna, he just left me. He was bored. He admitted more than once that I just 'didn't turn him on any more.'   I wish I *had* done something to justify what he did to me. Then I might have had some control of the outcome. That was what I wanted most—to control the outcome. At the time, I would have given my right arm if he had just been willing to put his mistakes behind him and be committed to our marriage— to being a father to our children.

"Maybe you should stop and look at the eternal perspective here, Janna. You've fixed the problems that drove him away to begin with. You don't have any reason to suffer guilt and regret over that. And if he's willing to make it right, *you* are the one who will be held accountable if the marriage doesn't make it. Do you truly have justifiable cause to divorce him when he's done everything possible to make it right? Can you justify how a permanent break-up would affect your children when there's nothing but some hurt feelings to explain it?"

Janna was so stunned she could hardly speak. She finally managed to tell Karen that she had some things to think about, and assured her that she wasn't upset by the things that had been said. But for days after their conversation, Janna most certainly *was* upset. She tried to tell herself that Karen had no idea how she felt. But in fact, Karen had *been* there. Her husband hadn't even had the courage to admit he was cheating while it had been going on for months. Karen had discovered it and confronted him. Only then had he left her.

Just when Janna was beginning to think that she could swallow what Karen had told her, Hilary called and asked if they could go out for dinner after their dance class. Janna gave her the latest trauma report of her life, just as she'd done with Karen, perhaps hoping for some assurance that she was justified in divorcing Colin. Surely she could use an objective point of view in this.

Hilary told her about an aunt, her mother's sister, who had gone through a similar situation when Hilary was a young teenager. This aunt had lived close by and spent a great deal of time crying to Hilary's mother through the ordeal. Janna listened to specifics of the story that Hilary remembered, relating to them in ways she didn't want to admit. Her heart ached for this woman who had suffered through the same type of betrayal and hurt. The twist came when

Hilary finished by saying, "But they're together and doing great. My aunt swears that their marriage is better than it ever was before."

Janna said nothing more. She wondered why the possibility of such a thing seemed so incredulous to her. The following day, she called in sick and spent the day in bed. At first she just lay there, mulling everything around in her head. Then she began reading bits and pieces of many books and articles and scriptures, praying to make sense of all this. Rather than finding peace, she felt terribly uncomfortable reading phrases like "Judge not that ye be not judged," and "He that is without sin . . . let him first cast a stone."

But every time Janna tried to imagine herself telling Colin that she had forgiven him, images of Lily in his arms rushed into her mind. How could she be free of them? What could she possibly do? How could she ever learn to live with it?

Thinking that perhaps divorce *was* the answer, she considered it carefully. But the reality of being connected to Colin for the rest of her life only through their children, without really sharing his life, just didn't feel right. And yet she couldn't bring herself to comprehend getting over the hurt enough to be with him. It always came down to the same problem.

Paul called Janna, wondering why she wasn't at work. She'd stopped taking breaks with him right after Christmas, but he continued to come into the fabric store to visit with her while she worked. Feeling more irritated than flattered by his attention, she took the opportunity to tell him, kindly but firmly, that she simply wasn't in a position to pursue any kind of relationship—with him or anyone else. She thanked him for his friendship and got off the phone as quickly as she could without being offensive.

Feeling only an increase in her frustration, she dialed Sean's office and left a message for him to call. He called back late afternoon, saying right off, "Hi. What's up?"

"Something's wrong with me, Sean."

"Really? I thought you were doing pretty well."

"I am . . . except for that one issue. I just can't get past it."

"Forgiving Colin," he stated with certainty.

"That's right. I've read and studied. I've fasted and prayed. What am I missing? What's wrong with me, that I can't let it go?"

"I'm not sure I can answer that, Janna. You've reached a point where I really can't help you anymore. You have the tools to solve your problems now. It's up to you to put the pieces together."

"Okay," she sighed, "just tell me one thing."

"I'll try."

"What does Colin know that I don't know?"

"I don't understand."

"Well, obviously I've hurt him a great deal, but it doesn't seem to bother *him*. Of course, the issues are different, but . . . what has he got that I haven't got?"

"That's a tough one," Sean said, then he was silent for more than a minute.

"Well?" Janna finally said, wondering if they'd been cut off.

"I'm thinking . . . or should I say, I'm trying to be inspired." A moment later he added, "You know, Janna, I can only think of one thing I've seen from him that I haven't seen from you."

"Okay, what is it?"

"Empathy."

"Empathy? What does—"

"It's just that simple, Janna. I've seen Colin try very hard to understand where your head was; what you were going through. I think empathy is one of the biggest elements of Christlike love. Christ has perfect empathy for our struggles, because he was tempted in all things, and he suffered our pain. I don't know if that's the answer you need, but it's the only one I can come up with. Maybe if you understand how Colin really feels, you could come to terms with it."

"And how do I do that?"

"Don't ask me. It's between you and the Lord." Janna said nothing and Sean asked, "Does this mean you're working toward getting back together with him?"

"Not necessarily," she insisted. "I really don't know what I want. But I do know that I have to get past these feelings—if only so I can live with myself in peace."

"That's true," Sean said. "Well, good luck. Keep me posted."

Janna sat with her arms folded tightly for several minutes after she got off the phone. She wasn't entirely pleased with having to handle this on her own, but she knew if she didn't come to terms with it and get on with her life—one way or another—she'd never be able to cope. After thinking through their conversation again, Janna got down on her knees and just asked the Lord outright, "Please give me empathy. Help me understand what Colin has been through. Help me to get past this and forgive, and to know the steps that I should take at this point in my life, so that I might be able to do what's best for all of us."

Janna crawled back into bed and continued to think about it, but she still felt numb. She was still lying there when Matthew called to see if she was home so he could bring something over. Janna got dressed and made her bed before he arrived, not wanting him to think that she was returning to her old ways of hiding from life by staying in bed.

"We need to talk," Matthew said as soon as he came in.

"Okay," she said, sitting beside him on the couch. At times he seemed so mature for his age. She often wondered if his exposure to so much abuse at a young age had made him grow up too fast.

"I know all this stuff between you and Dad has nothing to do with me. And maybe it wasn't right for me to do this, but I prayed about it, and I just felt like I should."

"Okay," she said again, this time more warily.

Matthew handed her a thick envelope.

"What's this?" Janna asked.

"Dad wrote you a letter, right after Christmas. Then he said he didn't think he should give it to you, because you already had your mind made up. But it's just been sitting there . . . and, well . . . I didn't read it, but I did borrow it long enough to get a copy. He doesn't know I did it. He might get mad at me, but . . . I thought maybe you should read it."

Janna glanced at the envelope in her hands, saying with some hesitance, "Thank you, Matthew."

He stood up and moved toward the door. "I'm going to shoot hoops at the church. I'll see you tomorrow, probably." He left, then stuck his head back in. "Oh, happy Groundhog Day."

Janna smiled. "Same to you."

For hours, Janna tried to talk herself into reading the letter. She cleaned up the apartment and cooked dinner while it sat on the

counter. Finally she shoved it into a dresser drawer, certain it would
only confuse her further. She continued praying and attempting to
grasp hold of this *empathy* thing. But the peace continued to elude
her. Five days later she still hadn't read the letter, but she did find an
opportunity to prove just how strong she had become. When the
doorbell rang, the last person Janna expected to see was her father.

"Hello," he said as if she should be glad to see him. When she said
nothing, he added, "Haven't you got anything to say to your old father?"

"Something comes to mind about bad pennies turning up."

"Not very gracious, are you?"

"Should I be?"

"May I come in?"

"No," she stated.

Janna didn't hear much of what her father said after that. He
was attempting to convince her of his rights or something. She just
picked up the cordless phone and dialed 911.

"What are you doing?" he asked, seeming more concerned
about her indifference toward him as she ignored him to use the
phone.

"I'm making a phone call," she stated, then said into the phone,
"Yes." She stated her address and added, "There's a man at my door
who refuses to leave."

Miles Hayne left before the police arrived. She didn't apologize
or justify herself; she just made a call after they left to file a restraining
order. And when she went to bed that night, she was pleased to note
that there were no negative memories assaulting her; no fear. She
simply felt good about doing what had to be done to get rid of him.
She recalled then how Sean had told her that *the death of a fear is
really exciting.*

The positive feelings generated by putting her father out of her
life, once and for all, started to blossom inside her as she got ready for
work the next morning. She was rummaging through her jewelry box
in search of a missing earring when she noticed the gold locket that
Colin had given her as a graduation gift. She'd seen it many times
through the months of their separation, and had chosen to push it
away and ignore it. But now she felt somehow compelled to pick it
up. Carefully she turned it over, recalling the day he'd given it to

her—more than seven years after her graduation, when they had finally come back together.

Janna held the locket in her fist and closed her eyes, willing the memories closer. Just as she could almost taste the reality of Colin's love for her, the same old horrible images flashed into her mind. She opened her eyes, startled freshly by the presence of Lily Greene in her head. Janna cursed under her breath and tossed the locket on her dresser, resuming her search for the missing earring.

At work, Janna was dismayed when Paul came to see her. She politely reminded him that she wasn't interested. He only smiled and went back to work. But as Janna watched him walk away, turning back to wink at her over his shoulder, something happened inside of her that she simply wasn't prepared for. She hadn't even been thinking of Colin, but when Paul looked at her that way, she found it easy to imagine how Lily might have behaved toward Colin at the office. With Paul, it was seemingly innocent; Janna had no reason to believe that he was trying to seduce her or tempt her into committing sin. But then, with Colin it had been different. Or had it?

As Janna continued her work, measuring and pricing fabric remnants, she found her thoughts consumed with Lily. But this time, she wasn't imagining the intimacy between this woman and her husband, but rather the incidents that led up to it. She became so absorbed in her speculations that she called Colin the minute she got home from work.

"Okay," she said, "I want to know how it happened."

"What?" He sounded understandably baffled.

"I'm sick to death of trying to imagine how it happened. Maybe my mind is making it worse than it was. So just tell me what led up to it, Colin, and I'll assume you're telling me the truth."

Colin didn't know what had spurred this sudden interest, but he was anything but comfortable with it. Reminding himself that she was his wife and she had a right to know, he took a deep breath and just started at the beginning. He told her how he'd found Lily crying in her office, and how he'd given her a ride home a few times when she'd had car trouble. Then he told her about the evening he'd gone in to help her fix a light switch—the way he'd been feeling that day, and how a friendly embrace just turned into more before he hardly knew what was happening. He stuck to the facts and avoided the feelings, finishing with, "That's all there is to it, Janna." When she was quiet too long, he added, "Does the prosecution rest?"

"Don't count on it," she said and hung up.

Colin looked at the phone, wondering what the point of their conversation had been. He surmised that she was probably gathering her information to file for a divorce. Then he tried—without much success—to put it out of his mind.

Janna wandered restlessly around her apartment, putting the pieces together in her head. Some conversation. A ride home. Help with a repair. Didn't that describe her relationship with Paul as much as Colin's relationship with Lily? Up to that point, at least.

Janna noticed the locket on her dresser and picked it up. Rubbing it between her fingers, she pondered the empathy theory and asked herself a difficult question. *If I were Colin, and he had treated me the way I had treated him . . . and if Paul had been there to help me with something . . . and . . .*

"Oh, help," Janna muttered, sitting unsteadily on the edge of the bed. The feelings that overwhelmed her were so powerful that she actually found it difficult to breathe. "This is what I've been praying for," she said aloud, as if hearing it might help the reality penetrate. *Empathy.*

While Janna's mind became consumed with a heartache on Colin's behalf that she had never thought possible, she curled up on the bed and cried. When the emotion finally settled, she wasn't certain if there was still a future left for them together, but she believed for the first time since he'd brought his confessions home to her that she *did* have it in her heart to forgive him . . . with time.

The following morning as she was getting ready for work, Janna noticed a little card that she had taped to her mirror—a remnant from the self-help classes she had taken. It simply stated *Life happens from me, not to me.* She'd read it a thousand times, but in that moment, she fully absorbed it. Feeling much as she had the day before, Janna closed her eyes to soak up the closeness of the Spirit and what it was trying to teach her. Yesterday she had learned something about Colin; and today, she was beginning to comprehend something wonderful about herself. In a way, the changes had come so gradually that she'd not taken notice of how drastic they had been. But now, as she opened her eyes and looked into the mirror, what she saw surprised her. She was a daughter of God—a woman capable of making her own choices and accepting their consequences. She had the power and responsibility to change and direct her life into ways of righteousness and happiness. She was strong enough to forgive, and humble enough to accept God's love for her—more specifically, the healing sacrifice of Jesus Christ. She couldn't explain what had taken place, and she still wasn't completely certain what path her life would follow. But she knew that she was capable of putting the past behind her, and whatever she chose to do, she would do it with courage and determination.

It wasn't until late afternoon that Janna remembered the letter. She felt anxious to finish up her work and get home, then she went straight to the bedroom and dug it out. Taking a deep breath, she sat down on the edge of the bed and opened it. It took her more than an hour to read it, since she had to stop every few paragraphs to wipe the tears and blow her nose. When she finally got through the letter, she lay back on the bed among the scattered tissues and closed her eyes. She could almost literally feel Colin's love surrounding her. It always had been; she'd just been too clouded by hurt and abuse to truly feel it. But now . . .

Janna got on her knees and asked her Father in Heaven what path she should take, while in her heart she already knew the answer. She simply needed validation that it was right. By the time her prayer was finished, she knew what she needed to do. There was only one fear holding her back. In spite of all Colin's efforts to prove his love for her, she still wondered how he felt about Lily. He had told her he had no feelings for this woman, but for some reason, Janna still struggled to believe it. Perhaps it was jealousy, she reasoned. She'd made progress in understanding his part in all of this, but when it came right down to it, was she just plain jealous?

Concluding that she couldn't expect to have every question answered at once, she made up her mind to take the first steps. And since this coming Saturday was Valentine's Day, she figured it was as good a day as any to let her husband know she wanted to try again—if it wasn't already too late.

It was Janna's weekend to have the kids, so the first thing she did was make a call to Nancy. She felt certain Colin's mother would help her out, provided she didn't have any plans.

"The thing is," Janna explained, "I've been doing a lot of soul-searching. I think things are finally coming together in my head, but I need some time alone. I don't want to rearrange the schedule with Colin, so would it be possible to leave the kids with you this weekend? Of course I don't want to put you out, so if you have other—"

"Oh, we'd love to, dear," Nancy Trevor insisted. "It's been a long time since we've had them overnight. We'll look forward to it."

"Oh, you're so good to me—as always," Janna said. "If it's all right, I'll bring them over about four on Friday."

When Janna took the children to their grandmother's on Friday afternoon, she asked Nancy if they could talk for a few minutes. While Matthew kept an eye on the girls, the two women sat at the dining room table.

"What is it, dear?" Nancy asked gently.

"Well," Janna began, "there's something I've been wanting to tell you."

"Okay," Nancy said eagerly.

"You know, I've done a lot of thinking the last several weeks, and I believe I've learned a great deal."

"Really, like what?" Nancy asked. "If you don't mind my asking, of course."

"Oh, I don't mind," Janna said. "But a lot of it's difficult to put into words. It's like I had little bits and pieces of help and information that came from so many sources, and then it all just kind of . . . came together and made sense. But as I looked back over the years since I met Colin, I think I began to appreciate something that I missed before. And I guess that's what I want to tell you."

"I'm listening," Nancy said when she hesitated.

Janna took her mother-in-law's hand across the table. "I just want to thank you . . . for taking me in. Being a mother now myself, I wonder how I would feel to have my son bring home a fifteen-year-old girl and have her practically move in, knowing she had no family beyond her mother. You're a perceptive woman, and I know you must have sensed that I had problems. And then when I came back, bringing an illegitimate child and all the problems from the abuse, you just took us in, no questions asked."

Janna sighed, and emotion caught her voice. "I want to thank you, Nancy, for loving me unconditionally, even when—or perhaps *especially* when—I wasn't necessarily treating your son and grandchildren very well. You've never once criticized me, or passed judgment, or made me feel inferior." She laughed softly. "Of course, I did enough of that myself. But I hope I'm beyond that now. I think I can finally look at myself in the mirror and see a woman worthy of a good life."

Nancy smiled serenely and squeezed Janna's hand.

"Several weeks ago," Janna explained, "I was given a challenge in one of my classes to look at myself in the mirror every day and simply say, 'I am beautiful.' The first time I tried it, I couldn't do it. After a few tries, I finally got the words out, and then I cried and cried. But eventually it seemed to make a difference. And then one day when I did it, I thought of you. I think the way you accepted me actually helped me cross that bridge." Janna smiled. "I just wanted you to know that."

Nancy became too emotional to speak, but she hugged Janna tightly, murmuring how grateful she was to see her doing so well.

Janna sensed that she wanted to ask if there was any hope of her and Colin getting back together. But she said nothing, and Janna was relieved. She didn't want to talk about that right now. In spite of her plan, she really wasn't certain how all of this would turn out. She was taking it one minute at a time and trying to follow her instincts.

After hugging the kids, Janna drove the Suburban to Colin's house—the home where her children were being raised. She sat in the driveway for a few minutes before she got up the nerve to reach in her pocket for the key. She had sneaked Matthew's key long enough to make a copy. She wasn't certain why she hadn't let anyone in on her plans; perhaps it was a way of protecting herself if she decided to back out. Or perhaps it wouldn't work out the way she had planned it. She had no idea where Colin's head was now; for all she knew, he'd finally given up on her and gone back to Lily. Or perhaps he'd met someone else. No, she couldn't think of that now. She just had to move forward with faith.

Turning the key in the lock, Janna stepped warily inside. She closed the door and leaned against it, pausing to absorb it as *home*. Slowly, quietly, she walked from room to room. The beds weren't made. There were dirty clothes on the bedroom floors, and evidence of a hurried breakfast in the kitchen. But the house was relatively orga-nized, and cleaner than she'd expected. Janna cried as she stood in her children's bedrooms and pondered the love their father had for them. It was evident in so many little things. Then she stood even longer in the master bedroom, contemplating the pictures of herself spread over the dresser in various frames. Some were as old as high school.

Then, noticing the clock, she panicked. If she didn't hurry, her plan would be foiled.

Janna unloaded the Suburban, then parked it around the corner in a church parking lot and walked back to the house. She put food in the oven and fridge that she'd prepared ahead, and hurried to straighten things up and wash some dishes. Peace and hope surged through her as she worked. *She felt as if she'd come home.*

When Janna knew that Colin could arrive soon, she put music on continuous play, lit the candles on the table, and hurried upstairs to change clothes and fix her hair. She was just touching up her face when she heard the car pull into the driveway. Attempting to quell a rush of butterflies, she hurried to the upstairs landing and waited for him to come in.

CHAPTER FIFTEEN
Valentine's Day

*T*he irony was horrible. Colin dreaded going home. He hated the weekends when Janna had the kids, anyway. But tomorrow was Valentine's Day. All day he'd been aware of people giving and receiving gifts, looking forward to doing something special with spouses and sweethearts on the weekend. But he was going home to an empty house. He'd spend Saturday cleaning and doing laundry, then he'd probably visit his parents and buy groceries. Distracted by his thoughts, he shuffled into the house.

Suddenly, a feeling of deja-vu overwhelmed him. He could hear music playing, and the lights weren't off. They were dimmed.

"What are you doing here, woman?" he shouted and slammed the door.

Janna was about to go down the stairs when she heard him. Suddenly afraid, she backed up and hid in the shadows on the landing. Tears stung her eyes as she wondered why he would be angry with her. Had she waited too long? Was it too late?

"I'm not up to this, Lily," Colin shouted, moving gingerly into the kitchen, wondering where she was hiding. He could smell something cooking, and wondered if she'd actually had the nerve to come in here and use his kitchen as some ridiculous ploy to get his attention. When he saw the table set for two with his best dishes—and candles, no less—he felt angry.

"Lily Greene, come out and show your face," he shouted, fully expecting his voice to penetrate every corner of the house. "How many times do I have to tell you I'm not interested—that one pathetic incident is no basis for a relationship?" He peeked in the laundry room, then went back to the front room. "Are you hearing me, Lily? I want you to leave here, *now*. If you don't, I will!"

Janna heard him starting up the stairs and quickly dried her eyes. Her tears had swiftly turned to pure joy. He would never know what his innocent declarations meant to her. She now knew exactly where he stood with Lily, and there was no reason to question his honesty with her. If there was any remaining question at all, it faded when he stopped with his foot on the bottom stair to see her standing a few steps above him. His surprise was so absolute, so touching. He grabbed hold of the bannister and teetered slightly, his eyes delving into hers.

"I'm not Lily," she said.

Colin was too stunned to speak, too scared to move. He put all the information together again in his mind. Music, dimmed lights, candles, dinner in the oven, *Janna standing on the stairs, wearing the black dress she'd once refused to wear*. It was nothing short of a miracle, he concluded as she walked slowly toward him. He wondered for a moment if he was jumping to conclusions. The evidence contradicted everything he'd believed about her state of mind. But then, the evidence was all too romantic to be just an effort at making peace. Wasn't it?

As she stepped closer, Colin wondered if she'd cut her hair; but it was twisted elegantly into a big clip at the back of her head. He backed off the stairs and felt pulsebeats in his ears as she stood to face him. Without a word, she took his hand into hers. Colin looked down to watch her do it, as if he had to convince himself she was touching him. He looked back to her face as she took his other hand and put it at the small of her back. She set her hand on his shoulder, and without even thinking about it, he realized they were dancing. At first he felt afraid to get too close; afraid to look away, as if she might disappear. Then, as if it might prove the reality of her presence, he closed his eyes to test it. He pressed his cheek to her brow and felt her soften. He inhaled her fragrance, so familiar and yet so strange. He felt her face move next to his, and she nuzzled subtly against his throat. Tentatively he pressed his arm further around her waist, tightened his hand around hers. He expected to feel some sign that she was apprehensive or resistant, but she only became more pliable, more warm. He buried his lips in her hair and felt the emotion bubbling up from the deepest part of him. Something between a chuckle and a sob erupted from his lips, then the tears followed. Of all the tears he'd cried since he'd lost her, these were the most difficult to get out. They burned through his chest and eyes, carrying with them so much unvented emotion that his head nearly swam. He lost track of the time as he danced in a slow, steady rhythm, holding her against him, crying like a child who had lost his mother at the mall and had just found her again. His legs suddenly went weak and he sank to his knees, pressing his hands to her back, crying into the folds of her skirt. He felt her hands in his hair, then she lifted his face to her view, caressing away his tears with one hand, wiping at hers with the other. She knelt to face him and pressed her arms around his shoulders. Time lost all essence as he just held her, then she drew back slightly and gave him a tentative smile.

"We need to talk, Colin," she said.

He stood up with an embarrassed chuckle and helped her to her feet. "Yes, I believe we do."

"Over dinner, perhaps?" She motioned toward the kitchen.

"That would be great," he said. "Let me just . . . wash up, and . . ." He hurried into the downstairs bathroom and leaned against the closed door for a full minute, just trying to grasp the enormity of the miracle. He splashed cold water on his face and blotted it dry, uttering a silent prayer of gratitude that evoked a quickening of his heart. When he walked into the dining room, Janna was setting a basket of rolls on the table.

"Can I help?" he asked, wondering if she'd ever looked more beautiful. She turned toward him with a smile and positively glowed.

"There's some raspberry lemonade in the fridge you could get."

"I love raspberry lemonade," he said, retrieving the glass pitcher.

"I know," she smiled again as he filled the elegant glasses. He helped her with her chair then sat across from her, briefly mesmerized by her reality in the candles' glow.

"Should we bless it?" she asked, startling him.

"Of course," he murmured and bowed his head, saying a brief but sincere blessing on the food. In the prayer he expressed gratitude for being with Janna, and he felt some relief when she added an eager *amen*.

Janna dished up her plate and passed the serving dishes to him. He felt as if he was moving in slow motion. When he realized what he was eating, he said, "I love chicken cordon-bleu."

"I know," she replied.

"So," he said when the silence became unbearable, "let's talk."
She smiled and glanced down, but said nothing. "Or should I call
Sean and see if he's hungry?"

"I only made enough for two," she said firmly. "I think we can
handle this on our own. We just have to be completely honest with
each other."

"I wouldn't want it any other way," he said, but Janna didn't
make another sound until they were eating dessert.

"Why did you think Lily was here when you came in?" He hesitated and she added, "Has she been here?"

"No, but she got into my apartment once and was waiting for
me when I came home."

Janna was relieved somehow to know that Lily had never been
in this house. The thought was unsettling. But she realized he was
talking about the apartment that was now hers.

"What happened?" she asked.

"We talked. I told her about you, and why it would be so hard
for me to give up, and then . . ."

"Then?" she repeated when he hesitated.

"We danced. Then she left. Is there anything else you want to
know about Lily?"

"Is there anything else I *should* know?"

"Nothing that I haven't already told you."

"Then I just have one more question. I asked you once before,
but I need it verified."

"Okay."

"Do you love her?"

"No."

"Did you ever tell her you loved her?"

"No, Janna. I was as honest with her as I was with you. She
knows exactly where my heart is, even if she doesn't seem to want to
accept it."

"Accept what?"

"That I would pine away for a woman who hasn't given me the
time of day for more than a year and a half."

"Why have you?"

"Where do you want me to start?"

"At the beginning."

"The beginning was when I set eyes on a fifteen-year-old girl and felt as if I'd seen a glimpse of heaven. The middle is that we've been through too much together to just throw it all away because of a stupid mistake. The end is that every time I started to wonder if I was fooling myself to believe you'd ever come back to me, my Father in Heaven made it clear that I needed to hold on."

Janna glanced down and said nothing for a couple of minutes. "Which brings us to now." She looked up, and Colin caught something in her eyes that was unfamiliar. While he felt himself gradually becoming reacquainted with her presence, he had to admit now that something had changed. He couldn't pinpoint it, and the uncertainty frightened him.

"Yes, now," he said, wondering if this was all an attempt to heal the wounds in preparation for taking separate paths. She'd been kind. She'd made an effort. But he had no idea whether or not she'd forgiven him. She'd given no indication of where her head was concerning the future.

She looked around before speaking again. "It's a beautiful home, Colin. It's evident that you've done well with the children, and I'm grateful for that."

Colin began to feel nervous. This was beginning to sound like a lead-up to bad news.

"I've done a lot of thinking," she said, fidgeting with her napkin, "and, well . . . Sean told me, and I'm certain he told you as well, that no matter what happened, we needed to be at peace with each other for the sake of the children."

Colin felt a tangible smoldering in his stomach but fought to keep an even expression.

"I'm ready to be a full-time mother again, Colin. I miss my children. You told me that when I was ready, I could take the house and the kids."

Colin unwillingly slid his chair back and gripped the edge of the table with one hand. What was she saying?

She glanced down again, then she almost smiled. But it was difficult to tell if her smile was genuine, or an attempt to mask some other emotion.

"I only have one stipulation," she said, and in the moment before she went on, Colin could hear divorce agreements in his head. "I'm not moving into this house until it's absolutely clear that I want you here with me." Her voice cracked as she went on. "I wouldn't blame you for not wanting to put it back together after what I've put you through. Most men would have slapped me with 'incompetent mother due to mental illness' and taken the kids and never looked back."

Colin watched the tears roll down her face, reflecting the candlelight. "Most women in my situation would have been left with nothing but a monthly settlement that wouldn't even make ends meet. But me . . . I have seventy-eight little cards that all say: *I love you, Colin.* And every one of them came with a bouquet of flowers."

While Colin was trying to gather his wits and make his voice work, she stood abruptly and went into the bathroom. Colin was so stunned, so grateful, so in awe, he couldn't even move. She came out and turned on the bright kitchen light. She started clearing the table, and he stood up to help her. In silence she put the food away while he wiped off the table. She started stacking dishes in the sink, but he turned off the light and took her hand. "I'll wash them in the morning. Dance with me."

The CD had come back around to the same song they'd danced to before dinner. Colin held her close as they moved in time to the music. He noticed then that she was wearing the locket he'd given her years ago. He briefly touched it and saw her smile. He wondered how to alleviate the undeniable tension still hovering between them. It didn't take long for him to figure out that there was one very big thing that needed to be clarified.

"Janna," he murmured, his cheek pressed to her brow, "I want you to know how deeply I regret what I did. The hell has been so intense for me, there is no way to describe it. All I can do is tell you that I'm sorry. I wish it had never happened, and my deepest hope is that you can eventually find it in your heart to forgive me."

She pulled back to look at him, seeming surprised.

"No, Colin," she said, and he briefly panicked. "It is I who must ask your forgiveness."

Colin's brow furrowed. He instinctively held her tighter. "I don't understand."

"Well, it's not easy to explain, so bear with me. It has something to do with casting stones. You know, 'He that is without sin . . . let him first cast a stone.' I don't want to get into the details right now. Let me just summarize it and say that through a lot of praying, and fasting, and reading, and talking to Sean, the picture finally fell into place." Emotion bubbled out with her confession. "I know I treated you badly, and I wasn't a wife to you. And when I think of the kind of man I know in my heart that you are, I cannot comprehend the desperation you must have felt to do what you did."

Janna pressed her face to his shoulder to hide the tears. She stopped dancing, and Colin just held her until she took a step back and lifted her chin. "But all of that's in the past now, Colin. I only ask that you put away past hurts and judgments, and allow me to do the same."

Colin caught his breath as he studied her face. He understood that unfamiliar quality in her eyes now. It was the window to her spirit. A window clear with a love of life and a strong self-worth. A window clean from pain and fear, no longer streaked with the scars of abuse and self-degradation. What he saw before him now was the *real* JannaLyn Trevor. Her next statement only verified the truth of that.

"I am here for you, Colin. I'm offering you a fresh start with the woman I have become. I am a daughter of God with the ability to love and be loved. I am not only a survivor; I have the potential to *thrive* on whatever life may give me. I have the will and the courage to overcome whatever struggles may lie ahead, to face them with fortitude, not to cower in fear."

Colin touched her hair, her face, her hair again, too moved to speak. She was so beautiful, so incredible. It was a miracle.

"You know, Colin, we've been together a couple of hours, and you haven't even kissed me."

He chuckled. "I've been afraid to." She looked concerned and he clarified, "With the way you make me feel, I'm not sure I could stop with a kiss, and I didn't know if you were ready to—"

She pressed her fingers over his lips. "Stop talking and kiss me."

Colin held his breath as their lips meekly made contact. It only took a moment for her eagerness to become evident. He pressed his mouth over hers, absorbing its warmth as if she was water to a man long in the desert. She turned fluid in his arms, melding to him as if she had spent eternity waiting only for this moment. Her aura radiated complete trust and acceptance.

"Colin!" she gasped, throwing her head back in abandonment. For a moment, he felt as if he was doing something he shouldn't. Surely something right could not feel this good! Then the reality descended upon him like a balm to his soul. *She was his wife.* There was nothing more right or good than this. He pulled the clip out of her hair and tossed it, watching her rich curls fall down her back.

Janna looked into his eyes. "You really look adorable with those glasses on."

Colin chuckled with embarrassment, then he took them off and set them on an end table.

"You look adorable with them off," she added with a gentle laugh, then she kissed him again.

A memory caught Colin off guard when Janna pressed her fingers between the buttons of his shirt. He reminded himself that he'd been forgiven—by God and by Janna. The agony of unwanted memories was something he had to face privately. When Janna stopped abruptly, he almost wondered if she'd read his mind. She glanced down at her hands as they pressed beneath his shirt.

"Colin? You're not wearing your garments."

Colin took a step back, hating the sudden crash of reality into this magical moment.

"I was excommunicated, Janna," he said, as if she didn't know.

"Yes, but . . . you were re-baptized, and—"

"It takes at least another year to get back the priesthood and temple blessings."

Janna glanced away, unnerved by the alarm in his eyes. "I'm sorry," she said gently. "I just . . . didn't know."

"Does it make a difference?" he asked when the tension deepened.

Janna looked into his eyes and he saw them soften. "No, Colin. I only wish that . . ."

"What?" he implored, not wanting anything between them that might cause friction in the future.

"That I could somehow share the burden, since I share the responsibility."

Colin squeezed his eyes closed, overwhelmed with humility and gratitude. "Just hold my hand every day until we can go back to the temple together. That's all I ask."

She smiled and touched his face, easing back into his arms. "I can think of no greater pleasure," she said and kissed him. Before their lips broke contact, he had pulled her up into his arms. She kicked off her shoes on the stairs and laughed as he quickened his pace, practically bouncing her in his arms. He walked into the bedroom and had to stop a moment to absorb what he saw. The lights were dimmed. Soft music was playing. The bed had been turned down. He met her eyes and saw them sparkling. She had come here with every intention of spending the night. The thought warmed him so deeply that he laughed out loud.

"Welcome home, Mrs. Trevor," he said and kicked the door closed.

She laughed as they fell into the center of the bed. And the rest was like a dream—nothing short of a miracle. This was the JannaLyn he had loved from the start, a woman with strength and life and spirit. This was not the guarded, apprehensive woman he had been married to before. This was a woman flowing with life, free of inhibition and fear, giving completely of herself, and taking all he gave her as if she could scatter it in the heavens to create a new galaxy. He had never dreamed that any earthly experience could be so perfect, so ethereal. He had thought that after all his months of celibacy, he might be consumed with urgency. But he felt only a desire to make it last, to savor every moment, as if they could share this experience forever.

Long after it was over, they held each other in perfect contentment. Neither of them felt prone to speak, as if words might break the heavenly spell hovering around them.

"I love you, JannaLyn," Colin finally whispered, just this side of sleep.

"I love you, too, Colin," she replied and pressed her lips over his brow.

Colin eased her closer and murmured under his breath, "Thank you, Lord." Then he drifted to sleep in her arms.

Colin woke alone in the bed and briefly panicked. Had he dreamt it? Then he heard water running in the bathroom. Janna appeared a moment later, wearing his shirt. The morning sun illuminated her mussed hair and smeared makeup. But he thought she'd never looked more beautiful.

"Good morning," she said, sitting on the edge of the bed.

"Good morning." He took her hand and kissed it, then he growled like some kind of beast and pulled her into his arms. Janna laughed and kissed him.

Recalling that today was a holiday, he raised his brows comically, asking, "Will you be my valentine?"

"Only if it's forever," she replied, touching her nose to his. Then the phone rang.

"Don't answer it," he said, kissing her ear, her throat, her shoulder.

"It might be Matthew," she said, grabbing for the phone. He pulled her out of its reach. She laughed and lunged out of his arms, knocking the phone on the floor.

"Colin!" she giggled and quickly picked up the receiver off the floor, saying into it, "Hello." She heard nothing and repeated, "Hello?"

"I'm sorry," a woman's voice said. "I must have the wrong number." Then a click.

Janna looked at the phone dubiously.

"What?" Colin asked.

"It was either a wrong number, or it was Lily."

Colin took the phone and put it back where it belonged. "Either way, it was the wrong number." He threaded his fingers between hers and kissed her hard. Then the phone rang again. This time Colin reached for it, saying abruptly, "What?"

"Colin?" Nancy said. "Are you all right?"

"Oh, good morning, Mother. Of course I'm all right." Janna kissed him quietly, then laid her head on his shoulder as he leaned back against the headboard. "How are you?"

"I'm fine. Did I wake you?"

"No," he said. "I'm in bed, but you didn't wake me."

"I just thought I should warn you. Matthew's on his way over to get some clean underwear for Mallory. We had a little potty problem and ran out."

"Is she all right?"

"Oh, of course," she insisted. "I think she just drank too much root beer. And . . . well . . ." She sounded hesitant, and Colin wondered what was wrong. "I tried to call Janna to get some underwear, but . . . she's not answering. Colin," the tension in her voice increased and he felt anxious, "I don't think Janna wanted you to know I had the kids. She said she didn't want to rearrange the weekends with you, but she needed some time. Of course I was glad to help, but now she's not answering, and I can't help being concerned. It's not like her to spend the night somewhere else, or to leave that early. Do you think that—"

"Mother," Colin interrupted with a chuckle, "I can assure you that Janna is well and safe. She's home."

"But I just called over there, and—"

"Mother, Janna is in my arms."

"Oh, my," Nancy sighed. Then she laughed. "Really?"

Colin put the phone by Janna's mouth. "Good morning, Mom," she said.

"Is that proof enough?" Colin asked into the receiver, then he kissed Janna quickly.

"I take it things are going well," Nancy said in a voice that betrayed her joy.

"Everything is perfect. And if you'll keep those little monsters under control for just a while longer, we'll come and get them."

"Oh no," Nancy said. "We were planning on having them until tomorrow. We're going out for pizza and shopping to celebrate Valentine's Day, and they'd never forgive Grandma if she reneged. So you just enjoy your day, Colin. I'd say the holiday is appropriate. Make the most of it, and we'll see you in the morning."

"Well, if you insist," he chuckled. "I think I could probably find a way to fill the day."

After he got off the phone, Janna asked with mischief in her eyes, "Just how *do* you intend to fill the day, Mr. Trevor?"

"Well, since Mom insists on keeping the kids until tomorrow morning, I thought I could clean out the garage or something. And there's laundry to do, and—"

"Stop talking and kiss me, Colin Trevor," she said, and he did.

A minute later, they heard a noise downstairs. "What's that?" Janna whispered frantically.

"It's probably Matthew. Mom said he was coming over to get—"

"Dad!" Matthew's voice called as footsteps bounded up the stairs. Janna ducked under the sheet just as the bedroom door flew open.

"You need to learn to knock, son," Colin said. He saw Matthew's eyes take in the appearance of the room, including the woman's clothes on the floor. His eyes widened in apparent shock, then he looked as if he might cry just before he turned away and closed the door.

"Matthew!" Colin shouted as he realized what the boy was thinking. "Janna," he nudged her, "call him, quick. He thinks—"

"Matthew!" she shouted, bounding for Colin's robe on the hook behind the door. She threw it on and hurried into the hall. "Matthew! Where are you?"

The boy appeared at the top of the stairs, his eyes wide with surprise and relief. "Mom?"

"It's me, Matthew." She opened her arms. "Everything's all right."

Matthew hugged his mother tightly, then looked up to see Colin leaning against the bedroom doorframe, wearing only a pair of jeans, his hands deep in the pockets.

"Good morning, kid," he grinned, and Matthew hugged him as well.

"Hey, Dad," he glanced over at his mother, "you got it right this time."

Colin met Janna's eyes. "Yes, I sure did."

"I'm the one who got it right," Janna said.

"Uh . . . I'll just get those things for Mallory and . . . uh, let you two . . . well, you know."

Colin chuckled as he watched his son hurry into the girls' room. Matthew waved comically as he walked back past them and down the stairs.

"Hey, Mrs. Trevor," Colin said, nodding toward the bedroom, "let's uh . . . well, you know."

"You act just like him," she said with a little smirk as she sauntered into the bedroom.

"It's the other way around," he clarified, following her. "I'm the boy's father, remember?"

"Oh, I remember, all right."

More than an hour later, Colin left Janna sleeping and went

downstairs. He loaded the dishwasher, then mixed up German pancakes and put them in the oven. He was making some orange juice when he felt Janna's hands on his back. The reality made his heart quicken. He closed his eyes and offered a brief prayer of gratitude. *He couldn't believe it!*

"I love your Saturday attire," she said, pressing her hands around to his chest. Colin glanced down at himself. His feet were bare. His jeans were faded, with a number of holes. His sweatshirt was stretched out and stained.

"Yeah, it's great," he said with light sarcasm. "Wouldn't my clients love to see me now?"

"Right now," she turned him to face her and pressed a hand over his stubbled face, "you're mine."

Colin sighed in disbelief. "I love you," he murmured and kissed her. Then he eased back and looked at her. She was wearing the shirt he'd had on last night. "Ooh, I like your Saturday attire, too."

Janna smirked and eased back into his arms, kissing him as if she'd been as starved for his affection as he'd been for hers. Then the timer rang, and he had to turn around and get breakfast out of the oven.

"Wow," she said, "that looks beautiful."

"I took a few cooking lessons from my mother. I was going to bring you breakfast in bed."

"Well, in that case," she said, "I'll go back to bed."

Colin watched her walk away, then he finished making the juice. He took a tray upstairs a few minutes later to find her leaning against the headboard, looking at the book that had been on the bedside table.

"Sean's required reading list?" she asked, holding it up.

"Yeah," he smirked and set the tray between them on the bed. They fed each other breakfast, talking and laughing, while Colin kept trying to convince himself this was real. He made love to her again, marveling at the reality of her healing. Was this the Janna he'd always believed had existed somewhere beneath all her self-doubt and hurt?

In the quiet aftermath, he asked, "Is this real, Janna? Or am I going to wake up tomorrow and find you gone?"

"This is forever, Colin."

"You're . . . different, Janna."

She leaned up on one elbow to look down at him. "Is that good or bad?"

"It's incredible," he chuckled. "You're like . . . the woman I always believed you were inside."

"Sean says this is the *real* me."

"Sean's right again."

"Do you remember that movie we used to see every year in seminary?" she asked. "The *Johnny Lingo* thing?"

"I remember," he laughed.

"Well," she said firmly, "you're the man who paid eight cows for something that everyone in the village believed was ridiculous. I'm here to prove that you finally got what you paid for." She touched his face. "You believed in me. You loved me in spite of everything. You saw something in me that I could never see in myself."

"I would have paid a thousand cows to have what I have now," Colin said. "Instead, I've just paid for Sean's kids' braces."

Janna laughed and hugged him. "Was it worth it?"

"Every penny."

Janna laid her head on his shoulder, and he relished her closeness while his mind wandered into plans for the future that he'd hardly dared contemplate before now.

"Colin," she said, "there's something I have to ask you."

"Okay."

"I know it's touchy, but I have to know."

"Okay," he said, reminding himself that he had nothing to hide; no reason not to be honest.

"It has to do with Lily," she said.

Colin took a deep breath. He didn't like this, but he recalled Sean saying that it shouldn't be a taboo subject. It was a part of their lives that had to be faced and dealt with.

"When you were with her," she began gingerly, "did you . . ."

She leaned up to look into his eyes, and Colin felt his heart pounding. He didn't want to talk about this. Not here. Not now.

"Did I what?" he pressed, wanting to get it over with.

"Well, I just have to know . . . did you paint her toenails?"

Colin groaned and rolled his head into the pillow as she erupted with laughter.

"Well, you know," she said, "you always used to paint my toenails. Like you often told me, it was terribly romantic, and I just have to know if—"

"No, Janna," he growled facetiously, pulling her into his arms, "I never painted her toenails."

Janna touched his face, and tears brimmed in her eyes. "Then I forgive you."

Colin took a moment to absorb it, then he buried himself in her arms and cried until he dozed off. He awoke to find Janna rearranging the closet.

"What are you doing, Mrs. Trevor?" he called from the bed.

"I'm moving in," she said, tossing a little smile over her shoulder. "I brought a few things with me, but I need to go get some more if I'm staying. And we could use some groceries."

"Saturday *is* grocery day," he said. "And laundry day, and—"

"How about from now on, I do the shopping and the laundry during the week, and Saturday can be *play* day."

"That sounds divine," he murmured dreamily and held out a hand to her. "Come here. Let's talk."

Janna sat beside him on the bed. They held hands and talked for nearly three hours. Colin told her again of his regret for what he'd done, and his wish that he could go back and change the course of events that had thrown that match into the gasoline spill. But he emphasized all he'd learned—his love for the Savior, and his appreciation for the Atonement in a way he'd never understood before. "Still," he added, "I wish I'd found some other avenue to learn such things."

Janna expressed similar feelings. "For me," she said, "I wish I could go back to the day when I first discovered I was pregnant with Matthew. I realize now, more than ever, how the choice I made to leave you was wrong. I've learned that even when a sin is committed, if we choose to put it in the Lord's hands and make it right, he helps us. And I believe he would have looked out for me if I had put it in his hands, rather than running. In a way, I've been running and hiding ever since. Even in our marriage, I was hiding from things that I should have been facing up to."

Janna told Colin that she respected the way he had immediately confessed his sin to her and, in spite of stumbling a little, he had quickly gone to work to make it right. She believed that in the long run, his choices had made a difference in their being able to put their marriage back together.

Janna talked about her mother's death, and how it seemed she'd never really healed from it until recently. And she spoke of her mother's life. "She was a good woman, Colin. But with everything I've learned, I can look back now and see that her attitudes affected me. She was an abuse victim herself, and I think, without realizing it, she encouraged me to look at myself as a victim. She wanted what was best for me, and I know she did the best she could. I only hope that I can teach my own children to take control of their lives in a righteous way, and avoid all the heartache that comes with dysfunction."

Colin expressed his own love for Diane Hayne, and his belief that she had been pulling for them on the other side of the veil.

Janna shared with Colin the steps of her progress, reminding him of the scripture that had given her hope years earlier—and again more recently. "Do you remember the 'walls of Jericho' thing?"

"I remember," he said, running his fingers through her hair.

"Well," she said, "it's like . . . when I got away from Russell, I escaped the walls. But it wasn't until these last few weeks that they finally fell. I know the Lord led me to that scripture, but I never would have believed that it would take this many years to fully understand what he was trying to teach me. Now I know. It's really true. By faith the walls fell down."

When the conversation finally ran dry, Janna touched her husband's face, grateful beyond words for all they shared. This time they had spent renewing their relationship emotionally and spiritually was evidence of how far they had come.

"I love you," she whispered and kissed him, then she got up to leave the room.

"Hey, where you going?" he insisted.

"I'm going to the apartment to get some of my things. Are you coming?"

Colin hurried to get dressed, hollering, "I'm not letting you go *anywhere* without me!"

Janna stuck her head back in the door and grinned. "I was hoping you'd say that."

The simple act of opening the car door for Janna and watching her get in provoked a childish excitement in Colin. He walked around the Suburban and got in himself, glancing over at her as he put the key in the ignition. Her expression was intently serious as she gazed at him through fluorescent green sunglasses with star-shaped lenses.

"What?" she asked when he just stared at her.

Colin laughed. "Where did you get *those?*"

"What?" she asked in a higher pitch. He pointed at her eyes, and she said with exaggerated enlightenment, "Oh, these?" She laughed again but left them on. "I think they belong to your daughter. She left them in the car when I took her to Grandma's."

Colin took her hand as they drove. He laughed again as she gazed out the window through Mallory's sunglasses, as if nothing was out of the ordinary. This was a Janna he'd not seen much evidence of since she was seventeen. And he loved it!

"You know," he said, briefly pressing her hand to his lips, "I think your daughter looks more and more like you."

"Which one?"

"Both, in a way. But especially Mallory."

"They are beautiful girls," she said.

"Just like their mother." Colin glanced at her, expecting to see some hint of disbelief in her expression. He couldn't recall that she'd *ever* accepted a compliment at face value.

Janna only smiled and said, "Between the two of us, we can't help but have adorable children." She laughed again, as if she were nothing but completely happy.

Together they loaded as many of Janna's personal things as they could fit into the Suburban, making plans to get the rest in the following two weeks before the end of the month.

"You know," Colin said, "if I don't have to pay rent on this place, we could probably afford a second honeymoon or something."

"You mean, just me and you, alone, for like . . . a few days? Maybe even a week?"

"That's what I mean."

"When can we leave?" she asked and laughed.

Colin helped Janna put her things away, then they went grocery shopping. They ordered a pizza and ate it by candlelight.

"Happy Valentine's Day," Janna said with a gentle smile.

Colin laughed. Oh, how appropriate! He'd never been so happy in his life. "Happy Valentine's Day," he repeated. "If I had known you were going to be here, I would have gotten you a valentine."

"Well," she smiled, "I have something for you, but it's not something I can wrap up."

"What is it?" he smirked with mischief.

Janna leaned closer and her eyes turned serious. "I'm giving you my heart, Colin—all of it. I've realized that right from the start, because of my personal struggles, a good portion of my heart was tangled up in hurt and fear. But I'm whole now, Colin, and I'm giving you my whole heart—forever."

Colin blinked back the tears and leaned across the table. The reality of touching her assured him that this was not a dream. Then something occurred to him.

"I do have something for you," he said. "I'll be right back."

Colin bounded up the stairs while Janna wondered what on earth he could be so excited about. He returned with nothing in his hands. "Close your eyes," he said, "and give me your hand. No," he laughed, "your other hand."

Janna held out her left hand and felt something slide onto her ring finger. She looked down and gasped. She met his eyes and found them sparkling. She looked back at her wedding rings, muttering, "But how . . ."

Colin laughed. "Matthew dug them out of the garbage," he said.

Janna cried as she flung her arms around his shoulders. "He's a sneaky little thing," she murmured.

"He's not very little anymore."

"No, but . . ." Janna pulled back and sniffled. "Did you know he copied a letter you wrote and gave it to me?"

Colin chuckled in surprise. "Why, that little . . . Is that why you came back?"

"Well, it didn't hurt any," she said and hugged him again, then he carried her up the stairs.

Somewhere around midnight, Colin lay across the foot of the bed, painting Janna's toenails a glossy wine color. "You have beautiful toes," he said. "They're so . . . *feminine*."

"Well, they've felt positively naked for a long time. It just never seemed right to not have them painted."

"You could have done it yourself," he said with a little smirk.

"No, I couldn't," she said warmly. "It just wouldn't have been the same."

Colin grinned and blew on her toes to dry them.

Lying awake far into the night, with Janna sleeping contentedly beside him, Colin marveled at the miracle. Even as he had hoped and dreamed that Janna would come back to him, he'd expected it to take time to achieve this kind of happiness between them. Or perhaps he'd never really comprehended this kind of happiness. Of course, there could be setbacks. But after what they had been through, he felt as if they could take on the world and win.

The following morning, they went together to get the children. Colin's happiness deepened as he observed them interacting with their mother. He'd not seen them together since Christmas. His parents' obvious happiness over their reunion was touching. But even that didn't compare to the way Colin felt as he walked into church holding his wife's hand. People were kind and friendly, and he felt his emotions hovering close to the surface as he introduced her, observing the welcome she received.

That evening they read out of the scriptures together and had family prayer, then Janna went upstairs with the girls to tuck them into bed.

"So," Matthew said, "this is way cool, huh?"

"Yeah," Colin laughed, "it's pretty cool."

"Mom's turned into a real babe."

"Son," Colin put a hand on his shoulder, "*that* is the woman I fell in love with when she was fifteen—only better."

"It's way cool," he repeated with a grin.

Colin went upstairs to find Janna reading the girls a barnyard story, while Mallory and Caitlin made animal noises.

"Thank you, Lord," he whispered, and just watched them.

CHAPTER SIXTEEN

"*I*s your day busy tomorrow?" Janna asked Colin as they were getting ready for bed.

"It's flexible, why?"

"I have an appointment with Sean. I was wondering if you'd come with me."

Colin laughed. "It would be a pleasure."

The following morning, Janna took the girls to Nancy's after getting Matthew off to school. Then she went to Colin's office and approached the front desk.

"May I help you?" she was asked by the young woman there.

"I'm here to see Colin Trevor."

"Do you have an appointment, or—"

"No, but . . . he's expecting me."

"Your name?" she was asked.

"*Mrs.* Trevor," Colin said, and Janna laughed when she looked up to see him approaching.

"Oh," Lucy said, "*Mrs.* Trevor." She stood up and shook Janna's hand enthusiastically. "It's a pleasure to meet you. I should have recognized you from the picture on Mr. Trevor's desk, but you're much more beautiful in person."

"Amen to that," Colin said and kissed Janna quickly.

"Janna, this is Lucy. Lucy, my wife, JannaLyn."

"It's a pleasure to meet you, Lucy," Janna said warmly. Then to Colin, "Are you ready?"

"I am," he said, adding to Lucy, "I'll be back mid-afternoon."

In the car, Colin said, "I still can hardly believe it, Janna.

Having you back in my life is not just an answer to prayers. It's a miracle. And you seem so . . . *happy*. Dare I say, happier than I've ever seen you?"

"I *am* happy, Colin," she said.

Sean's receptionist showed them into a room to wait. Once alone, Colin couldn't resist the urge to pull Janna into his arms to kiss her long and hard. Somewhere in the midst of it, they heard the door open, and both turned to see Sean's astonished expression. He closed the door and leaned against it, and there was no mistaking the tears in his eyes.

"I think you call this a success story, Dr. O'Hara," Colin said, hugging Janna tightly. "You're a genius."

Sean rubbed his eyes and glanced toward the ceiling. "I have partners in high places." Then he stepped forward and embraced each of them. He looked into Janna's eyes and said, "You are positively glowing, Mrs. Trevor."

She laughed and said, "I'm an eight-cow woman."

Sean spent the session reminding them of communication techniques they'd learned long ago but had since forgotten. He helped them set up some ground rules to avoid letting problems get brushed under the rug, and encouraged them to enjoy getting to know each other again. Before they left, he invited them to go out to dinner with him and his wife, Tara, on Friday. They eagerly accepted.

Colin took Janna out for a nice lunch, where they talked mostly about what he was doing at work. He couldn't believe how good it felt to be sharing such things with her in a way that had never been possible before. She told him about the job she'd had, saying that it had been good for her and she'd enjoyed it. But she'd decided that she wanted to be with her children, and she would only be working another three days. She told him about the sewing she'd been doing at home and how much she enjoyed it. She had decided that it was something she'd like to continue.

On the way back to the office, Janna said, "You know, Colin, I can't remember the last time I went to the temple. I let my recommend expire a long time ago, and I haven't renewed it. I guess I just wanted to wait until I got my life in order; I don't know."

"I can't remember the last time I went, either," he said. "I wish I could go now, but . . . it will have to wait."

"Well, that's what I wanted to talk to you about. I don't want to go back until you can go with me." He looked alarmed, and she clarified. "I've thought this through, and I've prayed about it. And for *me*, I think this is the best thing. Once I began to understand the full perspective of what happened to us, I had to admit my own accountability in your . . . being excommunicated, and all." She took his hand and squeezed it. "Perhaps this is a bit of a self-inflicted penitence. Or maybe it's just a desire to start fresh . . . together. Whatever it is, I want to work toward it with you. And when the time comes, we'll go together."

Colin laughed to keep from crying. "I'll be counting down the weeks."

The evidence of Janna's healing deepened as the days passed and they worked their family into a new routine. Colin was only too eager to help with the children when he got home from work, which was such an immense relief from having to do it all alone. But Janna kept the household running so smoothly that he felt almost guilty for being so happy, and to see his family doing so well.

Gradually he became accustomed to the new Janna, which she declared was actually the *real* Janna—the woman inside who had found it difficult to come out before now. She talked to him often about the things she'd learned and done, and he realized that he loved her more every day. Life was almost too good to be true. Colin wondered if any man had ever been so happy. There was only one thing that Colin really feared facing. He just prayed that facing it would not catapult them back into any degree of the misery they had endured in the past.

* * * * *

Colin walked in the door from work and heard Janna on the phone. "Okay, thank you," she said. "Yes, please let me know."

He kissed the side of her neck as she hung up. "Who was that?" he asked.

"Russell's parole officer," she answered coolly as she turned around to kiss him in a proper greeting.

"And?" He pulled back, certain this was the beginning of a whole new bout of misery.

"He's up for parole," she said, then went to the fridge to pull out some vegetables.

"And?" Colin asked, his voice growing deeper.

"And what? He's up for parole."

"The last time he was up for parole, you were . . ."

"Hysterical?" she provided.

"Something like that."

"I'm fine, Colin. Really."

"Aren't you . . . concerned?" he asked, wondering if he really wanted to know.

"Yes, but . . . I've put it in the Lord's hands. I'm certain everything will be fine."

"And that's it?"

"Colin," Janna took his hand and looked into his eyes, "I've learned a thing or two about fear in the last several months. Job said in the Bible that 'the thing which I greatly feared is come upon me.' Well, you know what, Colin? I think from the day I met you, I was afraid you would leave me."

Colin nearly held his breath as he began to perceive something he'd never considered before.

"It would seem," she went on, "that I have proven Job's theory to be correct. I have spent much of my life in fear. I finally took my problem to the Lord. In essence, I realized that I needed to be prepared for the worst. Then I put it in the Lord's hands. So, if my life is supposed to end at Russell's hands, so be it. But I won't live in fear anymore."

Colin wasn't certain if he appreciated her theory or not. He wanted to believe that she had truly overcome her fears, but a part of him wondered if she was in a degree of denial. She was doing so well otherwise that he didn't want to push it; but he had seen her fear of Russell in the past, and this just didn't make sense to him.

Still, it was easy to put thoughts of Russell aside as they left the children with Colin's parents and embarked on a second honeymoon. They drove in the convertible up through Idaho and into Wyoming, staying a night in Jackson Hole, another in a cabin at the foot of the Tetons, and then at the Old Faithful Lodge in Yellowstone Park. After sharing an elegant meal in the lodge dining room, Colin and Janna walked together under the stars.

"You know, Colin," she said, "I've probably done more thinking and soul-searching in the last several months than I have done in my entire life."

"Yeah, I know what you mean," he said, putting his arm around her shoulders.

"And there is no question that the Spirit has helped me understand a great deal that I wouldn't have been able to grasp otherwise. Do you know what I mean?"

"Absolutely."

"But . . . a couple of days before we got back together, I had this dream. The funny thing is . . . I had had the same dream once before."

"Really? When?"

"When I was in the hospital after Russell nearly killed me. I remember it helped me get through the depression."

Colin vaguely recalled some mention of the dream, and the memory became more clear as she repeated it now.

"It was like a scene from a war movie. I was in a field, with explosions and fire all around me. I knew I had to get out of there, but I was trapped. And then you were there. You picked me up and ran. The interesting thing is that . . ." Emotion edged her voice. "Well . . . the dream was exactly the same now as it was then. But I think it was only now that I understood it."

"Tell me," he urged.

"You never let go of me, Colin. But you fell . . . and you burned your hands. We finally got away, then I bandaged your hands, and I woke up."

Colin stopped walking and looked into her eyes as the analogy struck him deeply, though he didn't fully understand why until she explained it.

"I think the explosions and fires symbolized the abuse in my life and the way it was affecting me. And you burned your hands because you were in a dangerous situation—for the sake of trying to rescue *me*. I can't put it into words, really. But I think it helped me understand."

Colin sighed and held Janna close to him. He still had trouble believing they were back together, and able to talk so freely of their struggles. He only prayed that it would last.

A few days after they'd returned from their trip, word came that Russell had been released. Janna seemed a little disconcerted, but not terribly upset. That evening, she said, "I know you can't give me a priesthood blessing right now, but . . . do you think your father would?"

Colin tried not to think too deeply about what that meant to him personally. How he wished he *could* do it himself. But he said, "I'm certain he'd be honored."

The following evening, Carl and Nancy came over for dinner, then Carl gave Janna a beautiful blessing, promising her courage and protection. She was told there were children yet to be born to her, and she would see them raised.

Colin felt great comfort from the blessing, and Janna seemed relaxed and at ease. The following Tuesday, Colin left for work as usual, but he'd only driven a mile when he felt a distinct impression to turn around and go back. Noticing a strange car across from the house, he parked behind it and quietly entered the house through a side door. Memories came rushing back of Russell Clark coming into his home the last time he'd gotten out of prison. He was barely inside when he could hear Russell's voice, somewhere in the vicinity of the kitchen. His heart pounded with fear, and his stomach tightened with anger. Did the man have no goal in life beyond tormenting Janna? He was about to step in and let him have it when he heard Janna shout at him. Instinctively he held back, just to hear what she might say, and his fear quickly melted into pride. She truly had come a long way.

* * * * *

Janna wasn't terribly surprised to walk into her kitchen and find Russell standing there. Her heart raced with fear, but she was amazed at how quickly the things she'd learned took hold in her mind.

He looked different. She suspected that some ex-convicts would be more humbled, more prepared to face the world on its own terms. But the years in prison had only intensified the evil in Russell's eyes. He looked more gaunt. His aura was darker. The hypocrisy was catching up with him.

"What are you doing here?" she demanded.

"Need you ask, my love?" he said in a voice like the devil would have used when he gave Eve the forbidden fruit.

"Well, you might as well just leave now, because whatever you came for, you're not going to get."

Russell laughed as if this was all very amusing. "I've waited a long time to see you again, my love. You can be certain I won't leave until I get what I came for."

"And what is that? Some warped vengeance for having to face up to what you really are? You're a sick man, Russell. Do us all a favor and get a psychiatrist."

"My," he laughed, stepping toward her, "aren't we spunky!"

Janna resisted the urge to back away. She stood her ground and squared her shoulders. "I'm not the same woman who was your wife. And don't think for a minute that I will allow myself to be treated the way you treated me then. You will not—"

She was cut off as he reached out to strike her. She dodged his fist with little trouble. He grabbed her arm, but she turned and broke free. At that point her training kicked in, and in a matter of seconds she went for his eyes with her fingers, his throat with her hand, his ribs with her elbow. Then, without even blinking, she inflicted the ultimate pain on a male human being.

Janna took a sharp breath as she stopped to realize Russell Clark was curled up on the floor, moaning. She recalled the first time Sean had described the possibility of this moment to her, and how absurd she had believed it was. But she'd done it! Absorbing the picture before her in contrast to the fear and abuse he had inflicted on her, Janna realized how far she had come. She thought of the countless times he'd beat her into unconsciousness. She thought of the miscarriages he'd caused by kicking her. He was certainly incapacitated enough for her to call the police, but she didn't hesitate even a moment before she kicked him with as much force as she could muster. Russell groaned and curled up tighter. She felt certain that last assault wasn't very Christian, but it sure made her feel a lot better. Perhaps she had a ways to go in truly forgiving Russell, but she felt certain that conquering him physically would go a long way toward achieving that goal.

The moment Janna began to shake, she caught movement from the corner of her eye and looked up to see Colin standing in the doorway. He looked as stunned as she felt. She couldn't find the voice to ask what he was doing there before he said, "I came back because I felt like you needed me." He looked at Russell's groaning form on the floor and shook his head. "It would seem I was wrong."

"Well," she managed, "it's nice to know God had a backup plan." She took hold of the counter, feeling suddenly weak. "Actually, I *do* need you. I'm shaking. Could you call the police?"

"Yeah," Colin grinned, "it would be a pleasure. And maybe they'd better send an ambulance, too."

After Russell was removed from the house and the police left, Colin took Janna in his arms and just held her. "You were incredible," he said. "Watching you handle him was . . . *stirring.*"

"Really?" She looked up at him in amazement.

"Oh, yes," he smiled.

"When did you come in?"

"Just before you started telling him that he might as well leave now."

Janna hugged Colin close to her, wondering if she'd ever felt so good. She had just faced down Russell Clark and won. And on top of that, she had evidence that her Father in Heaven would see that she was protected; that he would be there to compensate for her weaknesses. Colin's prompting to return home was an undeniable witness that God loved her and was looking out for her.

To celebrate the conquering of Russell Clark, Colin took Janna to Salt Lake City for a nice dinner and a movie. They were standing in line at the theater when he heard a feminine voice say, "Colin Trevor, is that you?"

Colin turned to see Lily, holding hands with a man. His mind responded with a sarcastic, *Oh, this is just great.* But he smiled and said, "Hello."

While Colin was concentrating more on Janna, attempting to gauge her reaction, Lily said, "I'd like you to meet my husband, Brook."

"It's a pleasure to meet you, Brook." Colin shook his hand. He seemed like a decent guy, and he was glad to know that Lily had found someone.

Colin cleared his throat more loudly than he'd intended, saying cautiously, "You remember my wife, JannaLyn. Janna," he added, "I believe you've met Lily."

"Of course," Janna said so warmly that Colin was taken off guard. He watched Janna offer a genuine smile and shake Lily's hand. "It's good to see you again, Lily."

While Colin had expected some kind of tension from Janna, she looked up at him with nothing but love and acceptance glowing in her eyes. Even with this tangible reminder of a nightmare, it was evident that her forgiveness was complete.

"I was thinking about you a while back," Lily said to Colin. "These Mormon missionaries have been pestering me."

"They can be very persistent."

"I've noticed that," she chuckled.

"Are they stodgy?" Colin asked.

"Not really, but I am reading some of the stuff they gave me. I told them I'd once worked with a Mormon who was a pretty decent guy."

"Do I know him?" Colin asked.

Lily just smiled. Brook started telling Janna something he'd heard about the movie they were waiting to see. Colin listened until Lily discreetly said, "You appear to be doing well."

Colin grinned. "I've never been happier."

Lily glanced unobtrusively at Janna just as she laughed at something Brook had said. Her expression clearly told Colin she was amazed. And how could she not be? She was looking at two people who had suffered the deepest hurt and betrayal, yet Janna could smile at the woman her husband had cheated with, and have no hint of malice or jealousy. In fact, she glowed with a happiness that couldn't possibly be a cover for anything beneath it.

"It's pretty amazing," Lily said. "Would I be presumptuous to ask how you did it?"

Colin put his arm around Janna as her attention turned back to him. "It's a Mormon thing," he said, looking into Janna's eyes. "We call it *forever.*"

The line started to move, and Colin was relieved to be freed of the conversation. As they went into the theater and sat down, he realized that he felt good. Seeing Lily was not a reminder of the hell he'd been through, but rather a landmark of how far they'd come.

"You were great back there," he said to Janna, putting his arm around her shoulders.

"What?" she asked.

"With Lily."

"Oh," she smiled. She'd honestly forgotten. "How is that?"

"No apparent jealousy or malice—toward her or me."

"It's in the past, Colin."

"I know, but—"

"If I thought too long or too hard about it, I could feel a little unnerved. But what good would that do . . . for me? For our marriage? And who knows? Maybe we needed Lily to force us to face up to some things we should have faced up to long before she came around. If it weren't for Lily, maybe we'd still just have a run-of-the-mill marriage with lots of skeletons in the closet."

"When you put it that way," Colin said, "maybe we should send her a thank-you note."

Janna laughed. "I don't think so, but . . . well, from what little she said, maybe what you did for *her* will make her take notice of what those missionaries have to tell her."

"Yeah," Colin said with chagrin, "I'm sure she was impressed by the high values and moral character of her Mormon colleague." His sarcasm had a bite of self-recrimination.

Janna touched his face with complete acceptance and said, "In the long run, yes, I believe she was."

"Maybe, but if I had just—"

"It's in the past, Colin. You know what Sean would say."

"I know. He'd say there's no place for regret, and I know that's true. But there are still times when I think about it and—"

"Then don't think about it. It's wiped clean."

"I know, and I'm grateful for that, Janna, but still, I—"

"Colin." She pressed her whole hand over his mouth. "I love you. Now stop talking and kiss me."

Photo by Nathan Barney

About the Author

Anita Stansfield published her first LDS romance novel, *First Love and Forever*, in the fall of 1994, and the book was winner of the 1994-95 Best Fiction Award from the Independent LDS Booksellers. Since then, her best-selling novels have captivated and moved thousands of readers with their deeply romantic stories and focus on important contemporary issues. *To Love Again* is her eighth novel to be published by Covenant.

Anita has been writing since she was in high school, and her work has appeared in *Cosmopolitan* and other publications. She views romantic fiction as an important vehicle to explore critical women's issues, especially as they relate to the LDS culture and perspective. Her novels reflect a uniquely spiritual dimension centered in gospel principles.

An active member of the League of Utah Writers, Anita lives with her husband, Vince, and their four children and a cat named "Ivan the Terrible" in Alpine, Utah. She currently serves as the Achievement Days leader in her ward.

The author enjoys hearing from her readers.
You can write to her at:
P.O. Box 50795
Provo, UT 84605-0795

Special Note: As a result of her research in preparation for writing *To Love Again*, Anita has compiled a bibliography of books related to the topics addressed in her novel. The list includes a variety of publications dealing with self-help, personal development, overcoming abuse and codependency, and strengthening relationships. If you would like a copy of this bibliography, please send a self-addressed, stamped business-size envelope to the address above.